THE PROMISE OF HOME

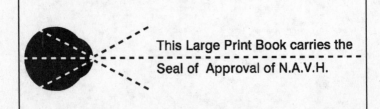

This Large Print Book carries the
Seal of Approval of N.A.V.H.

THE PROMISE OF HOME

A MILL RIVER NOVEL

DARCIE CHAN

THORNDIKE PRESS

A part of Gale, Cengage Learning

GALE
CENGAGE Learning·

Farmington Hills, Mich • San Francisco • New York • Waterville, Maine
Meriden, Conn • Mason, Ohio • Chicago

GALE
CENGAGE Learning®

LIBRARY OF CONGRESS CATALOGING-IN-PUBLICATION DATA

Chan, Darcie.
   The promise of home : a Mill River novel / Darcie Chan. — Large print edition.
      pages cm. — (Thorndike Press large print core)
   ISBN 978-1-4104-8120-7 (hardback) — ISBN 1-4104-8120-4 (hardcover)
   1. Interpersonal relations—Fiction. 2. City and town life—Vermont—Fiction. 3. Large type books. I. Title.
PS3603.H35558P76 2015b
813'.6—dc23   2015025035

Published in 2015 by arrangement with Ballantine Books, an imprint of Random House, a division of Penguin Random House LLC

Printed in the United States of America
1 2 3 4 5 6 7 19 18 17 16 15

For my loving family,
and for everyone who
has ever had to find the strength
and courage to begin again.

PROLOGUE

Courage is a kind of salvation.

— PLATO

January 2, 2013

With a last wave at the window where she stood looking down at him, Nick was gone.

In the terminal at Southern Vermont Regional Airport, Karen Cooper wrapped her arms around her son, Benjamin, and pressed her cheek against his head. She squinted through bloodshot eyes as her husband ducked into the turboprop for his flight to Boston. There, he would leave the small plane and board a transatlantic jet that would take him to Charles de Gaulle Airport in Paris and then on to Riyadh. The Middle East again — the land of 120-degree temperatures, sandstorms, danger, and uncertainty. The place Nick had already spent so many years, wishing every minute that he could be home with her and Ben.

7

The place he hated to be almost as much as she hated his being there.

Almost.

For nearly a decade, Nick had served in the Air Force, stationed on the other side of the world most of that time. She'd held down the fort at the bases where they'd been stationed, caring for Ben, their only child, and working part-time as a teacher's assistant. While Nick was deployed, most of their interactions had been measured in minutes chatting on the phone and later, on Skype or Facebook. There were a few precious weeks between deployments and during the holidays when he had been able to come home for a visit.

The rest of the time, she had lived with constant worry. There were the darker feelings, too, which she struggled to keep from pulling her under while her husband was away.

Finally, a little over two years ago, Nick left the military. They moved from Lackland in San Antonio to the little town of Mill River, in southern Vermont, where she had grown up. An aircraft systems engineer, Nick found a job at GE Aviation in Rutland. She was hired at the elementary school, and Ben adjusted beautifully to the move. They'd finally purchased a home of their own. After years of rentals and military housing, living in their own cute three-bedroom Cape Cod and knowing they wouldn't have to pack up and move for another deployment had felt like a dream.

She should have realized that, like all dreams, it wouldn't last long.

Nick was among the first to be laid off when the economy sputtered. The newest employees had the least seniority. Her salary alone wasn't enough to cover the bills, and their savings were significantly depleted after making the down payment on the house. But Nick had promised her that they would return to her native Vermont after his military career was over. They had scrimped and saved for years to qualify for a mortgage. And now they were settled in their new house. They were thrilled by how Ben was thriving in his new school. Finally, they were living in the cozy, loving community she considered her one true home. They were not about to surrender their dream without a fight.

"I could easily do maintenance, but none of the airlines are hiring. There's always contracting work, though," Nick had said as they sat at the kitchen table late one night. His voice had been quiet, hesitant, as if he hated to even bring up the possibility.

"You would have to go back."

"Yes. For a while. But the money would be great, a lot better than a military salary. Do you think you could make it through one more stretch apart? It might not be for long. The economy's finally on the way up. In six months or a year, I might get reinstated at GE."

Six months or a year.

Karen felt as if they were moving backward. She squeezed Nick's hand as she let his words sink in. It was all she could do to hold it together. But Nick's brown eyes were fixed on her as he waited for her reply.

"I thought we were past being apart for months at a time."

"I know, so did I. But short of moving again, I don't know what other options we have. Besides, this is your home. *Our* home. I don't want us to lose it or have to leave Mill River any more than you do."

Karen felt the darkness — which was how she thought of the clinical depression that had plagued her for years — trying to force its way through her defenses. She had been stable for quite a while, thanks to a new antidepressant and careful monitoring by her doctor. Still, Nick's long absences didn't help her condition, and she knew what she would be risking by going along with his proposal. She knew, too, that by asking her next question she would be giving in, and she waited a few moments to compose herself. Finally, she whispered, "Where would you go?"

"Nowhere near any hostilities. Not Iraq or Afghanistan, although we're about pulled out of them completely. Maybe the UAE or Qatar. Somewhere stable, with a U.S. presence and more tolerant locals."

"You make it sound like it's already a done deal."

"I've made some calls," Nick admitted. "Just to see if it was even a possibility. And it definitely is. Lots of guys I've worked with are already well established with the big contractors. I just need to give them the go-ahead, and they'll hook me up."

"What happens if nothing's changed with the economy by the time your contract's up?"

"We just have to have faith that it will be okay."

"I can't stand the thought of us living apart again. And Ben . . . it's meant so much to him to have you home."

She looked into Nick's eyes and saw inevitability. Her pain was reflected there, too, interspersed with his own hurt and disappointment. But in his gaze, Karen also recognized her husband's incredible fortitude. His strength and resolve were two of the things she loved most about him.

"I know. But we've all done it before. Can't we make it another year, honey? Can you stay strong for me one more time? I don't know what else I can do, and at least I'd be earning enough to give us a savings cushion. I can keep an eye out for openings while I'm gone. I may be able to line up something for after the contract is up, and if not, we'd have a little time to decide what we should do."

She squeezed Nick's hand in silent acquiescence. He reached over and cupped her face, wiping one of his big thumbs gently beneath her eye. "One more year. But this will be our last separation," he said. "You have my word. After this, whatever happens, we stay together."

The ground crew detached the portable rolling stairway from the turboprop as the aircraft door swung closed. Karen pulled Ben closer as the plane began to back away from the terminal. She didn't want her son to see her cry, but when she tried unsuccessfully to stifle a sob, he turned around. There was no avoiding it.

"It'll be okay, Mom," he said, stepping back into her arms. "He'll get to visit in the summer, and before you know it, it'll be Christmas and he'll be back for good. Maybe I'll even be taller than you by then."

"At the rate you're growing, I wouldn't be surprised," she said with her cheek pressed against Ben's temple. "I wouldn't be surprised at all."

Once the small jet had taxied out to the runway where Karen and Ben could no longer see it, they walked back through the terminal and out to the parking lot. They didn't speak much on the short drive home, which was just as well, because Karen was lost in her thoughts.

She worried that their time together as a family in Mill River might make this separation harder for her son. At last Ben had experienced what it was like to have Nick home at the end of each day, like most other fathers. For once, he'd had both parents attending his basketball games and other school events. Ben and Nick had begun to spend more time alone together on the weekends, doing "guy things" in which she had no interest. At least they'd had a little time together, and Nick had been there to see Ben transform from a little kid to an almost-teenager.

Still, it made her heart ache, how her son seemed to accept Nick going away again so easily. She told herself it was because Ben was a little older now and more emotionally mature. It was easier than admitting that, for her son, having his father live half a world away was simply the norm.

Karen exited the highway. With snow-covered rooftops and strings of holiday lights still illuminating the streets, the little town of Mill River rose up in the distance. She took a deep breath, slowing the car to turn into her driveway before they entered the quaint business district along Main Street. Here she had friends, a job, and their own lovely little home. For so many years, she had longed to bring her family back to the place where she'd had such a happy childhood. Closing her eyes and picturing her husband and son together in Mill River almost gave her a sense of peace. Besides, it would be better this time. *She* was better, and she could survive in this place.

"Well, Mom," Ben said as he turned to her, "I guess it's just you and me again."

"Yeah," Karen replied with a forced smile. She felt the dark wisps of emotion teasing, seeking a handhold on her soul, and she shuddered. "But only for one more year. We can make it for one more year."

She silently repeated the reassurance she had just offered her son. *I can make it one more year.*

For her family's sake, she would try. She had no other choice.

CHAPTER 1

On a bright Saturday in October, Claudia Simon looked eagerly out the passenger window of a pickup truck driven by her fiancé, Kyle Hansen. Kyle's daughter, Rowen, was in the backseat, and they were headed up the long, curved driveway to the McAllister mansion, the huge home plated in white marble that overlooked the town of Mill River, Vermont. The trees alongside the driveway were in peak autumn color, and the leaves floating down as they passed carpeted the pavement in a brilliant mosaic of red, orange, and gold.

"It's so beautiful," Claudia said. "It seems almost magical, like the colors are just dripping everywhere."

"Yep," Kyle said. "Definitely one of the best things about living in Vermont."

Rowen leaned forward between the two front seats and grinned. "Imagine how it'll be in the winter, when it's time for the wedding! I'll bet there will be lots of snow! And maybe ice will get stuck on all these trees, like crystal."

"That would be gorgeous," Claudia said. She glanced down at her left hand, where the diamond in her engagement ring gleamed in the late-afternoon sunshine.

"And romantic," Rowen said. "Especially with all the Christmas decorations."

"I've always wanted a holiday wedding," Claudia said. She looked across at Kyle and smiled. "And this place is so close to the church, and so amazing, at least on the outside. It could be the perfect place for the reception."

"It's nice on the inside, too," Kyle said, "but we'll have to see what Ruth's plans are. It may not even be ready by December."

Kyle pulled up to the large paved area in back of the marble house. Ruth Fitzgerald's Buick sedan was already there, parked next to an older Subaru Impreza. As he cut the engine, the back door opened. Ruth appeared and waved them inside.

"Hi there," she said. "I've been waiting for you. Would you believe the kitchen is almost finished? Come in and take a look!"

Rowen skipped ahead, darting past Ruth into the house. Claudia smiled at Ruth and

18

took Kyle's hand as they walked toward the door.

The back door of the house opened into a small mudroom. From there, Ruth led them into a wide, sunny kitchen. Claudia smelled paint and wood and window cleaner. In fact, a bottle of Windex and several rags rested on the counter. She and Kyle were silent for a moment as they looked around the room.

Directly in front of them, a professional stainless steel range gleamed. It was nestled between dark cherry cabinets that ran the length of the wall and continued around the kitchen. Other new appliances interrupted the cherry — a commercial refrigerator and freezer, two dishwashers, and a small wine storage unit. The tile backsplash behind the range complemented the rich pattern of the floor tiles. Veins of brown and gold in the new quartz countertops sparkled in the sunlight streaming through the window.

"Oh, Ruth, it's beautiful," Claudia breathed.

"It is," Ruth agreed. "It's almost too pretty to cook in. Emily DiSanti's managing the renovation. She's done a wonderful job so far."

As if on cue, a striking woman with red hair entered the kitchen. She held a plastic shopping bag. "Ruth, I've got the hardware for the cabinets, and I — Oh, hey, guys."

"You all know each other, don't you?" Ruth asked.

"Sure, of course," Emily said.

"It's nice to see you again," Claudia added.

"I don't know if you've heard, but Kyle and Claudia are getting married," Ruth said. The smiling, grandmotherly lady seemed to puff up with scarcely contained happiness. Claudia couldn't help but smile along with her.

"Yes, I heard," Emily said. "You know how fast news travels in Mill River. But congratulations! You must be so excited."

"I'm going to be the flower girl," Rowen chimed in, hugging Claudia around the waist.

"And you will be perfect, my dear," Ruth told her. "Emily, I'm glad you're here. Kyle and Claudia are planning a holiday wedding, and they were wondering whether the bed-and-breakfast will be open by then."

"We were hoping our immediate families and maybe the wedding party could stay here," Kyle said. "Since we'll be married at St. John's, it would be so convenient."

"I told them that the center hall would be a lovely place for a reception, too," Ruth said as she looked over Emily's shoulder toward the rest of the house. "But I said we'd have to ask you about it."

Emily set her bag on the floor and took a deep breath. "Well, if everything goes according to plan, we'll probably be finished in time. We've already taken care of most of the big things that needed to be done — the electricity upgrade, the new boiler for the radiators, the replacement windows. The drywall crew should be done replacing walls this week, too."

"Why did you need to replace walls?" Claudia asked.

"Mainly because lots of them were plaster and cracking beyond repair. Painted drywall is much easier to maintain. Plus, since it's an older property, covering plaster walls and replacing windows takes care of lead paint hazards."

"And my lovely new kitchen is done," Ruth added with a gleeful look around the room.

"Yes. The owner's suite is coming along nicely, too. Other than that and a few plumbing upgrades, there will be only cosmetic work to do."

"How many rooms will you have?" Claudia asked.

"Bedrooms, you mean?" Ruth asked. "Six,

not including the owner's suite. And each one has its own bathroom."

"That's exactly how many we'll need," Claudia said as she looked up at Kyle. "Two for your parents and brother, two for my family, and one apiece for the other grooms-men and bridesmaids."

"And where would you two stay?" Ruth asked with a mischievous, puckered smile. "Surely you wouldn't spend your wedding night at home."

"Well, I think —" Claudia began.

"Oh, no," Kyle interrupted, and Claudia turned to look at him again. "We'll be out of here that evening. We're not leaving for the honeymoon until after Christmas, but I've got something in mind for our first night as a married couple."

"You didn't say anything to me about that," Claudia said in a mock protest. She poked him gently in the ribs.

"Of course I didn't." He grabbed her hand to protect against further jabs.

"Where are we going?"

Kyle smiled but didn't answer. Instead, he spoke to Ruth. "So, what do you think about us maybe being your first custom-ers?"

"It would be an honor to host your families and your reception," Ruth said.

"Oh, I can't wait to show you the whole house! You'll be able to see how perfect everything will be. That is, if we can be ready. Emily, are you sure we can commit to it?"

As Claudia watched, a fleeting look of concern passed over Emily's face. It was gone in an instant, though, replaced with a wide smile.

"Absolutely. It'll be close, but I'll make it happen."

In the master bedroom on the second floor of the marble mansion, Emily turned off the edge sander she had been using and shifted into a sitting position on the floor. Without the noise of the machine, she could hear Ruth chatting with Kyle, Claudia, and Rowen on their way out. She tried to ignore the stress that had been building after she'd agreed to have the house ready in time for Kyle and Claudia's wedding. True, she had plenty of experience working to meet deadlines, and she had brought enough old houses back to their original grandeur to know what remained to be done in the McAllister mansion, but it wouldn't be easy. Between her part-time job at Turner's Hardware and the odd jobs she did on the side for her mother's real estate listings, she wouldn't have a spare minute for the next two months.

Emily sighed and got back on her hands and knees. Using a small handheld sander to remove the final bits of old finish on a wood floor was her least favorite part of the refinishing process. She took some comfort in knowing that this was the last room, though. She had finished the wood floors on the lower level during the summer, and the floors in many of the other bedrooms upstairs needed nothing but a good mopping and waxing, since they had never been used. Emily continued working her way around the room, crawling along the windows and into the closet.

It was then that she felt the crack in the floor beneath her hand.

She switched off the sander. The crack seemed to run perpendicular to the planks of the wood floor, and her first thought was that she might have to completely replace several of the pieces of wood. When she looked closely, though, she saw that the crack wasn't a crack at all but one side of a well-camouflaged rectangle that had been cut into the floor.

In fact, it looked like some sort of trapdoor.

"Emily?" Ruth's voice called, and the

sound of footsteps on the stairs followed soon after.

"In here," she replied.

Ruth entered the room, slightly out of breath. "Goodness, I don't know if I'll ever get used to such a big staircase."

"A big staircase for a big house."

"Yes. I guess I'm ready to head home. I just wanted to check to see if you needed anything."

"No, I'm good," Emily said. "I'm going to leave, too, as soon as I'm done edging in here. I'll vacuum first thing in the morning and then get going on the stain. I'll lock up everything, as usual." Her hand was still resting on the floor, and she felt the crack leaving an indentation on her palm.

"Thanks, honey. You have a good night."

Once Ruth had left the house, Emily jumped up. Her toolbox was on the floor near the base of the stairs, and she descended quickly to grab one of her putty knives and a flashlight. Then, back in the master bedroom, she entered the closet and knelt down. The thin blade of the putty knife just fit into the crack. It was difficult, but she was able to pry up a chunk of the floor, a rectangular lid, which she set aside. She switched on her flashlight and peered down into a hidden compartment. The space was perhaps two feet deep. The only thing inside, other than dust and cobwebs, was an old hard-sided briefcase.

Emily took hold of the dusty handle and pulled it out. The case was made of smooth tan leather. Unlike most modern cases, which used combination locks, the brass locks on either side of the handle had keyholes. To her chagrin, the locks were engaged. She shook the briefcase gently. It wasn't heavy, but a soft rustling noise from inside told her that it wasn't empty, either.

Maybe the key to the briefcase is still in the compartment.

Again, she shone the flashlight down into the hole. She was more careful this time, moving the light slowly and running her fingers through the dust at the bottom of the compartment in the hope of finding a wayward key. She found nothing, and the disturbed dust rose in a cloud that sent her into a sneezing fit.

When she had recovered, she took another good look at her find. A small bronze plaque attached to one corner of the case was engraved with P. MCALLISTER. Obviously, it had belonged to a member of the McAllister family and eventually, Mary McAllister. Which meant that now, like everything in the McAllister mansion, it was the property of Ruth and her husband.

I can drop it off at the Fitzgeralds' apartment on the way home, Emily thought, but telling herself this did nothing to lessen her intense curiosity about what was inside the old briefcase. Surely she could find a way to open it without breaking the locks. The case was in remarkable condition and probably valuable as an antique. Plus, she reasoned, it would be a favor to Ruth, since she and her husband would be able to inspect its contents easily.

Of course, if I open it, I'll be able to see what's in it, too.

A part of her was ashamed at her willingness to justify and commit such an inappropriate invasion of privacy. Still, that part wasn't strong enough to prevent her from going back to her toolbox in search of a small screwdriver or a long nail — or anything else that might help her coax the locks on the briefcase into revealing what was inside.

As the afternoon gave way to a chilly evening, Father O'Brien drove carefully down the main road leaving Mill River. However, instead of following the curve of the road around and through the old covered bridge spanning the river for which the town was named, he turned left into a driveway and parked.

As he had recently started to do before meeting with someone in person, he snapped his fingers several times, first on one side of his head and then the other, to make sure he could hear them properly. For a nonagenarian, he was in excellent health. His vision was still remarkably good; he'd easily passed the vision test the last time he had renewed his license. But his hearing was another matter. He'd finally had to get hearing aids for both ears, and they were simultaneously a godsend and a major annoyance. When they were inserted and functioning normally, he could hear quite well. But getting them adjusted to the proper volume in each ear, and making sure the batteries had enough juice, was a constant struggle. Today he had been called to the home of Karen Cooper, one of his parishioners, and he knew it was especially important that he be able to hear everything clearly once he was inside.

A car in desperate need of a new muffler drove by just as he stepped down out of his pickup truck. He suddenly felt a bit dizzy, and he kept his hand on the doorframe until the sensation passed. Maybe his hearing aids weren't quite as calibrated as he

28

thought, or maybe the unusually loud noise of the car was too much for them to handle. He snapped his fingers again to reassure himself, then approached the front door of the Cooper residence. Jean Wykowski, Karen's next-door neighbor, opened the door before he'd even raised his hand to knock.

"Hello, Father. Thank you for coming so quickly." Jean's expression was grim.

"Hello, Jean," he said quietly. He could see over Jean's shoulder into the kitchen, where Karen and her son, Ben, sat at the table. "You said on the phone that Nick's gone missing?"

"Yes, they just got word," Jean said, her voice barely above a whisper. "No one's seen him in four days, since he went out for supplies."

"Oh, my," Father O'Brien said.

"They've got people out looking for him, troops mostly, but some private security teams, too. Karen's taking it pretty hard."

Father O'Brien nodded and went to the kitchen.

Karen looked up at him with bloodshot eyes. "Thank you for coming, Father."

"Of course," he replied. Carefully, he pulled out the chair next to her and sat down. He waited for Karen to speak.

"I know Jean told you they can't find Nick," she said. "Four days ago, he and a colleague left work in the morning and never came back. They were supposed to pick up some things for the shop, and they made it to the warehouse and signed for the supplies, but after that . . ." Her voice trailed off. She took a deep breath. "Someone from his company called, a man. I wrote down his name and number. He said they have people searching for them, retracing their route and all that, but no other information *at this time.*"

Her voice broke as she struggled to finish her sentence. Jean came up behind Karen to put an arm around her shoulders. Ben sat silently across from his mother and stared down at the table. Father O'Brien tried to think what he could say that would bring some comfort.

"Karen, I know Nick is a good man. He's smart and strong. Whatever happened, wherever he is, we have to believe he'll find a way out of the situation. We have to trust that God is looking out for him. Now, listen to me, Karen. You've got to stay strong for Nick, and for your son here. Both of them need you."

Karen nodded through her tears, and Ben glanced up at him for the first time.

30

have to worry about while Seamus
are away."

table fell silent save for the sound of
dle scraping against the inside of the

king about his father and brother's
ng departure was perhaps the only
that could have pulled Michael's at-
away from his hunger. They weren't
to Burlington this time. Instead, his
and brother would use the last of the
's cash to travel to New York, where
ad heard that men were being hired
rk on the construction of a great
connecting the various boroughs of
York City.

counting on you, Michael," his father
ued. "You'll have to take care of your
r and grandmother while we're gone.
lot of responsibility."

ill, Father," Michael said quietly. "I
se."

e the food was served and his father
d his eyes after saying grace, Michael
ed up his spoon. He had intended to
eat slowly so his food would last
r. Still, he couldn't help but take a
first bite. The hot stew burned his
h and his throat when he swallowed,
quieted the ache in his stomach.

Father O'Brien took Karen's hand and
Ben's hand. "Will you join me in asking our
Heavenly Father to protect him?"

Karen nodded, and he and Ben bowed
their heads. For a moment before he closed
his own eyes, he watched Karen's son. Ben
was growing up so quickly, and yet he was
still so young, perhaps twelve or thirteen. It
was a difficult age, at the beginning of the
transition from childhood to adulthood, an
impressionable time during which the boy
would need his father more than ever. He
knew exactly how Ben must be feeling. Even
now, in the sunset of his life, it was all too
easy to remember himself at Ben's age, sitting at his family's table and facing the great
uncertainty of his own father's absence.

CHAPTER 2

Saturday, March 17, 1934

From his place at the dinner table, Michael O'Brien watched his mother ladle stew into his father's bowl. His stomach was gnawing at itself, and he tried to ease the uncomfortable feeling by fidgeting in his chair.

"Be still, Michael," his grandmother whispered from her seat beside him. "You'll get yours in a minute."

"Thank you, Anna," his father said as he accepted the bowl from his mother. "This smells delicious."

"Way better than that Hoover stew they were serving in Burlington." Seamus, his brother, sat next to their father with his mouth scrunched up in disgust. At twenty-two years old, and over seven years his senior, his brother was a grown man. They had always been opposites. Seamus was brash, impulsive, even rough at times, whereas Michael was quiet and studious.

Seamus and their fath the textile mill in Winoo been laid off when the Desperate for income, t menial jobs with tl Administration in Burlin for the program had run the two of them had tak few miles into the city ea of finding odd jobs. The kitchen regularly.

"In times like these, you ful for any food you're g said quietly to Seamus there's plenty of meat, th He's become quite the hu

Michael smiled, please praise, even though it ha empty stomach.

"He has," his father agr rel's the best wild game th did you get, son?"

"Six."

"Well." His father smiled They breed like rats in the will never run out of them spring on its way. There'll crop of them, and other thi So long as you've got you ing fresh meat is one thi

It was safer to eat his bread first, and he dipped his piece into the rich gravy in his bowl. While he chewed, he watched the four other members of his family.

His father, Niall, sat at the head of the table. He was tall, with thinning brown hair that faded to gray at the temples. His prominent shoulders were hunched forward as he ate. His tough, sinewy arms evidenced his long years of hard work at the mill.

Anna, his mother, was meek and soft. She had dark hair and a fair complexion. With her dainty wrists and dimpled elbows, she appeared doll-like next to the lean, rugged form of his father.

"This is good, Anna," his grandmother said from the chair next to him. Her name was Elizabeth, but almost everyone called her Lizzie. She had a raspy voice and was as wiry and tough as her son Niall. Several of her teeth were missing. Michael knew his grandmother was partial to his mother's stews because not only were they delicious, but also everything in them was tender and easy for her to eat.

"I'll sure miss your cooking, Mother," Seamus said. "No telling what we'll be eating while we're gone." Michael's brother was a fiery-tempered, younger version of their father, except that his hair was dark, like their mother's.

"Now, son, you ought not to worry your mother by saying things like that," Niall said. "We'll be fine. And we'll be able to look forward to better times, and more suppers like this, once we're home."

"You're sure you'll travel tomorrow, then?" Michael noticed a slight tremor in his mother's lip as she waited for a response.

Niall nodded with his mouth full. "We'll catch a train leaving Burlington in the morning. We should be to New York by nightfall."

"I just hope there will be enough work to go around," Lizzie said. "Seems like the projects in Burlington ended soon after they started. It would be a shame for you to get all the way to New York and find nothing available."

"The real shame is that the projects around here were only designed to last the winter, and most of them weren't anything of substance," Niall said. "If the government wants to pay people, it should be for something more than make-work. At least the bridge in New York will be something that's lasting and useful."

"And they ought to pay bridge workers a decent wage," Seamus said.

Father O'Brien took Karen's hand and Ben's hand. "Will you join me in asking our Heavenly Father to protect him?"

Karen nodded, and he and Ben bowed their heads. For a moment before he closed his own eyes, he watched Karen's son. Ben was growing up so quickly, and yet he was still so young, perhaps twelve or thirteen. It was a difficult age, at the beginning of the transition from childhood to adulthood, an impressionable time during which the boy would need his father more than ever. He knew exactly how Ben must be feeling. Even now, in the sunset of his life, it was all too easy to remember himself at Ben's age, sitting at his family's table and facing the great uncertainty of his own father's absence.

CHAPTER 2

Saturday, March 17, 1934

From his place at the dinner table, Michael O'Brien watched his mother ladle stew into his father's bowl. His stomach was gnawing at itself, and he tried to ease the uncomfortable feeling by fidgeting in his chair.

"Be still, Michael," his grandmother whispered from her seat beside him. "You'll get yours in a minute."

"Thank you, Anna," his father said as he accepted the bowl from his mother. "This smells delicious."

"Way better than that Hoover stew they were serving in Burlington." Seamus, his brother, sat next to their father with his mouth scrunched up in disgust. At twenty-two years old, and over seven years his senior, his brother was a grown man. They had always been opposites. Seamus was brash, impulsive, even rough at times, whereas Michael was quiet and studious.

Seamus and their father had worked at the textile mill in Winooski, and both had been laid off when the hard times hit. Desperate for income, they had accepted menial jobs with the Civil Works Administration in Burlington. The funding for the program had run out, though, and the two of them had taken to walking the few miles into the city each day in the hope of finding odd jobs. They ate at the soup kitchen regularly.

"In times like these, you should be thankful for any food you're given," his mother said quietly to Seamus. "And tonight, there's plenty of meat, thanks to Michael. He's become quite the hunter."

Michael smiled, pleased at his mother's praise, even though it had no effect on his empty stomach.

"He has," his father agreed. "And squirrel's the best wild game there is. How many did you get, son?"

"Six."

"Well." His father smiled. "You keep it up. They breed like rats in the trees. The woods will never run out of them, especially with spring on its way. There'll be a whole new crop of them, and other things to hunt, too. So long as you've got your good aim, having fresh meat is one thing your mother won't have to worry about while Seamus and I are away."

The table fell silent save for the sound of the ladle scraping against the inside of the pot.

Thinking about his father and brother's looming departure was perhaps the only thing that could have pulled Michael's attention away from his hunger. They weren't going to Burlington this time. Instead, his father and brother would use the last of the family's cash to travel to New York, where they had heard that men were being hired to work on the construction of a great bridge connecting the various boroughs of New York City.

"I'm counting on you, Michael," his father continued. "You'll have to take care of your mother and grandmother while we're gone. It's a lot of responsibility."

"I will, Father," Michael said quietly. "I promise."

Once the food was served and his father opened his eyes after saying grace, Michael snatched up his spoon. He had intended to try to eat slowly so his food would last longer. Still, he couldn't help but take a huge first bite. The hot stew burned his mouth and his throat when he swallowed, but it quieted the ache in his stomach.

It was safer to eat his bread first, and he dipped his piece into the rich gravy in his bowl. While he chewed, he watched the four other members of his family.

His father, Niall, sat at the head of the table. He was tall, with thinning brown hair that faded to gray at the temples. His prominent shoulders were hunched forward as he ate. His tough, sinewy arms evidenced his long years of hard work at the mill.

Anna, his mother, was meek and soft. She had dark hair and a fair complexion. With her dainty wrists and dimpled elbows, she appeared doll-like next to the lean, rugged form of his father.

"This is good, Anna," his grandmother said from the chair next to him. Her name was Elizabeth, but almost everyone called her Lizzie. She had a raspy voice and was as wiry and tough as her son Niall. Several of her teeth were missing. Michael knew his grandmother was partial to his mother's stews because not only were they delicious, but also everything in them was tender and easy for her to eat.

"I'll sure miss your cooking, Mother," Seamus said. "No telling what we'll be eating while we're gone." Michael's brother was a fiery-tempered, younger version of their father, except that his hair was dark,

35

like their mother's.

"Now, son, you ought not to worry your mother by saying things like that," Niall said. "We'll be fine. And we'll be able to look forward to better times, and more suppers like this, once we're home."

"You're sure you'll travel tomorrow, then?" Michael noticed a slight tremor in his mother's lip as she waited for a response.

Niall nodded with his mouth full. "We'll catch a train leaving Burlington in the morning. We should be to New York by nightfall."

"I just hope there will be enough work to go around," Lizzie said. "Seems like the projects in Burlington ended soon after they started. It would be a shame for you to get all the way to New York and find nothing available."

"The real shame is that the projects around here were only designed to last the winter, and most of them weren't anything of substance," Niall said. "If the government wants to pay people, it should be for something more than make-work. At least the bridge in New York will be something that's lasting and useful."

"And they ought to pay bridge workers a decent wage," Seamus said.

"How long will you stay, Father?" Michael asked.

His father's face sagged into an apologetic frown, and he paused to swallow a mouthful of stew before he answered. "I suppose we'll stay as long as we can. If we're hired on, I expect there'll be work to do at least through the summer and into next fall. I'd guess they'll want to do as much as can be done while the weather's good."

"If you get steady work, that will be all we could ask for," his mother said. "You mustn't worry about us here. We'll be fine, the three of us. The animals and the garden will keep us busy, and Frank is nearby if we need him."

Michael smiled. Uncle Frank's visits were something he hoped would happen more often. His mother's brother was a priest at the Holy Cross Mission in Colchester, and he was always cheerful and pleasant. He often brought a small surprise or treat when he came to the house.

"I'm thankful for that," his father said. "We may be gone until next winter, if the work and the wages are good."

"What if things turn around here? What if the mill calls you back?" his mother asked.

"You should send word to me, but I doubt it will happen. Orders had all but dried up when I left. If anything, the mill may close completely." His father leaned back in his chair and looked earnestly at his family. "They say Roosevelt has all sorts of plans to lift the country out of the depression, but I'll believe that when I see it. Until then, it'll be every man for himself. There are no jobs here, and I won't sit idle with a family to provide for. I'll take my chances in New York."

Michael heard his mother working in the kitchen soon after the first faint rays of sun came through his bedroom window. He turned his head and saw Seamus pulling his suspenders up over his shoulders. A large rucksack sat on the twin bed next to his brother.

"Sorry to wake you," Seamus muttered.

"I'm glad you did. How long have you been up?"

"A while. Didn't sleep much last night."

Michael threw back his covers and sat up. "How are you and Father getting to the train station?"

"Whibley offered to give us a ride. Said it was the least he could do after all the milk and butter we've given him."

Michael nodded. Aaron Whibley owned the farm next door. Anna usually gave milk and butter to the Whibleys, even though Niall often spoke with disapproval about the needy neighbors who had more children than they could afford to feed.

"Better get dressed," Seamus told him. "We'll be leaving soon."

Michael put on his clothes and hurried downstairs. The fire in the woodstove was starting to warm the room. His mother was packing up sandwiches while his grandmother and father sat at the table with cups of coffee. The plate in front of his father was already empty, and a rucksack similar to Seamus's was on the floor by the front door.

"I've got eggs in the skillet for you, Michael," his mother said, but he didn't feel like eating yet. His stomach was unsettled. What he really wanted was some fresh air.

"I'll eat in a few minutes. The wood box is almost empty." Before his mother could answer, he threw on his coat and hat and slipped out the back door.

The late winter air was biting cold. Still, he took a deep breath through his nose and enjoyed the clean, crisp scent of pine and impending snow even though the hairs inside his nostrils froze stiff. It was so different here, on his grandparents' old farm, than it had been at the mill tenement in

Winooski. He and his parents had lived here after the Great War, before his father had found work in the mill. True, the farm wasn't really a farm anymore — not since his grandfather had died and his grandmother had sold most of the cows — but it still had plenty of space to move around. He remembered running around the farm as a young child, when his grandfather waved at him from the barn and the pasture held a pair of sturdy Percheron horses and a good-size herd of dairy cows.

It was a godsend, really, that his grandmother had held on to the property. When his father and brother were laid off and they could no longer afford the rent for their apartment, the old farmhouse a few miles south of Burlington had given them a place of refuge. The nearly thirty acres of woods along the back of the property were ideal hunting grounds. With a decent flock of chickens and a good Holstein cow, plus a couple of mature apple trees and a large garden patch, the farm provided their family with basic sustenance. It wasn't income, but it was more than many families had these days.

The snow crunched beneath Michael's feet as he walked around to the woodshed. There, he filled his arms with the logs that he and Seamus had split. He realized that once his brother had left, many of the heavy chores would fall solely to him. There would be splitting wood, certainly, which was never-ending, and the more unpleasant work of cleaning up in the barn. After the snow melted and mud season was over, he would have to help his mother turn over the soil in the garden. Doing all that, on top of school and homework and hunting to supplement their dwindling food supply, would be a challenge. Perhaps he would have to leave school altogether.

A part of him wished that he could go with his father and Seamus. He'd never been outside Vermont or even outside Chittenden County, but the farm was close enough to the tracks of the Rutland Railroad that they often heard the whistles of passing locomotives. The thought of riding a train all the way to New York City was something out of a dream. What did the country look like between here and there? Were the people different? What sorts of towns might they pass through along the way? And the city itself, the city that supposedly never slept, must surely be a wonder to behold.

Someday he would see it for himself. In the meantime, he would keep his word and take care of his mother and grandmother while his father and brother were away.

Seamus had come downstairs by the time Michael returned to the house with the wood. His brother and father were buttoning their coats as his mother placed a cloth bundle of sandwiches in his father's rucksack. His grandmother, holding one of his late grandfather's old pipes, had pulled her chair closer to the woodstove. She had the stem of the pipe in her mouth, chewing it with the few teeth she had left. It was a sure sign that she was feeling as uneasy as he was.

As Michael deposited the logs in the box next to the woodstove, a horn sounded outside. "That's Whibley," his father said. He turned to the older woman sitting by the stove and put his hand on her shoulder. "Mother" was all he said, and Michael's grandmother looked up and squeezed her son's hand.

He turned to Michael next. "Son, I'm leaving this place in your hands."

"Yes, sir," Michael said. "I'll take care of everything."

His father nodded, and Michael thought he might say something more or extend a hand in a gesture of man-to-man trust, but instead, his father pulled him into a tight, quick embrace.

His mother was standing to the side, and his father turned to her last. "I wish you didn't have to go," she said as Niall took her in his arms.

"I know," he said. He kissed her tenderly and drew her against him, pressing his cheek against her hair. "I'll send word once we get to New York and get ourselves settled, so you'll know where to reach us."

His mother nodded and wiped her eyes. When she looked up at her husband, she seemed to be trying to smile.

Seamus followed their father in saying goodbye. He quickly hugged their mother and grandmother, giving them each a peck on the cheek, and he clapped a hand on Michael's back. "Hang in there, brother. And keep your fingers crossed for us."

"I will," Michael replied. His brother's tone of voice reminded him just how much younger than Seamus he was.

With his mother and grandmother, Michael stood in the open front doorway and watched the other part of his family squeeze into the cab of Whibley's old pickup. His father peered out the side window as the truck backed onto the road, and Michael focused on his father's steady gaze and nodded. His grandmother heaved a sigh. His mother said nothing but raised a hand, holding it up amid the newly arrived snow flurries until the pickup had disappeared in the distance.

CHAPTER 3

In the kitchen of Kyle's apartment, Claudia was trying to throw a salad together while he assembled sandwiches to grill. She opened his refrigerator and removed a withered brownish ball wrapped in plastic. "Is this what I think it is?" she asked, holding up the object.

"Oh," Kyle said when he saw what was in her hand. He gave her a sheepish grin. "That would be the iceberg lettuce, I think. I must've forgotten about it in there."

Claudia winced. Finding enough fresh vegetables for a salad was going to be a bigger challenge than she'd thought. "Okay . . . is there anything else lurking in your fridge that I should know about?"

"I'm not sure. There might be a few other things," Kyle admitted. "Sorry. You know I'm not great at fridge organization."

Claudia shook her head and set the lettuce on the counter. "Just so you know, I'm taking over that job once we move in together."

"That would be great! One more way we complement each other," Kyle said. He gave her a quick kiss before turning back to his sandwiches in the frying pan.

In spite of her disgust at the brown lettuce ball, Claudia smiled to herself. Since Kyle had asked her to marry him, she hadn't had a bad day. It didn't matter if the kids in her class at school got extra-rowdy or her alarm clock summoned her at an hour much earlier than she would have liked. Refusing donuts and pie from the bakery had become easy, with her gorgeous white wedding gown hanging in her closet. Even half-rotted Franken-produce in Kyle's fridge wasn't a big deal. A cloud of happiness seemed to have surrounded her, cushioning her against all the unpleasantness of life, and every glimmer of her engagement ring gave her mood a buzzy, giddy boost.

There was still the matter of the salad, however.

With a bit of trepidation, she started sorting through the contents of Kyle's refrigerator. She found some carrots and half a red onion that were good. There was a head of romaine lettuce, too. The outer leaves were dark and wilted, but the rest was fine. There were two cucumbers in one of the vegetable bins. The first one squished all over her hand when she grabbed it, but the other one was firm and edible. If she got lucky and found a can of olives in the pantry, she would be in business.

"You know, my brother called earlier today," Kyle said as Claudia washed her hands at the sink. "He said that he and his new girlfriend, Misty, were thinking about coming to Vermont while the leaves are at their peak. I told him they should visit this weekend, since it's getting late for good foliage. We could all have lunch or dinner together somewhere. Neither of us have met Misty yet, and it might be nice to spend some time with the two of them before the wedding."

"I'd love that," Claudia said as her happy, buzzy feeling ramped up to full power. Kyle's younger brother was a sweet guy — shy at first, but able to find humor in almost every situation once he relaxed and started to talk. "He knows you want him to be your best man, right?"

"Yeah. I asked him right after we got engaged. He's pretty excited about it. So is Rowen, since she's going to be our flower girl. She's nuts about Kev. Which reminds me . . ." Kyle turned to yell down the hallway. "Rowen, dinner's about done. Can you set the table?"

"I'll be there in a minute, Dad," Rowen called from her room.

"She'll be so thrilled if Kevin and Misty come for a visit," Claudia said. "How long have they been dating?"

"Just a few months, I think." Kyle paused and sighed. "My brother's never had great luck with women. His girlfriends have always turned out to be losers. But maybe this time will be different."

Claudia wanted to ask more about Kevin's dating history, but she decided against it because Rowen entered the room. Kyle's daughter was holding a book up to her face as she walked; somehow, she had made it to the kitchen without bumping into anything. Her expression brightened when she saw what Kyle had prepared. "Oooh, grilled cheese. Did you put tomato on mine?"

"Sure did. Sliced onions, too, just how you like it."

"What?" Rowen crowded up next to him at the stove. "But that's gross! I don't like onions on my grilled cheese. Are you kidding?"

"Yes. Gotcha." Kyle grinned down at her, and Rowen shoved him sideways once she realized that he'd been teasing her.

"I can't wait until we're all living together," Rowen said to Claudia. "Then he'll have someone to pick on besides me."

"Nah, he won't be doing much picking," Claudia said. She looped her arm around Rowen's shoulders and pulled the girl in for a hug. "We'll form a united front. You know, girl power! That way, you and I can pick on *him*."

Rowen laughed and squeezed her in return, and Claudia enjoyed another wave of pre-wedding bliss. As if it weren't enough to be marrying the man of her dreams, she was also gaining a precious stepdaughter whom she adored. Thinking about her soon-to-be-expanded family made her wonder again about Kevin and his new companion. Hopefully, Misty would also be someone whose company she would enjoy.

With a sigh, Emily slammed down the metal lid of her toolbox. The loud *clank* reverberated through the empty rooms of the McAllister mansion. Nothing she had in the box was small enough to fit in the tiny keyholes of the briefcase she had found. With her hammer and a chisel, she could easily break the locks and have the case open in a few minutes, and the idea was tempting. But besides the fact that the case wasn't hers, she couldn't bring herself to do anything that might damage it. She'd always been partial to antiques and furnishings of times past. She had built a career restoring old houses, after all. So, as curious as she was about the contents of the briefcase, she would baby it and find a way to open the locks properly.

Emily gathered up her purse and keys. There wasn't anything more she could do at the moment, and it was completely dark already. Her dog, Gus, was waiting for her at home and probably eager to be let outside.

She put the briefcase on the backseat of her car after she had locked up the marble mansion. On the short drive home, she thought about what she might have at her house that she could use to pick the locks. She had several small metal tools that she used to melt leftover bits of glass from her stained glass projects into beads. And there was no telling what she might find in her kitchen junk drawer.

Emily had just lugged everything into her house and let Gus run out to the backyard when someone knocked at her front door. Before she could get to it, the door opened and her mother stuck her head inside. "Em, it's me, honey. Are you home?"

"Barely," Emily said. "What's up?"

Her mother stepped into the foyer dressed in her typical real estate agent uniform — a tailored pantsuit and comfortable pumps. Since it was Saturday, she'd undoubtedly been out showing houses most of the day.

"I picked up two new listings today," she started, and Emily knew exactly where the conversation was heading. "They're both in pretty good shape, but one needs to have a few ghastly lighting fixtures swapped out, and the other has a really slow drain in one of the bathroom sinks. Do you think you'd have time tomorrow to take care of those things for me? I know I can sell them both quickly, but the drain worries me because it would show up on inspection."

"I'll try," Emily said, though she had no idea how she would squeeze in her mother's house maintenance projects. She was scheduled to open Turner's Hardware, where she worked part-time, in the morning, and she had been counting on having a solid block of time in the afternoon to finish the floors in the McAllister mansion.

"Thank you so much, honey," her mother said. "I don't know what I'd do without you. How are things coming with the new bed-and-breakfast?"

"They're coming. Ruth wants to have a wedding party stay there right before Christmas, and there's a lot to do before then. I'll probably be working up there most of tomorrow afternoon." Emily started toward the kitchen to let Gus back inside.

"I'll bet it's Kyle Hansen and Claudia Simon's wedding, right? Ruth was telling me they're engaged."

"Um-hmm." The big brown and white dog bolted through the door, tail wagging furiously. Emily managed to catch him by the collar before he could launch himself at her mother.

"Hello, Gus," her mother said, already backpedaling toward the front door. "I don't want to risk him jumping up on me while I've got my good clothes on. By the way, I'm off Monday, and I invited Rose and her family to supper. Ivy's coming, too, and so should you. A home-cooked meal would do you good after a long day of work."

"I'll try," Emily said again.

Her mother nodded and backed out the door, calling, "Okay, then. Have a good night, honey," as she closed it.

Emily released Gus and went to the kitchen. After she filled his bowl with dog food, she stood and stared into her refrigerator. She was starving but too tired to think about cooking anything. A simple peanut butter and jelly sandwich would do.

As she ate, she wandered from room to room, searching for something that would be suitable to pick the locks on the briefcase. There were some toothpicks in the junk drawer, along with an old nutpick, and she also gathered up a few of her smallest bead-making tools.

When she had stuffed the last bit of sandwich into her mouth, she took the old briefcase into the living room, beside a bright reading lamp, and sat down with it on her lap. She soon shoved the briefcase aside and flopped back in her chair. Only the toothpicks were small enough to fit in the keyholes, but they weren't strong enough to withstand the pressure she applied in trying to open the locks. One of them nearly broke off inside.

With fatigue finally overcoming her curiosity, Emily decided to take a long hot shower and go to sleep early. She would bring the briefcase to the hardware store in the morning, where she would have at her disposal umpteen different tools to open it.

Long after Ben had fallen asleep, Karen Cooper sat on the sofa in her living room. She couldn't bear to turn on the television, with its blaring twenty-four-hour news stations going on and on about the latest accidents and atrocities. From time to time, she glanced at the phone, willing it to ring, to bring her good news about her husband. *We've found Nick and he's fine,* she imagined a voice on the line telling her. Maybe he'd taken a wrong turn somewhere in Riyadh. Or maybe his vehicle had broken down and he and his colleague had had trouble finding someone to help them. As much as she tried to console herself with potential explanations, she knew very well that her husband would not disappear for four days unless something was horribly wrong.

The need to touch Nick, to reach out and grab his hand, to reassure herself that he was there with her, was as overpowering as it was impossible to satisfy. Not knowing what else to do, Karen reached under the coffee table where they kept the family photo albums, and moved several of them to the couch cushion beside her. These were their older pictures, taken when they were newlyweds and new parents. Smartphones and digital pictures hadn't existed back then, and the images in the albums were precious and irreplaceable.

She had forgotten about the evening when she'd been hugely pregnant with Ben and

Nick had decided to paint her tummy. He'd used her makeup to transform it into a face, complete with a protruding tongue made possible by her popped-out belly button. In between fits of laughter, they'd used the timer on the camera to take a close-up of Nick's face, with his tongue also stuck out, right next to her decorated stomach.

The next album held pictures of Ben as a four-year-old. She gently touched one of the few that included Nick. In it, he was dressed in fatigues, standing in front of their house on a Texas air base and holding their son on his shoulders. Both of them were smiling in the picture, taken just before Nick shipped out on a new deployment. As soon as Nick had left, she'd started to cry, and little Ben had kissed her wet cheeks "to make Mommy all better."

Karen looked down at the third album. It was the only one that was white. She couldn't bring herself to look at their wedding pictures inside. In fact, she found that she couldn't stand to continue looking at the old pictures at all.

After pacing around the room for a few minutes, she went to check on Ben. Her son was sleeping on his side with his mouth open and a gangly arm resting outside his covers. On the nightstand next to his bed was a stack of postcards and opened letters. Karen knew without looking that they were from Nick.

Silently, she entered Ben's room and lifted the postcard from the top of the pile. The front of the card was an aerial photograph of Riyadh. The city was vast and dusty and lacked even a hint of green. The orderly blocks of buildings with cars parked alongside seemed to go on forever, disappearing at the edge of the postcard into a grayish, blurred horizon. Nick was somewhere in that huge desert metropolis.

Or maybe he wasn't.

Pushing that thought from her mind, Karen flipped over the postcard. Her heart broke a little at the sight of Nick's slanted scrawl. The body of the message was short, almost cursory, containing only a mention of how hot it was getting and a promise to send a longer letter soon. It was the closing that got her, though.

Miss you and Mom more than ever. Can't wait to come home.

Love,
Dad

Karen struggled to keep her ragged breathing from waking Ben. She placed the postcard back on his nightstand and started backing out of his room. It was all she could do to get into the hallway and close Ben's door before she crumpled to the carpeted floor.

Pull yourself together, Karen. Stay strong. Nick would want you to stay strong. You're all Ben has right now.

And yet fighting against that internal voice of strength was a sinister undercurrent that threatened to haul her into a black abyss. She remembered the last time she had succumbed to it. It had taken a hospital stay and lots of therapy to pull her back from the brink. Despite the debilitating effects of the darkness — lack of focus or interest in things she enjoyed, fatigue, trouble sleeping, and a crushing feeling of guilt about her condition — she couldn't let that happen again.

From now on, until she got word that Nick was safe, she would keep up her routine. She would be a pillar of strength for Ben. She would summon up her courage and confront the fear and uncertainty bravely, as she knew Nick would. He would return to them. She believed that because she had to.

The alternative was unthinkable.

■ ■ ■ ■

In the parish house at St. John's, Father O'Brien had just settled into his recliner when the phone rang. He started and reached to answer it. An unfamiliar but pleasant woman's voice asked for him by name.

"This is Michael O'Brien," he told the caller.

"Hello, Father. My name is Julia Tomlinson. I'm a reporter with *America,* the Jesuit magazine, and I'm working on a story about clergy in the United States who continue to serve past the typical retirement age. I learned about you from the bishop of Burlington at a conference here in Manhattan last month. He gave me your private number."

Father O'Brien chuckled. "My number isn't really private, you know. Anyone can find it in the phone book. You're calling from New York, you said?"

"Yes, Father. Our headquarters are here in midtown."

"New York City." Father O'Brien paused as he tried to remember the last time he had been there.

"The reason for my call," Julia continued,

"is to ask whether I could interview you for my story. I've been doing some research, and I think you might be the oldest priest in the country with pastoral duties."

"That might well be," Father O'Brien said. "Of course, Ms. Tomlinson, I'd be happy to give you an interview."

"Oh, wonderful! And please, call me Julia. I could come up to Vermont this week or next if you have time to meet with me."

Father O'Brien chuckled again as he remembered the crowded streets and harried pedestrians in New York. "I have plenty of time, which is one of the wonderful things about Mill River. But even if I didn't, I would make time. Any afternoon this week would be fine."

"Why don't we try for Tuesday around one? I can meet you at the church," Julia said.

After he gave her directions to St. John's and ended the call, Father O'Brien leaned back into his chair. He removed the hearing aids from his ears and set them on the table next to the phone. Finally, his ears felt normal and natural, even if the deep quiet that surrounded him wasn't. "New York City," he said again, his voice louder than before, but with no one there to hear him, it didn't matter.

When he closed his eyes, picturing the skyscrapers and bustle of the city, he felt a kind of nostalgia. It wasn't a longing for New York — far from it. Instead, he recognized the memory of childhood wondering, the feeling of not having seen and wanting to see. It was almost as if he were a boy again, yearning to know what his father and brother were lucky enough to experience while he had remained at his grandparents' farm in the Vermont countryside so many years before.

CHAPTER 4

Saturday, March 31, 1934

Michael looked across the table at his mother. Their lunch had been meager — a bit of soup left over from the previous night's dinner and the last of a loaf of day-old bread — but she'd eaten very little.

"Mother, are you all right?"

"Just tired, that's all," his mother replied. "Here, Michael, you have this. I'm not really hungry." She pushed her plate and bowl across the table to him, and he didn't refuse it. "There's a bite of crust left in the kitchen, too," she added.

Michael looked at his mother's portion of soup and bread. "That's all right. This'll be enough."

As he finished her food, she reached over to pick up a postcard that had been wedged upright between the salt and pepper shakers. On the front was an image of the Hudson River Bridge in New York City, which had been completed only three years earlier. Niall had sent the postcard to tell them the address of the room he and Seamus had rented, along with a phone number where he could be reached in an emergency, and to show them something of the work they were doing.

The Triborough Bridge will be something like the one on the front of this card, Niall had written, *but bigger and connecting more pieces of the city.* He had promised to send money once he had been paid.

While his mother traced a finger down the edge of the postcard, rereading the message, Michael stared at the painting of the bridge on the other side. In the foreground was a street called Riverside Drive, carrying several fine-looking automobiles. The bridge rose up in the background, with great metal towers and steel support cables swooping majestically over the Hudson River. He was so fixated on the image that he didn't realize someone had knocked on the front door until his mother rose to answer it.

A strange man stood on the front porch. His clothes were dirt-covered and worn, and he hastily removed his hat. "Good day, ma'am," he said. "I was passing through, and I wondered if you might have any jobs that need doing."

"I'm sorry, we don't," his mother answered. She tried to shut the door, but the man took a step closer. Michael quickly stood up.

"Please, ma'am, I ain't had a proper meal in three days. Could you spare me anything to eat? Even a crust of bread, I'd be grateful for, if you have it."

"Anna, you best not be feeding hoboes," his grandmother hissed from her place at the table. His mother turned her head slightly, and Michael knew she had heard the admonition. No one spoke until Anna's soft voice broke the silence.

"Wait here," she told the man. In a flash, his mother went to the kitchen and grabbed the small, hard nub of the bread loaf left on the cutting board.

Anna, his grandmother said, but his mother ignored her again.

"I'm sorry it's not more, but we have very little," his mother said as she handed the crust to the man on the porch. "Now, you be on your way."

"Yes, ma'am. Thank you, ma'am," he said. Michael watched over his mother's shoulder while the stranger cradled the stale bread in both hands, as if it were a precious jewel, before scuttling backward off the porch.

"You're asking for trouble, Anna," his

grandmother snapped after the front door was safely closed. "There are too many strange men wandering about. You start feeding them, and they'll mark this place to let others know there's food to be had here."

"You didn't see his eyes, Lizzie. They were just . . . empty with hunger. Besides, the crust I gave him was hardly fit to be eaten."

"Just the same, don't do it again. You'll put us all at risk, especially with Niall and Seamus gone." His grandmother got up from the table and walked stiffly to the door. She put on an old coat and a pair of gloves. "I'm going to go check for eggs," she said before she left.

His mother started to clear the table, and Michael picked up his own dishes and silverware to help her. "Mother, I thought I might go hunting this afternoon," he said. Even though they had just finished lunch, he was beginning to regret his refusal of the hard crust she had offered first to him. His mouth began to water at the thought of the lovely ways his mother might prepare a rabbit or a nice grouse.

"We could use the meat," she said, "but first, I need your help. The root cellar needs cleaning out, and it'll go faster with the two of us. Besides, there's something down there I want to show you. Something your grandmother doesn't know about."

What frustration Michael felt at having to delay his hunting expedition vanished after hearing his mother's last statement. She set the dirty dishes in the sink and wiped her hands on her apron. When she put on her coat and went out the back door, he did the same.

The old farmhouse had both a front and a back porch, each shielded by an overhang. A door opened out of the floor of the back porch. From there, a steep stairway descended into a large root cellar.

"Your grandfather designed everything about this farm so well. It's really a blessing now, how our root cellar is hidden," his mother said as she pulled open the door and started down the stairs. "Even the hungry wanderers going door-to-door these days can't tell it's here. And it's so convenient to the house, not like some that are built out in people's yards. Imagine having to dig a path through the snow every time you need an onion!"

The root cellar was lit by a pair of bare lightbulbs protruding from the low ceiling. The thick, damp air smelled of cold earth. Shelves ran the length of the walls. A few mason jars containing pickled vegetables and fruit preserves sat on the uppermost levels. Pumpkins and Hubbard squashes rested on the lower shelves, along with empty jars being stored until they were needed. Nets of dried onions and garlic hung from hooks on the ceiling. On the floor beneath the shelving and forming a center aisle were wooden crates and bushel baskets placed side by side. Michael looked down the line at the containers of produce. There were separate ones for apples, potatoes, carrots, turnips, and beets. Not a single container was anywhere close to being full.

His mother started thinking aloud. "We'll need to go through and take out anything that's gone bad or started to grow. Hopefully, there won't be too many. We need to stretch what's left for quite a while yet. But first, while Lizzie's out of the house . . ." She walked to the far corner of the room. In a space between the wall and the end of the shelves on one side was a pile of burlap sacks they used when it was time to bring in the root crops.

"What I'm about to show you must stay between us, Michael," his mother said quietly. "But you're the man of the house now, and I want you to know about it." She bent over and reached behind the pile to remove a shiny wooden case.

"What is that?"

"It's . . . my insurance policy." She set the case on an empty stretch of shelving and opened it. Inside the rich mahogany, nestled in deep purple velvet, was a glowing set of sterling flatware. "This has been in my family a long time. My mother sent it to me years ago, even though my father would have abused her terribly had he known. He was a tyrant. When I married your father against his wishes, he disowned me and forbade everyone in the family to have contact with me."

Michael was shocked to be hearing about the taboo subject of his mother's parents. He knew very little about his maternal grandparents — only that they had lived in Boston and had cut off all communication with his mother. Never had his mother spoken to him about the reason for the estrangement. "Why did he disapprove of your marrying Father?"

"My parents were well-to-do, and I wanted for nothing growing up. Mama's family owned a big department store in the city. My father was a banker. Naturally, they assumed I would go to finishing school and marry well, preferably a gentleman they selected. It was especially important to them, I think, because Frank had decided to study for the priesthood, and they knew marriage wouldn't be in his future.

"They arranged several introductions for me, each one worse than the last. I couldn't imagine marrying any of the men my parents presented. I wanted to marry someone I loved, who loved me in return for more than my family's wealth. I'd seen my father's cruelty toward my mother all my life, and I didn't believe he or any man would beat his wife if he truly loved her."

"How did you meet Father, then?"

His mother smiled. "Your uncle Frank introduced us. Mama and I came out to Vermont to visit him a few years after he was ordained, and your father was up at the church with a delivery for needy families. Your grandfather did that often, you know. Donated milk and butter from the farm for the less fortunate. He was a good man."

"Times must have been much better back then."

"Financially, yes. Not like the twenties, but better than now." She traced her finger down the side of the wooden case. "Much better than now."

"If your parents wouldn't have approved of you marrying Father, how did you manage to do it? And when?"

"Frank helped me again." She gave a little

laugh. "I suppose it's true that my brother can be a bit devious at times. He certainly isn't like any other priest you're ever likely to meet. He always tried to shield me from our father, and he told me once that he felt guilty for entering the seminary because it would mean I'd be left at home without a big brother to protect me. Oh, he genuinely felt the call, don't misunderstand. But he knew, too, that the priesthood was his escape, and that marriage could be mine, if it were to the right man. He agreed with me that a marriage should be based on love.

"Your father and I wrote to each other secretly for nearly a year after we first met, and every time Mama and I came for a visit, Frank would make sure to let your father know so we could see each other. Eventually, your father raised the subject of engagement. He wanted to speak to my father before proposing, but he was the son of a dairy farmer. I knew my own father would never agree to meet him, much less consent to our marriage.

"It got worse once my parents grew impatient with my refusal to accept an engagement. My father was trying to force me into a marriage with the son of one of his partners at the bank. I panicked. I sent a wire to Frank, and he arranged for me to travel to his parish in Vermont. When I arrived, your father came up to the church, and we got married."

Michael looked at his mother as if seeing her for the first time. She was so small and quiet and deferential to his father. It was odd to hear her speaking matter-of-factly about her secret courtship and marriage. Could she really have been so bold and willful as a younger woman? Or was it that he simply didn't understand his mother's inner strength and what she was capable of doing?

"Did you go back home after you got married?" Michael asked in an incredulous whisper.

"I did. Or rather, *we* did. Your father and Uncle Frank and I went together. We thought my parents would take the news better if we were already married and there was nothing they could do to prevent it from happening.

"How foolish and naive we were! My father went into a rage when he realized what we'd done. He cursed at me, and Frank, too, for his role in it, and he tried to hit your father. My mother just cried. It was horrible. We left quickly and came here to the farm.

"We planned to stay until we could get

our own little place. Seamus was born two years later, and then the war hit. Your father volunteered to fight, along with his two brothers, even before the government passed the conscription law. They were all sent overseas in early 1917, once we were formally at war. I stayed here, with Seamus and your grandparents, while they were gone. Being here turned out to be a good thing.

"With my privileged upbringing, I didn't know anything about cooking or keeping house or taking care of babies — it had all been done for us. Your grandmother taught me about living on a farm, growing and storing food, cooking and cleaning, and raising children. She and your grandfather always felt it was important to be self-sufficient. By the time the war was over, I had learned so much about the work that goes into being a wife and mother."

Michael nodded. "What happened after Father came home?"

"Your father was the only one of his brothers to survive the war. It happened soon after they were all deployed. Even though his term of service hadn't expired, they sent your father back to the United States after his brothers were killed. After that, as his parents' only remaining child, he felt obligated to stay at the farm and help. He took a job at the mill only after Seamus was older and the income from the farm wasn't enough anymore. I think he always wanted to come back here someday and take over the farm and build it up, but after the crash and then your grandfather's death . . ."

His mother looked down at the case of flatware. "It was a long time after I got married before I heard anything from my parents. I never saw Mama after that last time being at the house, though eventually, she did start writing to me. Before she died, she managed to send this set of silver to me. It's by Towle Silversmiths, the rare Clover pattern from 1887. Twelve place settings and a matching server set. She begged me to keep it a secret from everyone — from your grandparents and even your father. She wanted me to have something valuable of my own, something that could be converted into money, in case I ever needed a way out of a bad situation. Mama sympathized with me, but she didn't dare go against my father. She was trapped and terrified by him. I think this silver was her way of providing me some sort of escape route that she never had."

Michael looked carefully at the flatware. There were tiny four-leaf clovers and clover blossoms etched into the silver. The designs were perfect, miniature likenesses of the clumps of clover that grew all over the farm in the summertime.

His mother carefully lifted a small round spoon from its place among the other, larger serving pieces. "The pieces aren't monogrammed. Mama knew engravings would diminish the value of the set if it needed to be sold. But she did have something engraved on this one special spoon for me. It's a sugar spoon." She held it out to him. "Look at the handle, in the little space between the clover leaves."

Michael took the spoon and squinted down at it. The dim light in the root cellar made it hard to read the fine script, but he tilted the spoon up and down until the minuscule etching was illuminated:

Anna

"And now, turn it over and look on the back of the handle."

He flipped it over and saw the words *My sweet girl* in the same tiny script, engraved into the thin silver surface. When he looked back at his mother, her eyes were brimming with tears.

"It was a little joke between Mama and

me. When I was a little girl, I used to sneak into the kitchen and eat sugar straight out of the bowl. The hired girls would scold when they caught me, but Mama was gentle. She always hugged me and said that I couldn't help it because I was her 'sweet girl.' "

Michael didn't know what to say, but he smiled and passed the spoon carefully back to her. After a moment, his mother gently placed the sugar spoon back in its place. He watched as she closed and latched the lid of the flatware case and hid it again behind the burlap sacks.

"Father and Grandma really don't know about it?"

"No, nor does Seamus, and you're not to tell them about it, either, Michael."

"But you've had it for so long, and we've moved more than once. How have they not seen it?"

"I've been very careful, and I change the hiding place from time to time," she said with a slight smile. "Now, Michael, I need to know — I can trust you, can't I?"

"Yes, Mother," Michael said. "You can trust me."

His mother nodded. "For all these years, I've honored Mama's wishes to keep her gift a complete secret. I've showed it to you only as a precaution, in case something happens to your grandmother and me while we're here alone."

"Nothing will happen to either of you. I promised Father I'd take care of everything, and I will."

"I know, Michael. You gave your word." His mother patted his arm before she took up two of the burlap sacks and began walking along the bins of vegetables, looking into each one. "Let's start at the end here," she said as she knelt down near the large potato bin at the end of the row. "Anything that's soft or rotten will go in one bag, and anything starting to grow that we can still eat goes in the other. The good potatoes, we'll pile up to go back in the box."

Together, they tipped the box forward and dumped the remaining potatoes onto the earthen floor. After a few minutes of silence, his mother looked at him with her brow furrowed. "I don't want you to think that my keeping the silver means that I believe I might need it someday to leave your father," she said softly.

"I didn't think that."

"Good. Marrying your father was the best thing I ever did. I keep the silver now only so our family has something to fall back on. I'd sell it if we were starving or desperate, but we're not — not yet, anyway. But I rest easier, knowing it's here. Since Roosevelt made it illegal to keep gold and took away forty percent of our dollars, silver is the only sure money. And I'd be afraid that your father and grandmother would want to part with it sooner than we should if they knew I had it — Oh!"

At his mother's loud gasp, Michael looked up from his sorting. She had picked up a potato that had gone bad, and its foul-smelling liquid had run all over her hand and down her arm.

"That's a really rotten one," Michael said. "It stinks worse than anything in the barn."

"It does," his mother agreed. She put the bad potato in the "rotten" sack and rose to her feet. "I'm going to go wash this off," she said, but she stood in place. She placed her clean hand over her mouth and clutched at the wooden shelving for support.

"Mother?" Michael quickly got to his feet. "What's the matter?"

"The smell," she said in a weak voice. "I just felt like I was going to be sick. I'll be all right once I get some fresh air."

"I can do the sorting myself," Michael said. "It won't take long."

His mother looked at him for a moment and then gave a resigned nod.

"Let me walk you upstairs —"

"No, no need. I can get myself upstairs, and I'll probably lie down for a little while. If you can finish down here, I'd be grateful. The sooner it's done, the sooner you can get out and get us something good for supper."

As Michael watched, his mother made her way slowly to the stairs and up out of the root cellar.

Once she was gone, he finished looking through the potatoes as quickly as he could and moved to the next container. The apples took the longest because there were more of those left. It was a relief to push the apple bin back into place. He could finally go hunting! Michael picked up the two sacks of inferior produce and selected one of the good apples from the bin to take as a snack.

He took the bag of still-edibles into the house and left it in the kitchen for his mother. The silence inside told him that she was in her room resting, and his grandmother hadn't returned from the chicken coop. Quietly, he slipped the long strap of his game bag over his head, removed his .22 rifle and a box of cartridges from the gun case, and went back outside. He would drop the rotten produce at the barn. His grandmother might want to feed some of it to the chickens, and the rest she could put in the compost heap beside the garden.

Michael started out, as he always did, by walking through the rear pasture toward the woods. At the corner of the field, just before the trees started, he passed a row of four large rocks that were purposefully placed. His mother walked down to the stones every spring to plant flowers among them. Now that he was older, he knew what lay beneath those rocks, and he knew not to bother his mother on those rare occasions when she visited them.

Only a few hours of daylight were left, at best, and Michael moved past the row of stones faster than he normally would have. He was focused on getting a few squirrels. There was a sweet spot in the woods where he could sit with a clear view of a grove of hickory trees. He almost always got a squirrel in that place, either perched on one of the bare branches or scrounging around for buried nuts.

Michael ended up bagging two squirrels in the woods before the sun dropped too low for him to continue. *It might still be bright enough to hunt outside the forest,* he thought, so he reloaded his rifle for the walk back to the house. If he got lucky on his walk home through the field, he might kick up a rabbit hiding in one of the frozen tufts of grass that extended above the snow. The last thing he wanted to do was miss an opportunity to add to his haul.

When he emerged from the trees, he followed the fence up through the pasture toward the house. The lights were on there, as well as in the barn. Undoubtedly, his grandmother was busy with the evening milking, and his mother was in the kitchen starting supper. That realization prompted him to move faster. The quicker he skinned and dressed out the squirrels, the quicker they would be cooked and ready to eat.

As Michael stepped onto the rear porch, his mother's scream snapped him out of his thoughts. He looked through the glass in the door and saw inside the looming figure of a man he didn't recognize.

CHAPTER 5

Late Sunday morning, Emily arrived at Turner's Hardware to open the store. Henry, the owner, rarely came in on the weekends anymore, and she was looking forward to the time between customers to work on unlocking the briefcase.

She put on her work apron, opened the safe, and loaded the till into the register. There were two boxes of stock that Henry had left for her in the back office, but it took her only a few minutes to unpack the packages of drywall screws and thin finishing nails. She slid most of the small containers onto the appropriate display racks, then put one package of finishing nails in her apron pocket. Next she walked around the end of the aisle to where the screwdrivers were displayed, including sets small enough to be used for jewelry or eyeglass repair. She placed one of those in her pocket as well.

Lined up on the far wall, there were spools

of rope, cabling, and wire that could be purchased by the yard. Emily snipped small pieces of two sizes of the wire and headed back to the front counter. On her way, she flipped the sign on the door to OPEN.

She had the locked briefcase up on the counter and was hunched over it, fishing the sturdier piece of wire into the keyhole, when her first customer arrived. She straightened up and smiled. "Hi. Can I help you?"

"Uh, yeah, maybe. Do you guys carry car air fresheners?"

"Sure, back in the auto section. Far corner on the left," she said as she pointed down one of the aisles.

"Thank you, ma'am."

Emily watched the man walk away from the counter. He looked vaguely familiar, though she didn't recall ever meeting him. Within a few minutes, she was again completely absorbed in working on the briefcase. The man clearing his throat as he stood before the register startled her.

"Oh! I'm so sorry! I didn't notice you coming back," she said.

"That's all right. I didn't mean to make you jump." The man smiled and put a package of evergreen-shaped air fresheners and a bottle of upholstery cleaner on the counter. "So, where's Henry?"

"He's off today," Emily said. "I usually cover the store for him on Sundays."

"And you are . . . ?"

"Emily DiSanti."

"I'm Matt Campbell." He reached out a hand, and she shook it. "Nice to meet you."

As soon as he said his name, Emily placed him. "You're one of the officers in town, right? The newest one?"

"Yes, ma'am. I'm off today, though."

Matt was wearing a flannel shirt and jeans. She had seen him only in passing and only in uniform. "The regular clothes threw me off," she admitted. "Here, let me ring you up. Is this stuff for the police department?"

"No, they're for my car. I just got a puppy —"

Her attention shifted for a moment as the front door of the store opened again. A woman with short black hair entered and walked down one of the aisles before Emily could greet her.

"Really? A puppy?" Emily said, focusing again on Matt. "What kind?"

"A shelter mutt."

Emily grinned. "That's where my dog, Gus, came from, too. Shelter mutts are the best."

"They are. I haven't named her yet. I

82

think she's part husky and part Lab, but who knows. Anyway, she's not housebroken yet, and I made the mistake of letting her sit in the passenger seat of my car."

"Ah." Emily laughed and started scanning his items. "Then you definitely need this stuff."

"Yes, ma'am. Unfortunately." He gave her a sheepish grin.

She smiled back. He had a handsome face that seemed to be getting better-looking the longer she spoke with him. He had also called her "ma'am" three times during their brief encounter.

"So, let me guess. You were in the military before you joined the police department?"

"Yes, ma' — Oh, I'm doing it again, aren't I? I'm sorry. Using 'ma'am' or 'sir' is second nature to me now. I'm trying to break the habit."

"That's okay," Emily said. "I've been called worse things."

"I was in the Marines for sixteen years. The last six before I got out, I spent in the Middle East — Iraq and Afghanistan — but the last time I had to decide whether to re-up, I felt like it was time to come home and do something else. Police work sounded pretty interesting. I like it so far."

"Mill River's a nice town," Emily told him

as she handed him his receipt and bagged his purchases. "I grew up here, and I moved back myself last summer."

"I actually heard a little bit about you," Matt said. "You know, when everything was going on with your sister."

Emily felt her cheeks start to burn. "Oh, right. Well, Rose and I are on better terms now." She smiled quickly. Matt continued to linger, and she began to get the feeling that he didn't want their conversation to end.

"That looks like a pretty old briefcase," he said. "It's in good condition, though."

"Yeah. It belongs to . . . a friend. I've been trying to get it open for her, but the keys are lost, and I didn't have anything at home small enough to fit in the locks." She looked down toward the far end of the counter, where her nails, wire, and tiny screwdrivers were scattered.

"Do you know anything about picking locks?"

"Well, no, not really, but I'm pretty handy. I'll figure it out."

"I can tell you that none of those things will work," Matt said, glancing at her makeshift collection of tools. "Look, let me make it easier for you. I've got a pick set at home. I need to go let my pup out for a break, but after that, I'll grab the tools and come right back here. I can pop this baby open for you, no problem."

"Really? I mean, that's so nice of you, but it seems like a lot of trouble."

"No trouble at all. I'll be back." Matt grabbed his bag from the counter and hurried out the door.

Why doesn't the hardware store carry lock-pick sets? Emily wondered. Henry stocked almost every kind of tool made, so it was odd to learn of something he didn't offer. More important, why would Matt know how to pick locks? Was it part of his military or police training? And besides, given that he *was* a police officer, and she was trying to open a briefcase she didn't own to view contents that weren't hers, wouldn't it be foolish of her to accept Matt's help?

Karen Cooper stood in Turner's Hardware, staring at a display of various kinds of rope.

Not that she intended to buy any, or use it . . . yet. It was more like she was giving in to a morbid curiosity that lingered deep in the back of her mind. She was merely looking at her options.

She'd been doing well this morning. After attending Mass, she'd swung by home to drop off Ben before going back out to do some shopping. At the bakery, she'd smiled and chatted with Ruth Fitzgerald and picked up a few pieces of pie. She was proud of herself for maintaining a cheerful facade, for sticking with her usual routine to provide a semblance of normalcy. All morning, except for a few brief minutes at St. John's, during the morning Mass and when Father O'Brien had spoken with her afterward, she'd managed to avoid actively thinking about her missing husband.

Overhearing the conversation between the woman behind the counter and the male customer had ruined her fragile balancing act. The man had mentioned that he'd been in the military, stationed in the Middle East, and his words had cut through the flimsy membrane containing the worry and despair Karen struggled to control. She was in front of the rope display, shaking and trying to get herself together, when she felt a hand on her arm.

"Excuse me, I wanted to see if you needed help finding anything . . . Are you all right?"

"Oh." Karen gasped and hurriedly wiped her cheeks. "No, I . . . uh, yes, I'm fine." She blinked and avoided eye contact with the red-haired woman next to her.

"Aren't you Karen Manning?"

Karen flinched at the woman's question

and glanced up at her. "Yes, I was. It's Karen Cooper now."

"I thought so! Do you remember me? Emily DiSanti? We went to school together. You were a year ahead of me."

"Emily?" Karen squinted at the woman's face. "Oh! You had an older sister, and I was in the grade between you two."

"Yeah, you're thinking of Rose. She and her family live in Mill River now. I do, too."

"I moved back a few years ago myself. My husband —" Karen paused. Why was it that every conversation circled back to Nick? She swallowed and tried to keep her voice steady. "My husband served in the Air Force for years, so we moved from place to place for a long time. We came back here to live once he decided not to reenlist."

"Mill River seems to have that effect on people. It calls to you when you've been away for a while." Emily furrowed her brow and hesitated before she said anything more. "Karen, are you sure you're okay?"

"I'm fine," Karen said, but her shoulders sagged as what was left of her composure slipped away. "It's just that . . . my husband is working in Saudi Arabia, and he went missing yesterday. I was trying to keep it together today, but I overheard your conversation with that man, and when he mentioned being stationed in the Middle East . . ."

"I'm . . . I'm so sorry," Emily said. "I don't know what to say. Does your family still live here? Do you have anyone close by?"

Karen smiled as Emily squeezed her arm. "My mother passed away years ago. Dad's nearby, in Rutland, but he has Alzheimer's. He lives in a memory care facility there. Sometimes he recognizes me, but he doesn't know who Ben is anymore, and he doesn't talk much."

"Who's Ben?"

"My son. He's thirteen. I can't believe he's a teenager already, but he is, and he's a great kid." She smiled at Emily through her tears. "My brother, George, lives in Seattle. Nick's family is in Texas, spread all over the state. His parents and sister live in Houston. I've been in touch with everybody. We're all just hoping and praying we'll get a call saying he's been found." Karen pulled her phone from her pants pocket and looked down at the screen.

"I hope so, too."

"They've got lots of people searching, lots of private security people from the company he's with, and some military. They'll find him."

"They will, I'm sure they will," Emily said quickly.

They stood in silence for a moment. Karen glanced at the ropes on the wall and then over at Emily. "I came in here for . . . lightbulbs. I'm all out of sixty-watt bulbs, or whatever fluorescent kind gives the same amount of light."

"Sure, we have them," Emily said, and she turned to lead Karen to a different area of the store. "How many do you need?"

Karen selected a box of bulbs and paid for them at the register. She gamely kept up small talk with Emily, but inside, she longed to rush home, climb into bed, and pull the covers over her head. Sleep would be a welcome, if temporary, respite. Perhaps the thick bedding would persuade her body and mind to relax enough to let it come.

Carrying a small brown bag and a steaming cup of coffee, Claudia left Ruth's bakery-café and headed up the street toward the police station. Even though the walk was short, it was wonderful to be out in the crisp autumn air with the bright sunshine warming her face. The sunny day and the brilliant fall foliage made everything in Mill River vibrant and happy. The fact that she was planning her wedding and on her way to surprise Kyle with lunch bolstered her upbeat mood, too.

She reached the door of the police station just as Kyle was coming out. "Hi," she said. "I brought you lunch." She held up the bag and the coffee cup.

"You're just full of surprises," he said, leaning down to kiss her. "What's in the bag?"

"Chicken salad and apple pie from Ruth's. Do you want to go to the break room?"

"Well, Ron just got here, so I was going to take a quick drive around. You want to come along?"

"Yeah." She smiled suggestively.

"Don't get any bright ideas, my dear. I'm on duty —"

"— which means you can't mess around, yeah, I know." She followed him to the department's Jeep Grand Cherokee and climbed into the passenger seat. "You really ought to loosen up a little."

Kyle rolled his eyes and started the engine. "So, you came from the bakery?"

"Yeah. Rowen was there, all set up at one of the tables with her homework."

"And probably something sweet, I imagine."

"Yes, she was working on a cupcake along with her book report."

Kyle chuckled. "That'll be another advantage of moving into your place. Rowen won't have a ready supply of baked goods downstairs."

"I don't know how you guys have managed to live in that apartment for as long as you have. I mean, it's a nice place, but I'd go nuts with the smell of pies and pastries constantly coming up through the floor."

They drove down Main Street, through the main business district and a residential area composed of small, older houses and a few trailer homes. There was a stand set up in front of one of the mobile homes. A stout woman with curly gray hair sat in a chair behind it.

"Daisy's still at it, I see," Kyle said as he slowed the Jeep and rolled the window down to speak to her. "How are you, Miss Daisy?"

"Hello, Officer! I'm just fine, thank you. Trying to sell what's left of my special Halloween potion." Daisy motioned to a line of large mason jars on the table, each of which was filled with bright orange liquid. "It's scary good, you know. There's lots of orange juice in it, and each jar comes with a secret spell to keep the ghosts and goblins away. Would you like to try it?"

Claudia watched as Kyle took a deep

breath and tried to give her an earnest response.

"It sounds nice, Miss Daisy, but I've got to finish my patrol and get back to the station. It's a nice afternoon to be out, though. You enjoy the sunshine!"

"I will, Officer," Daisy called as Kyle rolled up the window.

"I'd like to know how she comes up with those concoctions," Claudia said with a giggle once they were on their way. "And I wonder what's in her Halloween potion besides orange juice?"

"I don't think I want to know," Kyle said. He shook his head. "Daisy is something else."

They were approaching the old covered bridge on the edge of town. Once they were past it, Kyle turned onto a small highway. "I figured I'd drive out a ways, then head back through the country and stop at the new park, if you'd like," he said, and Claudia nodded her agreement. "So, what else do you have planned for today?"

"I've got a fitting for my wedding gown at two, with a woman named Pauline Albury. Do you know her?"

"I've heard the name, but I haven't met her," Kyle said.

"My landlady, Ms. DiSanti, recommended

her. She said Pauline does all the alterations on her business clothes, and you've seen how nice Ms. DiSanti always dresses."

"I can give you a ride over to her place once we get back into town."

"But then you'd see the gown!"

"Lay it in the back of the Jeep. I won't peek, promise."

"Nope, I'm not buying that. You'll just have to wait."

Kyle sighed. They came around a bend, and a lovely log cabin came into view.

"I really like Doc Richardson's place," Kyle said, motioning to the house, set back off the highway. "I like living in town, too, but you get more privacy out here."

"Do you want to look for a place in the country?" Claudia asked. "I mean, I know we're all going to live in my house for a while, but eventually?"

Kyle shrugged. "I dunno. I suppose when we're ready to buy something, we can check out everything that's available."

"Cool. Until then, we can snuggle up in *our* little house together."

Kyle grinned as he reached over and squeezed her hand. After another few miles, they turned onto a small paved road that headed up into the hills. There were small houses and farms along the roads, and several times, they came upon particularly stunning views. The trees were every color — flaming reds and oranges, golds and yellows so bright that they seemed to have an ethereal glow, and the deep dark green of evergreens scattered among the other hues. Kyle slowed the Jeep as they came to a large private pond, where they admired how the brilliant thicket of trees behind it was reflected perfectly on its still surface.

"Look how beautiful," Claudia breathed. "It's like a postcard."

"Yeah," Kyle agreed. "Scenery like this actually makes me look forward to fall patrols."

The road grew more narrow and curved again, passing by more houses and breathtaking scenery until it opened up into a straightaway. After a few moments, Kyle turned right onto a smaller road. A new split-rail fence appeared, running for several hundred feet until it formed a corner at an asphalt driveway and a large wooden sign that read HAYES MEMORIAL PARK AND RECREATION AREA. There were a few other cars in the newly paved parking area. Kyle pulled into a space next to a minivan. A small hatchback was parked on the other side of the lot.

"I haven't been here since the dedication

in September," Claudia said as she exited the Jeep. "It's even more gorgeous now that the trees have turned."

On one side of the park, picnic tables and metal charcoal grill boxes were placed strategically among a group of bright red sugar maples. There was a large open field beyond the tables where a man was throwing a football with a gangly teenager. On the opposite side, a swing set and two configurations of shiny playground equipment reflected the sunlight. A woman sat on a bench watching two young children climbing up a ladder to a slide. Beyond the playground area were tennis and basketball courts and a baseball field, as well as a fenced-in area where dogs could be exercised off-leash. A wide walking path ringed the entire park.

"Let's go sit down," Kyle said. He had the brown bag and coffee cup, and together they walked to one of the picnic tables. As Kyle ate, Claudia put her elbows on the table and leaned back with her eyes closed. Every few minutes, a burst of cool autumn breeze rushed over her face and caused a surge of colored leaves to rain down around them. Soon the weather would turn frigid, and it would be months before the sun's warmth returned. But this winter would be warm in other ways. She stole a glance at Kyle and smiled.

"I wonder what this place looked like when Samuel Hayes was alive," Kyle said. "Father O'Brien said it was a Morgan horse farm back then. There used to be a big barn right where we're sitting."

"And a farmhouse up on that little hill past the ball field, I remember him saying," Claudia said. She looked in the direction of the hill. An elegant monument of a mare and a young woman now stood on top of it, along with an engraved plaque describing Mary McAllister's gift of the land for the new park. "It's great what they've done with the property, though. I'll bet there are towns ten times the size of Mill River that don't have a park as nice as this." The sound of voices in the distance caught her attention. She squinted toward the parking lot, where the woman from the playground was shepherding her children into the minivan. A few minutes later, the two people who had been tossing the football climbed into the hatchback and drove away.

She and Kyle were alone . . . with the Jeep.

He had just finished his sandwich and pie and had taken the lid off the coffee. She waited as he drank it, watching impatiently as tiny wisps of steam rose from the cup.

Finally, she tucked her hands inside the sleeves of her sweatshirt and crossed her arms.

"You know, it's getting pretty chilly with this breeze," she said. "Do you mind if we go back to the Jeep?"

"No, I'm about done, and we should get going, anyway. Ron'll be expecting me back soon."

When they reached the vehicle, Claudia opened one of the rear doors and quickly climbed into the backseat. "C'mon," she said to him in a low voice.

"What? What are you — Oh no, we can't, Claudia. Seriously, I could be fired, and —"

"Shhh, I've got goosebumps. Just climb in and cuddle me for a few minutes. We won't do anything more."

"I don't believe you," he said, but he got in and closed the door anyway. As soon as Kyle was seated, she swung her leg over him and pulled herself onto his lap. "Claudia, it's broad daylight. Somebody else could show up any minute —" he started to say, but she took his face in her hands and kissed him.

"The windows are tinted, and no one else is here. We'll be quick. Just relax," she whispered, and didn't give him a chance to reply. Her hands moved to the buckle on his duty belt, trying to figure out how to undo it while she kept his mouth busy.

"God, Claudia," Kyle gasped. He grabbed her wrists. For a moment, he restrained her. She could tell by his breathing, though, that he was starting to feel the moment.

"Please, baby, I've wanted to do this for a long time," she murmured. After she kissed him again, a tortured expression passed over Kyle's face. She smiled triumphantly when he cursed under his breath, released her arms, and dealt with the buckle himself.

Afterward, they put on what clothes they had removed and lounged for a few minutes on the soft leather seat. Claudia reached up and gently touched Kyle's face. "Thank you. That's one off my bucket list."

"Seriously? Having sex in a car?"

"Not just any car. *This* one."

He rolled his eyes and leaned his head back on the seat. "Well, I suppose there are worse things."

Claudia smiled. "*Waaaaay* worse," she agreed as she rested her head against his shoulder.

Suddenly, the radio in Kyle's duty belt crackled, and Ron's voice came through the speaker. "HQ to Hansen, come in, over."

They both started, and Kyle grabbed the radio from its holster. He put a finger to his lips and gave Claudia a stern look before he spoke. "Hey, Ron, what's up?"

"Hey, Kyle. We just got a call from the Village Market. One of their customers locked her keys in the car with the engine running. The car's an older-model Chevy. Do you think you could jimmy the door for her?"

"I can try," Kyle said. "I'm heading back into town now, so I'll stop over there before I come back to the station."

"Ten-four. I'll let them know. Ron out."

"See? It's fine. No one saw, and nobody will ever know," Claudia said with a mischievous grin. "And don't tell me you didn't enjoy yourself." She followed Kyle's lead, though, when he quickly got out of the backseat and climbed into the front.

Kyle shook his head. "You're unbelievable," he said as he started the engine. "Reckless, full of bad judgment, and, and —"

"— and what?"

He looked at her, and his expression softened. It seemed he was trying to suppress a grin. He reached out a hand and tucked a strand of her mussed-up hair behind her ear. "*Very* naughty."

Claudia smiled. "And?"

"Drop-dead gorgeous."

Her smile grew wider. "And?"

"*Mine.*" Kyle leaned across the seat and gave her a slow, lingering kiss.

Claudia was happy down to her toes. And she knew she would never again think of Mill River's new "recreation area" in quite the same way.

Father O'Brien was in the sacristy at St. John's, removing his vestments after the morning's Mass. The celebration had been relatively uneventful, other than the short announcement he had made at the end about Karen Cooper's missing husband. He had asked everyone in attendance to say a prayer for Nick's quick and safe return.

He had spoken with Karen after Mass, once the other church members had offered her their words of comfort and left. She'd insisted that she and Ben were holding up as well as could be expected, but her pasty complexion and baggy, swollen eyes indicated otherwise. What concerned him even more was the expression he saw in her eyes — or, rather, the lack of it. There was no spark there, no trace of hope or anger or resolve, any of which he would expect to see in the eyes of someone in her situation. Her eyes were blank, emotionless. He had seen other people's eyes look that way, and

100

it had scared him every time.

Father O'Brien stood at the altar, looking out at the pews to make sure all was in order, when he suddenly realized how tired he was. His head felt as if it were spinning, and his knees were a bit wobbly. Perhaps it was because he hadn't eaten breakfast that morning?

Of course that's it, he thought. He'd had his usual coffee and a small glass of juice, but he'd gotten so absorbed in making a few last-minute changes to his homily that he hadn't had time to eat anything. Carefully, he left the church and walked the short path to the parish house.

In his kitchen, he grabbed a banana to eat while he grilled a sandwich. The heat from the stove burner felt good as it radiated toward him, and it reminded him of the paperwork for the new heating assistance program that Jim Gasaway had requested he look over. The weather was already getting colder, and winter was a few short months away. He wanted to make sure that the funds Mary McAllister had left for the program could be used as soon as possible.

When he closed his eyes, he could still envision Mary's smiling face. His dearest friend had been gone nearly nine months. He missed her terribly, especially in the quiet moments he had to himself. It comforted him to know that he was helping to carry out her wishes to care for the people of Mill River. Throughout her lifetime, she had done so much for her community, and her estate would provide even more help to those in need.

Still, there were limits to what Mary's love could do. If she were alive, he undoubtedly would have told her of Karen Cooper's situation, of his prayers for Nick's safety and the well-being of Karen and her son. She would have shared his concern. He knew, too, that as much as Mary would have wanted to help, there would have been nothing she could have done to find Nick Cooper and return him to his family.

CHAPTER 6

Saturday, March 31, 1934

For an instant, Michael was too shocked to move. A second scream from his mother launched him into action. He threw open the door and raised his rifle.

The large man in the kitchen towered over his mother. He stood with his back toward Michael, holding her firmly by the wrists and pushed up against the counter. She was struggling against his hold, kicking and thrashing, but she was no match for the man's strength.

"Take your hands off her!" Michael yelled. Never before had he aimed his gun at a person. He pressed his cheek to the side of the rifle, trying to steady the weapon in his trembling hands. The man turned, revealing a dirt-streaked face and an unkempt beard. Michael made eye contact with the intruder and took aim at his forehead. At that moment, two thoughts rose up in his mind.

The man was standing in close proximity to his mother, which would make firing extremely risky.

His loaded rifle held only a single shot.

"Or what, little boy?" In an instant, the man had produced a knife and whirled his mother around in front of him, where he held the blade to her throat. "Careful. You wouldn't want this knife to slip, now, would you?"

Michael stayed frozen where he stood. His finger was positioned just in front of the trigger, and his heart was hammering in his ears.

The intruder squinted at him before stretching his mouth into a taunting smile. "Come on, now, pretty lady. Tell this little boy of yours to put the gun down before you get hurt."

"Please, Michael," his mother gasped. "Do what he says." Her head was turned, pressed back against the intruder's chest, and she was looking at him out of the corners of her eyes. Michael could see how forcefully the man held the knife against her neck by the way her skin rose up around the point of the blade. It would take only one jab, one slight flick of the intruder's wrist . . .

"Be a good lad, now, and listen to your mommy," the man growled.

Michael's eyes made brief, intense contact with those of his mother before he focused again on the intruder's face.

"Please, please, Michael —" his mother began again, but the *crack* of the rifle next to his ear prevented him from hearing what more she said.

The intruder's head snapped backward. The hand holding the knife dropped away from his mother's throat as its owner sank to the floor.

Michael rushed forward and grabbed his mother by the arm. She stepped away from the body convulsing at her feet. A drop of blood appeared on her neck where the intruder's blade had nicked her skin, but she didn't seem to notice as she hugged Michael close.

"Anna? Anna, what's going on? I was halfway across the lawn with the milking and heard a shot." Lizzie came through the back door, out of breath after running from the barn. His grandmother looked down at the dead man and then at the rifle that Michael held. "Michael?"

"I came in from hunting and he had her pinned against the cupboard," he whispered, lowering the butt of his rifle to the floor. "He had a knife."

His grandmother stared at him, her mouth

open far enough that he could see the gaps where her teeth were missing. She walked over to the body and peered down at the man's face. "You shot him right through the eye."

"He didn't have a choice." Anna finally found her voice, although the tears were coming and she seemed to have difficulty speaking. "That man had a knife at my throat, and he would've killed us both — or worse — if Michael hadn't done it."

"Anna, come sit down," his grandmother said. She pulled out a chair, and Michael helped his mother over to it. "Thank goodness you're all right. Thank goodness. Maybe now you'll listen to me about feeding strangers who show up here. You can't trust anyone you don't know during times like this. Do you hear me? You can't trust *anyone*."

"It's all right, Grandma," Michael said in a soothing voice. "Now's not the time for scolding."

His grandmother had worked herself up, and she, too, was looking unsteady. Michael carefully leaned his rifle in a corner near the kitchen door and pulled out a chair for her next to his mother.

"You're right," she admitted as she sat down, "but we do have to worry about what

106

to do with him." She jutted her chin in the direction of the dead man on the floor. "Why don't you check his pockets, Michael? See if he's carrying identification."

Michael hesitated, not wanting to go near the body.

"We should call the police," his mother said, but his grandmother vigorously shook her head.

"Not so fast, Anna. We wouldn't want Michael to get into any trouble. We know it was self-defense, but you'd have to convince the authorities of that. What if they didn't believe you? Michael could be arrested. And they'd probably want to know where Niall is. If they contacted him, you know he'd leave his job and rush home."

His mother was silent for a moment. "That's true," she said slowly. She wiped under her eyes with the heel of her hand. "I'm not hurt, after all, and I wouldn't want him to lose that job or worry about us here."

"In my experience, the police sometimes make a mess of things," his grandmother said. "No, this is something we should deal with ourselves, if we can. Now, Michael, go see what that fella had on him."

He steeled himself and went over to the corpse. It had pretty much stopped twitching, but there was no avoiding the gruesome sight of the man's face, with blood filling the eye socket and spilled in rivulets down his cheek. The man obviously hadn't bathed in some time, as the stench from his body was acrid and nearly overpowering. Gingerly, Michael reached into the pockets of his filthy coat and pants. When he found nothing, he pulled open one side of the coat to reveal a bulging interior pocket.

There was a soiled, wrinkled handkerchief tucked inside, along with a gold pocket watch, two quarters, and a crumpled one-dollar silver certificate. Michael brought the items to the table for his mother and grandmother to see. "The watchcase is engraved. 'B. D. Woods,' " he read, looking down at it. "But it might not be his."

"From the looks of him, I doubt it is," his grandmother said. "And if there's nothing in the way of solid identification, then good. If he's a nobody, he won't be missed. We ought to wait a little longer and then bury him while it's still dark."

"Lizzie," his mother said in an anguished whisper, "I don't . . . I *will not* allow him to be buried out there. Not out there with my . . . my —"

"I didn't mean *there*," his grandmother said. "Of course not. The ground's frozen anyway. No, the only place we could dig a

108

grave for him would be underneath the haystack beside the barn."

"We'd have to move a ton of hay," Michael said. "It's covered in snow, too. It would take hours to expose a big enough piece of ground."

"So, we'd bury him, on Easter Sunday, no less, and then what?" his mother asked. "Would we just go about our business, knowing all the while that there's the body of a criminal festering out there next to the barn? What if someone does come looking for him? No, we're not going to bury him here. Absolutely not."

"Then what do *you* suggest, Anna?"

Michael looked from his grandmother to his mother. He didn't want the man buried anywhere on their property, either, but what else could they do? "Could we move him . . . the body . . . to some other place?" he suggested.

"Not us," his mother replied. "But maybe someone else could. I'm going to go call Frank. He'll know what to do."

For as much of his early childhood as Michael could remember, there had been no modern conveniences of any kind in the farmhouse. It still had no indoor plumbing, other than a hand pump at the kitchen sink that drew up water from the cistern. The electricity now supplied to his grandparents' farm was a recent upgrade made possible only by the farm's close proximity to the main road, where the power lines had been run. Residential telephone service was still a luxury reserved for wealthy city households, though. If his mother needed to make a phone call, she had no choice but to drive to a Union Oil station on the edge of Burlington, where there was a public call box.

Michael was putting his rifle back in the gun cabinet when he heard the familiar rumbling of the family's truck outside. His mother was back already, and when she came through the door, the relief on her face was plain. "I got hold of him at the rectory. He's already started the Easter Vigil, but he said he would come as soon as he can."

"Well, good," his grandmother said. She had just retrieved the pail of milk she'd left midway between the house and the barn and put it down in the root cellar, where the milk would keep for the time being. "In the meantime, we ought to move the body onto the back porch. From the looks of it, he's probably crawling with lice, and that stink is god-awful."

His mother nodded in agreement. "I'm

going to be sick if I smell him much longer. Michael, you take his feet. Lizzie and I will grab his hands. Maybe the three of us together will be able to drag him out back."

"We need something to put over his head or we'll have a bloody mess smeared on the floor. Anna, where are the old burlap sacks we use for the garden vegetables?"

Michael glanced at his mother in time to see her flinch at the question.

"Oh! I know right where they are. Just give me a minute." His mother made meaningful eye contact with him before she hurried out the back door to the root cellar.

They managed to drag the body from the kitchen. It was all they could do to get it outside and position it in the corner of the back porch, where it was out of the way. His grandmother fetched an old horse blanket from the barn and covered the body.

The three of them stood outside, resting after the exertion of their task. It was a relief to get some fresh air, even though it was cold, and Michael had no desire to go back into the bloodstained kitchen. He realized that his game bag was still suspended across his shoulder and chest. "Mother, I got two squirrels while I was out," he said in a quiet voice. "Should I go ahead and dress them?"

"You might as well. I have no appetite

whatsoever, but after we clean up the rest of the mess in there, I suppose I should finish cooking. Frank might be hungry when he gets here."

Grateful for his mother's answer, Michael headed for the barn.

Onion, the family's Holstein, lowed and shifted in her stall when he flipped on the lights. Michael passed her on his way to a supply closet at the end of the barn, where he grabbed an old bucket that was no longer used for milking. He carried it back to a worktable pushed up against the end of the stalls. Tabby, the resident barn cat, meowed hopefully from the hayloft as he took off his game bag and removed the squirrels and his hunting knife.

"You already had your milk for the evening, old girl," he said to the cat. "But maybe you could do with a bit of squirrel liver as well." His mother didn't care for liver of any kind, and she rarely served it because she couldn't stand the odor of it cooking. Of course, that smell would have been an improvement on the stench already in the kitchen.

Michael took hold of the first squirrel and readied his knife to cut through the fur on its back. It usually took him less than ten minutes to field-dress a squirrel, but tonight he found it difficult to force the knife through the pelt to begin the process of skinning the animal. His hand, no, his whole arm was shaking. Slowly, he put the knife down and began to take deep breaths. For some reason, he felt unsteady, as if the tremors in his hand were spreading up into his shoulder and throughout his whole body. The barn began to spin, and it was all he could do to stumble over to one of the milking stools and sit down.

He had killed a man.

The very hands that rested on his knees, the hands that were suddenly unable to do what he wanted them to, had held a rifle and ended a man's life. Up until now, he hadn't allowed that realization to sink in, or maybe he'd been in shock and incapable of any rational thought. The weight of it, regardless of the man's actions toward his mother, was immense.

He had done it in defense of his mother's life. He was acting out of instinct and a duty to protect his family and the farm, as he had promised he would. His father or his brother, and even his feisty grandmother had she been in his position, would have done the very same thing. He was pretty sure that killing to protect another wasn't a sin. And yet, the slight recoil of the rifle shot that had killed the intruder seemed to reverberate again and again in his hands and in his mind. Each replay of the memory battered him with a wave of guilt.

At that moment, Michael wished more than anything that he could speak with his father. The Great War had ended before he'd been born, but his father had fought in it and survived. Surely, his father had to have shot many enemy soldiers to emerge from the trenches in once piece. Maybe he would have some advice about how to get past it — the reality of having killed another person, the shock and the remorse of it — even if the killing had been in self-defense or the defense of another.

His mother had cautioned him not to bring up the war in any conversation with his father. "It haunts him, Michael," she'd said once when he'd found an old photo of his father wearing his Army uniform. "Your father wouldn't tell me much about it, but I know he must have seen and done things he never imagined he would. He was quiet for a long time after he came home, and after all these years, he still cries out in his sleep sometimes. He lost both his brothers, bless their souls. War's cruel like that, you know. It can take away people you love. It can change a man, the kind of person he is, at

114

his core, and not in a good way. Thank goodness *that* didn't happen to your father. He came back from the war the same man I married, but I respect his wishes not to talk about it. He wants to move forward with his life, not be caught up remembering the horrors he experienced across the ocean."

In the quiet of the barn, Michael realized that even if his father hadn't been hundreds of miles away, there would be no way he could confide what he'd done and ask for guidance. Both his mother and grandmother had made it clear that what had happened with the hobo was not to be revealed to Niall. He wouldn't disobey them.

He remained on the milking stool for several more minutes, until his breathing steadied and his trembling stopped. Tabby made her way down from the loft and, purring loudly, began rubbing the length of her body back and forth against his shins. He reached down and picked up the cat, holding her gently as he scratched behind her ears and under her chin. Her thick, soft fur against his cheek and the low, monotonous rumble of her purring relaxed him further. If only life were as simple for him as it was for Tabby. With a bed of hay, daily rations of mice and milk, and an occasional bit of affection, she was perfectly content.

Michael's second attempt at skinning and gutting the squirrels was successful. Once the carcasses were completely dressed out, he dropped the livers on the floor for Tabby and collected the pelts and entrails in the old bucket. The frozen ground was too hard for him to bury them, so he disposed of them on the manure pile behind the barn before he went back to the house.

The kitchen smelled much better when he brought the cleaned squirrels inside. His grandmother had mixed up a bucket of borax cleaner and was on her hands and knees, scrubbing the floor. The blood spatters on the cabinets and countertop were gone. His mother had cleaned herself up as well. Wearing a fresh dress and apron, she stood in front of the stove, stirring a pot of simmering vegetables.

"These just need rinsing," he told her as he left the squirrels in the sink basin and pumped some water to wash his hands. "They're young ones. The skins came off easily." The cold water running over his fingers and palms was tinged pink as it carried away the last traces of his squirrel cleaning. He focused on lathering the soap and tried not to think about the body on the back porch.

"Good." His mother came to the sink to

finish preparing the squirrels for cooking. "If they're tender, they cook faster."

"Well, that's about the best I can do," his grandmother said as she slowly straightened up. She placed her hands on her waist and arched her back. "No trace of anything left, as far as I can see. Michael, would you mind getting rid of this water for me? My back's had about all it can take for one night."

"Sure thing, Grandma." He glanced down into the borax bucket. That water, too, was colored pink. Although his stomach was empty and supper would be much later than usual, he doubted he'd feel like eating anything even when the food was on the table.

"Not inside, though," his mother said quickly. "You can leave the scrub brush on the porch, but I don't want that filthy water anywhere in the house. Why don't you dump it behind the barn? With any luck, it'll help keep the mice away."

Michael nodded. He picked up the mop bucket and went out the back door again, past the covered, lifeless mass that lay in the corner. As he emerged from the darkness behind the barn with an empty bucket, he heard the drone of a car engine coming up the driveway. He came around to the front, where the porch light glowed in anticipa-

tion, as a sedan with a cross and ST. JO-
SEPH'S CHURCH printed on the door was
pulling up to the house.

His uncle Frank had arrived.

CHAPTER 7

Once Karen had left the hardware store and Emily was alone again, she pulled a peanut butter sandwich and a bottle of water from her purse and sat down on a chair in the back office. Her thoughts wandered as she ate — she was worried about Karen and what might have happened to her husband. The radical fighters who had recently over-run parts of Syria and Iraq were shockingly brutal in their treatment of both civilians and prisoners, and they openly sought to kidnap Westerners.

Thinking about Karen's missing husband made her feel more and more disturbed, so she redirected her thoughts to the briefcase. As her curiosity grew, she kept looking at her watch, counting the minutes that passed before Matt returned with his lock-pick set. When she heard the bell on the front door ring to signal the entrance of a customer, she left what remained of her sandwich on the desk and hurried to see who had come in.

"Sorry it took me a little while," Matt said as he placed a small leather case on the counter. "I would've been back sooner, but the pup was more interested in playing than doing her business."

"Oh, that's okay. I totally understand," Emily said with a smile. "It's so nice of you to offer to help me." She grabbed the briefcase and slid it down in front of him. "Do you really think you can open this?"

"Oh, sure. Just gotta find the right tool. These keyholes are tiny." Matt unzipped the lock-pick case. Inside, several thin, oddly shaped metal instruments were held in place by tiny elastic straps.

"They look kind of like things a dentist might use," Emily said. "Especially that one — it looks exactly like that nasty little hook they use to scrape your teeth."

Matt laughed. "Yeah, I thought the same thing when I first saw them." He selected one of the tools and carefully removed it from the case.

"So, how did you learn how to pick locks? You're the first person I've met who owns an actual lock-pick kit."

"It was part of some specialized training I went through," he said. " 'Covert entry training' is what the Marines call it. It's not as easy as some people think, but it's a good skill to have. You never know when you might be locked in or out of some place."

"Or some *thing*."

"Exactly." Matt grinned. "May I?" he asked, gesturing toward the briefcase. When she nodded, he held it up and squinted into the tiny keyholes. Then he carefully set it back on the table. "The locking mechanisms inside are probably pretty old, but if they're not rusted shut, I'll definitely be able to open this."

He paused and looked squarely at her. Emily wasn't sure why he was hesitating.

"That's great! Go right ahead."

Matt continued to regard her, but the look on his face was strange. His smile — his whole demeanor, really — exuded kindness and confidence, but his eyes gleamed with mischief. Though she didn't know what scheme Matt was attempting to perpetrate, it was apparent to her that he was up to something.

"Before I do, maybe we should talk about what I'll get in return," he said.

"What do you mean, what you'll 'get in return'?" Emily asked slowly. She put her hands on her hips and took a step back. "I thought you were doing me a favor."

"Oh, I am," Matt said. "I was just think-ing that maybe, in return, you'd be willing to let me buy you dinner sometime. Or lunch or coffee. Whatever you'd prefer. It doesn't have to be anything big . . . I'd like to get to know you better."

Emily studied Matt's face. His expression was relaxed but serious. There was no hint of a smile. Although his eyes still shone with a cheeky glimmer, she decided that this wasn't a joke. "That's sort of underhanded, don't you think? Offering to help and then putting a condition on it? Especially a condition like that?" Emily struggled to keep her voice steady as she seesawed between feeling delighted by Matt's interest and annoyed by his proposition. "Look, I'm not like most women. I'm very straightforward. I don't like being manipulated or pressured into something. I don't play games with people. And, I'm good with tools. The only reason I haven't opened this briefcase myself is because I didn't have what I needed. But now that I know what tools to get" — she glanced down at his kit — "I can easily order a set like that and open the damn thing myself."

"I didn't mean to upset you," Matt said quietly, still with the sparkle in his eyes. "The only reason I asked you out is because

I suspected you *are* different than most women. And I'm sure you'll be able to open this by yourself . . . eventually. It'll take a little time for you to get a set of tools like these, though, and while you're waiting for them to get here, you'll be wondering what's inside the case. I can tell you're really curious about it. And even when you have the tools, like I said, the locks on this briefcase are old. You could break them easily if you don't have experience opening locks. I'd hate for that to happen, since it belongs to your friend."

Matt's tone was playful but sincere and not patronizing. Emily was torn. He was cute, definitely, but acknowledging that fact brought with it a huge wave of guilt and uncertainty. Plus, she hated having her prowess with tools called into question, and she had been completely caught off guard by his approach. Finally, her instinct to throw up a defensive wall won out.

"I might've been interested in hanging out if you'd asked me straight up, without trying to coerce me. So, thanks, but no thanks. You can keep your sharp little tools. I can think of a few places they'd fit quite nicely." She gently closed the case on his kit and pushed it toward him with a smile. "Have a nice day."

Before he could react, she picked up the briefcase and escaped to the back room. After a few moments, once she'd heard the bell on the door jingle, she peeked out to be sure that Matt had left. One of the store's business cards was facedown on the counter with something written on the back. Grudgingly, Emily went to the register and picked up the card. There was a phone number scrawled on it, along with a short note: *In case you change your mind.*

Less than an hour after Kyle had dropped her off at her house, Claudia was headed out again. She carefully laid her plastic-covered wedding gown on the backseat of her car and drove the short distance to another house in town. Pauline Albury lived six blocks away, on the other side of Main Street. Claudia parked in the driveway of the neat two-story house. A colorful needlepoint sign in one of the windows read THE STITCHERY, and beneath that, a neon sign glowed in the shape of a scissor and the words TAILOR AND ALTERATIONS. She had just reached the porch with her gown draped across her arms and a bag containing her shoes looped over one wrist when the seamstress hurried out the front door to meet her.

"Hello there, I'm Pauline. You must be Claudia. Here, let me help you with that." Pauline held open the door and swooped an arm beneath the lower part of the gown to support it as Claudia carried it inside.

"Thank you," Claudia said once she was through the door. "It's pretty bulky."

"Most of them are, dear. Let's bring it over here, into the sewing room, that way," Pauline said as she gestured toward a door leading from the foyer. "There's a tall rack just inside here where we can hang it."

They entered a large carpeted room that looked like a newer addition to the house. Once Claudia had heaved the dress up onto the rack Pauline had mentioned, she took a look around the room and smiled. It was a cozy sewing heaven.

The rack was to her left and positioned next to a good-sized fitting booth with a curtain that could be pulled across for privacy. Beyond that, in the corner of the room, were some steps leading up to a small platform and a three-way mirror. Shelves filled with bolts of fabric and packages of quilt batting took up the other corner. A plush-looking sofa was pushed up against the wall opposite her, beneath a window that was slightly raised to allow in some fresh air. To her right were a long quilting machine and a sturdy-looking sewing machine. On the wall above the sewing machine, a rack held dozens of spools of thread in every color imaginable.

Pauline's friendly demeanor and comfortable appearance coordinated perfectly with her work environment. She had a kind, smiling face and gray hair that she wore pulled back in a loose bun. A full work apron was looped around her neck and tied in back at her waist, and a pair of reading glasses hung from a silver chain against the top of the apron.

"What a nice place you have here," Claudia said. "It doesn't look too big from the outside, but once you're in here, wow. It seems like you've got everything you need to sew anything."

"You're right, I do," Pauline said with a proud little grin. "You said on the phone that Josie DiSanti told you about me?"

"Yes. She's my landlady, and as soon as she heard I was getting married, she mentioned you and how your work was always perfect."

A little color crept into Pauline's cheeks at the compliment. "How sweet of her! I've done tailoring for Josie for a long time. And I've done lots and lots of wedding dresses for young ladies in town. Now, let's get you into your gown, and we'll see what needs to be done."

When Claudia emerged from the dressing room, Pauline clasped her hands and sighed. "That is a gorgeous dress. Where did you buy it?" She stepped forward to help Claudia fasten the row of buttons that ran up the back of the bodice.

"You might not believe it," Claudia said. She was holding up the long skirt, looking down at the low-heeled dress shoes she wore. "I found a place online that had some gowns on final clearance, and they had this one in my size. Except it's too long, and it's a little saggy around my shoulders."

"It's loose here in back, too. But all those things are easily fixed. Could you come up here for me?"

Claudia stepped carefully up on the platform in front of the three-way mirror. "How long have you had your shop here?"

"Oh, about fifteen years," Pauline said. "Just stand nice and straight, now, so I can measure for the hem." She was crouched down at Claudia's feet, moving slowly around the bottom of the skirt and pinning it so that it ended just above the floor. Pauline looked as though she was in her mid-sixties, at least, and Claudia was impressed at how lithe she was and how quickly her nimble hands placed silver pins in the shimmering satin. "I've always worked out of my home — lots of people in Mill River do. You know how it is in a small town like this. If your stove is broken or your pipes are leaking, there's always someone who knows how to take care of it, even if they don't have an actual storefront. You've just got to ask around to find out whom to call."

"Yes, or you hear about the person from somebody else in town."

"That's right. I didn't always have such a nice setup. I had to build up my business and save until I had enough to add on this sewing studio. It took a while, but it was worth it."

"Well, I'm glad I found you. I figured I'd need alterations for this dress, since I ordered it without trying it on. The price was great, though, and Kyle and I are trying to stick to a budget. We feel like we should pay for our wedding ourselves, but teachers and police officers don't make all that much."

"Oh, I know," Pauline said. "It's just not fair, if you ask me. Teachers and police and so many others with important jobs should make a lot more than they do. Your fiancé's Kyle Hansen, you said? He's only lived in

Mill River a few years. How did you two meet?"

"He came to my classroom to talk to my students about what police officers do," Claudia replied. "And I chatted with him afterward, since his daughter was in my class at the time."

"Um-hmm, just a little meeting like that's all it takes sometimes. He's quite a catch, that fellow. Everybody in town knows he's a real gentleman. All right, let me see if it's even."

Pauline had finished a complete circle around the skirt. The seamstress got to her feet and stepped back to inspect the future hemline. Tickled by her praise of Kyle, Claudia was about to gush something else about him, but when she looked at Pauline, she forgot what she was going to say.

There were at least half a dozen silver pins protruding from the part of the apron covering Pauline's left breast.

"That's pretty good," Pauline muttered as she walked around Claudia, staring down at the pinned skirt. "Could you turn slowly in a circle?" When Claudia didn't respond, she glanced up. "Honey, are you okay? You look like you've seen something awful."

"Pauline," Claudia gasped, "your . . . pins. Doesn't that hurt?"

The seamstress followed her gaze. When Pauline realized what had alarmed Claudia, she let out a cackle and reached out to lay a hand on her arm. "Oh! I'm so sorry. I'm used to everyone already knowing . . . I don't have a real bosom on this side anymore, just a foam falsie. See?" She poked the area surrounding the pins to demonstrate its softness. "I had breast cancer and a mastectomy twenty-two years ago. I could've had a reconstruction, but it seemed like such a grueling process. Plus, the implants back then weren't great. The saline ones leaked, and I didn't want anything with that silicone chemical going into my body. So, I decided to stay with my falsie. Bob . . . my husband . . . always told me he'd love me the same whether I had one boob or two, or none, and he has, for all these years. Besides, it makes a real handy pincushion."

Claudia relaxed. Even though she was astounded by Pauline's candor, she couldn't help but laugh. "Obviously. Sounds like your Bob is a pretty good catch, too. How long have you been married?"

"Going on forty-seven years. We were high school sweethearts. We got married at St. John's a few years after we graduated. Father O'Brien said our wedding Mass all those years ago."

"I love hearing stories like that," Claudia said. "Father O'Brien is going to marry us as well, so maybe that'll help our marriage be as long and happy as yours. You wouldn't have any advice for a bride-to-be, would you?"

"Funny you should ask. I like to give all my wedding clients a little advice with each fitting. Hold your arm out for me, would you, dear?" Claudia extended her left arm, and the seamstress stepped closer, gently pulling up the fabric of the gown on her left shoulder and upper arm, trying to determine how much the material needed to be taken in. Pauline's eyes sparkled, and a tiny smile puckered the corners of her mouth as she began pinning the material.

"I've seen that look before," Claudia said. "It's exactly how a few of my students look right before they say something a little bit naughty."

Pauline chuckled. "I was thinking how some of my best advice fits with the little surprise I gave you," she said with a glance down at her chest. "And that is for you to always be truthful to Kyle, and for him to be truthful to you. Falsehoods and little white lies never lead to anything good. And be careful when you decide what's false and what isn't. Sometimes things and even people aren't what they seem."

Late Sunday afternoon, Emily sat on the staircase in the McAllister mansion with the briefcase on her lap. Before closing Turner's for the day, she had called the Home Depot in Rutland. Unfortunately and somewhat surprisingly, like the little hardware store where she worked, it had no lock-pick sets in stock. She was set on opening the case, though, particularly after her encounter with Matt. Despite the fact that she had three new pedestal sinks to install in various bathrooms, despite the painting of the recently installed drywall that needed to be done, she had been tinkering with the briefcase for the better part of an hour.

Her toolbox sat open on the floor, where a hammer and a chisel tempted her from the top tray. *I could just break it open and tell Ruth I found it that way,* she thought. But she resisted. In addition to her love of all things old and vintage, she had always hated dishonesty. It made her feel fake and ashamed to lie about anything. Even her decision to delay telling Ruth about the briefcase was beginning to weigh on her, so outright lying to her employer and longtime family friend was out of the question.

Emily sighed and stared at the briefcase balanced across her knees. If she ordered a lock-pick kit online, she would probably receive it within a week, possibly sooner with expedited shipping. She reached into her pocket and pulled out the card Matt had left for her. Maybe she shouldn't have rebuffed him. She could have squelched her indecision, batted her eyelashes, and accepted his terms. If she had, she would have already found out what was in the briefcase, and she might have a date scheduled as well — what would have been her first date in years. Given the fact that she was on pins and needles about the contents of an old briefcase, she probably needed a date. Or *something* exciting.

For a few minutes, Emily turned the card around and around in her hands, thinking. Then she set the briefcase on one of the steps and stood up. In one corner of the room was a trash bag into which she had been putting used sandpaper and other refuse generated from her renovations. She ripped the business card into tiny pieces and added them to the bag. *I'll just order the lock-pick kit through Turner's and wait for it to arrive,* she thought. In the meantime, there was work to be done.

Emily was in an upstairs bathroom, hook-ing up the pipes to one of the new pedestal sinks, when she heard a man's voice calling to her from the back door in the kitchen. Still holding a large pipe wrench, she hurried downstairs to find Matt in the doorway.

"How did you find me?" she asked as he stepped into the house and shut the door behind him. She noticed that he held the lock-pick kit in one hand.

"I went by your house, looking for you. Your aunt was on her front porch across the street and told me you were up here working." He spoke quickly, the words tumbling out. "Look," he said, "I feel bad about what I said earlier. It was pretty assholish of me to condition my helping you on a date. I don't know what I was trying to do — be funny, I guess — but the more I thought about it afterward, the more I realized what a dumb move that was."

Emily squinted at him, trying to believe what she was hearing. When she remained silent, Matt hurriedly continued. "I'd be happy to open the briefcase for you. No strings or conditions."

Silently, she looked at him for a few moments longer and then shrugged. "Fine. I've got it in here." She turned and led him toward the staircase in the great hall.

Matt was all business as he sat down on

the stairs and placed the briefcase across his lap, as Emily had positioned it earlier. While she watched with her arms crossed tightly across her chest, he opened the lock-pick kit and selected a thin instrument with a long L-shape bend at the tip. He inserted the instrument into one of the locks on the briefcase and tried to turn it gently one way and then the other. While keeping pressure on the first instrument, he took a second one from the kit, a long thin tool with a slight hook, and inserted it as well. He drew the second instrument forward slowly, listening as he did so. When the second tool was almost completely removed from the keyhole, he turned the L-shaped instrument a little harder. The lock opened with a sharp *click*. "One down, one to go," he said.

"So you need *two* at the same time," Emily said, more to herself than to Matt. He heard, though, and nodded as he worked on the second lock.

"Usually. Most simple locks like these have pins of different lengths that come down and keep the plug — this middle-cylinder part of the lock — from turning. A key cut to reflect the lengths of those pins aligns them to allow the cylinder to rotate and unlock. If you don't have the correct key, you use a tension wrench — the one shaped like a long L — to figure out which way the lock turns and then keep some torque on it while you push the pins up with your pick. Doing that lines up all the pins, just like a key would, except a pick does it one pin at a time. Once all the pins are up and out of the way, the internal cylinder is free to turn, and — voilà!" As he applied pressure to the tension wrench again, the second lock opened.

"Wow," Emily said. It wasn't every day that she learned something completely new about tool use, and she had seen enough master carpenters and craftsmen at work to recognize genuine expertise. Matt clearly knew what he was doing, and she was impressed.

He placed the lock-pick tools safely back inside their case and stood to hold the unlocked briefcase out to her. "I assume you'll want some privacy when you open it," he said. "I'll see myself out."

"Thank you," she said as she accepted the briefcase.

"No problem. And again, I'm sorry about this morning."

Emily nodded, but she was no longer annoyed with him or focused on what he was saying to her. Her heart pounding in anticipation, she waited until she heard the back door close before she moved. Once she was sure he was gone, she glanced around the great hall, settling her gaze on a sofa draped in a white dustcover. She had already sat for a long time on the hard wooden stairs, and if she was going to park herself somewhere for another good while, it would be on something soft.

She placed the briefcase on one of the cushions and took a seat beside it. Carefully, she positioned her hands on the two smooth leather corners of the lid and steadily raised it up.

The cloth-lined interior was filled with letters. *There must be dozens of them,* Emily thought as she stared at the yellowish envelopes bundled together and secured by neatly tied pieces of string. She picked up the first bundle and untied it. The top envelope, and each of those stacked beneath it, bore postmarks from 1973 and were addressed in a looping, handwritten script to Mrs. Mary McAllister. She turned the envelope over and saw a return address on the flap from Mrs. Anna O'Brien.

Emily didn't know who Anna O'Brien was, but she and everyone else in town knew of Mary McAllister, the late recluse who for seventy years had been a secret benefactor for the people of Mill River. Carefully, so as not to rip the delicate, aged stationery, she removed the letter inside and unfolded it.

My dearest Mary, the letter began. Emily's eyes flew down the page, scanning for anything of particular interest before she read it carefully:

. . . I must express again my gratitude to you for these letters. I've become somewhat isolated in my old age, and it is so kind of you to take up a correspondence with me when Michael suggested it. As his mother, I'm grateful that he has such a dear friend in you. He works too hard and too much — he always has — and his life has been anything but easy . . .

CHAPTER 8

March 31–April 1, 1934

In the front passenger seat of the church sedan, Michael sat quietly as his uncle Frank pulled out of the farm's driveway onto the main road. Behind them, the entire backseat was taken up by the body of the hobo. Once Uncle Frank had arrived at the farm and said a prayer for the dead man's soul, the four of them — Michael and Frank, Anna and Lizzie — had wrapped the stinking mass tightly in the old horse blanket and dragged it around the house to the car. Now he and Frank were taking it away, but where, he didn't know.

"Will you tell me now where we're going?" he asked once the farm had disappeared into the night behind them.

"To a place where the presence of a dead body won't raise suspicion," his uncle replied.

"The cemetery, you mean," Michael said.

His uncle pursed his lips and nodded slowly, but his gaze didn't deviate from the road.

"But the ground's frozen."

"Yes, it is. Still snow-covered, too."

"Then how?"

His uncle merely smiled. "It's a good thing we haven't had a storm in the past few days. The roads are clear, so we'll have no trouble getting there or getting you back home before dawn."

Michael leaned his head against the seat. It was obvious he wouldn't get more information until his uncle was ready to give it.

"I'm going to say again, Michael, how important it is that you never speak of what we're doing to anyone. Not even your mother or grandmother. If they don't know, they won't have information to give if anyone ever comes asking for it. Do you understand?"

"Yes."

They rode in silence for the rest of the short drive. The village of Colchester was dark and quiet as they turned into the parking area for a small stone chapel. Instead of stopping there, his uncle guided the sedan around to the back and onto a narrow drive that looped around the cemetery. His grandfather was buried there, but Michael hadn't been to his grave in years.

"We keep this driveway shoveled as best we can so we can get to the vault."

"Vault?" Michael thought of the bank vaults he'd seen in old silent westerns. The image in his mind was one of a gleaming steel fortress with a spinning, six-handled lock on the outside and piles of money inside. "The church has a vault?"

"Yes, a receiving vault. Before the ground freezes, we dig a few graves in the cemetery, but we can't know for sure how many we'll need during the winter. Once those graves are used, we hold the bodies of the deceased in the receiving vault until spring. Until we can bury them properly."

It was then, in the narrow beams of the sedan's headlights, that Michael saw where they were going. At the far end of the cemetery, tucked against the hillside that sloped up and away from the looping driveway, was a small, nondescript structure. It seemed to be made of the same stone as the chapel. There were no windows, only a door facing out toward the cemetery. The top third of the door was open but secured against unlawful entry by closely spaced iron bars.

His uncle parked in front of the vault and

cut the engine. "Wait here," he said. Before Michael could reply, his uncle was standing before the door to the vault, fumbling with a ring of keys, and making the sign of the cross as he opened the heavy door and went inside. After a few moments, the door opened again, and Michael saw the front of a cart emerge. He hurried to get out of the sedan.

"Quickly, now," his uncle said. Frank opened the door to the backseat on his side and motioned for Michael to do the same. "We've got to pull him out onto here," he said while he positioned the cart as close to the sedan as he could and then turned a crank on the end to lower the top surface until it was even with the car seat. "Once we do, it'll be easy to get him inside."

Michael glanced around. The cemetery was absolutely silent. The night was clear and cold, easily in the single digits, but he didn't feel it. Even with just the two of them, getting the corpse out of the backseat seemed to be far easier than loading it had been. Maybe it was the adrenaline pumping through him, fueled by his fear of being seen, or maybe it was because the body had stiffened and was easier to move. At any rate, before he had fully come to terms with what they were doing, his uncle pulled the loaded cart inside the vault.

The cold, dim interior was narrower than Michael had expected. The air inside was damp and still. A large cross gleamed on the interior wall opposite the door, and beneath it were stacked several plain wooden coffins. "We always keep some simple pine caskets in here for families without the means to buy one," his uncle said as he followed Michael's gaze. "Since it's just the two of us, it'll be easier to move this fellow without a casket."

The other two walls of the vault were lined with what looked like identical rectangular cupboards, complete with metal pull-handles. "Most of this side is already full," his uncle said, gesturing with his left hand. "We'll put him in one of the boxes on the right. The spring thaw is only a few weeks away, so this side won't come anywhere close to filling up before graves can be dug again." Michael watched as his uncle unlocked the door of a cupboard with another of the keys on his ring and lined up the cart with it. It took a moment of cranking to raise the wrapped body to the necessary height, and then together they pushed it into the cupboard.

Michael stood quietly as his uncle offered another set of prayers and blessings before closing and relocking the cupboard door.

"This will do for the time being," Frank said. "I'm the only one with access to the vault, and no one will be able to find him here or even think to look for him here. Now, let's get you back to the farm so your mother doesn't worry." His uncle pushed the coffin cart into the far corner and ushered him toward the exit.

"What do you mean, 'for the time being'?" Michael had experienced a moment of relief when his uncle had locked the cupboard. But it was a temporary solution, and he soon realized the answer to his question. Nobody could remain in the vault once the weather warmed. He began to feel jittery and sick to his stomach.

"The vault has to be emptied and disinfected no later than mid-May."

"Then what? How are we —"

"Don't worry, Michael. I won't let anything bad happen to you and your mother. I know exactly what we're going to do. We just have to wait a few weeks for the right moment to come. I'll need your help then, like tonight, but the next time we're out this late in the graveyard will be the last time. After that, you won't have to worry about this whole thing ever again."

On the way back to the farm, they rode

with the windows down in order to air out the sedan. For a while, Michael closed his eyes, enjoying the feeling of the fresh, frigid wind whipping against his face. When his lips, nose, and ears were numb, he pulled up the collar of his coat and covered his face with his gloved hands.

His uncle noticed his discomfort. "It's all right," he said as he rolled up the driver's-side window. "Put your window up, too. I've still got the ride home, and I can park with the windows open once I'm back at the mission."

"Uncle Frank?" Michael said once he could move his lips enough to speak.

"Yes?"

"I was thinking that maybe . . . before you go, you could hear my confession."

His uncle glanced over at him, and the look of surprise on his face reminded Michael so much of his mother's. His mother and his uncle bore a strong sibling resemblance. Frank was tall and burly, but he and Anna shared the same dark hair and snapping blue eyes, as well as a whole host of expressions.

"If you're feeling guilty about what happened, you shouldn't, Michael."

Michael barely managed to whisper a response. "I killed him."

"Yes, but you acted with the intent to protect your mother and yourself. You had no choice, and the action you took was reasonable and justified. If you hadn't, he would have harmed and quite possibly killed you and Anna and Lizzie as well. Saint Thomas Aquinas told us that it is our duty to preserve your own life and those lives under your protection. Killing in furtherance of that duty isn't a sin. The death of your attacker was an unintended but acceptable effect of your actions."

"I've told myself that . . . or some version of it . . . but I still feel like I've done something horribly wrong."

His uncle smiled. "You sound like so many boys who came back from the Great War. Killing another person for any reason is something that feels unnatural and wrong to most people. I've counseled so many soldiers who made it home but are shaken to the core because of what they had no choice about doing over in Europe. Michael, trust me when I tell you that you needn't confess anything about the business with the tramp."

"Not even hiding him in the vault?"

"*I'm* the one who made the decision to hide him in the vault. *You* are entirely without fault in the matter. As for what involvement you had in the man's death, I'll say it again — you've done nothing wrong. The man had no identification. You had no idea who he was or how to find out. He broke into your home and held Anna at knifepoint. You killed him in a sin-free, completely justifiable manner, and I blessed his body and prayed for his soul — on Easter Sunday, no less — before we moved him and once we got him into the vault. Because of what we did tonight, he'll be laid to rest in consecrated ground. There's hope that his soul will meet with God's mercy. It's better that he end up in the church cemetery than alongside some road or in the middle of the woods."

"He's going to end up in the church cemetery?"

"He's there now, isn't he?" His uncle looked over at him again and winked. "I aim to keep it that way."

Despite his continued misgivings, the corner of Michael's mouth twitched up in a smile. He understood then how right his mother had been when she'd told him that his uncle was different than any priest he'd ever met.

They arrived back at the farm just as the sky was turning gray with the impending dawn. Lizzie was already in the barn, and she came out to wave at them as they pulled up to the house.

"Remember, now, not a word to anyone," his uncle said, and Michael nodded. His uncle's admonition reminded him of his mother's secret silver hidden in the root cellar, and he couldn't help wondering whether Frank knew about it. He felt a powerful urge to ask, but he suppressed it. He had promised his mother he would not speak of it to anyone. It was strange, how quickly he had become a receptacle of secrets. His new burden of information was heavy, but he was determined to manage it.

His mother was pouring a cup of coffee as they came inside. She had dark circles beneath her anxious eyes.

"Everything's fine," Frank said immediately, and Michael was happy to see some of the tension leave her face.

"Good," she said. "I was about to make some breakfast. Can you stay?"

"If it's quick," his uncle said. "I need to be back to say Easter Mass in just a few hours. While you cook, though, I'm going to take a look around outside. Sometimes hoboes mark a property where they've been treated well, and the mark attracts others who wander by."

His mother nodded. "Michael, could you

fill the wood box? It's nearly empty. After breakfast, I'll heat a tub of water so you can take a bath. I imagine you need it."

"A bath sounds good," he told her. He'd never really minded bathing in general, unlike Seamus, who had always hated the weekly washing. But today it would be an exquisite treat.

He was coming from the woodpile with an armful of logs when he heard his uncle shout to him. Frank was standing at the end of the driveway, next to the mailbox, beckoning him to come over.

"I'll be right there," Michael yelled. He deposited the logs inside before he came back out and jogged down the driveway.

"I wanted to show you this," his uncle said, pointing to the thick wooden post on which the mailbox was mounted. The bottom half was buried in snow, but on the top half, a symbol had been marked on the post:

"What is it?" Michael asked.

"A hobo mark," his uncle replied. "It's a crude, universally understood symbol for a loaf of bread. Someone put it there to tell others that food is given out here."

"Mother does that, gives out old stale pieces of bread to people who come to the door, even though Grandma tells her not to."

"After what happened yesterday, I doubt she'll do it again. But we're going to get rid of this so any other wanderers who come by don't see it." His uncle took a handkerchief from his pocket and rubbed the symbol until the black lines were smudged and the image completely obscured. "You should keep an eye out, Michael. Check here and around the property every few days. If you see any other marks here or anywhere else, get rid of them any way you can."

They walked back to the house, where each brought in another armload of wood. Anna was moving around the kitchen table, scooping scrambled eggs from a frying pan and depositing them on plates.

"That coffee smells good," Frank said. "And the eggs, too."

"I'll get a cup for you," Lizzie said, starting to rise from her seat at the table, but Frank patted her shoulder as he brushed past her.

"No need, I can help myself."

Michael had pulled out his chair to sit

down when he looked over at his mother. She was standing on the opposite side of the table, holding a spatula and the nearly empty frying pan, but had stopped dishing out the eggs. Her face was unusually pale, her gaze distant and unfocused. She took an unsteady step backward.

"Mother?" he asked. "Mother, are you all right?" He remained standing, ready to reach out to her, and his question prompted his uncle and grandmother to turn their attention to her as well.

"Anna?" his uncle said, but she didn't reply or even acknowledge that she'd heard him. The heavy cast-iron pan fell from her hand, hitting the corner of the table and sending bits of egg flying. A half-second later, it landed on the wood floor with a loud *thunk,* and Michael watched his mother's eyes roll back into her head as she collapsed.

CHAPTER 9

Having spent the morning in bed, Karen forced herself to get up and dressed when the old clock on the wall in the foyer chimed to announce the noon hour. No one had called the landline or her cellphone during the morning, and she shot a nasty look at them both as she carried them into the bathroom with her. What she wouldn't give for any bit of news about her husband.

Where is he now? she asked herself periodically during the day. Maybe he was being rescued or on his way back to the base. Her heart leaped at the mere thought. Maybe he was bound and blindfolded, a hostage of some radical group. *Or maybe . . .* She always tried to stop herself there, before her thoughts entered the most terrifying realm of possibility. Images from news stories about other Middle East kidnapping victims were seared into her mind. Images of beaten and bloodied prisoners, of kidnappers brandishing long swords in front of video cameras before inflicting unthinkable agony on their hostages . . .

Nick is smart and strong, she told herself. *He'll figure out a way to free himself, if he's been kidnapped. He'll fight to get back home to Ben and me.*

And, Karen knew, he'd expect her to fight just as strongly.

When was the last time she'd really fought for something or someone? Her monotonous struggle with depression didn't quite fit the bill. Oh, she had a good temper, once she was sufficiently provoked, but just the idea of getting her dander up seemed exhausting right now. Still, she remembered a time, three or four years back, when she'd done exactly that.

It was before they'd moved to Mill River. Ben was still in elementary school, and he'd started coming home from school ravenous. At first, she'd chalked up his increased appetite to a growth spurt, but after it had continued for several weeks, she became worried.

"I don't know what's happening with you," she'd told her son as he went straight to the refrigerator after arriving home. "You're acting like you're not eating lunch at all. The school's food isn't that bad, is it?

153

What did they serve today?" She hadn't eaten at the school that day, since she worked there only part-time, on Tuesdays and Fridays.

"I don't know, Mom," Ben replied. Strangely, he didn't look at her. Instead, he kept his focus on the contents of the refrigerator.

"What do you mean, you don't know? You did eat lunch, didn't you?"

Ben didn't reply.

"Ben?" She took hold of his arm and pulled him around to face her. She'd fully intended to scold him for ignoring her, but the look on his face told her that something was wrong. "Answer me, Ben. Did you eat lunch today?"

"No."

"Why not?"

"I didn't have money for lunch."

"What? Why would you say that? I give you money to buy a lunch ticket each week."

Ben paused for a minute before he quietly answered her. "Because they keep taking it."

"Taking it? 'They'?" Karen's voice rose as she realized what her son was telling her. "Who's taking your lunch money?"

"Two big kids. From the middle school."

"Do you know who they are? Do you

know their names?"

"Not really. One of them is Billy, I think. I don't know the other one, or their last names."

"And where does this happen?"

"Usually on the bus, on Mondays. The first time, they twisted my arm and said they'd hurt me worse if I didn't keep giving them the money for the lunch ticket. Or if I told anybody."

Karen remembered him favoring his left arm about a month before. He'd told her he wrenched it swinging on the monkey bars.

At that moment, she felt a searing rage unlike anything she'd ever experienced. She was ready to rip her son's prepubescent bullies to shreds, regardless of the fact that they, too, were children. She would allow *no one* to harm her only child, and it was all she could do to keep her voice steady as she drew Ben into her arms and tried to reassure him.

"You're being bullied, Ben, and you did the right thing, telling me. I love you so much, and I promise you that I will not allow it to continue. Nobody is going to hurt you again."

The very next Monday, she and the middle school principal met Ben's bus as it arrived at the school. Ben exited and stood beside his mother. They waited as other students filed out until her son nodded. The principal cleared his throat and stepped forward as the final two passengers — two tall, older boys — came out of the bus.

"Good morning, Billy and Darren. Walk with me, please. We need to have a little chat in my office."

One of the two kids had glanced around to glare at Ben, but Karen caught his eye and stared him down with the wrath of a mother grizzly protecting her cubs.

The boys denied any wrongdoing until the principal had them empty their pockets. Only then, when they had produced the five- and ten-dollar bills she had subtly initialed before giving them to Ben that morning, were they forced to admit their actions. School suspensions for the two had followed quickly, and Karen smiled to herself as she remembered the boys showing up at her home with their parents to apologize to Ben.

If only all wrongs could be righted so easily, she thought. Karen feared the worst and prayed constantly that Nick would be found alive and unhurt and returned to her in one piece. The uncertainty of the situation taunted her, forced open her imagination to any number of nightmare scenarios, each worse than the previous one. She moved from the sofa only when the silence and the uncertainty became too much to bear. If she sat alone in her house for one more minute, she really would lose it.

Even as she felt increasingly helpless in her struggle against the familiar darkness — which seemed to be growing stronger, despite her efforts to keep it at bay — she realized the importance of minimizing the time she was alone. Her work as a teacher's assistant kept her busy on Tuesdays and Thursdays, but today was Monday. Ben was at school and wouldn't be home until closer to three o'clock. Right now, there was only one place she could think to go to find some semblance of companionship and comfort without having to hear and try to respond to questions about Nick.

The Alzheimer's care facility where her father lived was only fifteen minutes away, on the north side of Rutland. She visited frequently, and the receptionist smiled when she came in. "Hello, Mrs. Cooper. Nice to see you. Willie's just gotten his lunch, but you can go ahead in, no problem."

"Thank you." As she signed her name in the visitors' log, Karen returned the smile of the woman behind the counter, though doing so made her face feel like brittle, immovable plastic.

Her father was seated at a table in his room. An attendant sat next to him, holding a spoon of food she had scooped up from a tray in front of him.

"Hi, Maureen. I can help him with that," Karen said. She approached her father, put a hand on his back, and bent to kiss him on the cheek. "Hi, Daddy."

He said nothing as he turned to look at her. His face reflected childlike innocence, but his expression was empty emotionally and devoid of recognition.

This first contact at the beginning of every visit was the hardest part for Karen. Each time she arrived, she carried the dread of seeing her father's vacant stare as well as a sliver of hope that her father would indicate in some small way that he knew her. She searched his eyes, focused on every twitch of his facial muscles as a possible sign that there was something left of him, of memories of his family and of her, inside his diseased mind.

But when, like today, there was nothing to indicate that she hadn't been erased from her father's memory, her sliver of hope became a sliver of glass, painfully slicing its way deeper into her heart.

She understood what Alzheimer's was doing and would continue to do to her father. Nevertheless, she wondered whether his memories of her were still there somewhere, locked away inside the darkest recesses of his brain. It comforted her to think they were, and that even as his disease entered the most advanced stage, he hadn't truly forgotten her.

"I'm Karen," she told him as Maureen relinquished her seat and left the room. "I'm your daughter, and I came to visit you."

"Oh." His brow furrowed, and Karen held her breath. Then his forehead was smooth and relaxed again, and he didn't say anything more.

"Here, Daddy, let me help you with your lunch."

Karen sat down beside her father. His lunch tray held meatloaf and mashed potatoes with gravy, along with peas and a dessert serving of fruit salad. She picked up the spoon the attendant had left. It held a small bite of the meat and potatoes, and her father complacently opened his mouth for it. He chewed very slowly, and Karen watched him carefully to make sure he was able to handle the food without choking. At some point, she knew, his disease would rob him of his ability to chew and swallow.

She focused her gaze on the side of her father's face. His strong jawline was unchanged by time. As a younger man, he had worked so hard to support their family. Sometimes he'd had to take a second job to make sure she and her mother and brother were taken care of, and he'd always done it without hesitation or complaint. And yet, he managed to spend enough time with her and her brother to maintain close relationships. It made her all the more grateful that she was able to help care for him now, to return some of the love he had given her in a tender, tangible way.

"Are you ready for another bite? Here you go, Daddy." As he worked on chewing the second mouthful, she looked him over carefully. Her father had gotten noticeably thinner over the years after his diagnosis, but his weight had stabilized after he'd entered the care facility. He was clean-shaven and wearing his typical outfit of gray sweatpants and a long-sleeved T-shirt, each of which had a sewn-in tag that read WILLIAM MANNING.

Karen waited to give him another spoonful and looked down at his feet. He was wearing clean white tube socks and his usual house shoes, navy corduroy with sturdy rubber soles. How many times had she stood on those feet as a little girl?

She remembered a period during her childhood when he had worked as a truck driver. The money from that job had been enough to support the family, but it had required him to be away from home most weeknights. Back then, every Friday had brought great excitement when he arrived home, and Saturday nights were more fun than a party. Her mother always fixed a big dinner on Saturday evening, doing her best to make up for the lack of family time during the workweek. And after dinner, before they gathered around their old television set to watch a program or a movie together, there was the dancing.

Her parents always went first, swaying around the living room to whatever love song her mother chose while Karen and her younger brother, George, sat on the sofa, groaning and covering their eyes. When their mother disappeared to the kitchen to tackle the dishes, George would put on the latest pop hit, and he and their father would dance themselves silly, trying to one-up each other with their latest moves. Her father had actually tried to breakdance once. The memory of him lying on the carpet with his legs up in the air, attempting to spin around on his back, still elicited giggles from her.

Karen's turn was always last. She chose a song once in a while but usually humored her father by letting him put on Louis Armstrong's "What a Wonderful World." It was his favorite, and she liked it, too. When she was very young, she would stand on his feet as he maneuvered them both around the room. Slowly but surely, as the years passed, the song had become their anthem. They danced to it to celebrate her making the honor roll in middle school and after her high school graduation. It had been the obvious choice for their father-daughter dance at her wedding.

As she grew up and went through various stages of life, the words of the song took on new and deeper meanings. Even during times of great sadness — her years of living an ocean apart from Nick, and her mother's sudden passing from a brain aneurysm twelve years ago — the song had given her strength. It was a celebration of the beautiful things in life and the friendship and love between people. It was a song of hope.

"Here's another bite for you, Daddy. Peas this time." Karen gently inserted the spoon in her father's mouth. "You're doing such a good job with your lunch." Her father continued to stare straight ahead as he chewed, as if he were alone in the room.

She wasn't sure what prompted her to start talking about Nick's disappearance. True, she had left her house wanting to avoid discussing her missing husband, and she knew her father was no longer capable of carrying on or even understanding a conversation. Maybe that was just it. Though he was no longer himself, the man sitting next to her was still her father. She still loved him dearly and felt comfortable talking to him. But whatever words she uttered would disappear into the room without a reply. It was a one-sided unloading of fear and anxiety, stress, anger, and sadness, and a release she desperately needed.

"I'm so afraid, Daddy," she choked out after she had told him everything. "I don't know if I'll ever see him again, and I don't think I can go on if he doesn't come home. I know I've got to, somehow, for you and Ben, but I can feel the depression pulling me under again. It's so much stronger this time, Daddy. Some days I wish I could just die."

Karen stopped speaking, shocked by hearing herself say those words. It was the first time she had articulated her recent suicidal thoughts. Overwhelmed, she set the spoon down on her father's lunch tray and covered her face with her hands.

After a few minutes, as she struggled to compose herself, she realized that her father had turned to stare at her. His brow furrowed again, and he seemed to study her face. Slowly, he raised a hand and touched her wet cheek with one finger. "Louie?"

Her initial surprise at his question quickly turned into grateful elation. It was the first time in several weeks that her father had said anything meaningful. Even though it was one word, she knew what he was trying to ask.

"Sure, Daddy, we can dance," she said, gently taking his raised hand and squeezing it.

There was a portable CD player on a shelf in the room, with a small stack of discs beside it. Karen rose and went to the shelf, selected one of the CDs, and loaded it into the machine.

The instrumental introduction to the song seemed to have no effect on her father, but when he heard Louis Armstrong's gravelly voice, he turned toward the music, then looked at her and smiled.

"Can you stand up, Daddy?" she asked with her hand outstretched. After a moment, her father grasped it and got to his feet unsteadily. She kept hold of his hand as she slowly positioned herself in front of him and placed his other hand around her waist. She began to sway in place, in time to the music, and her father followed her lead. Their role reversal wasn't lost on her, but it didn't matter. She was so thankful for this moment, a father-daughter dance that might well be the last she would ever have with him.

When she looked up at his face, his eyes were closed, but he was smiling. She was reminded again of how wonderful the world was, and how their special song was one of strength, and love, and hope.

On Monday after school let out, Claudia stopped by the bakery on her way home. While she usually tried to limit her visits to the bakery and its myriad delicious and incredibly fattening offerings, it was time to start thinking about a cake for her wedding. The fact that Ruth would be making it was all the better. Claudia had yet to try something from the bakery that wasn't superb.

Humming to herself, she pulled open the door to the bakery and was surprised to see the DiSanti sisters talking at the counter. Emily held a disposable cup of coffee in one hand and a takeout bag in the other. Emily's older sister, Rose, was standing behind the register. Claudia regularly saw Emily around town and had spoken with her several times, but it had been several months since she had seen Rose. With her perfect blond hair and fashionable attire, Rose was the last person Claudia expected to see working the counter at the bakery.

She would never forget the day last July when the sisters had moved to Mill River. After backing her U-Haul truck into Emily's car, Rose had been anything but apologetic. The only other time Claudia had had any contact with Rose was the day a few weeks after their initial meeting, when she and Daisy Delaine had found Rose's son, Alex, unconscious in the yard after falling out of a tree. *It'll be interesting to see how she behaves,* Claudia thought now. *The two times I've seen her, she's been either totally rude or understandably hysterical.*

The sisters stopped talking and looked toward the bakery door as she entered. Emily gave her a warm smile. "Hey, Claudia. How's it going?"

"Hi. Pretty good," Claudia said. "I came by to see Ruth, if she's here. I wanted to look into ordering a wedding cake."

"Oh, how exciting!" Emily said with what seemed like genuine enthusiasm. "Sounds like a lot more fun than what I'll be doing in a few minutes."

"Which is?" Claudia asked.

"Replacing an old, leaky toilet," Emily said casually. "I'm just picking up a sandwich for my dinner before I head up to the mansion to work for a while longer."

"Wow, you're putting in long hours," Claudia said. "Is everything coming together?"

"Yeah. I think the inside will be spectacular by the time your big day's here, but there's a lot to do right now. I've gotta run — hey, you remember my sister, Rose?"

"Of course." Claudia made eye contact with the older DiSanti sister and smiled cautiously.

"I can try to help you with cake questions," Rose said quietly. "I've been covering for Ruth when she needs a little time off."

"I'll leave you both to it," Emily said as she headed for the door. "See ya."

"So, when are you getting married?" Rose asked once Emily was gone. "And congratulations, by the way."

"Saturday, December twenty-first. We figured a holiday wedding would be beautiful, and we'd get to see our families right before Christmas. Kyle's mom is going to stay with Rowen so we can get away for a quick honeymoon sometime between Christmas and New Year's." To Claudia's surprise, Rose was smiling and listening attentively. "I have to be back teaching on January second, and Kyle doesn't have much time off, either, but we didn't want to postpone a honeymoon until the summer."

"So, it'll be short but sweet," Rose said. "Where do you plan on going?"

"Sanibel Island, in Florida. Neither of us has been there, but it's supposed to be quiet and beautiful, and it's known for tons of gorgeous shells washing up on the beach."

"And it'll be much warmer than Vermont in December," Rose said. "It sounds really nice. What are you thinking about in terms of a cake? Ruth will be back tomorrow morning, and I could leave her a note with the basics, at least."

"We'll have about sixty guests," Claudia said. "Our colors are silver for the bridesmaids' gowns, with red roses. I thought it would be nice to have part of the cake chocolate and part vanilla so that people can have whatever they prefer."

"Hmmm." Rose was taking notes on a pad of paper. "You know, I think Ruth has a photo book here somewhere." When she knelt behind the counter, Claudia peeked over it and saw her pulling out and examining various binders and books from a shelf. "Here it is," Rose said as she stood up and laid a three-ring binder open on the counter. "All the photos in here are of cakes Ruth has made. Take a look and see if you like any design in particular. Or if you have a picture of a cake you like from a magazine or something, you can bring that in and show her. She could probably duplicate it."

Claudia barely heard the end of Rose's sentence. The photos in the cake binder were stunning. There were so many tiered master-pieces, some covered with delicate icing flowers and others with smooth, elegant exteriors highlighted by swirls and pearls and ribbons. She flipped the page and gasped.

The picture there took up a whole page. The cake was a non-traditional design, with the various layers held on separate platforms that rose higher and higher, like a spiral staircase. The icing was smooth, but each layer had glistening bands of lavender around the base and a spray of matching lavender roses cascading over the top.

"This one is amazing," she told Rose. "Simple and really beautiful."

As Claudia stared at the picture, the bell on the bakery door rang, but she didn't realize that someone had come up to stand beside her until Daisy spoke.

"Oh, Miss Claudia, that is such a beautiful cake!" the little woman with gray, curly hair breathed as she peeked over her arm at the picture. "Maybe it has a special potion inside to make it float in the air like that."

Claudia smiled down at Daisy and then made eye contact with Rose. Rose smiled in return and spoke kindly to Daisy. "I think Ruth actually calls them floating tiers. She has the stand in back. It's made of clear plastic, so the cake layers look like they're hovering in midair."

"Well," Daisy said, shaking her head in wonder. "It must still be a pretty special cake."

"If she could do this for us, but with silver around the layers and red roses on top, it would be perfect. Plus, each layer could be a different flavor." Claudia smiled as she envisioned cutting into one of the layers to reveal a moist, chocolate interior.

"Let me just make a note of the one you liked," Rose said as she scribbled the additional information on the paper. "That way, Ruth can get a better idea about pricing before she calls you. And Daisy, I'll be with you in just a minute."

"Oh, sure, Miss Rose. I'm not in a hurry.

You must be so excited about your wedding, Miss Claudia. I just know it'll be beautiful, especially with a cake like this one. Maybe someday I'll get to go to a wedding." Daisy sniffed and smiled up at her.

If it were anyone else, Claudia would take the comment as an inappropriate request to be invited to the wedding, but Daisy was so sweet and innocent. Claudia believed she was simply expressing a sincere desire without any ulterior motive.

"Hmmm," she said, looking into Daisy's face. "Well, you know, Daisy, wedding invitations always come in the mail."

"The mail? Are you sure, Miss Claudia?"

"Yep, they always come in the mail. And you never know when you might receive one."

"I suppose that's true," Daisy said. "I think I'll pay more attention to my mail. I sure like checking each day to see what's in the mailbox. You know, there might be mail waiting for me right now!" An excited look came over her face. "Miss Rose, I think I'll come back a little later, if that's okay."

"Sure, Daisy, I'll be here until five."

"Thanks, Miss Rose. See you around, Miss Claudia."

Claudia chuckled under her breath as Daisy rushed out the door. As she waited for Rose to finish writing, she began to imagine how her cake would look on a table on one side of the great hall in the McAllister mansion with the gorgeous layers spiraling up. She could picture her hands and Kyle's, holding bites of cake to feed to each other in front of everyone they loved . . .

"What? I'm sorry, I missed that," she said as she realized Rose had spoken to her.

"Oh. I was just saying that I never saw you after my son's accident this past summer. We were up at the hospital in Burlington for a few weeks after it happened, and then it was kind of crazy once we had Alex back home and Sheldon and I decided to stay here in town. I meant to call you a long time ago to thank you for everything you did for Alex when you and Daisy found him. I don't know what would have happened if you two hadn't been there."

"It's nothing," Claudia said. "I did what anyone would have. I'm just happy he's all right. I see Alex at school all the time, and he's always smiling."

"He does love it here," Rose said. "He's made lots of friends, and his teacher, Betty Martin, has done a great job keeping him challenged."

"Betty's a good friend of mine. She's commented so many times about how brilliant he is, and also that he's a really great kid."

A huge smile lit up Rose's face. "He is. Sheldon and I feel incredibly blessed to have him."

Claudia nodded. "Well, I should get going. Kyle and his daughter are coming over for dinner, and I'm late getting it started. Thanks so much for your help."

"Sure. I'll make sure Ruth sees this note first thing in the morning."

She was like a different person, Claudia thought as she left the bakery and went to her car. *Friendly, genuine, and normal.* She'd heard all the rumors about Rose being a closet drunk, and about the longtime feud between her and Emily. But the sisters had seemed quite civil toward each other, and Kyle had heard from Fitz that Rose had completed an inpatient treatment program for alcoholism. Maybe the sisters had worked out their issues, and maybe Rose was turning her life around. *Or maybe Rose is actually a sweet person, and I misjudged her based on my first impression,* Claudia thought.

Pauline had told her that "Sometimes things and even people aren't what they seem." It was an odd coincidence to recognize a possible real-life example so soon after visiting The Stitchery, and it made Claudia wonder what words of wisdom the seamstress might offer her at her next dress fitting.

When she arrived home, Claudia took in the mail and set her purse on the counter. There were several reply cards from the wedding invitations she had sent out, and she was still opening them when Kyle and Rowen arrived for supper.

"I haven't started cooking yet," she told them. "I stopped by the bakery to see about cakes on my way home."

"That's no problem, it's early," Kyle said. "I can help you in the kitchen."

"And I can watch the Discovery Channel," Rowen said with a toothy grin.

"Sure, go ahead," Claudia said.

"She's been bugging me to get cable," Kyle said as Rowen grabbed the remote control and made herself comfortable on Claudia's sofa. "You've spoiled her with all your channels."

"Compared with most kids these days, she doesn't watch much TV. Besides, you don't let her watch junk programs when she's here."

"True," Kyle said. "Everything in moderation. Although once we move in, that might be easier said than done."

"Have Fitz and Ruth found someone to rent your apartment once we're married?"

"Nope. Not as far as I know, anyway. They've still got time, though."

"Yeah." Claudia opened the refrigerator and started taking out various ingredients for dinner.

"Hey, I almost forgot. Kevin called me this morning," Kyle said. "He and Misty want to get together for lunch this Saturday and maybe go looking at the leaves afterward. I thought they could meet us at the bakery. We can go for a drive after we eat."

"Sure, that sounds like fun," Claudia said. She set a package of chicken and a jar of roasted red peppers on the counter. "Their wedding reply card was in the mail today, along with a bunch of other ones. The Swedhins, the Millers, and the Ottusches are all coming."

"That's great! It's probably a good thing we sent the invites a little early, before people had set holiday plans."

"Yeah. Listen, while we're on the topic of the wedding, I wanted to ask you about inviting one more person." Claudia closed the refrigerator door and cuddled up to Kyle.

"Oh, sure. Who?"

"Daisy."

Kyle's eyebrows went up. "Daisy? Seriously?"

"Yeah. I just ran into her in the bakery, and I don't think she's ever been invited to a wedding. It'd be a nice thing to do for her, and it'd totally blow her mind if she got an invitation."

Kyle shrugged and slipped his arms around her waist. "Okay. I wouldn't mind if she came. It might be a nice thing for her to be able to see the mansion at the reception, too, since she spent so much time up there with Mary."

"Thank you," Claudia said. "Not every guy would agree to having her come, you know. Just shows how lucky I am to be marrying you." She pressed her head against his chest as he leaned down to kiss her hair.

"I'm the lucky one," Kyle insisted. "There aren't many people who'd want to invite someone like Daisy. But I think you're right. If she's never been to a wedding, it'll be special for her. Something she'll never forget."

In the parish house Monday afternoon, Father O'Brien was looking over his schedule for the next day. He had an early-morning Pre-Cana meeting with Kyle

176

Hansen and Claudia Simon. While he had always conducted the marriage preparation courses for couples in his congregation, Kyle and Claudia wanted to complete the classes through a new program offered on the Internet. The technological world was largely foreign to him. Oh, he had a computer in the church office, and occasionally he managed to send an email or print out a letter. He usually left those tasks to Elsa Green, the wonderful lady who worked as his secretary in the church office. He was a painfully slow typist, and just the concept of the Internet or the World Wide Web or whatever they called it these days was quite intimidating.

He had agreed to let Kyle and Claudia complete their classes by computer only after learning that the United States Conference of Catholic Bishops considered the online program an acceptable alternative to regular classes, and only upon the condition that they meet with him a few times in person as well. How learning something by staring at a computer screen could ever be as good as learning it in a class, with a real-life teacher, he didn't know.

The only other item on his agenda for Tuesday was the interview with Julia Tomlinson from *America* magazine.

Interview requests like hers had come up once in a while throughout his years of service, particularly once he was older than seventy-five, typically the mandatory retirement age for priests. He expected questions about his education and training and the reason for his unusually long tenure and service exclusively to the Mill River community. There might be a bit of additional press coverage stirred up once the interview was in print. Before long, it would fade away, and he would continue on as usual.

As Father O'Brien stared at Tuesday on his day planner, the items scribbled there suddenly became a bit blurry. He blinked a few times and removed his reading glasses to rub his eyes. It was the second time in a week he'd had trouble reading something. *It must be eye strain,* he told himself. *I've been reading more than usual these past few days.* After his experience with his hearing aids, the last thing he wanted to do was get used to a stronger prescription for his glasses, but a trip to the optometrist appeared inevitable.

He sat back in his chair, smiling a little as he remembered himself as a much younger man with perfect senses. After a minute or so, he pulled out the large bottom drawer in his desk and removed a small box. It was in this box that he had consolidated his few and precious personal possessions. Among those items was a portrait taken on the day of his ordination. He'd been in his early twenties, with smooth skin and a full head of hair. Those parts of his appearance had changed dramatically, but his twinkling blue eyes were the same, as was the hopeful smile that still appeared in the mirror today.

Beneath the portrait were some black-and-white photos in various stages of turning yellow. He lifted them out and slowly looked through them. His father and mother in their wedding portrait. His mother, Anna, and her brother, Frank, standing together as children. A family shot of himself, his older brother, Seamus, their parents, and their grandparents standing in front of the farmhouse. He gave a soft, wistful sigh as he gazed at the images. It was a sad truth that for quite some time, he had been the sole surviving member of his family.

Other photographs in the box were of Mary McAllister, his closest friend, who had passed the previous spring. She'd hated seeing any image of herself, but she had allowed him to take her picture from time to time so long as he didn't show her the image afterward. He especially liked his photo of Mary standing beside Ebony, her beloved black Morgan mare. It had been a warm day in late spring, and the breeze had lifted Mary's hair and Ebony's mane in a gust. Mary was wearing an eye patch in the picture, the one she always used to conceal the gruesome injury her husband had inflicted on her, but she was hugging the black mare and smiling.

Other than photographs, there were two objects in the box. A black marble figurine of a horse sat heavily in one corner. It was the carved likeness of Ebony that had been used by Mary's late husband to rob her of sight in one eye and disfigure her permanently. Despite the terrible damage it had inflicted on her, Mary had kept and loved the figurine, and Father O'Brien had taken it as a keepsake after her death.

The last item in the box was a dainty silver teaspoon that Mary had given him. This delicate, sparkling object was his most prized possession. The smooth, convex back of the spoon bore an inscription that read: "To my dear friend, love, MEHM." Mary had been the first person to whom he had confided his greatest source of shame — a compulsion to steal and hoard spoons, with which he had struggled most of his life. If truth be told, he still battled on a daily basis to keep from acting on the sinful habit.

Mary had known of his spoon problem, but she had accepted him as a friend in spite of it and even conspired to assist him in certain ways. She had given him the engraved teaspoon so he would possess at least one spoon that was not sinfully obtained.

Father O'Brien gently traced the edge of the spoon with his finger. The memory of Mary's thin, jaundiced face when she had presented it to him at Christmastime last year was still fresh in his mind. In the months since Mary's death, he had come to view the beautiful teaspoon from her own flatware as a symbol of the most important parts of his past. It — all spoons, really — reminded him of his struggle as a teenager to care for his family in his father's absence. More than anything, this one spoon reminded him of Mary and how he had loved her with all his heart as the sister he never had.

CHAPTER 10

April 1, 1934

"Mother!" Michael yelled. Both he and his uncle Frank lunged around the kitchen table toward her, and Frank managed to catch one of her arms before her head hit the floor. Once they reached her, they gently lowered her down.

"Anna? Anna?" Frank asked, gently patting Anna on the cheek.

"Here, here's a cool cloth for her," Lizzie said. Michael took the wet towel she held out and pressed it against his mother's forehead. A few tense moments passed before his mother's eyelids fluttered open. She focused her gaze first on Frank, then turned her head slightly to look at Michael.

"Anna? Can you hear me? You fainted just now. Are you all right?" his uncle asked.

"I think so," his mother said weakly. "I don't know what came over me. I've been feeling a little off yesterday and this morning, but I figured whatever it was would pass after a few days."

"Do you feel like you can sit up?" Michael asked, and when she nodded, he and his uncle helped her into a sitting position on the floor and then onto one of the kitchen chairs.

"Have some water, Anna," his grandmother said as she set a full glass on the table.

"Thank you, Lizzie. I — Oh, goodness, I spilled egg all over the floor."

"Don't you worry about that. I'll clean it up, and I'll see that Frank and Michael are taken care of," his grandmother said as she retrieved the frying pan. "You best go lie down for a while until whatever this is runs its course."

"That's right, Anna," Frank said. "Here, Michael and I will walk you back to your room."

His mother nodded and, holding on to the back of the chair, slowly rose from it. Michael and his uncle each put an arm around her waist and went with her down the hall, where they helped her lie down on her bed.

When they returned to the kitchen, Lizzie was staring out the window above the sink. "She's resting," Frank said, as she turned to face them. "Mrs. O'Brien, did you have any idea Anna wasn't feeling well? Did she say anything to you?"

"No, nothing. Although she did say that the smell of the hobo was making her feel sick before we dragged him out on the back porch."

"She almost got sick yesterday morning as well, when we were cleaning out the root cellar," Michael said quietly. Both his grandmother and uncle looked at him with surprise. "There was a rotten potato. It made a horrible stench when she picked it up, and she had to leave quickly. I didn't think anything of it, though. The smell of it about made me sick, too."

His uncle and grandmother exchanged a worried glance. "Maybe Anna's right, and it's just a brief problem that will clear up quickly," his uncle said.

His grandmother sighed and turned toward the window again. "For Anna's sake, I hope you're right. But it doesn't sound to me like something that will be going away anytime soon."

"You don't think . . ." his uncle said. "Didn't the doctor tell her it would be unlikely? Especially after the others?"

Michael knew then what possibility his uncle and grandmother were discussing, and it scared him. He couldn't bear the thought of seeing his mother stiff and unmoving, like the body he'd helped to hide during the night. Almost as disturbing was the thought of a new stone being added to the small cluster of markers in the pasture.

"Yes, and risky at her age," his grandmother said. "But he didn't say it would be impossible."

The next morning, when Michael rose for school, it was his grandmother who was in the kitchen fixing breakfast.

"Good morning," she said as he appeared. "Your mother was up earlier, but she looked so puny that I sent her back to bed. I think she fell asleep again."

"It's good that she's resting."

"Yes. She needs to keep her strength up."

Michael didn't know what to say to that, although his grandmother's statement stirred up the uneasy concern that had been lingering inside his belly since his uncle's visit the previous day. "I'll be right back. I'm just going to fill up the wood box," he finally said.

"All right, but be quick about it, or your eggs will go cold."

After breakfast, Michael grabbed his books and cap and headed down the driveway. He made it to the end just in time to catch the old brown bus that provided transportation to Edmunds High School for students who lived in rural areas.

He had always been an excellent student. English, Latin, and history were his favorite classes, but his marks were strong in every subject, which pleased his mother greatly. It was part of the reason he hadn't been allowed to go with his father and brother to New York. "Your father needs you here," his mother had said, trying to temper his disappointment at his father's decision to seek a job in a different state. "He needs to find work, but he'd never leave Grandma and me here by ourselves for a long period of time. Besides, we both want you to finish school. Your good grades could get you into college, you know, and with a higher education, you'll have so many more options than your father or Seamus. Try to have patience, Michael. There'll come a time for you to venture out into the world, too."

The ride to the tall, brick school building on the corner of Main and South Union streets went quickly. The school day, though, seemed to drag on forever. Michael was distracted and spent much of the day staring out the great arched windows of the classrooms. His thoughts wandered from the events of Saturday night in the graveyard, to his mother's health, and to his father and brother working so far away. It was a relief when classes were dismissed for the day and he was back on the rickety bus to the farm.

He opened the mailbox before beginning the walk down the driveway, but what he found inside caused him to sprint the distance to the house.

"Mother! Grandma! There's a letter from Father!" he yelled as he burst through the front door.

They were sitting at the table with cups of tea as he entered. His mother's expression of joy did nothing to hide the dark circles under her eyes.

"Wonderful! I'll read it aloud," she said, and he gave her the letter to open. There was a piece of paper inside, covered with handwriting on front and back and folded around a five-dollar bill.

"Thank goodness," his grandmother said when she saw his mother place the bill on the table. "Quickly, Anna, let's hear it."

Michael set his books on the table and straddled a chair backward as his mother began to read:

March 26, 1934

To Mother, Michael, and my dearest Anna,
I hope this letter finds you well, and that my earlier postcard arrived without delay.

Seamus and I are fine and have been working steadily. A day's work brings each of us $4, which is the lowest rate of pay for a bridgeworker here, but we are thankful to have our positions. Most of our days are spent clearing debris to make room for access roads to the bridge site. We are both learning to weld so that we may eventually join the ironworkers, whose positions pay more.

The bridge will eventually connect three boroughs of New York City — Manhattan, Queens, and the Bronx. It is massive in scope and will surely take a number of years to complete.

We are staying in Queens, and the place is crawling with workers from all over the country. I have heard others in our tenement say that there are well over a thousand men working on the bridge. All were hired through the local union, even those like us from another state. Much of our first paychecks went to pay rent and purchase supplies and also to buy local names and addresses so that we could be hired on under the requirements of the union. It seems to me an illegal scheme to line the pockets of the union, but it was the only way we would be given work. I pray the $5 I am enclosing will see you through until I am able to send more.

I believe our positions here will hold out for some time. If all is well at home, we plan to stay as long as possible, hopefully until winter. Of course, you should send for us immediately if the need arises.

I'll write as often as I can. Seamus and I miss and look forward to hearing from you.

With all my love,
Niall

For a moment, no one spoke. Michael watched his mother's face. She held the letter after she finished reading it aloud and stared at it. As her eyes moved quickly through the words again, her hand moved slightly on the surface of the table to feel the thin edge of the money. When she had finished reading the letter a second time, she folded it back into its envelope and smiled.

"Well, Anna, you look like you're feeling better today than you were yesterday, and this letter is even more of a relief. Besides, we didn't properly celebrate Easter yesterday. What do you say we have something special for dinner tonight?"

His mother turned to his grandmother. "What did you have in mind, Lizzie?"

"How about chicken stew? One of the old hens has stopped laying. She's already been through two molts, so she's about finished. Besides, two other hens are brooding their eggs, so there'll be plenty of chicks to replace her."

Michael's mouth watered at the thought of eating stewed chicken with rich golden gravy. It was a rare treat indeed, as their current flock was barely big enough to keep the family in eggs.

"All right. If you'll go take care of the hen, I'll get some water boiling to blanch the feathers. Tomorrow we should go into town for gas and groceries. We're about out of everything."

Michael almost skipped out the door to attend to his chores. Splitting and carrying wood, even cleaning out Onion's stall, didn't seem so bad now that they knew his father and brother were established and able to send support. His mother seemed to have turned the corner, and other than the troubling unfinished business with Uncle Frank, it looked like everything was falling into place.

He would complete the school year and work on the farm during the summer. They could plant a huge garden, and when his father sent more money, they could start buying some livestock to build up the place. Having a pig or two and some more chickens would make next winter easier. Onion would have a calf later in the spring as well. They could sell it for additional income or keep it, if it turned out to be a heifer.

He would do everything he could to help his mother and grandmother throughout the fall. His father and brother would return home, and the family would be reunited and secure. Maybe his father would decide to stay and make a run at farming. Maybe, with the continued implementation of Roosevelt's policies, the country would be on more stable financial footing by then.

It was an optimistic outlook, he knew, but it was the first time in a long time that he had any reason to feel hopeful. *Such a change, from only a letter and a single bill,* he mused. And yet, those flimsy pieces of paper gave him a strange reassurance that everything was going to be all right.

CHAPTER 11

On Monday evening, Emily stopped work in the marble mansion earlier than she normally would have, even though it was difficult to leave the house and lock the door knowing how many projects awaited completion inside. Part of her wished she hadn't promised her mother that she would come to dinner. *But I can't work all the time,* she thought. Besides, she hadn't seen her nephew, Alex, whom she adored, in over a week, and after days of eating on the run, the thought of a home-cooked meal was especially appealing.

She was the last to arrive at her mother's house, which was directly across the street from her own home. The rest of her family had an equally short journey. Rose, Alex, and her brother-in-law, Sheldon, were her neighbors in the little house on the corner lot next door. Her great-aunt Ivy ran the town's indie bookstore, The Bookstop, from the cute bungalow on the corner lot across the street from Rose's place.

It was odd to think that after years of being estranged and living thousands of miles apart, she and her older sister were neighbors and on speaking terms. Even funnier was the fact that her family, with their four residences, had essentially taken over one end of Maple Street. It reminded her of the old Italian and Eastern European neighborhoods in Chicago, where different units of the same extended family often bought up all of the homes on a given street or block.

The smell of her mother's exquisite red sauce greeted Emily as she knocked quickly on the door and went inside.

"Aunt Emily!" Alex said as he came bounding from the kitchen. "You made it just in time!"

"Good! I'm starving." She put her arm around the boy's shoulders and pressed her cheek down against his blond hair. "How've you been? Anything interesting going on at school?"

"I'm going to try out for the school musical next week. They're doing *Oliver Twist*. I really liked the book."

"And you'll be able to learn your lines like that," Emily said as she snapped her fingers.

Alex was ten years old and a gifted child with a true photographic memory. He could perfectly recall anything he'd read even once.

Sheldon was sitting on the sofa reading a newspaper. "I told Rose that if he gets bitten by the acting bug, it's her fault."

"Aunt Emily, did you know Dad first saw Mom when she was onstage in a play?" Alex asked.

"Yeah, I did," Emily said.

"That was a *looong* time ago," Rose said as she came around the corner from the kitchen. "But it'll be fun for you if you get a part in the musical. Hi, Em."

"Will you and Dad come watch me? And you, too, Aunt Emily?" Alex looked around at the three of them with huge blue eyes accentuated by his glasses.

"If you get a part, you bet," Emily said.

"We absolutely will," Rose said. "But hey, why don't you go wash up? Your grandma says we're ready to eat." She rolled her eyes as Alex went down the hall toward the bathroom. "The sooner we get her and Ivy out of the kitchen, the better. Mom's barking orders, and Ivy's brandishing her cane."

Once they were all seated with full plates, Josie turned to Emily. "So, honey, tell us how the mansion's coming along. You're always working these days. I feel like I never see you anymore."

Rose snorted. "Talk about the pot calling the kettle black," she said, and the irony wasn't lost on Emily. Their mother was a workaholic. Josie's frequent absences necessitated by her expanding real estate brokerage had been their chief complaint while they were growing up.

With her stomach empty and her mouth full of homemade ravioli and meatballs, the last thing Emily wanted to do was stop eating and talk about the status of her renovation project. If only she could deal with the question and get her mother onto another subject quickly. "There's a lot to do, but it's taking shape. The floors are refinished, and the walls that needed it have been Sheetrocked. I'm working on updating the bathroom sinks now."

"Ruth told me that Kyle Hansen and Claudia Simon are planning to have their wedding reception there this December," Josie said. "They make such a cute couple, don't you think?"

"They're real sweet together," Ivy said with her mouth full. "By the way, this is excellent, Josie. Making ravioli's a lot of work, but it's worth it in the end."

"It is. Even if the person who's helping

you make it overstuffs the ravioli and then threatens bodily harm with a cane in response to gentle criticism."

"A little extra stuffing never hurt anybody," Ivy said.

"Except it can cause the ravioli to pop open in the boiling water and ruin the whole batch." Josie and Ivy glared at each other, but Emily saw a familiar sparkle in her mother's eyes, and Ivy's lip twitched like it always did when she was trying not to grin.

"So, going back to the house," Sheldon said to Emily with a careful look at Josie and Ivy, "what do you have left to do?"

Emily gave a little sigh. "Sanding drywall plaster, painting, swapping out plumbing and lighting fixtures. Plus some decorative things and a ton of paperwork to get it ready for inspection."

"And I suppose there will be more things that pop up as you go along," Josie said. "With houses, there are always surprises."

"Yeah, probably," Emily said. "But I'll get it finished in time for the wedding, no problem."

"Claudia came into the bakery this afternoon," Rose said. "I showed her some of Ruth's wedding cakes. She seems so nice, but a little naive. Almost like she's never lived anywhere but Mill River."

197

"She has, though, I think," Emily said. "When I met her last summer, she said she hadn't lived here all that long, so she must've come from somewhere else."

"You're right, Em," Ivy said. "She and Kyle are both transplants. I can't remember where Claudia's from, but he moved here with his daughter, Rowen, several years ago from Boston. He used to be a big-shot detective."

"Maybe he was a detective," Emily said, "but Kyle hardly seems like a big shot."

"Oh, I know," Ivy said in a more contrite tone. "I just meant that he had a big important job in a big city, and then he came here. I heard it was because he wanted his daughter to have a safer place to grow up after his wife died."

"He must like it, since he's stayed," Sheldon said. "I'm surprised how peaceful it is here. I never thought I'd enjoy living in a small town, especially after being in New York all those years."

"I still miss some things about the city," Rose said. "The restaurants, and the shows, and the shopping . . ." Her voice was wistful. "It's such a unique place, with so many different kinds of people."

"The people aren't all that different," Josie said. "They've got to have some values in common, or Emily wouldn't be preparing for a wedding between a big-city cop and a small-town schoolteacher."

"That's true," Rose said.

"Speaking of cops," Josie continued, "I ran into that newest one in town a few days ago. What's his name, Matt? The former Marine? He's just *darling.* So polite and good-looking —"

"— and single," Ivy added.

Emily realized where the conversation was headed and felt her stomach drop. She'd wanted to get her mother on another topic, yes, but *not this one.*

"You know, Em, I could introduce you," Josie said, but Emily was already shaking her head.

"No, Mom, I have no interest in dating anyone right now. I don't really have time with all the work I've got to do."

"Oh, but honey, it would be good for you to meet some people and get out once in a while. And Matt seems like a great guy, one who won't be single for long, if you know what I mean."

"Mom, I've already met him, okay? And, he was a total —" She looked over at Alex, who was listening attentively. "He didn't make a very good first impression."

"What do you mean?" Rose asked.

199

Emily paused, realizing that she had to be very careful about what she said. Her irritation with Matt stemmed from her possession of Ruth's briefcase. Ruth was her mother's best friend, and Emily didn't want to reveal anything at this point about finding and unlocking it. Or, rather, Matt unlocking it.

"He came into Turner's on Sunday morning. While he was there, he hit on me, and not in a way I appreciated. Let's just leave it at that."

That shut her up nicely, Emily thought, enjoying the satisfaction of causing her family's momentary silence. Her mother was staring with an open mouth. Rose, on the other hand, looked at her with raised eyebrows, and Emily knew her sister would press her for all the juicy details at the earliest opportunity.

"Aunt Emily," Alex asked after a few more moments had passed. "What does 'hit on' mean?"

Her sister jumped in to answer the question. "It's a way to describe what a man does when he sees a lady and wants to get to know her better," Rose said. "He might pay her a compliment — tell her she's pretty, for example, and ask her to go on a date."

"Did Dad hit on you?"

Rose coughed and nearly spat out the bite of food she'd just taken. Sheldon rolled his eyes as his balding head flushed pink.

"Well, yes, but in a very nice and polite way. He asked me out for a fancy dinner. Your father was always a perfect gentleman."

Too bad Sheldon couldn't give Matt a few pointers, Emily thought, although she was increasingly impressed by the fact that he had tracked her down later on.

"You're really pretty, Aunt Emily," Alex said with a dimple-inducing smile. "Did the man ask you to go to dinner?"

"That's sweet of you to say, Alex," Emily said. "And yes, he asked me to dinner, but I decided I didn't want to go out with him."

As she turned her attention back to her plate, Emily recalled Matt's appearance at the mansion, his sincere apology, and his quick, earnest assistance. She couldn't reveal the later part of their interaction without bringing up the briefcase. She began to feel guilty for casting him in such a negative light without also relaying his attempt to redeem his bad behavior. And, as Emily marveled again at Matt's skill with the lock-pick kit and remembered his handsome face and mischievous eyes, it

201

disconcerted her to realize that she was feeling something else — something she never expected, and which she hadn't felt in a long, long time.

At promptly one o'clock on Tuesday afternoon, a knock sounded on the parish house door. Father O'Brien snapped his fingers on each side of his head and, satisfied that his hearing aids were functioning properly, opened the door.

A woman with shoulder-length black hair and a kind smile extended her hand. "Father O'Brien? Hi, I'm Julia Tomlinson. It's so nice to meet you."

"And you as well, Ms. Tomlinson. You made it up here all right, I see."

"Oh, call me Julia, please. And yes, I drove up this morning. It was such a beautiful trip, and so wonderful to get out of the city."

Father O'Brien smiled. "There's no place quite like Vermont, and Mill River in particular. I thought we could do the interview in my church office. The furnishings in the parish house are quite old, but the chairs in my office are far more comfortable. I could show you the sanctuary, too, if you'd like."

"By all means. My editor wanted me to get a photo of you for the story, and both

202

those places sound like they might make for interesting shots. Lead the way."

Father O'Brien walked with Julia from the parish house to the church. Once in his office, he took his usual seat behind the desk. "Please, sit anywhere you like and make yourself comfortable," he said.

Julia pulled up a chair and took out a pad of paper. She also removed a small digital recorder. "Do you mind if I record our chat? I won't share the recording with anyone. I just like to have it on tape to make sure I get my quotes right."

"That's no problem," Father O'Brien said.

"Thank you. So, to get started, I have a short list of questions prepared. First, can you tell me a little about yourself? Things like where you were born, where you grew up?"

"Certainly. I was born up north, just outside Burlington, on my grandparents' dairy farm. I lived there with my parents, grandparents, and an older brother for several years. Eventually, my father decided to take a job working in a mill in Winooski, and we moved from the farm into rented quarters there.

"My father worked in the mill for many years, until the Great Depression hit and he lost his job. That was a difficult time. My grandfather had passed away by then, but my grandmother was still living, and she hadn't been able to sell the farm, times being what they were. We went back there, and I lived there until I entered the seminary."

"Your alma mater is St. John's Seminary in Boston?"

"Yes, but I actually started minor seminary at Cathedral College of the Immaculate Conception in Brooklyn. They had a six-year combined high school and college program back then. With help from my uncle, who was a priest, I was allowed to enroll partway through high school. I was a good student and managed to finish the high school part early." Father O'Brien enjoyed Julia's expression of surprise. "I applied to St. John's for my major seminary education. By that time, I wanted to be closer to home, in a place that was a little less frenetic. You see, I have a connection with New York just like you do, although the New York of my youth was very different from the city it is today."

"I'm sure it's changed a great deal since you last saw it. Or have you been there recently?"

"No, I've not been for many years now."

Julia was writing quickly. "I'm sure your family was happy when you came back north to St. John's. Were they supportive of your entering the priesthood?"

Father O'Brien paused. Not everyone in his family had lived to see him enter the seminary, but he had no desire to reveal that sad truth or dredge up the events leading up to it.

"My family was very supportive," he said. "My uncle Frank — my mother's brother and the priest I mentioned — was an important part of my life . . . of all of our lives. And my mother — Anna was her name — was especially keen on me pursuing a higher education."

"All right," Julia said as she scribbled furiously. She took a moment to skim over her notes before resuming her questions. "So, you were ordained in?"

"January 1941."

"And how old were you at the time?"

"Almost twenty-two."

Julia puzzled over his answer. "Forgive me, Father, but isn't that too young to be ordained?"

"These days, yes. Priests are required to be at least twenty-four now, and many are much older, with varied life experiences, at the time of ordination. But I'd finished my schooling early, and there was a war going on, don't forget. Military chaplains of all faiths were urgently needed. So I requested and received a dispensation to be ordained at a younger age."

"You expected to be sent into the war?"

"I knew it was a possibility, one that I welcomed, if that was the service needed of me. I ended up being assigned here, to Mill River, instead."

"Your tenure here is extraordinary, Father. I've never heard of another priest being allowed to serve so long in one place. I read a few other articles about you. One of them said that you received special permission to serve the people of Mill River indefinitely. Could you tell me about that?"

"Yes, it was another dispensation, granted to me long ago and honored by the diocese ever since." Father O'Brien could still see Mary as a young woman, lying unconscious in a hospital bed with her face heavily bandaged. And he would never forget Conor McAllister, Mary's grandfather-in-law, begging him to agree to look after Mary once he had passed on. It was Conor who'd had close ties with the bishop and had persuaded him to permit Father O'Brien to stay in Mill River.

"Has it been frustrating for you to be stuck here for so long?"

Father O'Brien pursed his lips as he

considered how best to answer the question. "In all honesty, there was a short period — while I was a very young priest — when I disliked the fact that I had been 'stuck here.' I wished for what might have been, had I not been asked and agreed to stay in Mill River, even though 'what might have been' wasn't even known to me. Maybe I would have traveled more, met more people, seen more things. Perhaps I would have taught in a seminary. The thought of teaching always did appeal to me. Or there might have been something else, some other role in which I could have been useful.

"That period quickly passed. I realized that I wasn't stuck in Mill River — I'd been placed here. It was God's doing that I ended up here. The people needed me, some far more than others. And I came to understand that I needed them as well. I've seen generations of the same family grow up here. I've been with them through the good times and bad, and I'm so thankful to have been here for all those times."

"Now you're, well, pardon my asking, but you're . . . how old, exactly?"

He smiled. "I've always thought that age was just a number. What truly matters is what's inside here" — he tapped his forefinger to his temple — "and here," he said, placing a hand over his heart. "I pray that I've accumulated enough wisdom over my many years to be of better service in my position, and I still feel very young at heart."

Julia smiled at him, and the wonder on her face was plain. "Do you think you'll retire anytime soon?"

Father O'Brien chuckled and leaned forward in his chair. "Julia, my dear, don't you think I would have retired long ago if I had any intention of retiring at all?" He winked at the journalist to make sure she understood that he wasn't being gruff or condescending. "Even if I did retire as pastor, I would immediately look for another way to serve and to work. I love what I do. I love the Lord and the people of Mill River. I fully intend to serve here as long as I'm able."

In Claudia Simon's fourth-grade classroom Tuesday afternoon, Karen was preoccupied with watching the clock. It wasn't because the students were being unruly or because she was eager to be done with work for the day. On the contrary, she was dreading the end of the school day, when she would leave the distraction of fourteen busy children and face another evening of uncertainty, not knowing whether her husband was safe or even alive.

She'd arrived early that morning so she could explain to Claudia what had happened and why she might not be completely herself. It was no surprise that Claudia had been completely supportive and sympathetic. Her supervising teacher was a sweetheart, and they'd worked together for months, since Claudia had taken the open fourth-grade position at the school. They were now friends as well as colleagues.

The classroom was quiet at the moment, with the children having gone to gym class. As Claudia worked on redoing one of the classroom bulletin boards, Karen sat at a desk grading the morning's math quizzes. It should have been a quick and easy task, but she kept looking up at the clock's minute hand inching forward and losing her place among the rows of math problems.

Just focus, she thought. *Worrying won't do anything to help you or Nick, and the kids will be back soon enough to take your mind off it.*

"How are your wedding plans coming?" she asked Claudia.

"So far, so good," Claudia said, stepping up on a stool to staple a border. "I'm trying not to stress over anything, you know? Kyle and I just want to keep things as simple as we can and enjoy the day."

"That's what matters. You'll remember your wedding day for the rest of your life, and you want those memories to be good ones."

Karen realized as she spoke the words how true they were for her. She and Nick had married during one of his brief breaks between tours, and so many things about that perfect day were seared into her memory. Seeing her mother beaming and crying as her father walked with her down the aisle to the altar. Hearing her father whisper in her ear — "You remember that you'll *always* be my little girl" — as he'd placed her hand in Nick's. And her new husband's face — strong and yet tender, with his own tear-filled eyes gazing down at her as he lifted her veil to kiss her — how many times during the past several weeks had she remembered that moment, held fast to it to keep herself going? How many times had she prayed to see that face again?

"Karen? Karen, are you all right?"

Only then did she snap out of her reverie and realize that the math quiz in front of her was peppered with tearstains. "I'm fine," she managed to say. "Talking about weddings . . ."

"I'm so sorry," Claudia said, but Karen shook her head.

"No, no, I'm the one who brought it up. I guess I shouldn't have, but it seems like everything I hear or see or say these days reminds me of Nick."

"I think that's entirely normal, given the circumstances," Claudia said. The teacher came closer and touched her arm. "Would you like some water? I could run down to the lounge and get a bottle for you."

Karen nodded. "That would be nice, thank you."

Claudia left the room, and Karen tried to compose herself and focus on her work. She had made it through another quiz when the cellphone in her pocket began to vibrate. The number that flashed on the screen caused her heart to skip a beat, and her hands began to tremble as she answered the call.

"Yes? Yes, this is Karen Cooper," she said to the representative from her husband's company. "Do you have new information about my husband?" She listened to the woman on the other end of the line, but as the words began to register, the pounding of her heart and the new flood of tears made it impossible for her to speak or to even keep the phone to her ear. She dropped it on the surface of the student desk in front of her and, shaking, gripped the edges of the desk until her fingers were numb.

The guttural, heart-wrenching sound that rose up and escaped her throat was one of unmistakable grief.

CHAPTER 12

April 20, 1934

On his way home from school on a Friday afternoon, Michael checked the mailbox and found it empty. That there was no letter from his father waiting was a minor disappointment, but one that would be reversed in due course, he was sure. After all, they had received the first letter and the five dollars only a few weeks ago, and they needed to allow time for his father to be paid again and for another letter to reach the farm.

The absence of a letter did little to spoil Michael's happy mood, because the past two weeks had been wonderful. His mother and grandmother had done some much-needed shopping with the money his father had sent. The pantry was restocked, the truck's gas tank was full, and there had been a bit left over to save. His mother had seemed better, too. She hadn't had any other fainting episodes, and she'd been unusually cheerful, whistling or sometimes humming to herself as she worked in the kitchen.

Michael came through the front door and hung up his book bag, cap, and coat. The house was strangely quiet. "Mother? Grandma?" He went into the kitchen, where a pot of something that smelled wonderful was simmering on the stove. Everything seemed especially clean, too, he noticed. The floors were damp, as if they had been freshly scrubbed. The counters and table were tidied up, and there were no dirty dishes in the sink basin. *Maybe Mother's in the root cellar,* he thought. *And Grandma might be in the barn.*

Just then his grandmother entered the kitchen from the hallway that led to the bedrooms. "Your mother's taken ill again," she said with a worried look on her face. "She seemed fine this morning and into the afternoon. Better than fine, really, because she started the spring cleaning. Just after she got supper going, though, she got sick again, and worse this time. Everything she ate came back up. I've been giving her soda crackers and sips of water, but even that won't stay down. I think, Michael . . . I think we should have a doctor look at her."

It took Michael a moment to process his

grandmother's words. "Should I go call for one?"

"You'll have to, because I don't want to leave her alone, and she's in no shape to drive. Go over and ask Mr. Whibley for a ride to the Union Oil call box. See if you can reach Dr. Washburn before his office closes for the day. And hurry, Michael."

So many thoughts ran through his mind as he rushed next door and then rode the few miles with his neighbor to the filling station with the public telephone. He wished so much that their farm had a telephone, even if its use was reserved for emergencies. He wondered how his family could afford a doctor's visit right now, especially a home visit, even if his mother's health demanded it. He was reeling from having his weeklong good mood replaced by a sense of precarious insecurity. More than anything, he was deeply concerned about and afraid of what was happening with his mother.

Time slowed to a crawl after Whibley returned him to the farm. Michael sat in the parlor, watching the minute hand of the old clock on the mantel. His grandmother was back in the bedroom, sitting with his mother, as they all waited for the doctor to arrive.

The sound of a car pulling up brought Michael to his feet. He opened the front door before the doctor had even gotten out of his car.

"Hello, Michael. Good to see you. So, your mother hasn't been feeling well, has she? I'll do my best to change that."

"Thank you, sir. She's inside resting." He led the doctor down the hallway to his mother's room and knocked gently on the door. "Mother? Grandma? Dr. Washburn is here."

His grandmother opened the door and quickly ushered the doctor inside. A look at Michael as she closed the door clearly communicated that he should remain outside the bedroom.

He turned and walked halfway back to the parlor before he stopped. It was wrong to even think about eavesdropping, and his cheeks flushed with shame as he stood silently in the hallway. Still, he began to creep back toward the bedroom, knowing all the while that he was going to listen at the bedroom door.

At first, it was hard to hear what was going on inside. Michael pressed his ear tight against the door and hoped it wouldn't creak. Only then could he make out the doctor's low voice quietly asking his mother questions and his mother answering weakly.

". . . remember when the last time you bled?"

". . . not sure, maybe a few months ago? It's not regular, and I don't really keep track very carefully anymore."

"And when was the last time you ate a normal meal?"

"I think three days ago, at breakfast. I haven't felt like eating much at all."

"Are you able to drink anything? Water? Milk?"

"I try, but it usually doesn't stay down."

There was a minute or so of silence before the doctor began to speak again. "There's no doubt you're with child again, Mrs. O'Brien. About six or seven weeks along, I'd say. Your extreme nausea troubles me. No one knows for sure why this sickness occurs in expectant mothers. Recently, there have been articles published by experts in the medical community indicating that nausea and vomiting like yours are largely psychosomatic. That is, some subconscious part of a woman's mind is fighting against the child she's carrying, resulting in the physical symptoms known as morning sickness. Of course, I'm aware of your medical history and the difficulties you've suffered trying to bear children. Given these new articles, however, I feel it my duty to ask —

do you truly want another baby? Could it be that your attempts to bear another child were influenced by the wishes of your husband?"

"What?" His mother's voice carried as much shock as Michael felt after hearing the doctor's insinuation and question. "Of course I want another child. So does Niall, but I can assure you, Doctor, that my own desire is both great and wholly independent of my husband's wishes. Why, I'd give my own life if doing so would allow this baby to survive."

"She very nearly did give her own life the last couple of tries, which you well know," his grandmother said. There was anger in her voice, and Michael could envision the wrinkles around her eyes becoming more pronounced as she glared at the doctor. "How could you believe that Anna doesn't want another child?"

"I don't believe that exactly, ma'am," the doctor said, and his voice took on an appeasing tone. "Of course she would *consciously* want the child she's carrying. If the current theory is correct — that the subconscious mind is the root cause of morning sickness — she might not be aware of such resistance."

"I can assure you, Doctor, that I want this

child with *all* of my mind, be it conscious, subconscious, or whatever," his mother said. Her voice sounded louder.

The doctor sighed. "Then perhaps the nausea is the result of some sort of stress you're experiencing. You said your husband will be working out of state for an extended period?"

"Yes."

"It can't be easy to hold down this place on your own, not knowing when he'll return."

"I'm not on my own," his mother said, and Michael could hear her frustration building as she spoke. "I have Lizzie and Michael here, and they help me plenty. If anything, the fact that Niall has found good, steady work has been quite a relief, even if it means he won't be home for a while. In times like these, a family has to make sacrifices. One of ours will be time spent apart, if it means that my husband will remain employed."

"Well. I suppose the important thing for now isn't why you're having this sickness but how we can get you feeling better. Your pulse is rapid, and you're showing early signs of dehydration. It's important that you continue to try to drink as much as you can, even if it comes up afterward. Water, fruit juices, any kind of liquid. It may be easier if you sip fluids in between meals. I'm sure you remember that a tea made with sugar and gingerroot is often very helpful in reducing nausea."

"Yes. So are soda crackers, especially in the morning, although they haven't helped me so far."

"I'll give you a prescription for a new vitamin formula that's being recommended for cases like yours. When you go to the drugstore to pick it up, you might also get a bottle of cola syrup, which is sold over the counter. And I want you to stay in bed and rest for the time being. Let's see how it goes over the next twenty-four hours. I'll come out to check on you tomorrow around this time."

Michael heard the creaking of bedsprings, presumably from the doctor standing up or his mother shifting position. Whichever the cause, the sound prompted him to back away from the door and slip down the hallway. He heard the bedroom door open almost as soon as he reached the kitchen, and the doctor and his grandmother joined him.

"I'd like you to keep a close eye on her, Mrs. O'Brien," the doctor said. He turned toward Michael. "You, too, son. Don't let your mother do anything to exert herself. Make sure she takes the medicine I prescribed and that she drinks often."

"Doctor," his grandmother said, "seeing as how I don't drive and Michael is too young to hold a junior license, we'll be hard pressed to get the medicine before the pharmacy closes. Would you be able to give Michael a lift into town? He could pick up the prescriptions for Anna and walk back here."

"That's no problem at all. I was planning to go back to the clinic, anyway."

"Thank you. I have one other concern, that being the bill for your services. We're extremely short on cash. I guess most folks are these days. We can pay the four dollars for today's visit, but after we buy medicine for Anna . . ."

The doctor was quiet for a moment and then offered his grandmother a resigned smile. "Why don't we consider tomorrow's follow-up part of today's visit? I know there isn't a family in the area that isn't struggling financially, and you folks have been patients of mine for a long time."

"We would appreciate that very much, Doctor. Thank you."

The doctor nodded. "I'll make note of it on the bill. Have a good evening, Mrs.

O'Brien. Are you ready, Michael?"

"Yes, sir, I'll just get my coat."

"All right. I'll go start the car."

As soon as the doctor had left the house, his grandmother grabbed his wrist. "You'll need some money for the medicine. Wait here." She went quickly down the hallway to her room and returned a few moments later.

"Here," she said, shoving a five-dollar bill into his hand. "Most of what your father sent went to buy groceries and gas, so use this for the prescriptions. And you be careful to bring back the change."

Michael looked at the money in his hand. "Grandma, I thought you told the doctor . . . Where did you get this?"

"It's not your business to ask, Michael, but I'll tell you anyway." His grandmother gave him a wry smile. "It came from that vicious tramp who attacked your mother. Do you remember the gold watch you found in his pocket?" she whispered as she glanced out the front window. "When your mother and I went to town after your father sent money, I told her I wanted to go to the drugstore to get some liniment for my arthritis. While she shopped for groceries, I did just that. But first I walked over to the loan office."

Michael knew about the loan office. It was the only one of its kind in Burlington, tucked away on the corner of a street on the edge of town. He had passed by it on occasion, and the front window was always stocked with fine jewelry and sparkling watches. The other items on display routinely changed. There might be a crystal vase or sterling candlesticks. He had seen a lovely, shiny guitar once, suspended from two ropes near the top of the window. Another time, there had been a new-looking console radio positioned at the very front, with the jewelry and watches flanking it.

The loan office was run by a sweaty Russian named Igor Borisov. Michael knew this because his mother had described the man, and she had made clear that he was never to go there. "It's a place of shame and desperation and last resort," she'd said. "Not only that, but Mr. Borisov has a reputation for being slimy, and not just in the physical sense." But his grandmother hadn't had a privileged upbringing like his mother's. Having lived and worked on a farm her entire life, she was used to doing whatever was required to scrape by.

"You took a loan against the watch?" Michael asked.

"I *sold* the watch," his grandmother said.

"I figured we didn't need it lying around here, where it might raise suspicion if someone saw it. And Borisov gave me twenty dollars for it. Twenty dollars! It's a good thing, because I have a feeling this won't be the last time we have the doctor out here for your mother. Don't you dare breathe a word of it to her. She wouldn't approve of me going there or telling you about it. Do you understand me?"

Michael nodded. He was trying to wrap his mind around what his grandmother had done, as well as the fact that there was now a new secret he was responsible for keeping.

His grandmother pulled his coat from the hook by the door and held it out to him. "You best get out there. The doctor's waiting for you."

The doctor's vehicle, a Cadillac town sedan, was by far the finest car in which Michael had ridden. He couldn't help but stare at the rich wood trim and the myriad gauges positioned across the dashboard behind a gleaming glass panel. The soft velour upholstery on the plush seats caught on the skin of his rough, chapped hands, and the polished chrome door and window handles reflected his image.

"You're quiet," the doctor observed as he drove out onto the road. "Worried about your mother?"

"Yes, sir."

"We'll monitor her closely. She might improve and get through the roughest part of the sickness on her own."

"And what if she doesn't, Doctor? What if she doesn't get better?"

Dr. Washburn sighed. "It's been several years since her last time expecting. There are some new treatments available. They're in-hospital treatments, mind you, but they're usually very effective."

Again Michael retreated into his own thoughts. He had a great deal to worry about, chief of which was his mother's troubling condition. He prayed that she would get better quickly, on her own. If she didn't, what would happen to her if she went to the hospital? How would they ever be able to afford the treatments offered there? Perhaps his father would soon send more money, enough to cover any unexpected medical expenses. There was also the money his grandmother had gotten for the hobo's watch.

Michael thought again of his mother's secret silver in the root cellar. How right she had been to conceal it from his grandmother, who'd had no qualms about visiting the loan office. She undoubtedly would have demanded they sell the set long before now.

He hoped only that his mother wouldn't be forced to cash in her "insurance policy" to save her own life.

CHAPTER 13

"Karen? Karen, what's wrong?"

Claudia's worried voice barely registered with Karen, and it took her a second to realize that the teacher had returned to the empty classroom.

"I just got a call about Nick," she managed to stammer. She was still sitting at the student desk. Claudia pulled up a chair and sat down, placing a hand gently on her arm. "They found his jeep. It was abandoned on a highway outside the city with two flat tires. The man he was traveling with . . . his body was still there, in the front seat."

"But . . . Nick wasn't there?"

Karen shook her head, too upset to speak.

Claudia's forehead bunched together in the middle. "Isn't it a good thing?"

"The Jeep was riddled with bullet holes," Karen gasped. "The windows were shot out, and the driver's seat was stained with blood."

"Oh, Karen. I don't know what to say."

Karen glanced into the teacher's eyes, but she only cried harder when she saw that Claudia's eyes had welled up and she felt the teacher's arms close around her.

"Karen, you shouldn't be here," Claudia said gently. "You're too upset, and the kids will be back soon. I don't think you should drive, though, not right now. Why don't you let me find Ms. Finney? I'm sure she'd agree with me, and maybe she could find someone to take you home."

Although the last place she wanted to go was home, she nodded in agreement, and Claudia hurried out the classroom door. When she returned a few minutes later, she was accompanied by Leona Finney, the school's principal, as well as Jerry Strand, the vice principal.

Leona touched Karen's shoulder as she bent to speak to her. "Karen, Claudia told me about your phone call. I'm so sorry about what's happened."

"We all are," Jerry added. "Why don't you get your things together? I'll drive you home in your car, and Leona will follow us and take me back to the school."

"Th— thank you," Karen stammered. "But, I really don't want to go home right now. Could you . . . would there be any way

228

you could take me to St. John's instead? I think I'd like to see Father O'Brien."

"Of course," Jerry said. "It might be better to be with someone right now."

"And Karen, you should take all the time off that you need," Leona said in the same kindly tone Karen had heard her use to comfort upset children. "I'm surprised you didn't say anything to me about your situation. I can't imagine trying to work when you're dealing with something like this."

"I only found out about it on Saturday," Karen replied. "There's nothing I can do except wait and hope and pray. I thought it'd be better to come to work. I'm just trying to stay strong and keep going for Ben. And for Nick."

In the marble mansion, Emily was up on a tall ladder with a handheld vacuum sander, checking to make sure the plastered drywall screws and seams had been sanded properly. She was planning to begin painting the new walls later in the week. So far, she had found that the drywall crew she'd hired to put up the Sheetrock had done a good job. Most of the walls were perfectly smooth, with only a few isolated spots requiring a pass with the sander.

Early in her career, her first time hiring

drywall subcontractors had been a disaster. One of the crew members had obviously been new or incompetent or both, because on many of the walls, the drywall screws had been left flush against the wall instead of being drilled in far enough to form small concave pits to hold plaster. Once the plaster had been applied over the too-far-out screws, entire walls had been covered in neat rows of convex bumps, like tiny plaster belly buttons. She'd insisted that the subcontractor redo those walls, but the second effort had set her project back over two weeks.

Emily came down from the ladder and moved it across the room to another wall. Before she went back up, she caught sight of the old briefcase sitting on the floor beside her toolbox. Even though she couldn't afford to waste time doing it, what she really wanted to do was park herself in a comfortable spot and continue reading through the letters.

It was strange, how she'd been completely drawn in by the old correspondence. Normally, she disliked gossip and preferred to steer clear of other people's business. Soap operas and reality shows — heck, most television — held no appeal for her; her own life had been so full of tragedy and drama that she saw no point in getting caught up in the problems of people who didn't even exist. But the old letters were different. Many of them contained stories about Father O'Brien as a child. Despite the gross invasion of privacy, she found it fascinating to read about the distant past of someone she knew. It was also interesting to read letters written to the mysterious late Mary McAllister, whom she knew about but had never met. With their fine cursive handwriting revealing secrets of a time long ago, the letters seemed to beckon to her from their leather enclosure.

Screw it, she thought. *One letter won't take much time.*

She went to the briefcase and pulled out the next letter in the bundle she'd been reading. Already, she had made her way through the earliest batches of correspondence from Anna O'Brien to Mary McAllister. Most of those had been filled with the written equivalent of polite conversation between two people who didn't know each other well. Over the years, though, as the two women became friends and then each other's confidantes, the letters had become much more personal in nature.

Emily sat down on the floor cross-legged

and took the folded paper from the envelope. Her eyes skimmed through the opening pleasantries until she came to the heart of the correspondence:

. . . Frank never told me what he and Michael did with the body, although I never asked him about it. I suppose I didn't want to know, and it was safer that I didn't. I know carrying that around was difficult for Michael. He changed after the shooting, Mary. He didn't hunt for pleasure anymore. In fact, he went out only if we needed game to eat. He became quieter, too, more withdrawn. Michael has always been sensitive and introspective. He's outwardly calm, but he feels things intensely, and I know killing the man who attacked me didn't sit well with him, even though his doing it saved my life . . .

After she finished the letter, Emily reread it, trying to make sense of the new information it contained. *As a teenager, Father O'Brien had shot and killed a man in defense of his mother.* She never would have guessed that the kindly priest had such a secret in his past, but knowing it gave her a new appreciation of his fortitude. His actions were perfectly justified and understandable. *In fact,* Emily admitted to herself, *even though Mom has her faults and has wreaked havoc with my life, if someone tried to hurt her, I'd use lethal force to protect her, too.*

She sighed and glanced up at the wall before her. It was getting to be late afternoon. The sun was sinking lower in the sky, and the tops of the walls were becoming obscured by shadows. Seeing places up there that needed to be sanded would be tough for the rest of the day. *And not only that,* Emily thought, as she looked over at her big dog napping on a cushion in the corner, *but Gus hasn't had a good run in a few days, and it's nice outside.* She could take him to the new park to stretch his legs, drop him off at her house, and return to the mansion to get some more work done on the plumbing in the evening.

"Gussie-pup, you wanna go outside?" she asked. In a matter of seconds, the brown and white dog was fully awake, whining in front of her with his tail rapidly wagging. Emily couldn't help but laugh as she rumpled his ears and walked with him toward the door.

At Hayes Memorial Park, she grabbed her water bottle and a plastic bag from the car, put Gus on a leash, and jogged with him toward the fenced-in area for dogs. Once they were through the gate, Emily unhooked Gus's leash and smiled as he dashed off to investigate the park's other human and canine visitors.

An older couple she didn't know watched a pair of wiener dogs chase each other in circles. A young girl and her mother took turns throwing a tennis ball for a large golden retriever. Another woman sat on a bench holding a leash and patting a mixed-breed dog sitting next to her and panting heavily. And in the distance, a man was bent over, playing with a small, fuzzy puppy.

Gus had already spotted the puppy and made a beeline directly for it. Emily chased after him, frantically calling his name. Her dog was usually loving and gentle toward both young children and puppies, but she didn't want his exuberance or size to startle this pup or its owner.

By the time she reached him, Gus had already sniffed the puppy in several places and was wagging ferociously as the man reached out to pet him.

"Gus! Gus, come here, boy!" she said. "I'm so sorry he charged up on you like that. He won't hurt either of you, he just loves puppies, and when he saw your —" As the man with the puppy turned toward her, Emily froze.

It was Matt.

His eyes widened at the sight of her, and neither of them spoke. Just as the silence began to grow awkward, Matt smiled and greeted her. "Hi."

"Hi."

"So, uh, this is your buddy, huh?" he asked, looking down at Gus. "He's pretty friendly. And big."

"Yeah, that's Gus," she said.

"This is the puppy I told you about. You know, the one who caused the problems in my car." He looked down at the little Husky mix, yipping continually and bounding around and through Gus's long legs. "I still haven't named her."

Emily scrunched up her mouth. "Given what she did in your car, I can think of a couple of names that might be fitting."

Matt exhaled loudly. "Yep. At the rate she's going, I'll be back for more upholstery cleaner before too long. The housebreaking isn't going too well."

"Ah." Emily nodded and looked across the park toward some of the other dogs. She was in that emotionally awkward place again, feeling flustered and slightly breathless in his presence but debating whether she wanted to continue their unexpected conversation.

"Oh, c'mon, Emily. I meant what I said up at the mansion when I opened your briefcase. I really am sorry for treating you the way I did. Can we start over, please?" He took a step closer and held out his right hand. "Hi, I'm Matt Campbell. And you are?"

She sighed and rolled her eyes, although not without noticing how muscular his arm was. "Haven't you heard the saying that you get only one chance to make a first impression?" She allowed a bit of playful sass into her own voice.

Matt dropped his hand and locked eyes with her. "Then let me make it up to you somehow. I'd really like to prove to you that I'm a decent guy."

Emily considered the possibility. Matt seemed sincere. He was so attractive, even in the old sweats and T-shirt he was wearing. *And,* she admitted to herself, *it's pretty fun, seeing him grovel like this.*

"Hypothetically, just how would you make it up to me?"

Matt shrugged. "I dunno. Maybe we could hang out. I'd still be happy to take you to dinner."

"So, we're back to that," Emily said, laughing and shaking her head. "Unbelievable. Look, I'll be very honest with you. I really don't have time to hang out. I've got a big work deadline looming over me, and I don't need any distractions."

"What about dinner? You have to eat, don't you?"

"Yes, but these days, it's mostly sandwiches on the run. If I'm not sleeping or doing something for Gus, or running the hardware store or fixing some issue with one of my mom's listings, I'm working in the McAllister mansion. I have no life, and it'll be that way for a while yet."

"It sounds like you could use a little downtime," Matt said. "Listen, if I can come up with something that would fit your schedule, would you agree to it?"

"I'm not sure anything will fit my schedule right now."

"I'm up for the challenge, if you'll give me the chance."

Emily was intrigued. As much as she hated to admit it, she was impressed by Matt's persistence and curious about how far he was willing to go with his groveling. "All right," she said finally as she extended her hand. "Hi, Matt. I'm Emily DiSanti. It's nice to meet you."

Father O'Brien was in his office at St. John's when his secretary knocked at the door.

"Father, Karen Cooper is here. She's terribly upset and asked to see you."

At once, he forgot the homily he was working on and followed Elsa into the nave of the church. Karen was sitting in the front pew with her head bowed. Her hands were in her lap, clasped around a large wad of Kleenex.

"I was just heading out for the day," Elsa whispered to him as she pulled on a cardigan sweater. "You be sure and give me a call at home if you need me."

Father O'Brien thanked Elsa and took a seat next to Karen. He waited for her to speak first.

"They found Nick's Jeep," she said. "His passenger was there, dead. There were bullet holes . . . blood in the front seat, but no sign of him. I came here from school. They excused me early, but I couldn't go home, and I didn't know where else to go. I feel like . . . Oh, Father, I just have this horrible feeling that he's gone."

Father O'Brien took Karen's hand. "I'm so glad you decided to come here, Karen. Is Nick's company still searching for him?"

"Yes. The military, too. And the Saudis."

"Then you — we — mustn't give up hope."

"I keep telling myself that, Father, but it's

so hard. I haven't told Ben yet. I'm not sure I should until we get more information, one way or the other."

"Tell me more about Nick," Father O'Brien said. If he could get Karen talking, help her focus on something other than the recent news, perhaps it would help her to calm down. "He's an engineer of some kind, right?"

Karen sniffed and dabbed her nose. "Yes, an aircraft systems engineer. He had a lot of training in the Air Force. He worked for a while at GE, but he got laid off. The job overseas seemed like his best option for now."

"What exactly was the job? Did I hear you say he was in Saudi Arabia?"

"Um-hmm. I don't know exactly what he was working on. Most of his work is classified, so I never get to hear the details. He was stationed on one of the Saudi air bases, though."

"He must have some fine technical expertise," Father O'Brien said. "Goodness, what I wouldn't give for just a bit of that. I can barely operate my computer. All the buttons and keys are so confusing. It seems like every time I press something, it beeps at me." He looked at Karen carefully. Her tears were coming slower, and she managed a wan smile at his computer comment.

"Nick is brilliant," Karen said. "I keep thinking that's the reason he was taken. He must know something important. Nothing else makes sense. Americans don't go missing in Saudi Arabia anymore, like they do in other places in the Middle East. At least that's what Nick said before he left. It's one of the reasons he felt safe taking the job."

"If that's true, then whoever has him will want to keep him alive," Father O'Brien said. "That's another reason to keep the faith. Listen to me, Karen," he said with a gentle squeeze of her hand, and she raised her tear-streaked face to look into his. "God loves you, and Nick, and Ben. Psalm 91 teaches us that the Lord is a refuge and a fortress, and that He will rescue and protect those who acknowledge His name. I believe deeply that God is watching over Nick right now, protecting him. And He's doing the same for you."

"I feel so hopeless and afraid, Father. Like I'm all alone. And," she added in a barely audible whisper, "it isn't good for me to be alone right now."

"Remember, you're not alone, Karen. You're not. God is always with you and with Nick. And, there are so many people in Mill River who care about you and your family.

If you need help, we'll be there," Father O'Brien said. "Our church family and our community are small, but both can do so much. Let me make a few calls. In the meantime, you're welcome to come here or call me anytime."

After they had said a prayer for Nick's safety and Karen had left, Father O'Brien put on his reading glasses and looked through his Rolodex for Elsa's home number. He rarely called his secretary at home. It was clear, though, that Karen needed assistance immediately, and Elsa could quickly activate the church support group. The volunteers on the list could provide meals for Karen and her son. They could also take turns visiting her or taking her for outings on the days she wasn't working. That way, she wouldn't be left alone with her worries for long stretches of time.

As he thumbed through the cards of members' addresses and phone numbers, Father O'Brien thought of some of the countless instances when the members of his church and others in Mill River had pulled together to help one of their own. There had been many surgeries and deaths. Car accidents had been another, more common occurence. Occasionally, a house fire or a bad winter storm had taken its toll on someone's home. Regardless of the reason, the people of the town always helped each other. Even he had been the recipient of his neighbors' love. Every evening for a full two weeks after the last town meeting, when people had come to understand the deep friendship that he'd lost with Mary's passing, someone from the town had brought him supper or stopped by to visit.

A support system like that could help people through the most difficult situations. But it was true that sometimes, assistance from friends and loved ones wasn't enough to avert tragedy or prevent a tragedy from getting worse. Even with his help, and help from his grandmother and uncle, his poor mother had suffered terribly after his father had left.

For Karen's sake, and for her son's, he could only hope that the grace of God and the loving hands of their friends and neighbors would see them through until Nick was found and returned safely home.

CHAPTER 14

Saturday, April 21, 1934

At dawn on the morning after Dr. Washburn's visit, Michael was awakened by his grandmother knocking on his bedroom door.

"Michael? Michael, get up. I need your help."

He thought at first his grandmother's voice had been a dream. He forced open his eyes and saw the faint sunlight beginning to illuminate his window. His grogginess quickly disappeared when his grandmother knocked again and opened the door.

"Did you hear me, Michael? I need you to do the milking this morning. Your mother's worse. She's been awake retching for nearly an hour, and I don't dare leave her. Thank goodness the doctor will be back today. Hurry, now."

Michael pulled on his clothes and nearly ran down the steps. His heart was beating fast, mostly from the shock of hearing his grandmother's words. Of course he would do the milking, but he wanted very much to see his mother before he went out.

His grandmother was standing at his mother's bedroom door with the doorknob in her hand, like a butler prepared to usher a guest out of someone's home.

"Can I go in? Just for a minute?"

"She's having a hard time at the moment, and you best take care of Onion first," his grandmother said. "The milk pail is in the kitchen. I scalded it last night. You can look in on your mother when you come back inside." Michael reluctantly headed toward the kitchen as she slipped inside the bedroom and shut the door behind her.

The family's Holstein was awake and shifting impatiently in her stall when he arrived at the barn. Carrying the empty milk pail and a bucket of warm, soapy water, he went to the opposite end of the barn, where a row of milking stations faced a feed trough against the wall. Once he had placed a ration of fresh hay and corn in part of the trough, he went to Onion's stall, opened the door, and grabbed her by the halter. "C'mon, girl, let's go," he said. Rather than follow him eagerly, though, as the cow did with his grandmother, Onion planted her feet and pulled against him.

Michael held up the shining milk pail. "Look here. You know what this is, don't you, girl? Come on, now, be a sweetheart and come get your breakfast."

The cow opened her mouth and lowed but didn't budge.

Michael sighed. He remembered the cows that his grandfather used to have — Holsteins, all, and every one of them sweet and docile. A few years ago, when the family had decided to return to the farm from Winooski, his father had purchased Onion from a farmer who was giving up on the dairy business. The young cow had already borne a healthy calf and proved to be a good milk producer. Unfortunately, they'd discovered once they got her to the farm that she was unusually stubborn and unaccustomed to being hand-milked. His grandmother had worked with her daily, and gradually the cow had grown used to the routine and to being handled. But his grandmother was the only person for whom the cranky cow would cooperate.

To their dismay, they also learned that the cow had a particular liking for wild onions. She eagerly sought out and consumed the dark green clumps with purple flowers that occasionally appeared in the pasture. The

245

wild onions, in turn, gave her milk an unpleasant taste and odor. The name Onion was fitting for her temperament as well as her preferred grazing.

Tabby, the barn cat, meowed a greeting from the hayloft. She arched into a stretch, watching as Michael scooped a handful of corn out of the feed tub and walked back toward the cow. "Here you go, girl. Let's try this again," he said as he held out the corn. Onion lowered her large, dripping nose to his hand, unfurled her wet tongue, and began licking up the grain. He took hold of her halter again and stepped back. To his relief, she walked forward with him, her attention fixed on the offering in his hand.

Slowly, he guided her toward the milking station he had prepared. Once the cow found the waiting hay and corn, he fastened the wooden stanchion around her neck. Next, he washed her udder and his hands with the soapy water from the bucket. Finally, he positioned the clean milk pail under the cow and sat down beside her on a milking stool.

Although he was a bit rusty, he'd often helped his grandfather with the milking when he was younger, and it didn't take long before he found a good rhythm and had nearly half the pail filled. Once the back half of the cow's udder had been emptied, he switched to the two front teats. It was then that Onion decided to act up. She lunged backward and, with her head secured by the wooden boards, threw the rear half of her body sideways toward him. He barely managed to stand up and move out of the way to avoid being knocked over.

"Gosh darn it, Onion!" He shoved his weight against the cow, trying to push her back into position, but this only caused her to kick out violently with her hind legs. As hoof collided with metal, there was a loud *crash,* and the milk pail and its contents went flying.

Twenty minutes later, Michael was fuming as he carried a scant half-pail of milk into the kitchen.

"That's all you got?" his grandmother asked as she stared down at the milk.

"No, but she kicked over the pail and nearly trampled me to death before I got this much. I ended up roping her rear legs to the stall before I could finish with her."

"She'll get used to you in time, I'm sure. She'll have to. I've got to attend to your mother until she's better, so you'll have to take care of the chickens and the milking."

"You're the only one Onion likes," Michael complained, although he felt his face flush scarlet with shame for doing so. "She's liable to kill me next time."

His grandmother was quiet as she took the pail from him. "Let me think about it. Onion's difficult, but I've had difficult cows before. Maybe I can figure out a way to make it easier."

Michael nodded. "How's Mother?"

"Asleep, but otherwise no change."

"I'm going to go sit with her for a few minutes."

"All right. Don't wake her, though. I'll fix us some breakfast, and then I'll need you to fill the wood box. We're running low."

Michael tiptoed to his mother's room and went inside. He winced when the chair beside her bed creaked as he slowly sat down on it, but his mother didn't stir. The rapid, shallow rise and fall of her chest was the only movement she made.

How different she looked than just a few weeks before, busily rushing around the kitchen, her dimples showing as she smiled and served dinner to the family. Her complexion was even more sallow, and her slightly parted lips were dry and cracked. *She's changed so much in such a short period of time,* he thought. *Lots of things have changed.*

Michael's gaze traveled down to his

mother's abdomen beneath the heavy bed-covers. He remembered seeing her midsection grow and change to varying degrees over the years. At first, learning that she was expecting a baby had been a source of happiness for the family. When Michael was a young child, Seamus was already doing a man's work. With his big brother and the rest of the family too busy to play or pay him much attention, Michael had been giddy at the prospect of having a younger sibling. After his mother's multiple losses, though, and increasing difficulty, their collective happiness repeatedly turned to anxiety and fear.

A part of him wondered if there was any truth to what Dr. Washburn had said — that his mother's sickness was caused by some part of her that truly didn't want the child she was carrying. Deep down, though, he didn't — and couldn't — believe such a thing any more than his grandmother did.

One of his earliest memories on the farm was of his family gathered in the far corner of the pasture, of his father placing a tiny, handmade wooden box into a freshly dug hole in the ground. He'd been so young back then and hadn't understood anything . . . what was in the box, why his mother tossed a handful of dirt in the hole and then dropped to her knees before it, why his grandmother held him close and prevented him from running over to his mother.

Maybe somehow it will be different this time, he thought. *Maybe things will be all right.* Even knowing the suffering and heartbreak his mother had endured in the past, there was a spark of hope deep inside him for her and the baby she carried. It burned brightly despite the absence of his father and brother, the weight of responsibility on his shoulders, and the secrets he harbored. It burned despite the fact, in so many ways, he felt utterly alone.

The rest of the day passed in a blur of chopping and stacking and hauling wood, mucking out Onion's stall while the cow spent some time in the pasture, looking in on his mother, and tending to his studies. In the late afternoon, he was seated at the kitchen table working out rows of arithmetic problems when his grandmother touched him on the shoulder. "It's about time for the milking again, and I have an idea."

He looked up to see that she was holding one of her old work dresses and the woolen hat she wore when she went out to the barn during the wintertime. "What are those for?" he asked, but as soon as the words left his mouth, he realized the answer to his question.

"They're for you. Now stand up and slip this over your clothes. You're skinny enough that it should fit around you."

Michael stood up, though he couldn't believe the indignity of his grandmother's plan. "You want me to wear a *dress* to do the milking?"

"*My* dress. And *my* hat. Onion will think you're me, and she shouldn't give you such a hard time. Now let me help you put it on."

Before he knew it, his grandmother had pulled the dress over his head. He grudgingly put his arms through the sleeves, frowning as she fastened the buttons up the front. His large hands and half of each forearm protruded from the end of each sleeve.

"What if someone sees me?" Michael asked. "I'll be a laughingstock. Besides, I can't believe this will work. Cows have a good sense of smell. She'll know right away that it's not you."

"No one will see you except Onion," his grandmother said as she pulled her hat over his head and fastened it under his chin. "With these clothes, you'll smell like me.

And oh, I almost forgot! You must whistle when you're around her. I usually do, and I think it helps to keep her calm."

"What should I whistle?"

"Anything. Songs from the radio or the movies, hymns, school songs, patriotic songs. She doesn't seem to care."

"Lizzie? Lizzie, are you in the house?" Anna's voice called weakly from the bedroom, and his grandmother turned in that direction.

"Yes, Anna, I'll be right there." Lizzie rushed into the kitchen, grabbed the clean milk pail, and handed it to him. "Hurry, now. The sooner you get out there, the sooner you'll be done."

Michael was left holding the pail as his grandmother bustled into his mother's bedroom and closed the door. With a resigned sigh, he headed to the barn.

Tabby was perched on a hay bale and greeted him with the usual meow. As he began to ready the milking area, the cat jumped down and began weaving around his ankles, purring loudly.

"No fooling *you,* is there?" he whispered as he scratched around her ears and under her chin. "I suppose you're ready for your evening milk." When he straightened up and glanced in the direction of Onion's stall, he realized that the cow was looking straight at him. Not for a minute did he think his ridiculous disguise would work. Nevertheless, he decided not to say anything else to the cat, in case his voice gave him away.

As he'd done in the morning, Michael went to the stall, grasped Onion by her halter, and pulled gently forward. The cow started to resist, so he quickly began whistling "Yankee Doodle." Onion cupped her long ears toward him, eyeing him suspiciously. Then she blew a long sigh through her nostrils and allowed him to lead her from the stall.

It was surprising how much faster the milking went with a little music. Michael whistled as best he could, going through songs as they popped into his head and squeezing in time to the rhythms. The entire milking session was uneventful and even pleasant, although by the time the pail was full and Onion was safely back in her stall, he had decided that it was the whistling and not his grandmother's dress that had made the difference. The next time he came to the barn, he would whistle again, but he would be wearing his own clothing.

Michael went back to whistling "Yankee Doodle" as he exited the barn. He was so focused on not spilling milk out of the very full pail that he was nearly to the house before he looked up and saw his uncle Frank and Dr. Washburn standing in the driveway, staring at him.

"Afternoon," the doctor said. There was a long pause as he seemed to grope for words. "Are you feeling all right, son?"

"Yes," Michael muttered, and he was nearly overcome by the rush of heat that entered his face. He could feel his cheeks and ears and neck turning a bright pink. How was it that he hadn't heard their cars drive up? Had he been whistling that loudly? "Yes, I'm fine. This . . ." He looked down at the bottom of the skirt wafting around his knees and quickly removed his grandmother's hat. "This was Grandma's idea. She made me wear her things to trick the cow into thinking I was her. Onion nearly sent me flying when I tried to milk her this morning." The two men continued to stare, and Michael felt his face burn hotter. "Grandma's been in with Mother most of the day," he added.

"Well," Dr. Washburn said with a polite smile, "it sounds like I should see her right away, then."

"Yes," Michael said, and he hurried ahead of the doctor and his uncle to open the door for them. "Go ahead down the hallway to her room. I'm sure she's expecting you."

"Thank you . . . *madam,*" Dr. Washburn said with a wicked grin and a tip of his hat as he passed. Uncle Frank followed with a bemused expression.

Michael's face was still flushed as he set the pail of milk on the kitchen counter and started unbuttoning the dress as quickly as he could. He couldn't even bring himself to make eye contact with his uncle.

"You know, Michael, my first thought when I saw you come out of the barn was to wonder how Lizzie had managed to grow taller at her age."

He glanced at his uncle with a wounded expression. Would this humiliation ever end? "Please don't say anything else, Uncle Frank. I don't think the clothes helped much, and I didn't want to wear them, anyway." Michael pulled the unbuttoned dress over his head and draped it, inside out, over one of the kitchen chairs. "I didn't expect anyone to see me."

Frank chuckled. "I know, I know. I won't needle you about it anymore. I've known your grandmother for a long time, and she has some crazy ideas. You went along with this one to humor her, and that was truly good of you. Something you did must've worked better than this morning, though.

How did you manage —"

His uncle's voice was interrupted by a commotion coming from his mother's room. There was her voice crying out unintelligible words, mixed in with the raised voices of his grandmother and the doctor. The bedroom door opened, and the doctor spoke loudly into the hallway.

"Father, could you come help us? We've got to get your sister to the hospital immediately."

CHAPTER 15

Just before noon on Saturday, Claudia walked into the bakery. She looked around and saw Kyle and Rowen waving from one of the corner tables.

"Right on time," Kyle said as she approached. He stood to give her a quick peck on the mouth before she sat down.

"So, Kevin and Misty aren't here yet?" she asked, but she'd barely asked the question before the bell on the front door of the bakery jingled again.

Kyle's face broke into a grin as he waved at a man who was a younger, heavier, and less handsome version of him. The man and a woman with long blond hair were standing at the front entrance. "Uncle Kevin!" Rowen called.

The couple turned toward them and smiled. "Hey, Kyle," the man said when they had reached the table. "Wow, Ro, you've grown a foot since I last saw you.

And Claudia, you still intend to marry this guy? No second thoughts?" He winked at Kyle and then pulled her into a hug as she laughed.

"Nice to see you, too, Kevin. And no, there are no second thoughts."

"There's still time, still time. Hey, this is Misty Lynn." He had his portly arm around Misty and ushered her forward as he introduced her.

"Hi." The woman shrugged and offered a limp handshake. "You can call me Misty. Everyone does. I'm not sure why Kevin always gives my middle name when we meet people." She smiled at Claudia, and her smile broadened when she looked at Kyle.

"I'm glad to meet you," Kyle said, while Claudia smiled and nodded. Misty sounded like Betty Boop with a strong Boston accent, and Claudia had to work hard not to giggle.

"So, what do you say we eat and then head out to look at the leaves?" Kyle asked. "You have to place your order at the counter here, but they'll bring it to your table when it's ready."

"This is a nice little place," Kevin said, looking around after they all sat down. "Smells great, too."

Claudia followed Kevin's gaze and saw

that Rose had appeared behind the counter and was chatting with Ruth. Misty didn't say anything in response to Kevin's comment about the bakery. She only sniffed and crossed her arms with a doubtful look on her face.

"That's right, the bakery had closed for the day the last time you came down," Kyle said. "Well, Mill River doesn't have Boston's restaurant selection, but Ruth — that's the owner of this place, Ruth Fitzgerald — she could definitely hold her own there. She makes the best pie you'll ever have, hands down."

"It's *really* good," Rowen chimed in. The toothy smile on the little girl's face was so enthusiastic that they all had to laugh.

"I believe you," Kevin said. "Remember when I slept on your couch the last time I visited? Around five or six in the morning, I woke up smelling sweets. God, I don't know how you stand that. If I lived in that apartment with the pie smell coming up through the floor, I'd be drooling instead of sleeping."

"You'd be drooling and *eating,*" Misty said.

"Probably," Kevin said with a laugh, but Claudia was surprised at the tone of Misty's comment, which seemed to carry an undercurrent of mild disgust. She was even more surprised to see Misty smiling at Kyle again.

"We're pretty used to the smell," Kyle said with a chuckle. "But Rowen and I are going to move in with Claudia once we're married, at least until we can find a bigger place, so there'll be no more bakery-scented dreams for us after that."

"Hey, Uncle Kevin, do you want to come see my Halloween costume?" Rowen asked. "It's upstairs in my room."

"Oh yeah? What are you going to be this year?"

"I'm not going to tell you, but I'll give you a hint. It's got something to do with the bakery. Dad's been helping me with it."

"The idea was all hers," Kyle said with a proud look at his daughter. "It's original, if I do say so myself."

"All right, you got me," Kevin said. "Let's just put our order in, and then I'll come up with you and your dad, how's that? It'll give Misty and Claudia some time for girl talk."

In a few minutes, after Kyle had given their order to Ruth at the counter, Claudia found herself alone with Misty.

"So, Rowen's going to be a donut for Halloween," she said. "Or rather, a donut hole. She's got an inner tube that she's painted

260

to look like a donut, and she's going to rig up straps so she can stand in the middle of it while she walks around trick-or-treating."

"Ah. That's cute," Misty said. Kevin's girlfriend smiled but did not continue the conversation, so Claudia tried again.

"So, Misty, what do you do? For work, I mean?"

"I'm a receptionist at a nail salon," Misty replied. She held out a hand and wiggled her long, fake, perfectly manicured nails. "They give me discounts, which is cool, but I'm thinking about looking for something better. You know, something not as boring, with better pay. What do you do?"

"I teach fourth grade."

Misty snorted. "That's a tough job for the money. I don't know how people can stand to be teachers these days. I could never deal with a bunch of bratty kids."

"The salary leaves something to be desired," Claudia admitted, "and I'm not wild about all the standardized testing we do, but my kids are great. They're bright and pretty well behaved. I like seeing them learn and grow. Most days I really enjoy my job."

"That's good," Misty said. "So, I've been wondering . . ." She leaned across the table, and the scent of her strong perfume became even more noticeable. "Where did Kyle pick you up?"

"We actually met at my school," Claudia said. She was slightly taken aback by Misty's phrasing of the question. Being "picked up" was something that happened in the dark recesses of bars or clubs, something that preceded a cheap one-night stand. "Kyle came over to teach my class about being a police officer last year. We talked a little afterward, and you know, one thing led to another. How did you meet Kevin?"

Misty flipped her long hair forward over one shoulder, causing an intense wave of her perfume to hit Claudia. "I was looking to change my car insurance. Kevin was the guy who helped me when I stopped by the insurance office, and we started talking. He ended up asking me out." She shrugged. Boredom passed over her face as she pulled her phone from her purse and began texting.

Claudia began to get a sinking feeling in her stomach. She had envisioned, even anticipated, a happy meeting with Misty where they would discover that they had mutual interests and personalities that clicked. Kevin's girlfriend, however, was turning out to be something entirely unexpected, and not in a good way. There was an awkward pause before Claudia blurted out the only thing she could think of to fill the silence.

"What kind of perfume are you wearing, by the way? I don't think I've ever smelled it before."

"It's Rush, by *Gucci*," Misty said in a nonchalant voice, but with plenty of emphasis on "Gucci." She glanced up from her phone. "Kevin got it for me."

"Ah. It's . . . nice. Very distinctive." *Or at least it would be if she hadn't doused herself with it.*

"That's exactly what I thought," Misty said. "I like things like that — clothes and shoes and other designer stuff that not everybody has. Like this bag." She put her phone back in her handbag, which had been resting on the seat of the empty chair beside her, and stroked her hand across the front of it like a model from *The Price Is Right*. "It's *Channel*. Isn't it amazing? It wasn't cheap, but it's definitely worth the money, I think."

Although Claudia was tempted to correct Misty's pronunciation, she decided against it and simply smiled at the woman. "It's a very nice bag."

Misty gave a half smile and refocused her attention on her phone.

Claudia's own purse was hanging on the

back of her chair. It was a sensible black leather shoulder bag from JCPenney, and she loved it. Even if her salary had permitted her to spend exorbitant amounts on luxury goods, she couldn't have cared less about high-end labels. She liked things that were reasonably priced, practical, and well made. Misty's blatant brags and superficiality were really starting to annoy her.

"Here's the first part of your order," a woman's voice said. Claudia looked up to see Rose standing beside the table, holding a tray of beverages. "I'll be just another second on the sandwiches." Before she had a chance to say hello, Rose was heading back toward the counter, so Claudia busied herself by removing the mugs and glasses from the tray and distributing them to their proper places on the table. The clicking of heels alerted her to Rose's return. Strangely, there was a slight smirk on the elder DiSanti sister's face.

Rose lowered the second tray. After she transferred the plates of sandwiches to the appropriate place settings, she stacked it inside the empty beverage tray. Rather than returning to the kitchen, though, she lingered beside their table, squinting down at Misty's purse. "That's quite a handbag you have there," Rose said, her voice rich with admiration.

Misty looked up from her texting, her smile smug and wide. "Thank you. I just got it."

Rose nodded and took a step closer. "May I?" she asked, holding out a hand, and Misty passed the purse to her. "Beautiful. This is one of the nicest *Chanel* knockoffs I've ever seen."

Claudia straightened up in her chair. Rose maintained an innocent expression, despite her heavy emphasis on "Chanel." Misty was staring up at Rose with her mouth slightly agape.

Even though Misty seemed to have been rendered speechless, Rose didn't give her a chance to say anything. Instead, she pointed with one of her own perfectly manicured nails at the front of the handbag. "The stitch count here isn't too far below what a genuine bag would have, and there are only a few places where the diamonds in the quilted pattern are stitched unevenly. The logo around the lock looks almost perfect, too — they just reversed the way the C's are supposed to overlap. But other than those few things, no one would ever know. Knockoffs are totally the way to go, if you ask me. Who can afford a real *Chanel* bag in this economy? They're thousands of dollars." She handed the purse back to Misty and picked up the empty trays. "Anyway, I hope you ladies enjoy your lunch." Rose turned on her heel and walked back toward the counter.

Misty's face turned a bright scarlet, and she stared down at her handbag before resting it again on the empty chair.

Claudia turned to look over her shoulder at Rose. From behind the counter, Rose caught her eye and winked. Claudia bit down on the inside of her cheek to keep from grinning, and she breathed a huge sigh of relief when Kyle, Rowen, and Kevin returned to the table a few moments later.

"So, did you two have a nice chat?" Kevin asked, the hope plain on his face.

"Oh, yeah," Misty said flatly.

"We did," Claudia agreed. She smiled sweetly at her future brother-in-law, but inside, she felt only pity. He obviously hadn't realized it yet, but Kevin was dating another loser.

As Claudia finished her lunch at the bakery, Karen Cooper made her way down the street to Turner's Hardware. Ben was at the middle school attending a weekend basketball clinic, and a Saturday afternoon alone stretched far before her. As she put

266

one foot in front of the other, Karen alternatively got lost in her thoughts and then snapped back to reality. Her reason for visiting the hardware store was irrational, she knew, and she kept pushing it to the back of her mind before it would slowly but surely make its way back to the center of her thoughts.

Since the discovery of Nick's abandoned Jeep, there had been no information on his whereabouts or the search for him. A representative from the personnel department in his company had told her that because Nick's disappearance had been formally declared an abduction, his salary would continue to be direct-deposited into their joint account for the time being. It was but a small comfort.

"How long will that happen?" she had asked the stranger on the phone.

"I'm not sure, ma'am," the man had replied. "It all depends on how long until he's found. In other cases, salary and benefits have been paid for a full year after a person has gone missing."

Other cases? she thought. *There have been other cases? How many other cases?*

"And then what? What if the person hasn't been found by then?"

The man on the phone had cleared his

throat. "Well, usually by that time, other determinations and declarations have been made, for insurance purposes and whatnot, so the salary is discontinued. But ma'am, it's very early to be thinking about that right now. Our focus is currently on finding your husband."

Though she and Ben relied on Nick's salary to pay most of their bills, she would have traded every cent of it to have him home and safe. What would she do in a year if Nick were still missing? She was having trouble making it through the days already.

Karen took a deep breath to steady herself as she entered the hardware store. Emily was behind the counter, leaning on her elbows as she read a handwritten letter of some kind. "Hey, Karen," she said. "How are you?"

Karen forced a smile. She knew that what most people really wanted to hear when they asked her that question — if they were aware of Nick's disappearance — was whether she'd received any news about her husband. "I'm doing all right, I guess. As best as I can, under the circumstances."

Emily nodded. "I've thought a lot about you since you were last here. Have you heard anything more? About Nick, I mean?"

"No, not yet, anyway."

"Oh. Well, I know you'll get some good news soon. But what brings you by today? Are you after more lightbulbs?"

"Um, no. This time, I need duct tape."

"Aisle three, near the back."

"Thank you."

Karen walked quietly down the aisle as Emily went back to reading. Instead of stopping at the tape displays, she continued on around the endcap until she stood before the ropes she had seen the last time she had visited the store.

Is this really the best way? The voice of irrationality surfaced again in her mind. *It might be painful, or it might take a long time.*

Karen shook her head quickly and went back to the tape section. She picked up a thick, steel-gray roll of duct tape. Feeling its familiar heaviness was like meeting an old friend. How many times had she used it around the house? Duct tape had seen her through broken windows and broken toys. It had braced cracked chair legs, covered holes in upholstery, and helped her leaning Christmas tree stand perfectly upright. During all those times when Nick had been deployed and she'd had to take care of something around the house, duct tape had so often been her go-to item.

She was about to head to the checkout

when something caught her eye. A little farther down the aisle, packages of box cutters and their replacement blades hung neatly on display hooks.

Another possibility, the irrational voice said in her mind, *but messy and almost certainly painful.* Deep down, Karen didn't really believe that she could use her own hand to inflict direct, painful, physical harm to herself. She didn't want Ben to see or find her after she had used such a method, either.

Ben.

Remembering her son had always helped her during times like this, when she began to contemplate doing the unthinkable. Her love for him ran as strong as her bones and as deep as the breath at the bottom of her lungs. From the moment of his birth, he had been her anchor, the reason she fought against the darkness and remained tethered to the land of the living. The thought of him being traumatized by something she were to do, or of her leaving him in the world alone to fend for himself, was always enough to force the irrational voice in her mind back into silence.

Until today.

But Ben is older now, the voice told her. *He's closer to adulthood. He could go live with your brother's family in Seattle. He would make it. He can make it now without you.*

Karen stared for another moment at the box cutters and then walked back toward the rope. The strong, vibrating hum of her cellphone in her purse startled her. She quickly grabbed and answered it. "Hello?"

"Hello, Karen. It's Father O'Brien calling. I was just wondering how you're doing today."

"Oh." She felt a bit light-headed, having been pulled so abruptly out of her reverie and also awash in disappointment that the call hadn't come from someone with information about Nick. "It's nice of you to check on me, Father. I'm . . . I'm doing okay."

"I'm glad to hear that. I take it you haven't received any other news about Nick?"

"No, nothing today. Not yet, anyway."

"We'll just continue to hope for the best. I wanted to tell you that I've spoken to some folks about the situation with Nick, and there are many people who've offered to help you and Ben through it. I was thinking of walking over to Ruth's for a late lunch. Would you care to join me? I'd love some company, and that way, I could tell you all about it."

"I'm not very hungry, to be honest with

271

you, Father, but . . . a cup of coffee sounds nice."

"Wonderful! And maybe once we're there, something will spark your appetite. You need to eat, even if it's just a little, to keep up your strength."

His kindly, paternal tone made her feel as if she were a young child refusing her vegetables, and she had to smile. "I know, Father."

"All right. I'm going to leave the parish house right now, and I'll meet you there."

"I'm actually right next door to the bakery, at the hardware store," she told the priest. "I'll go in and get us a table. See you in a few minutes, Father."

Karen brought the duct tape to the register and fished around in her purse for her wallet.

"Find everything all right?" Emily asked.

"Yes," she replied. A small flicker of light thwarted the darkness and warmed her anxious, aching heart when she thought of the elderly priest coming to meet her at the bakery. "I found everything I needed today."

CHAPTER 16

April 21, 1934

At the Mary Fletcher Hospital in Burlington, Michael followed his uncle, grandmother, and a nurse down a series of hospital corridors until they came to a double door with a sign above it that read WOMEN'S WARD. Beyond the door, they entered a great room with a tall ceiling. Large windows were spaced high along the wall on either side. A hospital bed was placed beneath each window, along with a curtain that could be pulled on a track to surround the entire bed for privacy, if needed. A wall running half the length of the room divided it down the middle, and there was an old radiator and a nurse's supply station positioned up against the short end of the wall that faced the double door.

"Right this way," the nurse said, and she led them to the bed farthest down on the right side with the privacy curtain drawn completely around it.

Michael took a deep breath as he stepped inside the curtain with the others. His mother was lying on her back, asleep. One of her arms was resting outside the stiff white sheets that covered the rest of her body. There was tape holding something against her wrist — a needle, it looked like, that seemed to have been inserted and left there. A thin, light brown, flexible hose ran from her wrist to a large glass container of clear liquid that was suspended, upside down, by some sort of frame next to her bed.

"What is that attached to her?" Michael asked in a voice barely above a whisper. He had never seen anything like the apparatus to which his mother was connected. His grandmother, wide-eyed and uncharacteristically quiet, looked at him and shrugged.

"Intravenous fluid therapy," said a man's voice behind him. Dr. Washburn stepped inside the curtain. "It's a new treatment available for patients who are dehydrated. More and more hospitals are starting to offer it for hyperemesis gravidarum, which is the severe sickness that expectant mothers sometimes have. We insert a hollow needle into a vein, usually in the wrist, as we've done with your mother. Through that needle and the connecting rubber line you see here, we can insert fluids directly into her bloodstream. It's more than fluids, really. We can give medicine through the connecting line, and the glass there contains water, glucose, and saline. Sugar and salt, in layman's terms. They'll replenish her body and stabilize her, hopefully enough to allow her to start eating and drinking on her own."

"How long does she have to take this therapy?" his uncle asked.

"It varies," the doctor said. "Some patients need fluids for only a few days and recover fully in as little as a week. Others take longer. We'll want to make sure she's properly hydrated, able to eat and drink on her own, and that her kidneys are functioning normally."

"Will this treatment prevent her sickness from returning?" Michael asked.

"It might," the doctor said, "or it might not. It's very difficult to predict. The goals, of course, are to return her to good health and ensure that the child she's carrying survives to term. But there's nothing more we can do for her tonight except to let her rest and let the fluids start to help her." The doctor glanced down at the nurse meaningfully.

The nurse acknowledged the hint with a small nod. "I'll escort you back to the waiting area," she said. "If everything goes as planned, you should be able to see her each day she's here during normal visiting hours."

Michael took one last look at his mother before following the nurse from her bedside. Seeing her weak and helpless in the sterile white bed left a terrible feeling of uneasiness in his stomach.

During the ride back to the farm, his uncle brought up the subject of his father. "I wonder if we shouldn't contact Niall. It's one thing for Anna to be sick at home, but it's quite another for her to be hospitalized. She was never admitted to the hospital before."

"Absolutely not," his grandmother snapped from the backseat. "He would leave everything and come home, and then where would we be? There's nothing he or any of us can do for her right now. Anna's getting the care she needs, and we'll need his salary to pay for it. Once she's well, she'll be back home with us, and everything will be fine."

Michael wondered how much it would cost for his mother to stay in the hospital.

"Does he even know she's with child?" his uncle asked.

"Not yet," his grandmother said.

"Don't you think he deserves to be told?"

If I were in Father's position, I'd want to be told, Michael thought, but he dared not voice that opinion and agitate his grandmother even more.

"Anna's been in this same position lots of times, and most of them have ended badly. There's no point saying anything to Niall while it's so early. If she gets to where it looks like the baby has a chance, then yes. Until then, we'd best keep it to ourselves. Besides, that's what Anna wants. She told me as much herself."

Uncle Frank was pulling up to the house, and Lizzie opened the car door and got out the moment the wheels had stopped turning.

"There's no crossing her, is there?" his uncle asked as they watched her go inside.

"No."

"Michael, I've got a busy week ahead. I won't be able to come out to the farm, but I'll check in on your mother as often as I can. I'll get in touch immediately if there's any change for the worse, and if she's still in the hospital next Saturday, I'll drive out then and take you and Lizzie to visit her."

"I'll let Grandma know about next

Saturday. Thanks for everything, Uncle Frank."

"Don't mention it," his uncle said. "Oh, and Michael?"

Michael had already opened the car door, but he paused and turned to look at Frank.

"Next Saturday night, I'll need you to come back to the mission with me," his uncle said in a low voice. "We'll need to move what we left there to a final resting place."

CHAPTER 17

Late Saturday afternoon, after closing Turner's for the day, Emily went to the marble mansion to start edging the newly finished walls with paint. Rather than being focused on her work, though, she was preoccupied with the old letter from the briefcase that she had read most recently.

. . . I can't even begin to describe how ill I was. Nothing stayed down, not even water, and I started feeling so weak. Michael came to sit with me one morning, and I could tell by the look on his face that the sight of me scared him. I know he was desperate to help me. He washed my face with a cool cloth and told me how happy he was for the baby's coming, but there was nothing he could do to ease my sickness. It was heartbreaking for me. A mother is supposed to care for her children, and even though he was nearly fifteen, he was still my child, still in need of my care, and I couldn't provide it . . .

I was convinced that I would die before she was born. The hospital was necessary but terrible, with strange tubes and fluids inserted into my body, and nurses hovering, inspecting everything that went in and came out. And seeing Michael's face when he visited, full of love and concern and fear . . . that was nearly enough to kill me. What if I didn't make it? What would become of him?

So, Anna's pregnancy had complications that, back in the 1930s, would have been life-threatening to her and the baby. *Medicine has come a long way,* Emily thought. Her sweet nephew, Alex, had nearly died as a result of a head injury. Without the doctors, surgeons, and advanced medical technology of today, including the advent of medevac helicopters, the little boy would have perished. Emily couldn't imagine how her life would have changed if Alex had died.

She was painting slowly, still awash in gratitude, when she heard the back door of the marble mansion open and her sister's voice echo through the house. "Em? Emily?"

"In here." She set the paintbrush and small can of paint she'd been holding on the foldout tray at the top of her ladder and carefully climbed down.

"Hey," Rose said as she entered the room. "I brought you a sandwich from Ruth's. Your usual, chicken salad on rye with two pickles on the side. Figured I'd save you a trip over there to pick up your dinner."

"Oh. Thanks," Emily said, accepting the bag Rose held out to her. "That was really nice of you." It was still odd, being on speaking terms with her sister. The truth was, she still wasn't sure their relationship could be repaired, but she'd agreed to try if Rose did. So far, the effort seemed to be working. "How do you like working at the bakery?" she asked as they walked to the kitchen, where she stuck the bag containing the sandwich in the refrigerator.

Rose shrugged. "It's not bad. It helps out Ruth, and it keeps me busy while Alex is in school. That's one of the things they stress in AA meetings — you gotta keep yourself occupied. If you sit around with nothing to do, it's easier to slip up and start drinking again."

"Makes sense," Emily said. She looked at her sister and smiled a little. "I'm glad you're sticking with the program. I know it's hard, but you're doing a good job at it."

Rose nodded at her and then looked down at her high-heeled shoes. She didn't say anything, but Emily could see the tickled smile on her sister's face and the color that crept into Rose's cheeks.

"You know, this house is amazing, even though you're not done yet," Rose said suddenly. "I can't believe it's been up here for all these years, and nobody had any idea what was inside."

"A few people knew," Emily corrected her, "but yeah. It's a shame. Since you're here, why don't I show you around really quick? I'm excited for when it'll be open, even though I'm stressed out over all the stuff I have to finish. There's no way I was going to tell Ruth she couldn't open in time for Kyle and Claudia's wedding, but I knew I'd have to cram about a year's worth of work into three months to pull it off."

Emily led Rose back into the great hall and up the staircase to begin the tour.

"Look at that millwork," Rose remarked as they peeked into a couple of the bedrooms. "It must've been custom-made."

"Absolutely. I've worked in several other older homes, but even in the most expensive ones, you rarely see woodworking of that quality. Here's the master suite, which will probably be called the honeymoon suite," Emily said as they entered the largest bedroom, the one with the huge windows overlooking Mill River. "The view is amazing."

"Wow," Rose said as she stood before the window looking out. "Can you imagine, all those years that Mary McAllister was up here by herself, watching over all of us?"

"I know," Emily said. For a moment, she and Rose stood together silently, gazing out over the last of the brilliant fall foliage and their little hometown.

"The artwork, too, is stunning," Emily said, pointing up at the walls as they came back down the stairs. "Horses and Vermont countryside, mostly, all originals. And look at the antique lighting fixtures." Rose craned her neck to stare up at the ceiling, especially the huge chandelier hanging over the great hall. "I've had a time, trying to find incandescent bulbs to fit some of them. All they make these days is fluorescents and LEDs. Ruth may need to have them retrofitted or maybe swap them out entirely at some point. It'd be a shame to have to get rid of them, though."

They'd reached the bottom of the stairs, and Emily went to a light switch on the wall. "The big chandelier's on a dimmer switch, see?" She lowered the light in the room to demonstrate.

"Romantic," Rose said with a grin.

"Yeah," Emily agreed. "I don't blame Kyle and Claudia for wanting to have their wedding reception here."

"Speaking of which," Rose said, "you should've heard this idiot woman Claudia was with at the bakery earlier. Kinda reminded me of my bartending days, when I used to hear people say all sorts of crazy stuff. Anyway, this woman — Misty, her name was — came in with Claudia's future brother-in-law. She was so loud and obnoxious that I couldn't help but overhear their conversation, and the more I heard, the more pissed I got."

Emily's mouth dropped open as Rose recounted Misty's rude behavior, and she burst out laughing when Rose described how Misty had bragged about her "Channel" purse.

"I guess I got my bitch on," Rose admitted, causing Emily to laugh even harder, "but I really couldn't help it. Claudia's a nice person. Naive and innocent, maybe, but really nice, and she didn't deserve to be treated like that."

"Claudia *is* nice," Emily agreed. "I'm glad you were there to help her out."

"Soooo," Rose said, and Emily knew immediately that her sister was changing the subject to one she didn't really wish to discuss, "tell me what happened with that Matt Campbell person at the hardware store. You know, the time you mentioned at Mom's? When he hit on you?"

Emily rolled her eyes. She was so conflicted about Matt — what kind of person he was, how she was starting to feel about him, and whether she was ready to feel that way about anyone. Rose was eagerly waiting for her response, but she didn't know what to say, and she preferred not to say anything at all.

"I really don't want to get into it."

"Oh, c'mon, Em. I'm dying to know. Besides, we used to tell each other everything."

"Rose," Emily said, struggling to keep her annoyance from creeping into her voice, "things are different now than when we were kids. I mean, look, I'm glad we're talking again. I really am. And it's great that we're both back here in Mill River. But I've become a pretty private person over the years. It's not you — I just don't like to share relationship details with *anyone.*"

Also, Emily thought, *things aren't nearly back to the way they used to be, and you have a lot of nerve pressing me for personal information when we weren't speaking a few months ago.*

As her sister stared at her with a crestfallen look, a loud knock at the back door interrupted the silence. A moment later, a man's voice called out, "Emily?"

Rose looked at her with wide eyes and raised eyebrows. "Are you expecting someone?"

"Hello? Who's there?" Emily said loudly. She shook her head and shrugged, although she recognized the voice and knew *exactly* who had come through the door.

"I probably should have called you before I came over, but I just decided — Oh." Matt hesitated as he came into the great hall carrying a large picnic basket and saw Emily standing there with Rose. "Sorry, I didn't realize someone else was here."

"Um, Matt, this is my sister, Rose Frye. Rose, this is Matt Campbell."

"Nice to meet you, Matt, and don't worry about it," Rose said. "I was leaving anyway." Her sister hurried past him, heading for the back door. Once Rose was behind him, she pointed at Matt and gave an enthusiastic thumbs-up. Emily kept a poker face and focused her attention on Matt.

"What are you doing here?" she asked him

once her sister had left the house.

"Well, you said that you'd have dinner with me if I could figure out a way to work it into your schedule. So, I decided to bring you dinner here," he said, holding up the picnic basket. "I brought a blanket to spread out on the floor to keep anything from falling on the wood you just refinished." He turned the basket slightly, so she could see a rolled blanket strapped to the side of it. "What do you say? Are you hungry?"

Emily couldn't help but smile. *This* was an impressive gesture, not to mention an original and thoughtful one. Matt looked really good, too — clean-shaven, and wearing a dark plaid flannel shirt and nice-fitting jeans. She thought about the chicken salad sandwich waiting in the refrigerator, but she'd had the same thing for dinner the last three nights. How much chicken salad could a girl really eat?

"Maybe," Emily said with a cautious glance at the picnic basket. "Whatcha got in there?"

Matt grinned and started unbuckling the straps that held the rolled blanket in place. "Let's sit down, and I'll show you." He spread the blanket in the center of the great hall, well away from the ladder where she'd been standing earlier. Emily lowered herself into a cross-legged position and watched as he joined her and started to unpack the basket.

"Grilled chicken, still warm," he said as he lifted out the first container of food. "Baked beans, also warm," he said when he removed the second container. Matt then held up a bag of small oranges. "Clementines, room-temperature. And last but not least, beer and bottled water, both ice-cold." He set the oranges on the floor, removed the beverages, and looked at her sheepishly. "I wasn't sure whether you drink alcohol."

"I'm not my sister," Emily said. "I don't drink much, but I'll have a beer every now and then. Today, though, since I'm working . . ." She grabbed a bottle of water and twisted off the cap. "Did you cook all this yourself?"

"I grilled the chicken," Matt said. "The baked beans came out of a can. I figured I shouldn't push it, trying to cook something from scratch I'd never made." He took disposable plates and plastic forks from the bottom of the basket and handed one of each to her. "Here, help yourself."

"Thank you," Emily said. She took a plate and served herself a drumstick and some beans. "You know, I actually like canned baked beans. And they sound a heck of a lot better than a chicken salad sandwich for the fourth day in a row."

"Wow, you weren't kidding when you said you'd been stuck up here," Matt said. "What were you working on today?"

"Getting ready to paint," Emily said after she swallowed. "I have to edge and paint all the new walls, which were put up to address a lead paint issue. It's going to take me forever, but I don't want to go over budget by hiring a crew to do it, since I'm perfectly capable myself. I'd rather subcontract out for things I don't have the expertise in. This chicken is great, by the way."

"Thanks," Matt said. "What do you have left after the painting?"

"Some plumbing things, mostly updating fixtures. I've been ordering updated toilets and sinks and swapping them out as they're delivered. I've got to stain and seal the wood floors. They're all sanded, but I didn't want to finish them until the walls are painted and dry, just in case. I have a stained glass image that I want to install in the window above the front door. Then there are a bunch of smaller things — installing new deadbolts in all the rooms and hanging new flat-screen TVs. I'm sure there will be more stuff that comes up."

"That's a lot for one person to do," Matt

said. "How did you . . . I don't mean any disrespect at all by asking you this, but how did you learn how to do this? Restore houses, I mean?"

"What, you mean you don't think women can build or restore houses?" Emily looked at Matt sternly enough to cause him to stop chewing. His eyes grew wide with alarm, and he threw up his hands and tried to speak with his mouth full, but Emily laughed.

"Don't worry, I was just messing with you. I'm not offended at all. I actually get that question all the time. I started fixing small problems in high school. My mom's a real estate agent, you know, and every time she got a new listing, she'd let me take care of whatever I could so she wouldn't have to mess with hiring a professional." She paused, carefully planning what she would tell him next. "After I left Mill River, I started working as an assistant to a contractor, and I took some courses at technical schools. Eventually, once I'd been through enough renovations to feel comfortable handling everything about them, I got a contractor's license and starting taking jobs on my own."

"I'm impressed," Matt said. "Did you

know you wanted to do this for a living early on?"

Emily took a deep breath. The correct answer was *no. I was going to be an art teacher,* she thought, *until my world was shattered and plans to finish college went out the window.* But she wasn't sure whether she wanted to say anything about that to Matt.

"No," Emily replied, "but I knew I wanted to do something creative. This just happened to be the work I ended up falling into. You told me you were in the Marines before you came to Mill River. Was that the career you always planned on having?"

Matt nodded. "Yeah, definitely. I went to the Naval Academy down in Annapolis right after high school. After I graduated, I was on active duty for sixteen years. Did three tours in the Middle East, two in Iraq and one in Afghanistan. I made it to the rank of lieutenant colonel, and I was considering re-upping, but I got offered an early retirement package. It was a nice deal, and I didn't want to spend more time in the desert on another redeployment. Besides, Congress ended up cutting the military's budget the year after I left. Several of my friends who stayed in had their positions eliminated, so I might've been forced out, anyway."

"I don't think there are too many people out there who haven't had some sort of problem with the economy we've been in."

"I totally agree, and it's sad," Matt said. "I was happy to get the job with the police department. Not everyone in my class at the academy had a job lined up." He pulled two of the clementines from the bag and tossed one gently to her.

"So," Emily said as she turned the miniature orange around in her hands, "you already know a little about my family. Tell me about yours."

"Okay," Matt said. "I have two older sisters, Margaret and Samantha. Meg and Sam for short. They used to gang up on me when I was growing up. I got bullied into wearing nail polish and having tea parties."

Emily snorted. "Is that why you joined the Marines? To get back in touch with your masculinity?"

Matt chuckled. "Could be, now that you mention it. Those Marines sure worked me over. They did their best to beat my sisters' influence right out of me, but you know, it isn't completely gone. I'll tell you a secret." He glanced at her sideways, the corner of his mouth curved up into a sly grin. "I can still brew a mean cup of Earl Grey."

Emily laughed. She pictured Matt handing her a mug of hot tea before sitting down to snuggle with her on some cozy sofa. It was startling, how natural and realistic the image seemed. It was also a bit disconcerting when she realized that she *liked* the idea of being cuddled up with him.

"My mom and dad are still married . . . fortysomething years now. And still living in the house in Maine where we grew up."

"That's a long time," Emily said, and wistfulness crept into her voice before she realized it. "Are you close with them?"

"Very," Matt said. "My sisters, too, surprisingly, after everything they did to me. Meg lives outside Boston. She's married with two boys and works as an ICU nurse. Sam lives in Maine, not too far from my parents. She's an accountant and has her own business."

"Sounds like a nice family."

"Yep, we're pretty typical. Do you like having your whole family here in town? Your sister and your mom, I mean."

"Yeah, I do, actually. And my great-aunt, Ivy, too. She's my mom's aunt. That's all I've got in terms of family, other than Rose's husband and son. My dad died when I was two, so I never knew him or his side of the family. My grandmother on my mom's side died before I was born, and my grandfather was killed in Vietnam. I never knew them, either."

"That's rough." Matt paused, seeming to consider his next comment carefully. "You and Rose seem to be getting along better now. Compared to this past summer, I mean."

Emily sighed. "We're trying. We used to be close, growing up, and we're trying to get back to that. It'll take time, though."

"What happened to make you not close? Not that it's any of my business," Matt added quickly. "If you don't want to talk about it, that's fine."

Should I tell him? she asked herself. *He could probably ask around town and someone would give him the scoop. If he really doesn't know, it might scare him off if he thinks I'm not ready for someone else. Hell, maybe he already knows and he just wants to hear my take on the situation. Besides, I'm over it. I'm over . . . Andy.* She took a deep breath.

"Well, back when I was in college, I was dating a guy. He'd arranged to come down to Mill River over spring break and surprise me with an engagement ring. My mom sent Rose to the train station in Rutland to pick him up, not realizing that she'd been upstairs sleeping off a drinking binge. There was an accident on the way back. Andy was killed. Rose was injured, but she survived, obviously."

Matt had stopped chewing and was staring at her. "I really don't know what to say. That's . . . horrible. Worse than horrible."

Emily shrugged. "It was. And is. But I really need to move past it. All those years after the accident, I felt like I was drifting. I don't think I ever came to terms with what happened until I moved back here, to Mill River, last July. I just want to go forward, try to forgive Rose, and build a real life for myself. It's easier said than done, but I'm working on it."

"That's a lot to forgive. I don't know if I could do it if I were in your situation."

"I hope you never are." She smiled at him. "But you have only one life, and I finally decided I'd spent enough of mine being miserable. I wanted to be happy again, really happy, and I realized that would never happen unless I stopped living in the past."

"Yeah, I think I know what you mean. When I came out of the service, I was pretty messed up for a while. I didn't have any PTSD problems, like some of the guys did, but it took some time before I could relax easily and focus on the future. And some of the things I saw . . . like guys being blown up or shot right in front of me . . . I don't think I'll ever be able to get those images out of my head."

"I can't imagine seeing something like that."

"Most people can't. It changes you for sure. Makes you realize what you have and what other people have given up so you can have it."

Emily nodded. Neither of them said anything, but strangely, the silence didn't seem awkward. Instead, it was almost a moment of mutual reflection.

"I love these," she finally said, holding up the clementine that he'd given her, "but I think I'm going to save it for a snack later. I know we haven't been sitting here long, and I don't mean to be rude, but I should get working again. I need to get a lot of the edging done tonight to stay on schedule. This has been great, though. A lot nicer dinner than I would've had, and with unexpectedly pleasant company to boot."

"I guess the picnic idea was a good one?" Matt asked with a smile. He was turning his own clementine over and over in his hands. "I have another idea. What would you say if I helped you with the painting?"

"What?"

"I'm serious," Matt said. "I'm off tomorrow, so I could stay tonight and help you edge, and then I could help you roll the rest of the walls in the morning. And when I'm not on duty, I can help with some of the other things, like the locks on the bedrooms."

"Oh, goodness," Emily said, "I couldn't ask you to do that."

"You didn't ask. I'm offering," he continued, and his earnest expression made Emily feel strange, as if her heart had started to glow. "Look, I understand you've got a lot on your plate for the next few months. I'd like to spend more time with you any way I can. If that means I have to work for a . . . lady contractor . . . that's cool with me."

Matt's eyes sparkled as he watched how she'd react to his razz, and Emily couldn't help but smile. She rested her hands on her knees as she pondered his offer. "Do you know how to paint?"

"Sure. My parents' house got painted inside and out every five years. My sisters and I did most of it once we were old enough."

Emily squinted at him. "I couldn't pay you anything."

"I'm not asking for payment."

"You are, in a way," she said. "You want

my company." The quid pro quo nature of his offer made her feel cheap.

"C'mon, Emily. We'd be no different from any other man and woman normally spending time getting to know each other, except that the time we spend would happen here. For now, at least."

"What if I decide I'm not interested in getting to know *you* any further? Or if I decide that I can work better without you here?"

"You're the boss," Matt said simply. "You call the shots. Whatever you say goes, no questions asked."

Emily felt a rush of emotion, a warm, fuzzy feeling spreading throughout her body. Maybe Matt was just a smooth talker, but since their initial contact at the hardware store, his words and his intentions had seemed honest and sincere. If they were, she realized that he might just be the rarest of creatures: a handsome man who was accomplished, intelligent, and thoughtful, one with a good sense of humor who was capable and self-confident enough that he wasn't threatened by who she was or what she did for a living. Plus, he liked dogs.

There had been only one other person in whom she had found all of these qualities, and that person was no longer living.

It scared her to feel the way she did and to think about giving Matt the answer he desired. But it was an answer she wanted to give him, too.

She had been alone a long time. Maybe that was about to change. Maybe she owed it to herself to find out.

"All right," she said quietly. "Let's get to work."

CHAPTER 18

Saturday, April 28, 1934

Michael and his uncle reached the Holy Cross Mission in Colchester just after eleven o'clock. Instead of driving into the cemetery on the narrow road that circled it, they left the sedan in its usual parking spot outside the rectory and walked into the graveyard.

As his uncle had instructed before leaving the farm, Michael was wearing mucking boots and work clothes. He had brought a lantern and a sturdy stick he had whittled sharp at one end.

The graveyard was dark and preternaturally still. Without a hint of a breeze, the dormant trees that stood interspersed among the headstones were great sentry-like pillars with bare, outstretched arms. The snow that had blanketed the cemetery several weeks earlier was gone. In its place, between the dark, wilted patches of grass, the mud was slick and several inches deep, stubbornly persisting as spring continued to coax the cold ground to warm and soften.

"Right over here," his uncle whispered over his shoulder as he turned from the paved road to walk down one of the rows of headstones. Michael followed him to a spot in the middle of the row, beneath the branches of one of the trees. A great mound of earth was piled near the tree trunk, and two shovels were stuck upright in the dirt. Next to the pile was a freshly dug grave.

"The grave diggers barely got through the ground," his uncle said. "They managed, though, which is lucky for us."

Michael shuddered, growing fearful about what his uncle had planned. "Uncle Frank, what are we going to do?"

"You'll see. First, give me the lantern." Michael did as he was instructed, and his uncle took him by the arm and guided him closer to the hole in the ground. "This was dug today, for the first burial of the spring Monday afternoon. A grave needs to be five feet deep, measured from the bottom of the casket to the surface. We need to make this one a little deeper, at least another eighteen inches. I'll hold the lantern. You jump down there, and I'll pass you a spade."

"What if someone sees us?"

"Not likely, at this hour. But if I see someone coming, I'll tell you, and you keep low and quiet. I'll walk over to the path and make the excuse that I was inspecting the grave for tomorrow's burial."

Michael stared at his uncle. "Would someone really believe you're out inspecting a grave just before midnight?"

"Yes. Once thing I've never had is a problem with credibility." He raised his chin higher, as if to call attention to his white collar. "Now, let's get you down there. The quicker you dig, the quicker we can be done."

Michael hopped into the grave and took the shovel and stick his uncle handed to him. "What am I supposed to do with this?" he asked, holding up the stick.

"Push the sharp end into the side at one end, flush with the ground you're standing on. That way, you'll be able to gauge how much deeper you've gone."

Even with the light from the lantern, the pit in the earth was a dank, cramped place. Michael worked at a feverish pace, using the shovel to cut through tree roots and throw out fresh dirt. The sweat ran down his face and dripped off the end of his nose. He ignored the pain from blisters forming on his hands. He began to get a stitch in his side from the effort, but he pushed through it, stopping every once in a while to glance down at the stick protruding from the dirt wall of the grave.

After what seemed like hours, Michael paused and looked up toward the lantern light. "Uncle Frank?" he whispered as he caught his breath. "Is this deep enough?"

His uncle peered down into the pit, where the protruding stick now pointed to Michael's knee instead of being on the same level as the sole of his boot. "Yes, that's nearly two feet. Come now, pass me the shovel and then grab on," he said, extending his hand. "I'll help you out."

Back on regular ground, Michael took several deep breaths. It was a relief to feel cool, fresh air on his face and not stagnant air scented by soil and rot.

"Let's go get what we left in the vault," his uncle said, thrusting the spade back into the dirt pile. Michael followed him, grimacing at the odor as they entered the storage structure. His uncle noticed his expression as he closed the door behind them. "You understand now why we hold burials quickly once the ground thaws," he said with a wry smile.

Michael looked around as his uncle

readied the coffin cart and unlocked the
cupboard containing the hobo's body. He
noticed that of the several charity caskets
that had been stacked beneath the cross the
first time he'd been inside the vault, only
one remained.

A knock on the door of the vault startled
him. He looked at his uncle, panicked.

"Hello? Is someone in there?"

His uncle stared in the direction of the
door before whispering to Michael. "I don't
recognize the voice. Now, listen carefully. I
need you to go over to that casket." He
pointed to the lone coffin in the shadows
near the far wall. "Act distraught, as if
someone you love is inside it. Keep your
head down and try not to make eye contact
with whoever this is. I don't want you to say
anything unless it's in response to a question I ask you. Do you understand?"

Michael nodded. His heart was pounding,
and he felt a bit light-headed. His uncle
gave a single nod and quickly relocked the
cupboard he'd opened and went to open
the door. Michael knelt before the spare
casket, glancing back just long enough to
see who had knocked.

A uniformed police officer stood on the
other side of the door.

Michael snapped his head back around

and bowed it as if in prayer.

"Good evening, officer. I'm Father Frank Lynch. May I help you?"

"Oh, hello, Father. I was just driving past the church here — my shift ended a little while ago, and I was heading home — and I saw the light on. Given the hour, I thought there might be someone in here who wasn't supposed to be."

"Ah. I appreciate your checking. I opened the vault for the son of one of my parishioners." His uncle spoke more softly, his voice filled with sympathy. "That's his father in the box there, the poor child."

Michael was kneeling before the casket with his back to the door of the vault, and he took his uncle's words as a cue. Slowly, he clasped his trembling hands together and rested them on the lid of the empty coffin. He also sniffed loudly.

"That is a pity," the officer said. "But why are you here at this hour?"

"Arrangements have been made for the boy's care. He's been staying at the rectory temporarily, but he'll be sent to live with an aunt in Maryland early tomorrow," his uncle replied. "Since the ground is barely thawed, we haven't been able to hold a burial yet. He saw my light was on and came to ask for a moment with his father to say goodbye before he leaves. I didn't have it in me to refuse."

"Well, if that isn't something. That's mighty good of you, Father, mighty good. I'm so sorry for intruding, just wanted to make sure everything was on the up-and-up."

"Of course, and it was no intrusion. You were just doing your job. Thank you again, Officer — ?"

"Kelly. Officer John Kelly. Good night, Father."

Michael didn't turn around again even when he heard the door of the vault swing closed. He let out a long breath, one that he seemed to have been holding for several minutes, and gasped with relief.

"You did well," his uncle said, placing a hand on his shoulder. "We'll wait a little while to make sure he's gone before we finish what we came to do."

They stayed inside the vault for another hour, and his uncle took a thorough look around outside before he unlocked the vault box containing the hobo's body. Once they'd pulled it onto the coffin cart, they turned out the light and carefully wheeled it to the grave site.

"There'd be no way the two of us could lower him down there in a casket," his uncle said as he peered down into the grave. "Even simple wooden ones weigh over a hundred and fifty pounds empty. You'd need at least four strong men, preferably six, to handle this fellow in a casket."

His uncle positioned the coffin cart parallel to the grave and then turned the crank on the end to lower the body as far as it would go. "All right, Michael," he said, kneeling beside the body, "we're almost done." Michael squatted next to his uncle, ready to push the body in and push the entire ordeal out of his mind. "On the count of three. One, two, three!"

Together, they rolled the body, still wrapped in the horsehair blanket, off the cart and over the edge of the grave. It hit the bottom with a muffled *thud*.

Frank grabbed the two shovels stuck in the dirt and handed one to Michael. In a few minutes, they'd shoveled enough soil over the body to cover it completely. "That should be fine," his uncle said.

"What if someone finds him before the funeral? Or what if an animal of some kind gets in there and digs him up?" Michael felt the panic rising again.

"Highly unlikely. I'll keep an eye on the grave, but he's well hidden. At the burial on Monday, a casket will be lowered on top of him and the grave will be sealed. This will be his permanent resting place."

"What if he has a family out there? They'll never know what became of him."

His uncle exhaled slowly before he began to speak. "He might have a family, or he might not. Given his actions toward your mother, I shudder to think how he would treat his own family. But this is one of those tough situations, Michael, where there are no good solutions. It isn't possible to do something right without somebody else getting hurt or paying a price. These situations will come up every once in a while during your lifetime, and you need to recognize them and choose which solution does the least harm and who should suffer that harm.

"With this fellow, we could've gone to the police and explained what happened, but there's no telling whether they'd have believed us. We don't even know if anyone can identify this man to notify his next of kin. We could have left him somewhere — a remote forest, maybe — where he might never have been discovered. Of course, he wouldn't have had a proper burial then, and if someone *did* end up finding him and linking him back to us . . . Well, you see how that would make for a very complicated situation.

"Leaving him buried here will avoid any problems with the law, and your father can stay at his job without being called home. True, the man's family, if he has one, will never know. They're the ones who pay the price, if it can be considered that. But I look at it this way: He's in consecrated ground, and my family is protected. That's two out of three positives, and the best choice, in my book."

As he'd done when they first left the body in the vault, his uncle quietly said a series of prayers and blessings. Michael stood alongside him, waiting.

In his mind, he replayed the horrible events of the night the hobo had attacked his mother. He wished with everything in him that, by some miracle, his memories of that night would disappear. Yes, the man had attacked his mother. Yes, part of him hated the hobo and realized that he'd been justified in taking the hobo's life. He knew that. He *knew* it. And yet the guilt was still there. He'd pushed it aside as much as he could while his mother was becoming more and more ill, but right now he wasn't as focused on her. That left an opening for the guilt to come roaring back.

In the dark, quiet cemetery, as he listened to his uncle pray for the soul of the *man* he'd shot, the *human being* he'd removed from the earth, Michael's eyes welled up and overflowed. For the first time that night, a wisp of wind brushed through the graveyard and over his face, cooling the moist paths down his cheeks. It left as quickly as it came, and all became still once again.

Chapter 19

Late on Saturday evening, after Rowen was asleep, Claudia was canoodling with Kyle on his living room sofa. It was the first time they'd been alone all day.

"So," Kyle asked in a soft voice with his arm around her shoulders, "I'm dying to hear what you thought of Misty."

Claudia sat up a little straighter. The whole afternoon with Kevin and Misty had been miserable. "She is beyond awful," Claudia said, and Kyle gave a chuckle. "Shallow, self-absorbed, obsessed with designer things that cost a fortune. The way she acts around Kevin — I wonder whether she really likes him at all. And he seems so taken with her."

"I know," Kyle said. "She's another loser."

"Exactly. But why can't Kevin see that?"

"It's so typical of him," Kyle said. "Kevin is *the* nicest guy you'll ever meet. He'd give you the shirt off his back if you needed it.

But he's always had problems with women. He's a little overweight and insecure about it, so he tries to compensate by being funny and really accommodating. Like, almost naive-pushover-level accommodating. I think having Misty walk into his office and then agree to go out with him really blew his mind."

"I can just see it," Claudia said with her hand on her face. She could truly empathize with how Kevin must have felt. "I mean, I'm sure lots of men find Misty attractive, and if Kevin had problems meeting attractive women . . ."

"Exactly," Kyle said. "I still remember him calling me up the day he met her. By the time she left his office, they'd made plans to have dinner together, and he was gushing about how this gorgeous woman had dropped into his life and taken a huge interest in him."

"Maybe he's so enamored with her looks that he doesn't realize what she's really like as a person."

"Wouldn't be the first time," Kyle said, "although her looks don't hold a candle to yours."

"I'm relieved you feel that way. She smiled at you an awful lot."

"I noticed that," Kyle said as he rolled his

eyes. "Maybe it was just her nerves. I hope it was innocent."

"Trust me, it wasn't. She was trying to flirt with you."

"Maybe, although she's really an idiot if she thought it would be effective," Kyle said, drawing her closer. "I don't know why Kevin would be with someone like that, but I'll bet he didn't notice."

"You're sure not like your brother in that department," Claudia said as she leaned back into Kyle and rested her head against his shoulder. "You're good at reading people. Even now, when you look at me, I feel like you can tell exactly what I'm thinking." Slowly, she traced her finger up Kyle's chest. He caught her hand in his.

"You make it easy," he said. He pulled her closer as he kissed her, and the urgency of his touch left no doubt in her mind that she was right.

"This couch is a little small, don't you think?" she asked when she could. "Besides, Rowen might see us out here if she wakes up."

Kyle pulled back slightly and stroked his fingers down the side of her face. "Yeah, but wait. There's something I wanted to talk with you about."

"What?"

"I was thinking . . . it wouldn't be easy for us, but maybe we should sort of . . . hold off on certain things until our wedding night."

Claudia blinked and studied his face. "Seriously? I don't get it. First you tell me that I'm way better-looking than Misty. Then, you kiss me like that, so all I can think about is . . . you know . . . being with you, and then you tell me you don't want us to do that again until we're married. What is this, payback for me seducing you in the Jeep?"

"No, no," Kyle said with a laugh. "I suppose I didn't do a very good job of broaching the subject. We don't have to if you don't think it will be worth it, but . . . do you suppose that, maybe, it would make our wedding night even more memorable than it will already be?"

"Our wedding is still two months away. I don't think I can make it that long." Claudia freed her hand from his grasp and slid it back down his chest, then a little lower. "I'm willing to bet that you can't, either."

"It would be a challenge," Kyle said. "But imagine how it would be if we did. It might be like the first time all over again, but better. More . . . intense."

She thought back to their first night

together, the night of Valentine's Day, when an unexpected snowstorm had cut the power to Kyle's apartment. The thought of waiting for two months and then making love with Kyle on their wedding night in December, when the snow might be whirling around outside once more, sent tingles down her spine. Then again, she had no idea where they would be spending their wedding night or what the weather there might be like.

"I'd be willing to try it," she said finally, "but I have three conditions." She leaned over and kissed him again, a soft, sensual kiss with her lips barely brushing his.

"Tell me," Kyle said, although the look on his face seemed to indicate that he was no longer in much of a mood to talk.

"All right." She kept her face close, her mouth hovering over his as she spoke. "First, kissing is allowed, along with hugging and anything else we can do with our clothes on."

"Agreed," Kyle said. He leaned in again, but Claudia turned her face slightly and put her finger up against his lips.

"Uh-uh, I'm not finished," she said with a smile. "The second condition is that you have to give me a hint about where we're going to spend our wedding night."

"Hmmm. A hint?" Kyle pulled back, his eyes narrowed in thought. "I can do that. I'll even give you two hints."

Claudia's smile stretched wide as she enjoyed the feeling of gleeful anticipation.

"It's somewhere very private, with a very large bed."

"Those aren't helpful hints." She stuck out her lower lip in an exaggerated pout.

"You didn't say it had to be a helpful hint."

Claudia rolled her eyes. "Fine. I suppose I'd really rather not know, even though I'm dying to, because you want it to be a surprise, and I don't want to take that away from you."

"Thank you," Kyle said, drawing her tight against him. "It's only because I love you. I want it to be special, that's all. Now, what is your third condition?"

She didn't answer right away, but instead smoothed her hand down the side of his face and lost herself in his dark brown eyes before she kissed him again, hard on the mouth. He didn't complain at her delay in answering, just ran his fingers through her hair, cupping them gently on each side of her jaw. Only when his lips found their way down to her neck did she whisper her third condition.

"The last thing," Claudia began, then

gasped as his hands slid down her body. She covered them with her own and guided them beneath her shirt. "The last thing is that the starting date for your little plan is *tomorrow*."

On Sunday afternoon, Claudia walked to The Stitchery for her second fitting. Pauline met her at the door, just as she had for their first meeting. Claudia stifled a giggle when she looked down and saw three pins protruding from Pauline's "wearable pincushion."

"How is the wedding planning coming along?" Pauline asked.

"Everyone keeps asking me that," Claudia said with a laugh. "We've got things set for the ceremony and reception. Pretty much everyone has RSVP'd, and I've given Ruth a deposit for the cake. I wish there were a florist here in Mill River, but since there's not, I think I'm going to use Hawley's in Rutland for the flowers. Other than those things, Kyle is taking care of the honeymoon plans, and he's got some surprise in store for where we're spending our wedding night."

"Sounds like you've got everything under control," Pauline said. "You're ahead of the game on most of those things."

"Maybe. But I don't want to be stressing about anything on my wedding day. Nobody likes a Bridezilla, you know, so I'm trying to have everything in place well in advance."

"You're a smart girl for doing that," Pauline said. "Even if something unexpected happens at the last minute, I'm sure you'll find a way to deal with it and have a beautiful wedding. Things always have a way of falling into place. Now, I'm going to stop my yammering so you can get changed. Your shoes and gown are already in the booth there, ready for you to put on."

"Oh, good!" Claudia said. "I can't wait to see my dress!" She hurried down to the booth and went inside.

"If you need any help getting into it, dear, just call me," Pauline said.

When Claudia emerged from the booth, a huge smile was plastered on her face. "This looks so good, Pauline! The length is perfect with my shoes, and it feels like it fits so much better in the bodice and arms."

"As well it should," Pauline said with satisfaction. "Come on up here in front of the mirror so I can take a good look."

Claudia walked carefully up the steps to the three-way mirror, and Pauline began a detailed examination of the gown. "The sleeves do fit perfectly now," she said. "But

I think the bodice could be taken in a little more." She pinched the fabric a bit. "Does that feel too tight to you, as I'm holding it?"

"No," Claudia said, "but I don't think I'd want it any snugger than that."

"All right. I'll just pin this little part here, but other than this, I don't see anything else that needs to be altered."

"I think it's gorgeous," Claudia said. "I can't wait until Kyle sees it!"

"You're doing it the traditional way, then? The groom won't see the gown until the ceremony?"

"Yep. Although he teases me that he's going to sneak a look at it before then."

"And yet he's keeping your wedding-night accommodations a surprise? That doesn't seem fair."

"I may have to put a lock on my closet," Claudia said.

"Do you two have lots of family and friends coming?"

"Neither one of us has a huge family, but everyone we invited on both sides is planning to attend. Most of our friends are coming, too. It shouldn't be a huge wedding, though. We're expecting between fifty and sixty guests."

"Not huge by today's standards," Pauline agreed. "I take it you've met his family?"

"Yes, everyone is just wonderful. Except . . ."

"Except?"

Claudia gave a little sigh. "Oh, Kyle's brother has a new girlfriend. We met her yesterday, and she was a real piece of work."

"Really?" Pauline straightened up and came around to face her. "What do you mean?"

"We didn't have anything in common, and she seemed pretty disinterested in being there, except she smiled at Kyle a lot."

"Really? It's odd that she'd do that, especially in front of you and Kyle's brother."

"That's what I thought. Then again, she was rough around the edges, even borderline rude. Or maybe I'm just hypersensitive about other women noticing him."

"He *is* very handsome," Pauline said with a smile, then walked around Claudia, putting in a few final pins and checking everything over again. "I wouldn't worry about it at this point. Smiles are pretty harmless, and I'm sure Kyle is as honest and faithful as they come."

"True," Claudia said. "Besides, she and Kyle's brother live in Boston, so they're not down here in Mill River very often. And when they do come, I can keep my eye on her."

"I think that's wise. Your situation made me think of the perfect advice for you for this fitting."

"Let's hear it," Claudia said. She'd been wondering what the seamstress would say this time, and whether the advice would be as practical as her first lesson had been.

"Well. Even though you and Kyle have known each other for a while now, your wedding day will mark a kind of new start for you and your relationship," Pauline said. "It's the official beginning of your lives together as family. Your bonds have to be strong enough to weather hardships and tough times. Whatever you two have already been through in that respect, let it stay in the past. You'll have enough trying times to deal with in your lives ahead. Every new married couple does. What you don't want to do is let somebody or something come between you two and drag you down. Trust each other, enjoy the present, and focus on your future together."

After Mass on Sunday, Karen was heading to Rutland to visit her father. Ben was with her this time, slouched in the front seat and wearing the typical scowl of a sullen teenager.

"He's not going to recognize me, Mom," Ben said. "He never does anymore. I shouldn't have to come with you to see him."

"Maybe he doesn't recognize you. Or maybe he does but he has no way of showing it anymore. He's still your grandfather. He still loves you. If you were sick in the hospital, and unconscious so you had no way of knowing what was going on or who was there, wouldn't you want the people you love to come visit you?"

Ben turned his head to stare out the car window. "If I was unconscious, I wouldn't be able to tell, so I wouldn't care."

"I don't think you really mean that." She didn't say anything more, and she tried to overlook Ben's surly behavior as exacerbated by the stress and fear they both felt over Nick's absence.

Deep down, part of her hated dragging her son to the Alzheimer's care facility. For the past several months, they'd had almost the same conversation every time, and it was true that her father seemed to have completely forgotten Ben. That was what really got her. It was one thing to have her own hopes crushed after sitting with her father for hours without seeing the tiniest spark of his old self emerge. It was quite another to see *Ben's* hopes crushed at first, and now see them completely extinguished.

And yet, it was her father, and Ben's grandfather, who was in that facility. He was family.

As they drove on in silence, Karen allowed herself to reminisce about happier times in Mill River. On those nights when her father had come home from work after being away for days, their house had been filled to the rafters with joy. So, too, had it been later on, after she'd left home, when she'd return to visit her parents. There was no length of time or physical distance that could have broken their loving bond.

Karen believed with all her heart that the bond had also withstood the assault of her father's terrible disease. She had no proof. In fact, his behavior indicated otherwise, but still, she believed.

She would continue to bring Ben with her from time to time. Even if her father truly didn't recognize them anymore, being able to visit him was a blessing, and he was still deserving of love.

CHAPTER 20

Thursday, May 1, 1934

It took a couple of days after he and his uncle had buried the hobo for Michael to feel something close to normalcy. He hadn't slept at all that first night, when his uncle had dropped him back at the farm in the early hours of the morning. He'd sat in the tepid washtub of water his grandmother had left out for him, scrubbing his skin, trying to remove the mud and grime caked on the outside and to free the remorse festering just beneath the surface.

Sunday night, his sleep hadn't been much better. He'd slept, yes, but his rest had been fraught with vivid nightmares full of headstones and hoboes, the smells of blood and death and the feelings of being hurled into an open grave, and of wet earth falling in clumps, covering his face. He'd awakened on the edge of a scream in his dark bedroom. School on Monday had been difficult, too. He'd passed the day in a stupor, barely able to follow along in the various lessons. Monday night, finally, he'd collapsed into an exhausted slumber, the deep sleep that comes instantaneously upon one's head touching a pillow.

Today he'd awakened feeling refreshed and calm. School was fine if uneventful, and the early-spring sunshine was out in full force as he descended the steps from the school bus outside the farmhouse.

His good humor turned to elation when he found a letter from his father waiting in the mailbox. That excitement was tempered when he saw the St. Joseph's parish sedan parked in front of the house.

Fearful that his uncle had driven out to bring bad news, Michael ran down the driveway and burst through the front door. There, seated at the kitchen table, were his grandmother, his uncle Frank, and his mother.

"You're home!" he yelled, and swooped down to grab his mother in a hug. "I don't believe it! Are you all right now?"

"I'm much better," his mother said, laughing. "I still feel sick sometimes, but I've been able to drink and eat enough that Dr. Washburn let me come home."

"Thank goodness," his grandmother said.

"The hospital treatment worked a miracle."

"Medicine these days sure is something," his uncle agreed.

Michael just stood there, beaming at the three of them. Only when he moved to put down his book bag did he remember the letter in his hand.

"There's another letter from Father," he said, holding it out to his mother. "It was in the mailbox. I can't believe I forgot about it just now."

His mother eagerly took it and stuck her finger beneath the envelope flap to open it. "I couldn't ask for a better homecoming present," she said. "I'll read it so we can all hear." She unfolded the paper inside. Two ten-dollar bills were wrapped inside the letter, and she carefully laid them on the table and smoothed them flat before she began to read.

April 23, 1934

Dear Anna, Mother, and Michael,
I hope that all of you are well. I write this letter with a heavy heart, as I have considerable serious news to tell you.

Last weekend, Seamus was involved in a fight in a local pub. I was not there with him, as he went out cavorting with several other young men his own age. He did not return that night or report for work the next morning. The details about what happened are still uncertain. I do not know whether Seamus started the fight or was merely defending himself, but at some point, Seamus struck another man with a broken bottle and cut his throat badly.

The man was taken to the hospital and survived, thank the Lord. Seamus was arrested. The local authorities, it seems, are set on making an example out of Seamus by charging him with attempted murder. I don't know yet when a trial will be held, but I have spoken with a defense lawyer who has agreed to represent him.

My salary alone is easily enough to cover the rent on our shared room and other necessities, but I must also pay the considerable lawyer's fees if Seamus is to have any chance of avoiding conviction. I do not know what else I can do at present except continue to work. I have no other employment option, and I couldn't leave Seamus here in this predicament. But I fear that the twenty dollars I have enclosed for you is most likely the last money I will be able to send for some time.

I feel truly ill and helpless about Seamus. I blame myself for not advising him more strongly against visiting the pubs, but I wonder whether it would have made any difference. He is brash and strong-willed, as you know.

There's nothing more I have to say at the moment, other than to ask for your thoughts and prayers that some favorable resolution to the situation comes to pass.

With all my love,
Niall

By the time his mother had finished the letter, her trembling hands were clenched around the sides of the paper, and she could barely speak for the breathing that had become more and more ragged.

Every bit of the buoyancy Michael had felt upon seeing his mother at home had left his body. He was numb from shock, as they all were. The only thing that snapped his mind back into more active thought was the sight of his mother leaning over in her chair and retching on the floor.

"Anna!" His grandmother was up and around the table to his mother before Michael realized what had happened. "Listen,

Anna, you can't start this again. You have to be strong. Do you hear me? Seamus will be fine. Niall is with him, and he'll take care of it. Frank, Michael, help her to her room, please, while I clean up in here."

Michael went to his mother, as did his uncle, and they walked her down the hall and into her bedroom. Once she was lying down comfortably and his grandmother had cleaned the floor beneath the chair where his mother had been sitting, the three of them gathered solemnly around the kitchen table.

"We've got to figure out a way to make do without Niall," his grandmother said finally. "We've had a difficult time of things, to be sure, but I can't imagine what he and Seamus must be going through right now. Still, the hospital bill will be along any day now, and I shudder to think what it will be."

"How much does it cost to stay in a hospital?" Michael asked.

"It varies a little depending on what treatment the patient receives, but usually around six dollars per day," his uncle said.

Michael did the math in his head. His mother had been in the hospital for a week and three days. *Sixty dollars.* Even with the twenty dollars his father had sent, plus the money his grandmother had left from the secret sale of the hobo's watch, they were woefully short.

"We've got Doc Washburn's private bill coming, too," his grandmother said. "There's no telling whether Anna's out of the woods yet. She may need more medical care, and there's the birth to worry about. Plus, we'll need gas for the car. The electric bill is due each month and property taxes at the end of the summer. If Niall can't send anything more, I don't know how we'll manage."

"I'll help as much as I'm able," his uncle said, "but my stipend is meager. Priests do take a vow of poverty, after all." He was reaching into his jacket pocket as he spoke. He withdrew a creased leather billfold. It contained a five-dollar bill and two one-dollar silver certificates, and he took all of them and added them to the bills already on the table.

"What about the cow?" Michael asked. "We always have extra milk. You usually give it to the Whibleys, but couldn't we sell it? Or maybe make butter or cheese and sell that?"

His grandmother shook her head. "Nobody wants dairy products these days if they haven't been pasteurized, and we don't have the equipment to do that. Besides,

Onion's going to have her calf in a few months, and I'll have to dry her out to make sure she's ready to go again when the calf comes."

"We can sell the calf," Michael said.

"Yes, we can," his grandmother agreed. "Let's hope it's healthy and a heifer. We'd get more for a future milk cow. But it won't be enough."

"You never know. Niall might be able to sort out the mess with Seamus within a month or two," his uncle said. "The lawyer he's hired might be able to get the charges reduced or dismissed entirely. I can't believe Seamus would ever try to kill someone."

"Drink does bad things to that boy," his grandmother said. "There's no telling what he intended —"

"I can get a job!"

His uncle and grandmother looked at him.

"Grandma, I can get a job. That would bring in a little more money until Father is able to send it to us again."

"Michael . . ." The look on his uncle's face was a mixture of admiration and pity.

"There are no jobs to be had around here," his grandmother said. "If there were, your father would never have left."

"Maybe that will change in the summer. What if lots of men have left, like Father?

There might be places that have temporary work, and I wouldn't be picky. I can work inside, in an office or factory, or outside. There are lots of farms. Maybe one of them needs an extra hand?"

"I admire your optimism, Michael," his uncle said. "But I'm not as optimistic as you are that a situation would open up for you."

"Besides, until school's finished for the year, that's what you should concern yourself with," Lizzie said. "Your mother would want you to focus on your studies. We'll figure out something in the meantime." Uncle Frank nodded his agreement.

"I'm going to keep my eyes open for anything," Michael said. "I can ask around after school whether anyone has a job I could do for the summer."

His grandmother sighed. "No harm in asking, I guess. After I fix supper tonight, we'll have no fresh meat in the house, and I want to make sure your mother gets plenty to eat. There are a few hours of daylight left. Do you think you could go hunting and have time to finish your homework this evening?"

"I think I could," Michael said. He rose from the table, put on his jacket and cap, and went to the gun cabinet. His .22 was there, along with his game bag, where he had last left them. With the memory of the hobo's burial so fresh in his mind, though, the sight of the gun and the thought of using it again made him feel queasy.

He stood there before the cabinet, willing himself to reach for his gun and hunting supplies. He could feel his grandmother and uncle watching him. Their stares were becoming heavier and heavier until they forced his arm into action. He threw open the glass door of the cabinet and removed his game bag and a box of cartridges. Instead of taking the .22, his hand closed around the barrel of his .30-30 Winchester rifle.

"Are you going for squirrel?" his grandmother asked. "That's a lot of firepower for squirrels."

Michael turned around, the gun in his hand. "I don't want to use the twenty-two," he whispered. Before his grandmother or uncle could respond, he was out the back door.

To hunt squirrels, he would have headed for the woods. The rifle he carried was for larger game. It would be better to get something more substantial, something that would provide more meat for a longer period of time. This was especially true for two reasons. Since his father wouldn't be sending money for the foreseeable future, they would have to live off the food they could grow and hunt for much of the summer, if not longer. And, Michael admitted to himself, he truly didn't want to hunt anymore. After what had happened with the hobo, he wasn't sure he could bear to do it.

There was a small brook that ran along the edge of the pasture behind the barn. Since it was mud season, the melted snow had made the water level a bit deeper than usual, and the banks were slippery and soft. Rather than hop over it and continue into the forest, Michael turned and walked alongside it for a few hundred yards, past the orchard on the far end of the property, until the brush became a dense thicket. He took up a position behind the curved interwoven briars and tall stalks of dead grass from the previous year. It was damp and cold, sitting on the ground, but the spot offered him a well-concealed place with a clear view of the brook.

Michael tried to remain as motionless as he could, his rifle at the ready. Even if any game that might pass by didn't catch his scent, it would almost certainly spot him or hear him if he made a sudden movement.

He endured mosquito bites and ignored his nose or places on his back when they begged to be scratched. When his foot fell asleep from sitting cross-legged, he altered his position very slowly and deliberately, moving only a few inches at a time.

As the sun dropped below the trees and shadows began to loom over the thicket, he caught a hint of movement out of the corner of his eye. He turned his head slightly, carefully. In the distance, a young deer lowered its head to drink from the brook. It was either a doe or a button buck, he couldn't tell which from where he was sitting. Not that it mattered. Venison was venison.

Since it wasn't deer hunting season, taking the deer now would constitute poaching, but that didn't matter, either. He'd hunted year-round since he was twelve without license or repercussion, and he suspected the authorities had been overlooking hunting violations for some time. People were desperate these days, and hunting kept the hungry from increasing in number.

He slowly pressed his cheek against the rifle and took aim. The deer was perhaps fifty yards away, well within range. He had a perfect shot lined up through the iron sights, but he hesitated. Just the anticipation of hearing the gunshot and feeling the recoil against his shoulder made him feel queasy again.

Michael tried to steady himself. He took a deep breath and exhaled slowly.

The deer's head snapped up. It stared in the direction of the forest, its huge ears cupped forward, and then turned to look directly where he was sitting. Michael tried to be absolutely still. *You're going to miss your chance if you don't do it,* he told himself. *Your family is depending on you to provide for them. You promised your father you would take care of everything.*

Even from a distance, he could see the deer's large, dark eyes. He didn't want to kill it. He didn't want to kill anything ever again. But a deer would feed his family for a long time, and he couldn't bear the thought of his mother and grandmother going hungry.

Michael looked one final time through the sights and squeezed the trigger.

Fifty yards away, the deer jumped, ran a few yards, staggered, and fell.

He waited a few minutes and then walked along the brook until he reached the carcass. It was a button buck, its nubs of antlers just beginning to protrude from its head. The bullet had hit right behind the shoulder, ensuring a quick kill.

On the one hand, he was pleased that the deer hadn't suffered for long, as it might have if the bullet hadn't hit the vital chest area. But he was all too aware of his ability to ensure a quick demise, and the shot just reinforced this awareness. It also made him feel guilty, and a little afraid — of what he was, and of what he was capable of doing.

As quickly as he could, Michael took out his knife and gutted the deer. He saved the heart and liver, placing them in his game bag. Even after it had been field-dressed, he estimated that the carcass weighed a good eighty-five pounds. He was several hundred yards from the barn, and with a rifle to carry, he faced a difficult task in getting the deer back to the farm.

With his gun tucked in the crook of one arm and his other hand grasping one of the deer's rear legs, Michael trudged slowly toward the barn. He had to stop frequently to rest, or to kick away bramble or other vegetation. The hand he was using to hold onto the deer grew sore with fatigue. When he finally reached the barn, his clothes were soaked through with sweat, and the twilight had nearly given way to darkness.

Inside the barn, Michael sank heavily onto a bale of straw to rest for a few minutes. As soon as he caught his breath, he got a rope from the supply closet and suspended the carcass head-down from one of the thick wooden beams. Tomorrow after school, once the deer had had a chance to cool, he would skin and section it. After that, he would quarter it and debone the meat. It was a big job, getting a whole deer ready to be frozen or canned, but maybe his grandmother would help him once he had it in smaller pieces.

She was standing before the stove stirring a pot of soup when he came inside. His mother was sitting at the table, which had been set for dinner.

"Well?" His grandmother looked at him expectantly.

"I got a deer," he said without smiling. "It's in the barn, field-dressed."

"That's wonderful!" his mother said. "We haven't had venison in so long. Maybe I'll make a stew for supper tomorrow, if I feel up to it."

"Your venison stew is divine, Anna," his grandmother said.

Wordlessly, Michael put his rifle and ammunition back in the gun cabinet and returned to the kitchen. He placed his game bag on the counter for his grandmother to empty and began to wash up. He was exhausted and grimy, soaked through on his bottom from where he'd been sitting on the damp ground, and there was blood smeared on his hands and caked beneath his fingernails. He was drying his hands and thinking how, after supper, it would be lovely to have a rare midweek bath, when someone knocked loudly on the front door.

"Goodness," his mother said, flinching in her chair. "Who in the world could that be?" She went to the door and turned on the porch light before glancing out through the window. "Oh, dear Lord," she said in a frantic whisper as she looked back at them. "It's the police."

CHAPTER 21

After returning from their visit with her father, Karen was straightening up the kitchen while Ben sat at the table doing his homework for Monday.

Their visit had been uneventful. Her father hadn't given any indication that he'd recognized either one of them, even when she'd put on his favorite Louis Armstrong music. Sitting in the recliner in his room with his eyes half open, he'd hardly moved at all. Ben's mood had improved considerably when, after only thirty minutes, she'd decided they'd been there long enough.

"That's a relief," her son had said as they exited the care facility. "I hate this place."

Although she'd never admit it to Ben, she was feeling relieved, too. As hard as it was for her to see her father's deteriorating condition, the increasingly frequent days when he was unresponsive were so much more difficult.

Now that they were home, she was struggling to stay busy and to project some semblance of normalcy for Ben's sake. Every few minutes, her thoughts would drift to Nick, or something she or Ben said would involve him. Each time it happened, the worry and fear she felt over his absence would shoot up to the forefront of her thoughts like a poison dart. Although she really wanted to slip into her dark bedroom and take refuge from those feelings under her covers, she instead curled up on the couch under a warm throw.

"Hey, Mom, if I get all my homework done early, can we go do something fun?"

Now that she had made herself comfortable on the sofa, the last thing Karen wanted to do was go out again. "Like what?"

"We could go to the park and shoot baskets. Like Dad always does with me."

Karen knew she should agree to Ben's request. For some reason, though, she felt no desire to take her son to the park. She had no emotional reaction at all to his plea, not even guilt at denying him a reminder of his missing father. Some part of her knew she shouldn't feel that way. It wasn't normal; actually, it was a warning sign. But that realization, along with the small voice of her conscience urging her to give in to

Ben, was quickly stifled by a vast mass of apathy.

"I don't think so, honey. I really don't feel like going all the way out to the park, and besides, it'll be dark before long."

"Could I go over to Gabe's for a little while, then?"

Gabriel Wells was her son's best friend, a nice kid who lived with his family two blocks over. Gabe's father was a teacher in Rutland, and his mother worked part-time at the post office in Mill River. He had a younger sister named Sophie who occasionally tried to convince the boys to play Barbies with her.

Karen was thankful that Gabe was in Ben's life and that they lived close enough to easily spend time together. Their friendship was a good distraction for Ben while Nick was away.

Nick.

Deep breath. Steady. Focus.

"Sure. What kind of homework do you have?"

"Algebra. And I have to write a two-page book report for English."

"That doesn't sound too bad. *Robinson Crusoe?*"

"Uh-huh. I finished reading it last night."

"You're good at guessing what I was go-

342

ing to ask next," she said with a chuckle. The laugh felt strangely automatic — shallow, almost devoid of emotion, and disconnected with her inner self. "Did you like it?"

"Yeah, it was pretty good. Way better than *Little Women.*"

"I don't know about that," she said. "I really loved *Little Women.* Still do."

"That's 'cause you're a girl, Mom."

She smiled — another reflexive response, something she was supposed to do to appear normal but that she didn't feel. "Right, of course that's it."

"Hey, what's for dinner?"

"What sounds good?" She had no appetite, and she hoped that whatever Ben wanted would be simple to fix.

"Hamburgers."

"Again?"

"I love hamburgers," Ben said, looking up from the paper. "Sloppy joes are good, too. And spaghetti."

"All those things take ground beef, which we're out of."

"So just go to the store," Ben said matter-of-factly. "I'll stay here and finish my homework."

Karen closed her eyes. *You need to take care of your child,* the voice in her head said.

You need to get off this couch and go to the store.

"All right," she said. Reluctantly, she sat up, successfully pushing back against the strong force that wanted to tether her to the sofa. "If I'm going shopping, I'll get stuff for the week so I don't have to make another trip for a while. What kinds of vegetables do you want?"

Ben looked up at her with his lip curled.

"All right, I'll surprise you with the vegetables."

"Oh! Get some cereal, too — Frosted Mini-Wheats — milk, and some stuff for sandwiches. And we're out of bananas."

"Wow, that's quite a list. Maybe you should just come with me and do homework later?" she asked. Everything Nick had told her about the size of growing boys' appetites was absolutely true.

Nick.

Deep breath. Steady. Focus.

"Just kidding," she said with a smile in response to Ben's deer-in-the-headlights look of panic. "I know you hate food shopping. I'll be back in an hour or so."

"Okay."

"Remember, don't go out, and don't open the door for anyone while I'm gone."

"Mom." Ben rolled his eyes. "I'm thirteen,

344

you know."

"I know," she said. She kissed the back of his head as he looked down at the table, focusing again on his schoolwork.

At the little grocery store on the edge of Mill River, she pushed her cart purposefully, methodically, up and down every aisle, regardless of whether she needed something in it. Now that she was there, the store turned out to be a welcome change of scenery, a place where she wasn't alone but also wasn't bothered. She found it soothing to peruse a wall of salad dressings. The display of olives — green, with or without pimentos, black, kalamata — was fascinating. So many of the spices for sale in the display rack were new or foreign to her. What in the world was garam masala used for? And why would something so exotic appear for sale in Mill River's little grocery store?

Karen continued toward the meat counter, where she picked up ground beef and some chicken that was on sale. The store was running a special on sirloin steaks, too, thick ones that would be perfect on the grill. *Nick would love one of those,* she thought. *Marinated, then grilled medium-rare with onions and mushrooms on the side . . .*

Nick.

She'd done it again. It was impossible to avoid thinking about him for long, and although part of her wished she were capable of it, a bigger part knew she wasn't and wouldn't have it any other way.

There were two registers open at the front of the store. Karen glanced quickly at the people in line and, relieved that she didn't know any of them, pushed her cart into place at the rear of the line that was shorter. She had just finished putting her groceries on the moving belt when a man behind her asked, "Would you mind passing me one of those dividers?"

Karen quickly reached for one of the plastic rods to place between her groceries and his. "Thanks," he said when she handed it to him. He placed it on the conveyor belt and began to unload the few things he had in his shopping basket.

She realized that he looked familiar. For a few minutes, she discreetly studied him, trying to figure out where she'd seen him. It didn't take long for the answer to come to her. "Aren't you the new police officer in town?" she asked.

"Yes, ma'am. No uniform today, though," he said, glancing down at his old T-shirt and sweatpants. "I'm Matt Campbell."

"Karen Cooper. Nice to meet you," she

346

replied. "I saw you a few days ago, in the hardware store."

"Oh, really?" Matt said with a small grin. "Yeah, I ran in there looking for upholstery cleaner. New puppy."

"Ah." Karen smiled and nodded. "New puppy, new messes." Matt grinned at her, and his friendly demeanor encouraged her to continue the conversation. "I thought I overheard you tell the clerk that you served in the Marines before you became a police officer?"

"Yes, ma'am, I did, for sixteen years," he said.

"That's a long time," Karen said softly. "Thank you for your service."

"I was proud to do it," Matt said. "Though I'm glad to be back in the States permanently. Three tours in the Middle East were enough."

Karen smiled again, although she felt like crying. She busied herself by arranging her groceries on the conveyor belt and reading the tabloid headlines until the customer ahead of her in line had completed his transaction. When he'd taken his receipt from the cashier and pushed his cart through the aisle and toward the exit, Karen stepped forward.

"Hi," the cashier said to her. "Did you

find everything you were looking for?"

"Yes, thank you," she replied. Once she had removed her check card from her wallet, she glanced back at Matt again. "I was wondering . . ." she began, although when he realized she had spoken to him and looked her full in the eyes, she almost changed her mind about asking him the question. The intense, serious way he had focused on her reminded her so much of Nick. "I was wondering, while you were stationed in the Middle East, did you ever go on missions to rescue people held hostage by militants?"

Matt's expression transformed into one of surprise before a crease formed between his brows. "Personally, no, I never did, but lots of guys in my platoon had. Some of our missions were designed to keep abductions from happening in the first place. We were always being sent out on security patrols. Why do you ask?"

"I know someone whose husband has gone missing over there. In Saudi Arabia."

"Oh. Wow. That's tough," Matt said. Karen noticed him clenching his jaw as he seemed to grasp for words. "Kidnappings are way down from what they used to be, but it doesn't make it any easier for people who are still being taken, or for their families. There are isolated groups of militants and terrorists everywhere, even in countries we didn't invade."

"Yes," Karen agreed. "I've heard."

"If it's any comfort, tell your friend that our guys over there don't give up. If one of them goes missing or an American civilian gets snatched, there's no stopping until the person's found. They consider it a sacred duty to protect innocent people. I did, too, when I was over there."

"That's good to know," Karen said. She felt the moisture building in her eyes and turned away from Matt to swipe her check card through the electronic reader. "With that kind of loyalty, Mill River's lucky to have you." She hurried to sign the receipt and leave the store.

"Tell your friend I'm sorry about her husband," Matt said before she pushed her cart out of the aisle. "And tell her she should keep the faith."

"I will," Karen said softly. "I will."

In the marble mansion, Emily had covered the floor in tarps and set up her ladder. She was pouring a tray of paint when Matt let himself in through the back door. Gus, who was curled up on a large dog bed in the corner of the room, got to his feet and whined.

"Emily?" Matt called as he came into the room. "Hi. And hey, Gus, how's that good boy?" he said, bending down to pet the large dog. "He's keeping you company, today, huh?"

"Yeah. It's hard on him being alone so much, and this way I don't have to run home at set times to let him outside. He's hung out with me on lots of jobs." She looked at Matt's grubby attire. "I guess you're serious about helping. I thought after last night, you might bail on me."

She glanced up around the great hall, which was entirely edged in fresh off-white paint. Matt had been a huge help, although she hated to admit it. The fact that he was back, on his day off, no less, was even more impressive.

"Nah," Matt said. "We got the hardest part done yesterday. Brushwork is tedious, but rolling the paint on is a cinch. It can even be fun. And look, I brought snacks and some cold drinks." He held up two plastic grocery sacks.

"That's really nice of you, thanks!" Emily said. "You can put the drinks in the fridge if you want. I was just getting started."

When he left to go to the kitchen, she got Gus settled on his cushion and poured a second tray of paint for Matt to use.

"I'll get up on the ladder and do the upper portion of the walls if you can take the lower parts," she said, handing him a paint roller with a long handle. "You're taller than I am, so you'll be able to reach higher."

"Yes, ma'am," Matt said as he accepted the roller, but the crinkles at the corners of his eyes told her that this time, he had called her "ma'am" on purpose.

They worked for several minutes without speaking, the sound of wet rollers spreading paint reverberating throughout the room.

"You seem a little quieter than yesterday," Emily said. She didn't look at Matt as she spoke but instead fixed her gaze on the wall above her head. "Are you sure you're not having second thoughts about doing this?"

"Oh, no, I'm definitely where I want to be. I was just thinking . . . I stopped off at the store on my way over, and the woman next to me in line struck up a conversation. She said she'd overheard me talking to you last weekend in the hardware store."

"Really?" Emily lowered her roller. "That's weird. The only other person who came in then was . . . Oh. It was Karen. Karen Cooper."

"You know her?"

"Yes, she was a year ahead of me in

school. I didn't know she was living in town again, but I talked with her a little bit after you left. What did she say to you?"

"She wanted to know about military rescues in the Middle East, like whether I'd ever gone on a rescue mission while I was there. Said she knew someone whose husband has been kidnapped by militants."

"It's her husband she was talking about," Emily said quietly as a wave of sympathy spread through her. "After you left the store, I went to see if she needed help and found her crying. Karen's husband is a military contractor. He went missing in Saudi Arabia a few days ago. She was in the store again yesterday, and she hasn't gotten any new information."

"I had a hunch it might've been something like that," Matt said. "I wasn't going to ask any questions, but she seemed like she was on the verge of getting upset while we were talking. I feel so bad for her. And it brought back a lot of memories I wish I didn't have."

Emily paused, wondering whether she should satisfy her curiosity and ask about his time overseas. "Did you . . . did you ever free someone who'd been kidnapped? When you were still in the service, I mean," she said cautiously. "If you don't want to talk about it, I totally understand."

"No, it's all right," Matt said. He dipped his roller in a tray of paint and carefully placed it against the wall. "The truth is that I never went on a rescue mission like that, but there were times when I thought I might end up being taken hostage.

"The scariest time was once when I was in Afghanistan, on a night patrol with my company. We were in the mountains and started taking small-arms fire, but even with night vision equipment, we couldn't see where the enemy was hiding. We backtracked a ways, until they started firing rocket-propelled grenades from behind our position. We were surrounded. Ambushed, basically. One of our Jeeps was hit. Killed two guys and injured two more, even with armor reinforcements on the vehicle. It was just . . . chaos. The only reason we got out of there was because we called in an airstrike and got some cover. That, plus dumb luck, or Providence."

Emily was frozen in place. She hadn't noticed the paint dripping off the end of her roller or the way her free hand had tightened its grip on the aluminum rail of the ladder. Instead, as Matt quietly rolled a stripe of paint up the wall, she was seeing him again for the first time. Here was someone who was amazingly strong — who had willingly chosen to protect others, who had been thrust into violent, terrifying situations more than once and emerged with his life and self intact. The uncertainty and drama and difficulties she had experienced during her own lifetime seemed insignificant compared with what he had seen and done.

"I can't imagine how terrifying that must have been," she finally said. "I'm glad you made it out of there."

Matt nodded with his eyes on the wall. "Me, too."

At that moment, Gus got up off his dog bed, shook his collar, and whined. Emily exhaled a long slow breath, relieved at the opportunity for a break in their serious conversation. "Oh, that's the signal," she said as she began climbing down from the ladder. "Hey, Gussie-pup, you need to go outside?"

Gus came over to her, tail wagging, and whined again.

"All right. I'm going to take him out back — I won't be long."

Matt nodded and gave her an envious look as he applied more paint to his roller. "A well-house-trained dog is a beautiful thing."

When Emily came back inside, Matt was leaning against one of the unpainted walls in the great room drinking a Coke. He held out a cold bottle of water to her. "There's more soda in the fridge, if you'd rather have that," he said.

"No, water's great, thanks." She took a drink, then poured some of the water into a bowl beside Gus's cushion. "We're making good progress, don't you think?"

"Yeah. This wall's about finished, so we can move — Look out!"

Matt's warning came too late. As Emily walked backward, looking upward to see to the top of their newly painted wall, her heel caught on the base of the ladder. She tripped and fell, landing on her rear in Matt's half-full tray of paint.

"Oh my God," she said as she realized what she'd done. She felt a bright, hot flush of color spreading over her face and a cool, unpleasant wetness seeping through the seat of her overalls.

"Are you okay? Here," he said, extending his hand. She allowed him to help her up and then looked down at the tray, which was nearly empty. The paint that hadn't coated her butt had sloshed out onto the tarp beneath the tray.

"I cannot believe I just did that," she said, turning to try to see the damage. "So much for these overalls." It was impossible to see without a mirror, but she was painfully

aware that her whole ass was beautifully accentuated in "antique eggshell."

"Do you have something else that you can
put on?" Matt asked.

Emily sighed. "Not here. I'd run home for
a change of something, but I don't even
have a plastic bag I could sit on in the car.
Besides, there's so much paint . . ." She
twisted around enough to be able to see
thick off-white rivulets running down the
back of her legs. "I don't dare step off this
tarp, or I'll get it all over the floor."

"What about putting the tarp, or one of
the other ones that doesn't have too much
paint, around yourself?"

Emily looked down at the floor coverings
and shook her head. "They're too big. I
don't think I could drive wrapped up on
one of those."

"Well, I could drive you . . . Wait, I might
have something in my car that you could
wear. Let me go check." Matt bounded out
of the room.

She crossed her arms, trying to quell her
embarrassment and frustration. She had
always been independent and self-sufficient.
Being able to take care of herself was a
source of pride, something that heavily
influenced her sense of self-worth. After
years of working in a male-dominated trade

and having to repeatedly prove herself, she took pains to ensure that she would never appear incompetent in her skills or be forced to be reliant on a man. To her, being a damsel in distress meant that she was weak and inferior, but here she was, having to rely on Matt a second time to help her out of a bind.

Of course, the damsel-in-distress situation in which she now found herself was unique. Frustrating, but unique. And even a tiny bit funny.

After a few minutes, Matt came back into the great room holding a wadded pair of black sweatpants. "These have been in my trunk for a while, and I don't think they're all that clean," he said, cringing a little. "But you could slip them on long enough to go home and put on something else."

"Thanks," Emily said. "They're better than nothing, or what I'm currently wearing. Turn around for a sec, would you?"

When Matt's back was facing her, she unhooked and stepped out of the overalls and quickly pulled on the sweats. The pants were too big, but she was able to cinch them snugly around her waist.

"Not bad," Matt said when he saw how she looked.

"Could be worse," Emily agreed. "Er, it

was worse. I'll just run home for a minute and change. Wouldn't hurt to have a change of clothes and a few plastic bags up here, too."

"You'll need one to put those in," Matt said, motioning to the heap of her overalls. "I'll just stay here and get a start on the next wall. Gus'll keep me company, won't you, boy?"

From his cushion, Gus raised his head and gave an agreeable *woof*. His tail started thumping against the wall, and before Emily knew it, her loyal canine companion was sitting down next to Matt, leaning against his leg, and staring up at him with an adoring, tongue-baring doggie smile.

Matt gaped at Gus before starting to rub the dog's ears. "I swear, it's like he knew exactly what I just said."

"No doubt about it."

"You really think they can understand complex speech?" Matt shook his head. "We always had dogs growing up. They stayed outside in their doghouses, went hunting with me and my dad, you know. They were just dogs. We loved them, and they obeyed all the basic commands, but that's pretty much it."

"All dogs have a lot of potential to learn. But some are exceptional, especially if they spend lots of time with you. They can get to the point where they can understand pretty much everything you say and sense what you need better than you can yourself."

The words were out of her mouth before Emily realized what she had said. She was still embarrassed over the paint mishap and surprised that Gus seemed to be developing an interspecies bromance with Matt. But maybe, that was just it. Maybe her pup was trying to tell her something that no one else could, in a way that she couldn't help but understand.

CHAPTER 22

Tuesday, May 1, 1934

"Why would the police come here?" his grandmother hissed. "Michael, can you think of any reason? Or anything you should tell us?"

"No, Grandma. Unless someone saw me with the deer. It's the off-season." His heart was thundering so loudly that he could barely articulate his reply. Quickly, he grabbed his game bag holding the deer's heart and liver from the kitchen counter and shoved it into one of the cupboards. *Surely,* he thought, *in times like these, they wouldn't really arrest someone for trying to feed his hungry family, would they?*

His grandmother nodded her approval at his actions. "You best see what they want," she said, again in a whisper.

His mother quickly pulled open the heavy door. "Hello. May I help you?" she said.

Michael saw two men on the porch, one

dressed in a three-piece suit with an overcoat and hat, the other in a regular police uniform.

"Good evening, ma'am." The more formally dressed of the two men stepped forward and tipped his hat. He opened a bi-fold wallet and flashed a badge as he did so. "I'm Detective Richard Jensen with the Burlington police. This is Officer John Kelly."

For a moment, no one spoke. Michael's hand, resting on the back of a kitchen chair, tightened around the wood until his knuckles were white. The officer wearing the uniform was the same one who had stopped by the vault and spoken to his uncle four nights earlier.

Michael hadn't said a word to anyone about what he and his uncle had done, but he was frantic with worry. His thoughts returned to the officer who had stopped by the vault. He was almost certain Officer Kelly hadn't seen his face that night — he'd been careful to keep his back to the door of the vault. But perhaps the officer had suspected something even after leaving. Or maybe someone else had seen him and his uncle and reported them. *They're here because we hid the hobo in someone else's grave,* he thought.

"How do you do?" his mother asked calmly. "What brings you by this evening?"

"We're looking for a Mrs. Elizabeth O'Brien," the detective said. "Is there someone here by that name?"

His mother turned to make eye contact with his grandmother, who rose from her seat at the table. "I'm Elizabeth O'Brien," she said.

"May we come in?" the detective asked, and his mother nodded and stepped backward as the two men entered the house. "Mrs. O'Brien, I'm investigating an armed robbery that took place in Burlington last month. Bryson D. Woods, one of the city's most prominent businessmen, was robbed at knifepoint outside his home by an unknown assailant. Whoever it was made off with his wallet and a gold pocket watch that had been a gift from his father."

"That's terrible," his mother said as she came to stand by his grandmother's side, "but why on earth would this have anything to do with our Lizzie?"

"That's what we're hoping to find out, ma'am. You see, the watch that was stolen from Mr. Woods was located in the loan office in Burlington yesterday. The proprietor, Mr. Borisov, provided paperwork showing that he'd purchased the watch for twenty dollars from a Mrs. Elizabeth O'Brien, along with this address. So, you see, Mrs. O'Brien," he said, turning again to his grandmother, "we need to verify that you did indeed sell the watch, and also to understand how it came to be in your possession."

Michael stared at his grandmother. She was looking from Anna's surprised face to the two policemen, working her jaw slowly from side to side.

"I did sell the watch at Mr. Borisov's shop," she said evenly. "I found it lying alongside the road, a few feet from our mailbox. I knew it didn't belong to any of our neighbors, since none of us that live out here have money enough to buy a watch like that. For folks like us, the money's more valuable than the watch. My daughter-in-law here is expecting a child in the fall and was recently in the hospital. We needed money to pay the bill, and selling the watch seemed to be the easiest way to get it."

The detective was jotting down notes on a small pad as his grandmother spoke. When she mentioned his mother's condition, he saw the detective's eyes shift ever so slightly as his line of sight swept over his mother's abdomen. "Are you Mrs. O'Brien as well?" the detective asked Anna.

"Yes, I'm Anna O'Brien."

"Were you aware that the elder Mrs. O'Brien had found or sold the watch?"

"I . . . I knew that she'd found it," his mother stammered. "But I had no idea she'd sold it. I was quite ill at the time."

The detective nodded and made further notes on his paper. "And just to confirm, neither of you ladies saw anyone drop the watch?"

"No," his mother replied as his grandmother shook her head. "But being close to the road and the railroad tracks, we've had our share of wanderers passing by the place."

Michael saw his grandmother's posture stiffen slightly at his mother's answer, and he realized immediately that she'd said more than she should have.

"Is that so?" The detective reached inside his overcoat and removed a folded piece of paper, which he unfolded and held out to them. "This is a sketch of Mr. Wood's assailant. It was nearly dark when he was robbed, so he didn't get a very good look at the man. This is the best our sketch artist was able to do. Have either of you seen someone who looks like this?"

Michael's mother and grandmother leaned forward together to look at the image on the paper. "I don't recognize him," his grandmother said.

His mother took a moment longer to study the picture, bringing her hand up to touch her neck as she did. "I'm sorry. I've never seen this person before," she said.

"Rick, let the boy take a look," Officer Kelly suddenly said, and Michael started.

His grandmother took the drawing and passed it to him. For being based on a description limited by darkness, the image was remarkably accurate, and Michael's brow furrowed as he studied the grizzled beard, the large nose and deep creases in the face, and especially the cruel, beady eyes.

"No, sir," Michael said. "I don't know this man." He gave the drawing back to the detective.

Officer Kelly stared at him for a few moments, and Michael tried his best to keep a calm, neutral expression until the officer looked away.

Detective Jensen turned to his grandmother. "Are you aware, Mrs. O'Brien, that under the law, the money you received from Mr. Borisov should be returned to him, owing to the fact that the watch you sold him was stolen property?"

"I was not aware of that," his grandmother

said. "I'm not a thief. I'd give him his money back, if I had it, but as I told you, we no longer have it. We used it to pay my daughter-in-law's hospital bill."

Detective Jensen let out a long sigh. "I guess this is all we can do. We'll be in touch with Mr. Borisov, and we'll explain the situation. It'll be up to him whether he wants to take any further action." He glanced at Officer Kelly as he made a final note on his pad and then slipped it back in the pocket inside his overcoat. "It looks like our criminal made haste to clear the city and then jump a train after the robbery. Must've dropped the watch where Mrs. O'Brien found it. It's lucky for Mr. Woods, though. He was delighted when we recovered the watch. It was a gift from his father and worth far more to him in sentiment than its weight in gold. I'll be including your statements in my report," he continued, looking at each of them in turn, "but I suspect the matter will soon be closed. Thank you for your time."

"Of course," his mother said. "I'm happy we could provide the information you wanted."

Detective Jensen tipped his hat. "Good evening," he said, and the two men left the porch.

After the door had been closed and the police car had pulled out of their driveway, the three of them sank into chairs around the table.

"That was unpleasant," his grandmother said. She was leaning forward with one elbow on the table and her forehead in her hand.

"Thank goodness they're gone," his mother said. "Lizzie, why did you sell the watch? And why didn't you tell me you did it?"

"It was just like I said to the detective," she said. "You were sick, and we didn't have nearly enough to pay the bill. I didn't want to worry you about it. You had enough going on."

"Just the same, don't I deserve to know these things?" His mother put a trembling hand over her mouth and squeezed her eyes shut.

"Mother, are you all right?"

She nodded and moved her hand to wipe a few tears that had escaped her eyes. "I'm sorry, Lizzie. I know you were trying to do what you felt was right. It was just so upsetting, seeing him again in that drawing."

"It *was* a good drawing," his grandmother said. "Something about the expression was — well, it was —"

"Chilling," his mother finished for her. "Like he was right here again, leering at me."

"I pray that was the last we ever have to hear of him."

Michael remained silent, but he nodded in agreement with his grandmother. The secret of the watch was out, and its weight had been lifted from his shoulders. The hobo's body seemed to be safely hidden in the last place anyone would think to look, and if the police didn't return, the burden of carrying that secret might continue to become easier to bear. Perhaps, over time, it would disappear completely.

If they truly had put the matter of the hobo behind them, there was only the secret of his mother's silver remaining, but that was easily manageable. The well-concealed flatware in the root cellar, his mother's insurance policy, was no more than a family heirloom — a beautiful thing given out of love. It was nothing to worry about. Indeed, Michael was far more concerned about his father and brother, struggling in far-off New York City, and about his mother's health and the health of the unborn child she carried.

They had been through a great deal as a family, and he wasn't so naive as to think that they wouldn't face more hardship in the future. But they had made it so far. That fact gave him a renewed strength to see his family through, as he had promised his father, until they were all together again.

After school on Wednesday, Michael and his grandmother were hard at work in the kitchen. He'd skinned and quartered the deer, and each of them was using a sharp knife to strip every bit of meat from the bones. Had it been late in the autumn, the normal time for deer hunting, they could have kept the carcass hanging in the barn, preserved by the freezing outdoor temperatures. But now, with the outside temperatures growing warmer by the day, the meat would spoil if left outside, and only the tiny cold compartment in the refrigerator would allow them to keep any of the venison frozen. The rest would have to be canned.

"I feel as if I should be helping, too," his mother had said, standing at a distance from where they were slicing and cutting, "but I don't know whether my stomach could handle it. The raw meat smell . . ."

"Don't push it, Anna. We're making good progress here. Why don't you get some fresh air? Take a walk or maybe check the coop for eggs. The hens have been laying more now that the weather has turned. Once we're done, I'll keep out enough meat for venison stew, if you think you'll be up to fixing it for supper."

"All right. I should be able to manage that. I'll get some vegetables from the root cellar while I'm outside." She put on a jacket and went out the back door with the basket they used for egg gathering.

Michael focused on the job at hand. He was cutting the larger pieces of the deer into smaller ones, from which he then removed any large bones. His grandmother took each piece from him, checked to make sure no smaller bones or fragments were in it, and sliced it into small pieces or cubes suitable for making stew. It was an efficient partnership. He was particularly amazed by his grandmother's speed and skill in preparing the meat.

"So, Grandma, how many times have you done this, do you think? With venison, I mean?"

"Oh, I couldn't say. Hundreds, maybe. Too many times to count." A small smile played across her face. "I used to help my mother process game when my father and brothers came back from a hunt. I was the only girl in the family, you know, so it was up to my mother and me to take care of everything they brought back. And wild game was a staple for us back then, so there was a lot for us to do.

"Then I married your grandpa, and we had your father and his brothers. I didn't have a daughter to help me then, so I learned to do everything quicker. I had to, to get everything done. On a farm, the work is never-ending."

"Have you ever thought about what you might have done? If you hadn't met Grandpa, I mean?"

"I would have married someone else, I suppose. Don't know who. Once I laid eyes on your grandfather, I didn't even think about other fellows. When I was a young lady, I was expected to find a nice young man, settle down, and raise a family. And that's what I did."

"But did you ever want anything else for yourself? Like to travel? To see the country and meet new people?"

"No, I can't say that I wanted to travel. I grew up here, and I was always happy being here." She paused as she carefully removed the meat from one of the shank portions. "Other than to marry your grandfather and have a family with him, I can only think of one other thing I've ever really wanted.

"Your grandpa's family was well-off compared to mine. Not rich, mind you, but they had a prosperous farm and never went without. He gave me the most beautiful engagement ring when he proposed. He told me he ordered it special from a jewelry store in Burlington. It had a beautiful center stone, a rich red-brown garnet, surrounded by gems called opals. The opals looked like little rainbows when the light hit them. I'd never seen such a thing. It took me some time to adjust to having something so fancy."

Michael glanced down at his grandmother's left hand. She'd stopped wearing her plain gold wedding band a few months after his grandfather's death and now wore no jewelry at all. Still, in all the time he'd spent with her, he'd never seen her wear the ring she'd just described.

"Once we were married, we bought our own farm and moved here. After a few years and a few babies, the ring was too small to fit on my finger. I kept it in a little cloth pouch in my bureau. I figured someday, when we had the money, I could have it re-sized.

"Things got pretty tight for Grandpa and me for a while. We had a good herd going when our cows started getting sick. About

372

half of them died, and the ones who survived weren't producing enough milk to cover all our orders."

"What made them sick?"

"Bad feed, as best we could tell. We'd just had a new supply delivered, but once we took the cows off that feed and started them on a different batch, the ones that were alive recovered. Nearly wiped us out. Our milk production was down to a third of what it normally was, and we knew it'd be that way for at least a few years, until we could rebuild the herd. Your grandfather didn't want to, but he accepted help from his parents to make the payments on the farm until we were back up and running. It was the only time he ever took a dime from them. We had to feed a mess of growing boys, though, and replace the cows we'd lost. Even back then, cows and heifers weren't cheap.

"Your grandfather was feeling low about it, I could tell. He was proud of having his own farm, independent from his parents, and then to need them to step in . . . I hated to see him so discouraged. Weeks went by without any sort of light in his eyes, and I finally decided that I'd do what I could to help the situation. So, as much as I loved it, I sold the garnet ring he'd given me, and I used the money to buy three female calves. Gave them to him for his birthday. They were real young, and they had to grow up and have calves of their own before they'd produce milk, but they were ours, bought and paid for with our own money. I wanted to show him that we really were in it together, for better or worse."

His grandmother paused again, this time to transfer a pile of cubed meat to a large bowl. "I had to tell your grandfather where I'd gotten the money for the calves, of course, and I was honest with him. He was angry in the beginning, but eventually, he came to understand my way of thinking."

"What do you mean?" Michael asked.

"I told your grandpa that keeping a material thing, even one with sentimental value, was downright dumb if you could sell or trade it for something your family needed. I did what should have been done. A ring in a drawer, especially one that was too small for me to wear anymore, wasn't doing anyone any good. Besides, it had already served its main purpose, which was to help your grandpa show me how much he loved me, not that I needed a ring to understand that. Better to use it to invest in our family and help build our future."

"So that's why you sold the watch so

quickly."

"Yes and no. Yes, it had value that we could trade for money. But it was nothing like the ring. It had no sentimental value. All it did was remind me of that monster, the night he came in and threatened your mother, and I bloody well would've gotten rid of it one way or another because of that. Although I might not have sold it at the loan office if I'd known it was stolen."

Michael shuddered. He didn't want to allow the hobo into his thoughts in any way. "Grandma, I don't understand . . . what was the one thing that you really wanted?"

She sighed as she reached for the next chunk of meat. "I'm ashamed to admit it, but since your grandpa passed, I've wished I could see that ring again, maybe slip it onto my finger for just a moment. I suppose I was more attached to it than I cared to admit. I don't regret selling it for the calf money, mind you. I would do it again if I were in the same situation. But when I think about how loving your grandpa was . . ." Her voice wavered, and a bit of color rose into her wrinkled cheeks. "He always made me feel as beautiful as that ring. It would be nice to be able to see it one last time."

CHAPTER 23

On an afternoon two weeks after her last fitting with Pauline, Claudia stood in her closet at home, admiring her finished wedding gown. It was perfect, a sleek silk dress with just enough decoration to accent its elegance. She especially loved the bodice, which Pauline had taken in and adorned with tiny sequins and pearls, and the delicate, detachable lace train. Her shoes were tucked neatly in their box on the floor beneath the long plastic sheath covering the gown. All that remained to complete her wedding attire was a headpiece and veil, which Pauline was creating for her.

"Claudia?"

She heard Kyle's voice calling out, and she quickly shut her closet door and hurried out into the living room. "Hey. I didn't hear you come in," she said, standing on her tiptoes to kiss him. He was wearing his uniform. "Are you on your way home?"

"Yeah, just thought I'd swing by and see if you might want to have dinner with Ro and me."

"Sure! I don't have any plans. I was actually just looking at my gown."

"Oh, you picked it up already? How did it turn out?"

"It's *perfect,*" she said, clasping her hands together. "Pauline is amazing. She turned the Internet cheapie into the dress of my dreams."

"Wow. Maybe I should go take a look," Kyle said as he made to walk past her to the bedroom.

Claudia stepped in front of him and pressed her hands up against his torso. "Oh, no, mister. You're *not* seeing it until I come down the aisle."

"But you've made me so curious," Kyle said, grabbing her hands. "And since the dress is in your *bedroom . . .*"

"It's technically in my closet," Claudia said. "Besides, the bedroom is off-limits, remember? That was your idea, after all."

Kyle sighed. "I know, I know. I'm kind of regretting it now, especially since we have a few minutes alone, and there's the added bonus of being able to sneak a peek at your gown." He pulled her in for a kiss, which she didn't resist. And when he maneuvered her up against the kitchen table, she seriously considered throwing their no-sex-until-the-wedding plan out the window.

It was almost as if Kyle was reading her mind. "Maybe we should cheat a little," he said. "The bedroom is off-limits, but we don't have to go in there."

"Tempting," Claudia gasped, "but isn't Rowen expecting you home? If you didn't tell her you'd be late, she might get worried." As much as she wanted to take Kyle back to her bedroom and have her way with him, she was hell-bent on toeing the line on their agreement. She didn't want him to think she was a pushover or incapable of following through on something that was difficult . . . *extremely* difficult. With her resolve reinforced, she gently pushed him away.

"Oh, all right," he said, but his tone was good-natured. "We'll see if you're still holding out after another week or two."

"Don't worry," Claudia said. She tilted her head and gave him a provocative smile. "You have no idea what I'm capable of. Besides, it's already November. Our wedding will be here before you know it."

"I suppose," Kyle said. "Oh! Speaking of November . . ." He took another step backward and took a deep breath. "I talked to my brother today. He and Misty and my parents want to spend Thanksgiving with us."

"Oh." Although she had no desire to spend more time with Misty, Claudia genuinely liked Kevin, and Kyle's parents were absolutely lovely, the kind of in-laws she had always hoped for. "Well, that'd be okay, I guess. As long as I don't get stuck spending a lot of time with Misty one-on-one."

"That's unlikely, with all of us together," Kyle said, "but there's one more thing. They want to have Thanksgiving here."

"Here? In Mill River?"

"Yeah."

"Even if they didn't all stay with you, there's not nearly enough room for that many people to have dinner in your apartment."

"I know. That's why I kind of suggested that they'd be more comfortable staying in Rutland . . . and that we could have the dinner here, at your place." Kyle was talking fast, no doubt in response to the shell-shocked look on her face. "I mean, it'll be our place soon, and my parents wanted to see where we'd be living after the wedding."

"I've never prepared a big Thanksgiving dinner all by myself."

"I'm sure Mom would happily help out with the cooking. She's a whiz in the kitchen. I could help, too, with some of the simpler things."

Claudia took a deep breath and exhaled slowly. Now was not a time to get worked up. She truly enjoyed spending time with Kyle's brother and parents, who would probably be as excited as she about the upcoming wedding. Misty was a disaster, but being surrounded by the rest of Kyle's family might put a damper on her obnoxiousness. Although Claudia had never hosted a huge Thanksgiving meal, she was a competent cook, and with careful planning and some recipes and pointers from her own mother, there was no reason she shouldn't be able to handle it.

"Okay. Let's tell them it's a go."

"Seriously?" The relief on Kyle's face was plain. "Thank God. I was worried you'd freak out about it."

"Nope, not worth freaking out over. With a little luck, it'll be the first of many Thanksgivings we all have together, so why not think of it as a special occasion and make the best of it?"

"I love you," Kyle said, grabbing her up in a bear hug and nuzzling her face. "Thank you."

"Don't thank me yet," she said. "I've still got to roast a turkey without burning it up and resist the urge to shove Misty in the oven along with it. But I'll manage somehow."

"I know," Kyle said. "Hey, can I use your restroom?"

"You still feel the need to ask?" She laughed. "It's basically *our* bathroom now. Just don't go into the bedroom. I don't want you anywhere near my closet."

"Scout's honor," Kyle said. He left his keys and phone on the counter and left the room.

As she waited for him to return, Claudia leaned back against the sink. She was starting to think about what she would fix for Thanksgiving when a text message popped up on Kyle's phone. She had never given a second thought as to what was on Kyle's phone or who called or messaged him, but when she glanced down at the screen, she was surprised to see that the text included a photo of a familiar blond woman with a note below it:

Can't wait to see you again at Thanksgiving! xoxo Misty

In the parish house, Father O'Brien had just

started to think about what he could prepare for supper when someone knocked at the door. He wasn't expecting any visitors, but it was common for people in town to drop by with no notice. When he opened the door, though, he was surprised to see a middle-aged man wearing a white collar on his stoop.

"Father Grimaldi!"

"Hello, Michael," the younger priest said.

"My goodness, Leo, it's been a long time. Come in, come in!" He led his visitor into the living room and motioned for him to sit. "I'm curious about what brings you by. You're quite a ways from home."

"I know. I hope you'll excuse my coming without calling first," Father Grimaldi said. "I was on my way back to Burlington from a conference and thought I'd take a short detour, since it would save me a trip next week."

"Next week?" Father O'Brien asked. "You were planning on coming down to see me?"

"Well, to be honest, I wasn't, but the vice chancellor asked me to."

Father O'Brien picked up a grim undertone in his colleague's voice and realized that this was not a social visit. Father Grimaldi had long served as part of the administrative board of the diocese of Burlington, and to have been asked by the vice chancellor to come to Mill River meant that the matter he wished to discuss was serious.

"I'm guessing this is about the article," Father O'Brien said, taking a seat in his recliner, and Father Grimaldi nodded.

The interview he had granted to *America* magazine had appeared in the current issue. A complimentary copy, containing the story and a full-color photo of him sitting in his office, had arrived in his mailbox. As he'd expected, it had prompted the usual media flurry, with the *Mill River Gazette* and the *Rutland Herald* calling to inquire about doing stories of their own. What he hadn't expected was for the media in Burlington to pick up the story, or for the diocese to react negatively to his interview, because neither of those things had happened in the past.

"There is some concern," Father Grimaldi began. "First, over the fact that your tenure here has been allowed for so long. Lots of priests would love to serve their communities for longer than they're permitted before being moved or asked to retire. The article made highly visible the facts that you've never had to start from scratch and that you've been exempted from the mandatory retirement age. Can you see how that might cause some hard feelings?"

"I suppose, although I would argue that the duration of my service here has been far more challenging than many people would believe — more difficult in many ways than moving among other parishes might have been. As for the retirement age, it's common knowledge that there's a shortage of priests and of men entering the seminary. Why is it a bad thing for me to continue to serve, even at my age, since I'm perfectly capable of doing so?"

Father Grimaldi looked carefully at him. "It may be that they . . . the administration . . . is wondering whether you are, in fact, still capable."

"Ah, I see." Father O'Brien gave a chuckle and then leaned forward with a hint of a smirk. "They sent you down here to see whether I still have all my marbles, hmm? Be honest, Leo."

The younger priest gave a heavy sigh. "I won't lie to you, Michael, but you should know I won't lie to the administration, either. You're obviously fine, at least for now, and I'll tell them that. But you have to realize that there will come a time when your position will get to be too much for you. Look, despite the attention called to your unique situation in the *America* article, the administration doesn't want or intend to remove you."

Father O'Brien squinted at his colleague. "But?"

"But . . . the board thinks it would be a good idea to assign a young priest to Mill River to work with you. To learn from you. To get to know the congregation and the other people in the community. You could show this new priest the ropes, so to speak, and when the time comes, and I pray it wouldn't happen for a good long while, he would be ready to take over for you."

Hearing Father Grimaldi's proposition nearly moved Father O'Brien to tears. At a loss for words, he swallowed hard and blinked several times.

"Think of it as something that will help the people here," Father Grimaldi continued. "If there were another priest here, someone the people knew and trusted, it would be a much easier transition for them when . . ."

Father O'Brien nodded. He hated to think about leaving his people and his town, but it was even worse to imagine them arriving at St. John's to hear Mass said by a stranger. "I don't have a choice in the matter, do I, Leo?"

"No." The younger priest's low reply was barely audible to Father O'Brien, even with his hearing aids. "At least, not with respect to someone else being assigned to help out down here. You won't be forced into retirement, though, not so long as you're physically and mentally capable of serving. You'll be the pastor, and you can keep or delegate responsibilities as you see fit. They wanted me to emphasize that. You're somewhat of a marvel to the administration and to the bishop. I think they're convinced that the good Lord Himself has wanted you here all these years, and they're not about to interfere with that now. They just want to make sure there's a transition plan in place."

"When?"

"The administration was thinking early in the New Year."

Father O'Brien closed his eyes. The faces of the people in the pews at St. John's, of his neighbors, of the other wonderful people in town, of children he had seen grow up and have children and grandchildren of their own, began to parade through his mind. How many weddings had he performed? How many funeral Masses had he said? How many confessions had he heard? How many people had he counseled, embraced, and prayed with or for? Hundreds, maybe thousands. In this one little place for nearly his entire adult life, he had been enmeshed in their humanity, doing the best he could to help the best way he knew how. If he couldn't continue to do that, there would be nothing left for him to do.

Through the swirl of faces dancing across his eyelids, one became clearer and larger than all the others. It had been several weeks since Mary's face had appeared to him so vividly in his mind's eye. Usually, he remembered her quiet voice and her distinctive appearance best when he was experiencing strong emotion of some kind, and this time was no exception. Her expression was calm and soothing. She gave a barely perceptible nod, the kind of reassuring gesture she might have offered him during one of their long conversations. It was as if she were telling him that things were fine and would be fine. He didn't have to worry.

"All right," Father O'Brien said. He opened his eyes and nodded at the younger priest. "All right."

On Monday morning, Karen awoke suddenly five minutes before her alarm clock was due to go off. She sat up in bed and smiled. She'd slept soundly for the first time in many nights, and Ben hadn't needed to wake her in time to get ready for work or to say goodbye before he left for school. She chose not to think about the fact that her thirteen-year-old son routinely got himself up and out of the house without her involvement, or what that meant with respect to the quality of her parenting.

No, today was the first in nearly two weeks that she would have entirely to herself, and she wanted it to be a good day. Having time to herself presented its own difficulties, but since she'd spoken to Father O'Brien and he'd sprung into action, a day hadn't passed without someone in the community coming by to visit or take her out or bring her dinner. It had been wonderful at first. Knowing someone was scheduled to drop in had given her something to think about and look forward to. It had helped keep her from focusing on Nick's absence and her own tenuous mental state. But now, her refrigerator was a wasteland of partially eaten casseroles, and she was starting to feel like a child designated for constant supervision. The ideas of cooking a meal from scratch or having some time to spend as she wished were newly appealing.

She swung her legs over the side of the bed and stretched. Ben was still asleep. It had been a long time since she'd worn makeup, but after she'd dressed and wrangled her hair into order, she applied a bit of blush and lipstick. The color made a huge difference.

Feeling energetic, she went into the kitchen and started pulling things out of the fridge for breakfast. She heard the muted beeping of Ben's alarm clock through the wall, followed by the sound of footsteps and water running in the bathroom. Her teenager emerged in the kitchen a short time later. "You're up?"

The surprise on his face put a damper on her mood. She tried to ignore it. "Morning," she said, holding a plate out to him. "I made you a breakfast sandwich. Scrambled eggs, ham, and cheese on wheat toast, just the way you like it."

"Thanks, Mom," Ben said. He grabbed the juice on the counter and poured himself a glass, which he chugged before taking the plate. "You put on makeup," he observed with his mouth full of the sandwich. "How come you're all dressed up? You don't go to work on Mondays. You usually don't even get up on Mondays."

"I don't know. I guess I just felt good this morning," she said. "Thought I'd spruce myself up for a change and do some shopping, maybe go see your grandpa."

"Good, that way I don't have to go."

His relief took her mood a notch lower, and she gave him a look of disapproval.

"What? I'm just being honest."

"Maybe so, but it's insensitive of you to say things like that. You haven't spent much time with your grandfather. I know you don't feel all that close to him. But try to think of how it is for me, Ben. He's my father, and I love him very much. Imagine how it would be if *your* dad were sick like your grandpa is."

She hadn't meant to bring up Nick, but once she had, she felt her mood sink again.

Ben chewed a mouthful of his sandwich with a sullen expression. "Okay, Mom, sorry."

Karen doubted that he really was sorry, but she didn't want to lose what was left of a good start to her day by pressing the issue further. "You better take what's left of that and get out to the bus stop," she told him.

"There's nothing left, see?" he said before cramming the last biggish piece of the sandwich into his mouth. "Bye, Mom. See you after school." He gathered up his backpack and coat and rushed out the front door.

She took her time with her own eggs and toast and watched the morning news while lingering over a second cup of coffee. When she picked up her purse and headed outside to her car, she ran into her neighbor, Jean Wykowski, dressed in scrubs and heading for her car as well.

"Hi, Karen," Jean called to her with a smile. "You doing all right this morning?"

"Yep. You?"

"Doing fine. Well, about as fine as going to work gets. Any word about Nick?"

"No, nothing new for a while now."

"No news is better than bad news," Jean said, and Karen nodded in agreement. "By the way, Ron and I were talking, and we wondered if you and Ben would like to join us for Thanksgiving dinner this year. We're not having any other company, so it'd be just us and the boys, but we'd love to have you both."

"Oh, I hadn't even thought of Thanksgiving, but . . . Sure, that would be really nice. Let me know what I can bring. Better yet, maybe you and I can join forces in the kitchen and make it easier on ourselves."

"That would be great! I'll call you when it gets closer to the date. We can plan out the menu and decide who will make what."

"Sounds good," Karen said. She reached down, feeling for the handle on her car door. She was desperate to get inside and shut the door. "Have a good day."

"You, too," Jean called.

Quickly, Karen slipped inside her car, buckled the seatbelt, and started the engine. Rather than pull out of the driveway, she took her phone from her purse and stared at it until well after Jean had driven away.

How can we celebrate Thanksgiving without you, without knowing where you are? she thought. *Please, please ring. Please call me and let us know they've found you and you're okay. Please.*

To her great surprise, as she sat clutching the phone in her trembling hand, it *did* ring.

The name of the caller flashed across the screen: Maple Manor Assisted Living.

Still reeling from a good shot of adrenaline, Karen answered the call.

Thirty seconds later, she peeled out of the driveway. As she gunned the engine and headed north to Rutland, the words of the nurse supervisor rang in her ears again and again.

It's your father, Mrs. Cooper. We need you to come to the facility right away.

When she arrived, she ran inside, not bothering to stop at the information desk. There was a small group of people wearing scrubs gathered inside her father's room. Some were nurses and aides whom she recognized, but a few of the faces were new.

Her father lay in bed with his eyes closed while a woman in a white coat leaned over him, a stethoscope pressed to his chest.

"I'm Karen Cooper, his daughter. What happened?"

"Mrs. Cooper." The woman with the stethoscope straightened up and extended her hand. "I'm Rebecca Martin, the physician on call. The staff paged me a little while ago because your father seemed to be having some trouble waking up. His pulse and blood pressure are very low, and while I've been here, his respiration has become irregular. Am I correct in my understanding that your father has a do-not-resuscitate order in place?"

"Yes, he does." Karen wiped at her eyes. *How can this be happening right now?* "I also hold medical power of attorney for him. Do you have any idea what might be wrong?"

"It's difficult to tell without a thorough evaluation in a hospital, especially in a patient who's uncommunicative. One of his pupils is dilated. That, as well as his abnormal breathing pattern, are often symptoms of a stroke, but I can't make any definitive diagnosis without running some tests. In a case like this, absent a DNR order, I'd normally recommend that we rush the patient to the emergency room. We can transport your father there, if you'd like, but given his instructions, our treatment options would be very limited."

"No breathing machines, no shocking his heart or life support," Karen said softly. "He was always adamant about that, especially after his Alzheimer's diagnosis."

For a moment, nobody in the room spoke, and Karen could almost feel a blanket of finality descend over them.

Dr. Martin gave a slight nod, her eyes heavy with sympathy. "If there's anyone else you'd like to call, now would be a good time."

"My brother, George, in Seattle," Karen whispered. "I have his number in my phone."

"We'll give you some privacy," one of the nurses said, stepping forward to usher several others toward the door. "We'll be right down the hall at the nurses' station if you need anything."

Once Karen was alone with her father, she dialed her brother's number, but the call went straight to voicemail. "Georgie, it's Karen. It's a little after eight-thirty my time. I'm at the center with Daddy. They called me this morning. He's not doing well, and they think he may have had a stroke, and the doctor said he might not have much time left. I think you should get a flight as soon as you can. Please call me back when you get this."

She placed her phone in her purse and pulled a chair up beside her father's bed. He lay on his back with his eyes closed. One of his hands rested on the sheet before her, and she took it gently, holding it between her own as she spoke to him. "Daddy, can you hear me? It's Karen, your daughter. I'm right here with you. Right here."

For a moment, her tear-blurred eyes could no longer maintain their focus on him. She paused, bowing her head, willing herself to hang onto some semblance of composure while she was in his presence.

The sound of his breathing seemed to confirm the prognosis at which the doctor had hinted. He would take several deep breaths, followed by increasingly shallow breathing, when his chest would rise and fall rapidly. Then there would be a period of fifteen or twenty seconds when he didn't breathe at all before the cycle repeated. As the minutes and cycles passed, his breaths seemed to grow weaker, and the periods of apnea increased in duration. She took comfort in the feel of his warm hand, large and well padded as it had always been.

"If you can hear me, Daddy, the doctor

said you might not have much time. I want you to know that I called Georgie. He's on his way here right now. And I want you to know how much I love you. Nick and I, and Ben, and George and his family. We all love you so much."

She stroked his hand with one of her thumbs and took a few seconds to breathe, to steady herself enough to say goodbye. "I've told you before, but thank you again for everything you've given me and done for me. You were the best father, Daddy. The best father I could have asked for. My protector when I was little, my friend once I was all grown-up, and even now there isn't a day that goes by when I don't think of you, or something you taught me, or something we did together in the past.

"You've been sick a long time, Daddy, but you're going to be in a better place real soon. I just don't know what I'll do without you. I'm sure Mama will be waiting for you. She's been waiting a long time to dance with you in heaven. Give her a hug for me and tell her I love her, okay? I love you, too, Daddy, so much. I'll think of you every day, I promise. Every day for the rest of my life."

CHAPTER 24

May 31, 1934

Early on a Thursday morning, Michael rose and put on one of his nicer pairs of trousers and his best shirt. Downstairs, the house was quiet, although a glass of milk and a small paper bag containing two egg sandwiches — one for breakfast and the other for lunch — had been set out for him, probably by his grandmother. His mother's bedroom door was closed, and when he looked out the window toward the barn, he could see that the heavy wooden door had been propped open, as was his grandmother's habit when she went to do the milking.

Michael smiled to himself. His grandmother knew he had special plans for today, and in addition to the pre-packed sandwiches, she had given him the rare treat of a morning off from milking duty. How wonderful it was, starting the day in a good mood and knowing Onion wouldn't have a chance to ruin it!

On the kitchen table, tucked gently between the salt and pepper shakers, was the most recent letter from his father. Michael slid the letter from the envelope and began to read it silently, even though his mother had read it aloud the previous evening.

May 21, 1934

Dear Anna, Mother, and Michael,
I read your most recent letter with great relief. I am glad to know you are doing well and that things at home are fine.

I've not much news to report since my last letter. Seamus and I are both as well as can be expected. He is still behind bars, on account of my being unable to raise the funds to make his bail, and we are both anxious for his case to proceed. The prosecutor offered a plea bargain after the arraignment, but his lawyer advised him to reject it because it would require some jail time and would keep a felony on his record. The lawyer also believes the government's case is weak on a charge of attempted murder and that Seamus will be found not guilty at trial, if the case proceeds that far. It is possible that the charges will be dismissed or reduced once the prosecutor understands that Seamus has capable representation and is willing to go to trial. Unfortunately, his trial date has been set for the sixth of August, so we have another two months to wait.

I've been working long hours to be able to pay the lawyer's fees and have enough left to live on. One good thing is that I've applied to join the ironworkers. If I'm accepted, I would be working on the actual bridge structure, and for higher wages. It's difficult work, but I'd welcome it, as it would mean I'd have money to send home to you. I worry about all of you, and I'm ashamed that I've not been able to provide what I should for you . . .

Michael folded the letter back into the envelope, guzzled the milk, and grabbed the bag of sandwiches before leaving the house. He would eat his breakfast on his walk into Burlington.

The past month had flown by. His mother had spent another three days in the hospital during a relapse of her sickness, which had added another eighteen dollars to the hospital bill. Finally, though, her health seemed to have stabilized. She still struggled daily with feeling nauseated, and she ate and drank less than what she should, but she rarely got sick. Her expectant condition was starting to become visible — a slight rounding of her belly.

Although Michael dared not speak of it, he wondered what might have happened had recent medical advances been available to his mother in the past. It was amazing to think that doctors could now nourish and hydrate a person by inserting fluids into the body through a needle. It was expensive, yes, but the treatment had kept his mother from losing the baby she carried, he was sure. It might have saved her life as well.

If only intravenous therapy had existed five, seven, ten years ago, there might have been a houseful of siblings at the farm instead of a somber ring of stones in the pasture.

Not another stone this time, he thought. True, his mother wasn't due to give birth until early December. Months stretched out before them as a separated family, months in which his father might be unable to send them money, in which they would have to make do on their own. Michael was determined to do his part, to see his family through. And when his father returned home for the holidays, hopefully with Seamus, he would arrive to the joyous discovery of a new baby.

Michael walked quickly up the driveway to the main road. Somewhere in Burlington, or along the way, he would find a job. There had to be someplace that needed help for the summer. He didn't care what the job was — he was willing to work hard for whatever wages he could get. Anything was better than nothing.

He made it to the edge of the city after walking for an hour, and several minutes later, he stood at the intersection of Main Street and Church Street with the city's business district stretched out before him. There were shops and restaurants of all kinds, punctuated by dark storefronts of businesses that had failed. Those that had managed to survive the poor economy were just opening for the day. Store owners and employees were out sweeping the sidewalks in the mild fresh air. Ignoring a bout of nervousness, Michael focused on the corner coffee shop nearest him.

He removed his cap and stepped inside. There were some customers already seated inside, and the air was scented with coffee and bacon and warm maple syrup. Even after the egg sandwich, his stomach rumbled.

A waitress caught his eye. "Sit anywhere you'd like, hon. We've got plenty of empty tables."

He nodded and approached a small table, although he didn't sit down. "Ma'am, I'm not here for breakfast," he said in low voice when she came over. "I'm actually looking for a job."

"A job?" A few of the patrons in the restaurant glanced over at her shrill exclamation, and Michael felt a flush of heat color his face. "Sorry, hon, there's nothing here. It's just Luke and Larry behind the counter and me waiting tables. It's a wonder we're still here and getting paid, with business the way it's been. Good luck finding something, though."

Michael nodded and quickly left. He didn't know what he could do in a restaurant, anyway, except perhaps clear tables, and there was a whole street of places to try.

For the rest of the morning, he made his way slowly up the street, stopping into each business to make inquiries. He visited shoe stores and department stores and more restaurants and cafés. There was a store that sold radios and phonographs. Another one sold refrigerators, the sleek new white ones made by General Electric.

None of those places was hiring. At one o'clock, disappointed, hungry, and with feet aching from being squeezed into shoes that were too small and heavily worn, he sat down on the stoop of a shuttered business and ate his second egg sandwich.

Maybe Grandma and Mother were right, he thought. *Maybe it's still impossible for anyone to find a job around here.*

But he had to find *something.* His family was depending on him.

He stood up, stretched, and started out again. His hopes soared when he entered the grocery store his mother frequented and learned from one of the clerks that the store sometimes hired summer help.

"Let me get the manager so you can speak with him," the young man told him before leaving to fetch his boss.

Michael waited anxiously at the front of the store. There was plenty to be done in such a large, busy place. Deliveries needed to be unloaded and stocked. Groceries needed to be checked out and bagged for customers. The whole store itself needed to be kept clean and tidy. And, it would be a pleasant place to work.

"Here's Mr. Baird," the clerk said breathlessly as he approached. The older man following him had a kindly face and salt-and-pepper hair.

"Hello, sir," Michael said, extending a hand. "My name is Michael O'Brien, and I'm looking for a job for the summer."

"I expect you are — you and the whole city." The manager sighed as he shook his hand. "You look like a nice kid. Do you live here in Burlington?"

"Just outside the city a few miles, sir."

"Um-hmm. And how old are you, Michael?"

"Fifteen, sir."

Mr. Baird nodded. "I'm sorry to have to tell you, but I just hired a couple of kids, and I'm afraid that's all I can afford to hire right now, even paying reduced wages. I'm happy to take your name and address, though. If I have another position come open, I'll contact you."

Michael swallowed hard and struggled to keep his disappointment in check. "Thank you, Mr. Baird. I would appreciate that very much."

"You have a good day, now, son," the manager said, and Michael went back through the front doors.

One by one, he tried the rest of the businesses on Church Street. Without any employment prospects by late afternoon, he walked down a few of the other streets in the center of the city, stopping every so often to make inquiries. His desperation increased when he realized that the businesses had starting closing for the day. He was on a side street several blocks from where he had started in the morning when he looked up and realized that he was standing in front of the loan office.

The sign above the door was unchanged, a wrought-iron frame from which three gold balls were suspended, and the display of gleaming gold jewelry and watches in the front window was much the same. The other items in the window were different. A violin and bow rested in an opened case. A silver tea set and matching tray was arranged in one corner, and a pair of sterling candlesticks stood in the other. Up above, two hunting rifles were suspended, their shiny barrels pointing at each other and nearly touching in the center of the window.

Michael reached for the door handle, but as his fingers brushed the metal, he hesitated. Even though he had just turned fifteen, his mother might try to tan his hide if she learned that he had gone inside the loan office. Did he dare do it? And if he did, would it be to ask about a job or to satisfy his own curiosity?

He glanced nervously over his shoulder, but the sidewalk in front of the shop was empty in both directions. Without answering the last question, he pulled open the door and went inside.

It was much darker inside the loan office, and while his eyes adjusted to the change in light, his sense of smell enjoyed a moment of dominance. The air was heavy and musty and tinged with scents of damp cloth and grease and gunpowder. There was another odor, too, a distinct pungency emanating from a counter positioned farther in, against the wall. A woman was finishing up her business there. As she turned and came toward the door, the man behind the counter, who was undoubtedly the source of the odor, came into view.

Mr. Borisov fit his mother's description exactly. Light brown hair, curly and greasy, was slicked back from a high, shiny forehead. Beads of sweat clustered along the sides of the forehead and lined up along the brow, then ran in shimmering rivulets downward from each graying temple. A pair of gold-framed spectacles rested halfway down the man's nose and appeared ready to slide all the way down onto his bushy mustache. He wore a white shirt with the sleeves rolled up to his elbows, simultaneously exposing corpulent forearms while encasing doughlike rolls along his torso.

Michael quickly removed his cap and took another step forward. Mr. Borisov was writing in a ledger of some sort and gave him a cursory glance. "Yes?"

"Good afternoon, sir," he began. "Are you Mr. Borisov?"

"Yes. What can I do for you?"

"My name is Michael O'Brien. I've finished school for the summer, and I'm looking for a job. I was wondering if you had any positions available."

Mr. Borisov laid down his pen and stared at him. After Michael had finished speaking, there were a few seconds of silence before the man's laugh filled the room. "Job? You want job?"

"Yes, sir."

The man laughed again. "I haf people come in for many things. Sometimes loan, sometimes to sell something. Sometimes to ask for more time to pay loan. But never haf I had someone come here and ask for job. Tell me, what do you think you could do here? What kind of job do you want?"

Michael took a deep breath and quickly looked around. Behind the counter and on either side as high as the ceiling, the wall

407

was covered by small cubicles. The contents of many were visible — clothing, shoes, hand tools, small firearms, and any other common possession one might venture to use as collateral for a loan. The remaining cubicles contained items wrapped in brown paper, for privacy, he assumed. Larger shelves and display racks picked up where the cubicles left off, to accommodate larger items. There was a section of long-handled tools: shovels, rakes, axes. Another portion of the wall was covered in paintings of various sizes and styles. The shelves held everything from kitchenware and small appliances to mantel clocks and sets of books with elegant gilded spines.

"I could keep the place neat. Maybe help with the displays in the front window. Or whatever else you might need help doing. I learn quickly, and I'm a hard worker."

Mr. Borisov squinted at him and then shrugged. "Maybe you are hard worker. You look like nice boy. Skinny but clean. Speak good English. Why you want to work here, Michael O'Brien? Why not shoe store or grocery?"

"I've made inquires, sir, but they have no positions open. I asked at almost every place up Church Street and then some."

"This not good place for nice boy to work.

Besides, I always haf problems with O'Briens." The owner's tone was final and dismissive. Michael felt a surge of panic as Mr. Borisov took up his pen and bent once more over his ledger.

"Please, sir. Please, I've got to find a job. My father's gone away, and my mother's been deathly sick. We need cash wages to pay her hospital bills. She's expecting a baby, but it's just me and my grandmother trying to take care of her."

Mr. Borisov stopped writing but kept his gaze fixed downward. He remained this way for a good minute, and Michael scarcely breathed. Finally, he looked up with a stern expression. "All right. I gif you job as clerk. I teach what you need to know. Start Monday, nine o'clock to five o'clock closing time. I pay you only child wage, ten cents an hour. We try for two weeks. If you learn what I teach and work hard, we keep going. If not, you lose job. Do we haf deal?"

"Yes! Yes, sir, we do. Thank you," Michael said. He extended his hand for Mr. Borisov to shake, and the smell surrounding the counter suddenly wasn't quite as pungent as it had been. "I'll be here on Monday morning at nine sharp."

"Very good, Michael O'Brien. Very good. See you Monday."

As Michael stepped outside the store, he was nearly overcome with joy and gratitude. He sucked in the fresh air as he walked briskly down the street. The ache in his feet notwithstanding, he almost gave in to the urge to kick up his heels. *Against impossible odds, he had found a job.* If Mr. Borisov kept him on past the initial trial period, he would be able to earn more than forty dollars by the end of the summer — enough, when combined with what they already had and what they could get from selling Onion's new heifer calf, to pay the remainder of his mother's hospital bill, the electric bill, and the property taxes that would be due on the farm.

Once his initial euphoria subsided, he began to wonder whether he'd accepted Mr. Borisov's offer too quickly. Mainly, he wasn't sure how he could convince his mother to let him work in the loan office. She would never approve, he was sure, and he was afraid to tell her. After his inquiries, he felt reasonably sure that he wouldn't find another position in the city, but he hadn't tried finding a job at any of the farms outside of Burlington. It was possible he could find a summer job picking produce or as a farmhand. Though he had no way of knowing what sort of wages he might be offered, it would be respectable work. Did he really want to forgo those possibilities to work in the loan office?

He could tell his mother and grandmother about a job on a farm. But there was no guarantee he could find a farm job, and if he did, it would mean less money. Plus, there might be no possibility of farmwork once the summer growing season was over. What if his father were unable to send money even when autumn came? If he worked in the loan office, he might be able to leave school temporarily and continue working through the fall until his father straightened things out with Seamus or else came home.

Michael hurried along the street, knowing that his mother and grandmother would be expecting him home. As he fell into the rhythm of fast walking, he came to the solemn realization that if he wanted to ensure the safety and security of his family, he had no choice but to work for Mr. Borisov. That meant that he would have to hide the truth about where he'd be working — this new secret of his own — even if it meant being purposefully dishonest. It was especially important that his mother not find out, because she would be terribly upset, and that was the last thing she needed in her condition.

He arrived back at the farm just as the sun was nearly to the horizon. The Colchester parish sedan was parked in front, and he quickened his step, wondering why his uncle had come. *Has something happened to Mother? Has someone discovered the secret in the cemetery?*

In the house, his mother was seated at the kitchen table, holding a handkerchief. Her face was moist with tears. His uncle sat with her, clasping her hand, and they both turned when they heard him come through the door.

"Mother? Is everything all right?"

"It's Lizzie," his mother choked. "She died this morning. When she didn't come inside by noon, I went to the barn, looking for her. I've already called your father, and he's on his way home."

CHAPTER 25

On the Tuesday evening the week before Thanksgiving, Emily stood in the great room of the marble mansion. She stretched her back and yawned as she looked up and around at what she had accomplished.

The walls were freshly painted and bright, and the smooth wood floors gleamed with new stain and varnish. The trim and woodwork been painted or refinished as needed. Emily smiled as she approached the staircase. It had been painstaking work, stripping the stain from the beautiful handrail before sanding and refinishing it, but it looked brand-new.

The transformation extended to the rest of the house, down to the way the house smelled. The musty, stale air that had greeted her on her first visit to the marble mansion was gone, replaced by the scents of fresh paint and lumber and the leaves that had begun to rain down on the house and in the yard.

The bathrooms had been updated with new fixtures and mirrors, except the enormous cast-iron tub in the owner's suite. Ruth had asked her not to replace it because she loved antique claw-footed tubs, and Emily had been happy to oblige, since she would've had to knock out a wall to remove the behemoth.

The kitchen was now a fully modernized workplace for Ruth, complete with a professional stove, dual ovens, and quartz countertops. Emily had reconfigured the cabinets to allow room for a commercial refrigerator and freezer, as well as a long length of counter space that could be used as a coffee and breakfast buffet for guests. She had cut a second door in a kitchen wall, which led conveniently into the dining room.

Most of the heavy lifting in giving the mansion a makeover was finished. She would begin to tackle the smaller items on her list in the morning, but right now, all she wanted to do was go home and collapse.

Emily tidied up the corner of the great room where she kept her toolbox and her other belongings while she was working. There were a few used plastic paint trays in the corner, and she smiled as she gathered them up to throw away. The day she'd fallen into one of those trays had been a turning point of sorts. Learning about Matt's experience in the military had been eye-opening, and he'd handled her awkward mishap like a true gentleman when he could have made her feel even more foolish. In the few weeks that had passed since the paint incident, he hadn't made as much as a single joke or snide comment, which had further tipped the scales in his favor. Plus, he'd continued to show up to help her at the mansion on his days off.

It was hard to admit it, but Matt's volunteering days of his time to help her had been wearing down her own walls, the ones she kept close around her heart. She hadn't truly opened her heart to someone since Andy had been killed. Neither of her two serious relationships after that had worked out. She knew now that she hadn't been emotionally ready, but it was also true that neither of her post-Andy boyfriends had been anything like the wonderful man who had been ripped so suddenly from her life.

Matt, though, was turning out to be different. She'd forgiven his first attempt to get to know her as an epic fail at trying to be cute and clever. Throughout the hours and days they'd spent together in the mansion, she'd begun to feel more and more drawn to him. Of course, physically, he was extremely handsome. He also had the same quiet confidence and intelligence that Andy had exuded and that she found so attractive. She'd been surprised to discover that Matt had a goofball sense of humor, too.

On the third day he'd shown up to help her, she'd gone to use the restroom, leaving Matt and Gus alone in the bedroom they'd been painting. On her way back to the room, she'd heard someone singing in a strange voice, one that sounded like a higher-pitched version of Yoda from *Star Wars*. She'd tiptoed to the doorway and peeked in to see Matt holding up his index finger, bending it in time to his singing as if it were a little person. Gus was sitting on his dog bed, staring up at Matt with his ears pricked and his head cocked to one side. The tune was from "That Doggie in the Window," but Matt had altered the lyrics:

Who left that poor Gussie in the window?
The pup who's infested with fleas?
I know why that Gussie's in the window,
'Cause doggie farts smell worse than
    cheese.

Emily had clasped a hand over her mouth

to keep her laughter from giving her away. After Matt had sung the verse one more time, he made a loud raspberry, perhaps to further illustrate the last line in the song. Gus bounded forward with his tail wagging and gave a huge *WOOF.*

"You like that, boy? Huh? You wanna sing with me?" Matt reached down to rumple the dog's ears as she stepped into the room.

"You know, that wasn't bad. You might have a future as a pop star if the cop gig doesn't work out."

The look on Matt's face had been pure mortification and absolutely priceless. "Oh my God, you heard that?" He shook his head as a deep pink hue spread up his cheeks. "That was just something I made up while I was messing with Ruby. You know, she's definitely part husky because she sings with me when I, uh —"

"— serenade her?"

"Yeah." He grinned as the fuchsia creeping up his face made it all the way to his hairline.

It was at that moment that Emily had felt another shift. It was as if a long-frozen wall of ice had cracked, revealing an opening to her soul, and Matt's silly antics with Gus rushed right through it.

The feeling terrified her.

What she really wished for was a talk with her mother, the kind they used to have when they'd sit and laugh and discuss everything. Her mother's advice was nearly always spot-on, but they hadn't connected like that in months, not since her mother faked her own death in a crazy, last-ditch attempt to get her daughters back on speaking terms. Emily had forgiven her for the stunt, but she hadn't forgotten it, and she still didn't feel enough time had passed since the incident to resume their mother-daughter chats.

Eager to shower and crawl into bed, Emily went home. Once she was clean and Gus was back inside from his pre-bedtime trip into the yard, she slid under her covers and sank onto her pillow. The briefcase from the mansion sat on her nightstand, but she was too tired to read any of the letters tonight. She didn't want to think anymore about Matt, either, since her emotions were entirely unsettled. As she closed her eyes and began to drift off, she hoped only that somehow things would work out for the best.

When she arrived at the marble mansion the next morning, Matt was sitting outside the back door with a disposable cup from the bakery in each hand.

"You're here early," she said as she got

out of the car and opened the door for Gus to do the same. She also took a bag from the backseat containing the sweatpants — now freshly laundered — that Matt had loaned her after the paint mishap.

"So are you. I brought you a green tea from the bakery." He held one of the cups out to her, and the steam emanating from the small drinking hole in the lid curled up into the chilly morning air. "Mornings are getting pretty cold."

"Yeah. It won't be long before we're buried in snow. Thanks for this," she said as she took the cup. Gus went up to Matt and whined for attention as she pulled the key to the door from her purse. "Here, let's go inside."

In the kitchen, they took off their coats and gloves. "So, what's on tap for today?" Matt asked. He took a sip from his own cup.

"Well, I need to install a support for a flat-screen TV on a wall in each bedroom. While I do that, I thought maybe you could put in the new locks I got for the doors."

"Sure. Locks are my specialty," Matt said with a smile. "You have a drill here, right?"

"Yes, in the toolbox. I'll need to use it, too. Here, I'll put your stuff with mine." She took Matt's jacket and gloves and laid them beside her own on the kitchen counter.

"I've got deliveries of furniture starting right after Thanksgiving, so there's not too much time left to finish up —" She turned around in midsentence and nearly ran into Matt, who had stepped closer to the counter while she had her back turned. "Whoa, I'm sorry. I almost beaned you."

She had never been that close to him, and what air remained between them felt electrically charged. She was close enough to see the flecks of gold in his brown eyes and the day-old stubble around his mouth, to smell toothpaste and freshly scrubbed skin combined with the scent of the coffee he held. It was almost as if time stopped for a few seconds as her mind went completely blank.

Get ahold of yourself, she thought. *You have work to do.*

Emily got Gus settled on his dog bed, grabbed her toolbox, and headed for the stairs. Wordlessly, Matt took the heavy toolbox from her before they went up. She opened her mouth to protest.

"Don't you even," he said before she could get a word out. "I know you're usually very capable of lugging this around, but you almost bashed into me down there. I'm not sure you're fully awake yet, so I'll get it for you this one time. No telling what damage you might do with a large metal object." He shot a cocky grin over his shoulder as he bolted up the stairs with her tools.

"Hey!" She ran after him, taking the stairs two at a time, but she couldn't catch him before he'd reached the master suite and set down the box.

They worked methodically most of the morning, she using a stud finder and tape measure to insert supports for the televisions and he swapping out the old doorknobs for new ones with dead-bolt locks and adding chain door guards. They shared the drill back and forth as they needed it.

"Can I use the drill for a minute?" Emily asked. She had just marked a small X in pencil on the wall where she needed to place one of the wall supports. They were in the last of the six bedrooms that would be used by future guests.

"Yep." He passed the drill to her and returned his focus to measuring for the doorknob's new strike plate.

Emily took a few seconds to let her gaze run over the way Matt's shirt fit on his muscular torso before she wrested her attention back to the wall. Confidently, she swapped out the Phillips bit for a long bit, raised the drill, positioned the bit against the small X on the wall, and squeezed the trigger switch.

At first it felt like every other time she'd drilled a hole into a stud. The bit went easily through the drywall before encountering a harder surface. But instead of the steady, increased resistance that was typical once the bit hit wood, there was only a moment when it came up against a hard surface before it plunged forward. Even worse, a thin jet of water shot straight out of the hole into her face.

"Dammit!" she yelled. She yanked the drill away from the wall and set it down roughly. The muffled sound of rushing water could be heard coming from within the wall, and in a few seconds, it began gushing out beneath the baseboard.

Matt flinched and looked over his shoulder. "What happened?"

"I hit a water line."

"Oh, shit." Matt glanced down at the floor. "That's a *lot* of water."

"The pipe in the wall must've burst. Probably corroded from the inside." Emily was already bolting out the door, heading for the stairs. "I'm going to shut off the water. As soon as you hear me yell, go in the bathroom around the corner and turn on the sink — the cold water side, wide open.

It'll help run the water out of the pipe faster." She left before he could reply and raced downstairs, through the kitchen, and back into a small utility room. The washer and dryer were there, along with a closet where Ruth intended to keep brooms and cleaning supplies, the circuit breaker panel, and the main water shutoff valve.

"Matt, turn on the sink!" she hollered after she'd rotated the valve all the way closed. She had very little in the mansion that could absorb water, but she grabbed an old bucket from the utility room. On her way back through the kitchen, she turned on the cold water at the sink and took Matt's clean sweatpants from the counter. There was a roll of paper towels next to the clothes, and she snatched that up as well.

The water was already pooling on the floor when she reentered the bedroom. Immediately, she threw the sweatpants on the wet floor and started unrolling the paper towels.

"Sink faucet's on," Matt said as he bent to help her. "I shudder to think how much water is inside that wall."

"The wall is toast," Emily said. "I've got the kitchen faucet running downstairs to drain the pipe. Now, the most important thing is to get this water up before it soaks through to the ceiling below us. It'd be nice if I could keep the wood floor here from warping, but I think it's too saturated to avoid damage. Have you got any more clothes in your car?"

"I wish. I got embarrassed, having only dirty clothes in there to lend you, so I cleaned out my car and washed everything I had stashed in it."

"Well, we're going to need more things to sop up this water, and fast. I never should have taken my shop vac home." There was still standing water on the floor and more leaking out of the hole in the wall and the crack beneath the baseboard.

"Do you want to run and get it? Or I could go home and get towels," Matt offered, "but that might take too long —"

"Dog bed!"

Emily jumped up again, ran downstairs, and heaved a sleeping Gus off his large cushion and onto the floor. "Sorry, bud, I've gotta borrow this," she said as the dog whined and blinked. In seconds, she was back to the bedroom, where she threw the dog bed on the wet floor.

Another minute or so passed before the stream of water from the wall stopped. The flow from the sink faucet slowed to a trickle and then a fast drip before it, too, ended.

The dog bed functioned like an enormous sponge, soaking up much of the water on the hardwood. She and Matt tried to absorb the rest of it with his sweatpants. They took turns wringing them into the bucket or the bathroom sink until the floor was no longer a shallow lake.

When they finally stopped their frantic work, Emily sighed, and Matt shook his head. She was glad that Matt didn't try to say anything just then, because there wasn't a single thing he could have said to make her feel better. It was a huge setback. She would have to have the entire length of the corroded pipe replaced, dry the interior of the wall, replace and repaint the drywall that had gotten wet, and tear up and replace much of the hardwood floor.

"We need to get this wet dog bed off the floor," she said finally. "I'll throw it in the back of my car and deal with it at home. It was due for a washing, anyway." Emily tried to lift the cushion, but it was waterlogged and awkward.

"Here, let's both grab it," Matt said. Emily didn't offer any resistance when he took hold of one side and hoisted it up. Together, they carried it downstairs to the back door and out to Emily's car, where they loaded it into the rear cargo area.

"Do you want to go home and change?" Matt asked.

Emily looked down at her clothing. Everything from her work boots up to her knees was sopping wet from kneeling on the floor, and her face and the rest of her body had been thoroughly splattered by the water spraying from the punctured pipe. Matt was similarly saturated.

"Yes, but I want to take a look at the ceiling first."

She went inside to the dining room, which was directly beneath the bedroom that had flooded. The ceiling was lower there than in the great room, so she moved the ladder into the room and climbed up until she was high enough to touch it.

"Any moisture?" Matt asked as he held the ladder steady.

Emily moved her hand slowly along the ceiling, feeling for any trace of dampness and looking for any droplets of water that might have soaked through the bedroom floor. "Nope, nothing, at least not yet."

"With that much water, you'd think it would come through pretty quickly."

"Um-hmm. I don't think we're out of the woods yet. If it's dry this evening, I'll breathe a little easier."

"This is a solid old house," Matt said as

she climbed down. "Maybe the floorboards are extra-thick."

"Could be," Emily said. "Or it might be the insulation. Ruth wanted to make the place more energy-efficient, so I had a thick layer blown in between the first and second floors before the drywall crew redid the walls. That might cause some mold issues . . . I guess we'll just have to wait and see. I can't believe I hit a water line in the first place."

"You were using a stud finder. It obviously couldn't tell the difference between a stud and a pipe, so how could you have known?"

"I don't know. It was probably an old cast-iron pipe. I should have realized the wall where I was drilling separated the bedroom from the bathroom. If I'd been paying attention, I would have picked a different wall to drill."

"Maybe you need to take a little break. You're here all the time, working nonstop. It's easy to lose focus when you're tired."

"I didn't lose focus because I was tired." Emily looked Matt full in the eyes.

He took a step back and put his hands up. "If I'm distracting you, keeping you from doing your best work —"

"No, Matt, that isn't —"

"I won't come anymore if you'd rather I

not. I mean, I promised —"

"Matt!"

He stopped talking and looked at her, his face a mixture of wariness and disappointment.

"That's not it. I mean, yes, you're a distraction, but . . . a good one. You leaving is the last thing I want."

She couldn't believe she'd said what she did. For her to blatantly admit her feelings, *those feelings,* was so uncharacteristic of her. Maybe Matt was right in one respect — that the nonstop work had started to soften her self-control. She couldn't even bring herself to look at Matt. *What will he think of me?* she thought. *And am I really ready —*

She never finished the thought because Matt stepped forward and pulled her into his arms. With his face inches from hers, he hesitated only a moment, long enough for him to slip a hand behind her head, and for her to feel the warmth of his face emanating against her own, before he kissed her.

Emily didn't resist. Whether it was out of surprise or simply a feeling of relief at having a subconscious wish granted, she let him draw her closer, let herself enjoy the sensation of her body pressed against his.

Something in that sensation was vaguely

familiar. She realized it was because Matt was holding her exactly the way she liked to be held — gentle enough that she didn't feel trapped or overpowered, but firmly enough for him to convey his attraction, to show her his strength, and to make her feel secure. It was yet another way that he reminded her of Andy.

Still, Matt *wasn't* Andy. His mouth felt different, tasted different, as it moved against hers. His voice was nothing like Andy's, and his background and vocation . . . well, she never could have imagined Andy handling a firearm of any kind. Matt was an entirely different person, on the inside and the outside, and that was okay. *More than okay.* And all those times during the past several days when she'd thought about what this moment might be like, it hadn't been Andy in her fantasies. For the first time since she'd been with Andy, the person she was kissing was a person she truly *wanted* to be kissing.

"Do you know how long I've thought about doing that?" Matt asked in a low voice when they separated.

Emily touched the side of his face, slowly stroking her fingers down toward his mouth. "I think . . . maybe I've wanted you to —" She didn't know exactly what she was saying, and she didn't get a chance to finish her thought or her sentence.

For a moment, maybe longer, she lost track of time, where she was, what she had intended to do next. There were only feelings of giddiness and excitement and wanting more. She shivered, and Matt seemed to be able to read her mind. He was no longer tentative as he gently moved his mouth from hers and planted a trail of kisses along her jaw.

Emily struggled to come to her senses. There was so much work she had to get done. "Not that I want this to stop," she murmured, "but I've got that disaster to deal with upstairs."

"You mean *we've* got that disaster to deal with. I know," Matt said in her ear. "But since we've had one hell of a morning, and we've just now cleared up the matter of my presence here, will you please let me take you out for lunch? You don't have to call it a date, since we were going to get cleaned up anyway. I've got to let Ruby out of her crate for a bit, but we could go somewhere after that, just to relax for a little while, before we start in again." He kept his arms around her waist as he pulled back.

"I think a date somewhere outside this house is long overdue," she said with a wry grin. "Plus, while you deal with Ruby, I'll need to get some more tools and equipment from my place, and I have to call around and find a plumber who can help me replace the corroded pipe on short notice. I don't have the time to install a new one on my own. It might have to be run the length of the wall or longer . . . But it would be good to know the diameter of the old pipe before we leave."

Emily was already making a verbal to-do list, and she had every intention of breaking Matt's embrace to go back up to the flooded bedroom, but for some reason, she couldn't resist staying right where she was. In fact, she nestled closer and was secretly delighted when he took the hint and kissed her again.

"I thought you were going back upstairs?" Matt asked after another few minutes had passed.

"Um-hmm. I am." Still, she didn't move.

"I see. You know what I think?"

"What do you think?"

"I think you drilled that hole on purpose. You know, to make a huge mess and extend the time I'd be coming around to help you out."

She scoffed and playfully shoved his chest. "Don't flatter yourself, buddy."

"What? You're too good at what you do to

make a silly mistake like that, and it seems like you've enjoyed spending time with me. Especially just now."

Emily tried to keep a straight face, but a little smile broke through her resolve. "Well, everybody makes a silly mistake once in a while. I just picked the wrong spot to drill. And maybe I didn't think I'd like having you here in the beginning . . . but I ended up being wrong about that, too."

"I'm glad." As he released her, Matt took one of her hands, raised it to his lips, and kissed it. "Go measure the pipe, and then let's get out of here for a while. We can come back and deal with the wall later, together."

CHAPTER 26

Saturday, June 2, 1934

Again, the Colchester parish cemetery.

Across the expanse of headstones, he could see in the distance the grave in which he and his uncle had buried the hobo. Michael shuddered, even though the sunlight was intense and he could feel sweat beginning to moisten his shirt.

It *was* warm, not like the dank, earthy experience of the hobo's midnight burial. The perfect springtime leaves rustled in a gentle breeze as he and his family stood clustered around his grandmother's freshly dug grave.

It was like an odd dream, seeing his grandparents' headstone up close after such a long time, with the blank space for the year of death that would soon be engraved with 1934. It was even more surreal having his father there, standing with his mother's hand tucked in the crook of his elbow. Niall had taken the first train he could get to Vermont on Thursday night after receiving word, and he would return tomorrow — Sunday — and resume work the following day.

Throughout the earlier funeral Mass, and now, as his uncle conducted the burial prayer service, Michael couldn't rid his mind of the first glimpse he'd had of his father. He'd been gone just over three months, but his hair was thinner, grayer, and his lean build now bordered on gaunt. His mother had run out the front door at the sound of a vehicle pulling up to the house.

"Niall," she said before his long arms swallowed her to his chest. Michael watched from the doorway as they held each other, as his father pressed his hand to his mother's soft hair. They were oblivious to him, to the frigid night air, to the straining engine of Whibley's truck pulling out of the driveway.

It was only once they had come inside, after his father had greeted Michael and hugged him tightly, and after his mother had removed the heavy coat she'd quickly thrown on, that his father learned of his mother's condition.

"What was it that you wanted to tell me, Anna?" he asked, turning toward her.

"Show you," she corrected him. Slowly, facing him, she moved her hands down over her slightly protruding belly, pressing the material of her dress against it to accentuate its changed shape.

His father gasped. "You're . . . ?"

She nodded. "More than three months along."

"And you weren't . . . you didn't take ill?"

"I did, worse than before, but there are new treatments. I had to stay in the hospital for a little while, but this time I got better."

No one said anything. The silence in the room was broken only by his father's increasingly labored breathing.

"The hospital." His father shook his head, and his voice was pained. "I wouldn't have wanted you in the hospital alone. You should have sent word to me. I would have come."

"I know you would have," Anna said. She stepped forward and took one of his hands. "Please don't be upset with me. I know you would have come, but you might've lost your job, and I wasn't alone. I had Michael here with me, and Lizzie." Her voice broke as she spoke his grandmother's name. "She nursed me through the worst of the sickness. I . . . we . . . owe her so much. It's a wonder that her time didn't come until after I was through the worst of it."

"Not a wonder. It was Providence," his father said quietly. He took a step forward, reaching out with his hands to lay them tentatively on her belly. Before Michael knew it, his father had sunk to his knees. He slid his arms around his wife, drawing her closer until his cheek rested against the slight rounding of her middle.

"Oh, Niall," his mother said. She touched his hair, holding his head as tears ran down both of their faces.

Michael, too, found it impossible to maintain his composure, but his parents didn't seem to notice. As he stood against the back wall in the kitchen, he felt that his presence during their emotional intimacy was an inappropriate intrusion. Quietly, he slipped out the back door to start the evening chores.

On the evening after his grandmother's funeral, once he and his parents had returned to the farm, Michael was again in the barn when his father came in with a clean milking pail. "Your mother will have supper ready soon."

"I've got the stall cleaned out," Michael said as he came out of the feed room with a bucket of corn. "Just have the milking left to do."

"I'll give you a rest tonight," his father

said as he took up the bucket of soapy water waiting on the old table. "After I go back tomorrow, you're going to have a heavier load on your shoulders, at least for a while."

"You are going back, then? I didn't know if you would after you knew about the baby."

"I don't want to leave. But I don't have a choice. There's still no job here for me, and your brother still needs my help. I'll be back when the baby is due, though, job or no job. And I wanted to talk to you privately for a few minutes."

Michael didn't know what his father was about to say to him. He waited, remaining silent as he poured the bucket of corn into the feeding trough. Once his father had Onion positioned in the stanchion, he glanced up at Michael.

"Even more than before, I'll be relying on you, son," he said as he washed Onion's udder. "You'll be the only one here with your mother. She assures me that she's fine now, and maybe she is. Regardless of what she says — and I know how headstrong she can be — you are to call or send a wire to me without delay if her condition should take a turn for the worse. Is that clear?"

"Yes, Father."

"Good. And now that school's finished for the summer, you should look for a job

— any job, no matter how low the pay. Both of us will need to earn as much as we can, however we can."

Since learning of his grandmother's death, Michael had scarcely thought about the job he was scheduled to begin on Monday. He had assumed his father would disapprove of it, like his mother, but perhaps, based on what he'd just said, his father would have a different understanding about doing what was necessary to get by.

"I found a job already."

"Oh?" His father stopped milking and looked up at him, and Michael was encouraged.

"I went into Burlington last Thursday, before everything happened with Grandma. I walked around all day and talked to every business downtown, looking to see if they needed help. Only one of them did, but I got the job. I'm supposed to start working as a clerk on Monday."

"A clerk? That sounds like a plum job!" His father smiled. "Who offered it to you?"

Michael took a deep breath. "Mr. Borisov, at the loan office."

The smile melted from his father's face.

"I didn't expect Mother — or you — to approve," Michael said quickly. "But I asked everywhere in the city. There aren't any other jobs. Besides, you just told me that we need to earn money however we can. Mr. Borisov offered me ten cents an hour. It's not much, but won't it help?"

His father turned and resumed milking. "It's a poor wage, even in times like these," he finally said with an edge in his voice, "but it's something, and yes, it'll help. Still, you best not tell your mother, especially given her condition. Borisov robs good people of every shred of their dignity, and you'll not continue working for him any longer than is necessary, not after I'm home again. And you're not to let the job interfere with your schooling once summer's over, do you understand? I know lots of older kids have left school to work, but your mother and I agree that you'll not be one of them. We'll do whatever else it takes to get by."

"Yes, Father." So strong was the relief Michael felt at having confided his job secret that he longed to divulge the others as well, especially about the hobo, so he could seek his father's advice about how to rid himself of the guilt he carried — but he knew he couldn't. Even stronger than the need to unload the remaining secrets was the craving for his father's company. When his father was around, he felt that everything would be all right, even if there was a good chance that it wouldn't be. Michael wanted so much to be able to talk with him at leisure, to hear his opinions, to enjoy having the family engulfed by his steadfast presence. But there were only precious hours before his father returned to New York. He would savor the time, not taint it by unfurling conversations about difficult matters.

"You know, Michael, you've done a fine job these past few months. Seems like you've grown quite a bit while I've been away. I suppose doing a man's work has made you into a man."

Michael felt warmth spreading through his chest in response to the praise. "Thank you, Father. I promised you I'd take care of everything while you're away, and I aim to keep doing that."

"I know, son. I know you will."

His father stopped speaking as he focused on finishing the work at hand, so Michael crossed his arms over the walls of a stall and listened to the rhythmic spurts of milk entering the pail. After a while, Onion's head came up out of the empty trough. Michael thought of his grandmother's advice and tried to pucker his lips to whistle, but his mouth only trembled and refused to form the proper position. It was just as well. His father had already eased the full milk pail safely away from Onion's hooves, and the lump in his throat would have distorted any sound he managed to make.

Summer 1934
By the end of July, having worked for nearly two months at Mr. Borisov's loan office, Michael had learned more about the intricacies of the pawn business than he ever thought possible. His title was clerk, but he was expected to do anything and everything that Borisov didn't have time to do or didn't feel like doing. These tasks included maintaining and changing the display in the front window, polishing sterling silver items on display, sweeping the sidewalks every morning and the floor inside the shop every evening, fetching items from storage when their owners showed up to get them out of pawn, and wrapping and storing new items that Borisov took as collateral for a loan or bought outright. Michael also kept a daily tally of items that were originally accepted as collateral for a loan but whose owners had failed to repay once it had come due. Ownership of these items — the former, often cherished possessions of residents in and around Burlington — immediately transferred to Borisov.

Michael had also learned a great deal

about human desperation and the resulting hard choices it required. Never did a day pass without someone's loan coming due. If the owner of a pawned item appeared in the shop on the day the loan expired, the person might pay the amount due and take back the item. More often than not, a more unpleasant exchange took place.

Michael still cringed when he remembered the woman who had come in just before his two-week trial period had ended. Mr. Borisov had been in his usual place behind the counter, and the woman had stepped quietly forward, her hands clasped in front of her around a yellow pawn ticket.

"Mr. Borisov? I'm Martha McFadden. I brought my wedding rings and some other family jewelry to you about six months ago. This is the ticket. I've tried to put back enough to repay the loan you gave me, but seeing as how my husband still isn't working, I was wondering . . . would you have it in your heart to give us a bit more time?"

Mr. Borisov had taken the pawn ticket and flipped through his ledger until he found the entry. "One ladies' gold wedding ring. One ladies' gold pearl ring. One gold pocket watch." He was silent as he glanced over the notes for the entry. "Loan term, three months. First loan extension, two months.

442

Second loan extension, one month." He glanced up at the woman with an emotionless, almost nonchalant expression. "Sorry. Can only do two extension. Must pay loan balance today to get rings and watch."

Michael had been sweeping in the rear part of the store, but even from there, he'd been able to hear the woman's breathing become ragged as she began to plead.

"Please, Mr. Borisov. My husband doesn't know I pawned my rings or the watch. The watch is his, you know. He thinks he lost it somewhere in the house. His father gave it to him just before he died. It's the one thing he has to remember his father by. And the rings, if my husband finds out I don't have them . . . Please, I just need a little more time, just another month, to get the money together."

While the woman had been speaking, Mr. Borisov had stared down at the ledger, refusing to make eye contact with her. "Office policy is two extension, no more. I wish could help more, but I also haf bills to pay. Loan is loan. Times difficult for everyone."

At that point, the woman had started to sob and dropped to her knees before the counter. Michael had tightened his grip on the broom handle, willing himself not to stare or intervene in support of the woman.

"Please, please, Mr. Borisov, I'm begging you, I can't lose my things, I just can't. Please have mercy, Mr. Borisov. I'll bring you the money soon, I swear it. I'd give it all to you today if I could. Please . . ."

Michael didn't know how long the woman had stayed on the floor or how Mr. Borisov had managed to get her to leave the loan office. Michael had gone into the water closet at the back of the shop and stayed there until he heard nothing coming from the front of the store except the ticking of the various clocks displayed on the wall.

When he finally emerged, he took up the broom and resumed his sweeping. Mr. Borisov seemed entirely indifferent to what had just happened. He was still in his seat behind the counter, writing in the ledger. After a moment, he glanced up and held out the yellow pawn ticket left by the woman. "Find these things. Put in display two weeks. If no sell there, we save for gold buyer at end of month."

"Gold buyer?"

"Gold buyer come from Boston first Monday every month. Take what gold I haf, measure karats, give me eighty percent value in cash. He take silver, too, measure troy ounces. Also pay eighty percent for silver."

"Why only eighty percent?"

"Gold buyer haf expenses, too, and do all melting to give to government. Gold, silver only real money right now."

Michael nodded. The government had confiscated all monetary gold the year before and revalued it at thirty-five dollars per ounce. The resulting devaluation of the dollar had destroyed people's savings. It was no wonder that most people saw gold and silver as the only sure sources of value.

"So, the lady who was just in here, wanting more time on her loan . . ." Michael hesitated. He didn't want to ask the question in a way that would anger Mr. Borisov. "Do you ever give in when someone begs like that? I mean, she has a family to take care of. You can't expect her to repay a loan and let her kids go hungry."

Mr. Borisov shrugged. "I feel bad, but I haf business to run. My business help people. Give cash to people when banks say no. If I give extra extension to one person, I get hundred more, all wanting same thing, and my business lose. No more money come in. Kids go hungry every day, Michael O'Brien. Is sad but true. I haf four children at my home, and good wife, too. If I haf to choose which children hungry and which eat, my own children eat every time."

Michael had not considered that Mr. Borisov might have a family of his own. No one in town seemed to know much about him or interact with him, other than to take care of whatever unpleasant business they might have with him. It was true that there were a great many items for sale in the loan office — collateral of loans never repaid — but as the weeks passed, Michael rarely saw anyone come in to shop. Money was so scare that folks were making do with what they had or simply going without.

Fridays were Michael's favorite day. Mr. Borisov paid him four dollars in cash each Friday before he walked home. It was a joyous feeling, leaving the loan office with money in his pocket and a whole two days with nothing to do but work on the farm and spend time with his mother. Even mucking out Onion's stall was enjoyable, compared with seeing and hearing the hardship faced by Mr. Borisov's customers. And Michael was proud to give his wages to his mother, whose condition was now obvious and whose health continued to remain stable.

"I'm so proud of you, Michael," she'd told him one Friday in early August. "With this week's wages, you've earned more than thirty-five dollars since you started. You've kept food on our table, paid our bills . . .

By the end of August, we'll have the hospital bill completely evened up and maybe some left over to put back for when the baby comes."

Michael smiled as she embraced him. It was the first time he had heard his mother speak about the baby being born with utter certainty. Until this moment, he hadn't dared mention it for fear that this time would ultimately be no different than the others.

"Here, give me your hand," his mother said, and he extended it to her. She pulled it closer and pressed it, palm down, against her belly. "Keep it right there for just a minute," she whispered.

He stood and she sat still, waiting, when there was suddenly a surprisingly strong shove against his hand.

"Whoa, I felt it! That was strong!"

"I know. That was a kick. It always happens after I eat something."

Michael looked down at the table in front of her, where a plate held a half-eaten slice of bread. He couldn't help but smile again. "I'll bet he's going to be a strong baby," he said.

"Or she. Although, this one reminds me of when I was carrying you. I thought you'd kick me to death before you were born," his mother said. "And you were lots bigger than Seamus when you came out, although you've got some catching up to do now. I worry about your working so much. It might keep you from filling out as you should."

"I'm tall and thin like Father, that's all," Michael said. "But speaking of work, I've been meaning to ask you about something. I think I should speak to my boss, maybe ask him if I could stay on at part-time in the fall, at least until Father gets home."

"We'll see. Part-time might work if it doesn't affect your grades, and an education is the only way you'll do better for yourself than your father and I did. But selling shoes isn't too tiring, and the shops aren't open late."

Michael nodded. There were three shoe stores in downtown Burlington, and he'd told her he'd gotten a job in the one she liked the least.

"Radcliff's?" she'd said. "I don't care much for that store. Their prices are too high. Forelli's is better, with a better selection. But I suppose it's work, all the same." After that, his supposed place of employment wasn't a topic that came up often, though when it did, he tried to end the conversation as quickly as possible.

"I'm going to go cut some wood while it's

still light," he said.

"I'll call you when supper's ready," his mother said. "Before you get started, I wonder if you might bring me a few ripe tomatoes from the garden? It seems like I can't get enough of them these days." She rested her hand on the top of her belly, which protruded out far enough to form a little shelf.

"Yes, Mother."

He went into their vast garden, past the neat rows of carrots and chard and the hills of squash. The tomato patch loomed, its plants tied to stakes and yet still overgrown. A tangy scent hung in the air above vines heavy with tomatoes in various stages of ripening. Michael found three large globes, all a deep shade of red-orange. They were so perfectly ripe that they practically fell into his hand; he was careful to grasp them gently as he started back through the garden to the house. It was such a small, simple gesture, the picking of a few ripe fruits for his mother to eat, but it made him happy that she had asked and that he was able to do it for her.

If only everything could be so easy and honest.

CHAPTER 27

At noon on Thanksgiving Day, Claudia had already been in the kitchen for hours. A huge turkey was roasting in the oven. She had a tray of traditional stuffing and a healthier version made with quinoa ready to slide onto the top rack above the roaster. A pumpkin pie and a low-fat, sugar-free pumpkin custard, which she'd baked upon rising, were cooled on the countertop. A pot of green beans was sitting on the stove, ready to be cooked, and a large relish tray was in the refrigerator.

She sat down at the kitchen table to eat a quick cup of yogurt. There was a stitch starting to form between her shoulder blades, undoubtedly from hunching over the counter. Claudia stretched and worked through her mental checklist of things she had yet to prepare: sweet potatoes, corn, cranberry sauce, rolls, and gravy.

Also weighing on her mind was the text

message that Misty had sent to Kyle. Claudia had been ready to ask him about it before she'd decided not to, lest he think she was invading his privacy or doubting his commitment to her. It was a private message, after all, one that could have been sent as an entirely innocent expression of enthusiasm.

Then again, Misty had sent the text to Kyle's phone, which meant that she'd had to go through the trouble of getting his number somehow. And she'd written to Kyle that she couldn't wait to see "you" again — not "you and Claudia" or "you and your family."

You.

Claudia sighed and stabbed her yogurt with her spoon. She'd already let her insecurities get the better of her once with Kyle, and she believed with everything in her that he loved her completely. She didn't know what Misty was doing with her little message, or maybe messages by now, but she trusted Kyle. Unless he mentioned Misty's text to her, she needed to allow him the freedom and privacy to handle the situation as he saw fit. She also needed to pretend that nothing was bothering her when Misty showed up at the door for Thanksgiving dinner.

The sound of that door opening snapped her out of her thoughts. Kyle came into the kitchen a few moments later with Rowen in tow. "Boy, does it smell good in here!" he said as he bent to give her a kiss. "You've been busy, I see."

"Yeah, I was up early. So far, so good. I haven't started the kitchen on fire or anything."

"Impressive. My mom'll be surprised, too. I think she was expecting to pitch in with the food prep, but it looks like you'll have everything done."

"We got the crackers and cheese ball you wanted," Rowen said, holding up a plastic grocery bag. "Do you want me to arrange them on a plate for you?"

"That'd be great." Claudia stood up and took a large plate from her cupboard, which she handed to Rowen. "So, we'll have the crackers and cheese, plus a relish tray in the fridge, for people to snack on before the meal. Have you heard from your brother yet?"

"Yep. They picked up Mom and Dad and left the city around ten. They'll probably be here in a little over an hour."

"Okay. I was planning to have everything ready to eat around two, so that would be perfect."

"Finished," Rowen said, holding up the plate of cheese and crackers. "Now what do you want me to do?"

"Hmmm . . . you and your dad could set the table. I've got a new tablecloth and a dried-flower arrangement for a centerpiece — they're already sitting in there in the dining room."

"We're on it," Kyle said. "C'mon, Ro, let's give the cook some space."

Claudia turned back to the food preparation as Kyle and his daughter bustled in and out, taking plates and glasses and silverware from the kitchen. She peeled the sweet potatoes and sliced them into a casserole dish for microwaving. Next she rinsed the cranberries, placed them in a saucepan with some water and sugar, and set them on the stove to simmer. She turned on the burner beneath the green beans, then readied a pot for the corn. The stuffing would go in the oven in about thirty minutes, the rolls fifteen minutes before dinner. She would make the gravy once the turkey was out of the oven, when she could collect the drippings at the bottom of the roaster.

Kyle appeared in the kitchen just as she poured herself a glass of iced tea and sat down at the breakfast table. "Everything's set up out there," he reported.

"Where's Rowen?"

"Can't you guess?"

"Parked in front of the TV, watching the Discovery Channel?"

"Close."

"Animal Planet?"

"Yep. Hey, do you need me to do anything else?"

Claudia looked around. The pots on the stove were starting to boil, but strangely, everything was calm and under control. "Yeah, now that you mention it." She stood up, peeked around the corner to make sure Rowen was in the living room, and pulled Kyle close. "Can't you guess what else I might need?"

He answered with actions rather than words, and Claudia lost all track of time until the sharp *hiss* of a pot bubbling over on the stove startled them both.

"Whoops," she said, and reached over to reduce the heat under the pot of beans. "No harm done, it was just water."

"Good," Kyle said, bending to nuzzle the back of her neck. "You know, I could have my mom stay with Rowen tonight instead of going back to the hotel. Then I could come over here."

"Very tempting," Claudia breathed. "But we do have an agreement in place, remember?"

Kyle dropped his head and sighed. "You've got more willpower than I bargained for. I never should have suggested we hold off until the wedding."

"Only another month. Less, actually. And then we're going to have an amazing night."

Kyle chuckled as he backed away slightly. "All right, all right. You're the boss in the kitchen, anyway." He turned her around and began to massage her shoulders. "You're tense."

"I've just been bent over cooking for hours. I'm starting to get a crick in my back, right in the middle." Kyle moved his hands so that his thumbs pressed along her spine, and Claudia closed her eyes. "That's exactly where it hurts, right there. That feels awesome."

"Dad! Claudia! They're here! Grandma and Grandpa are here!" Rowen darted into the kitchen long enough to make the announcement before she ran to the front door and threw it open.

"They're early," Kyle said. "Must've been Kevin's lead foot."

Within seconds, Claudia's house was an excited mass of hugs and kisses and happy greetings. Claudia hugged Dave and Peggy, Kyle's parents, and Peggy had barely let go of her before Kevin slung his arm across her shoulders and gave her a squeeze.

Misty was the last to come in. She wore a jacket that was ridiculously light for late November in the Northeast, and her bleached-blond hair was pulled back in a messy bun. Her dark roots and dark makeup were even more pronounced than the last time Claudia had seen her. Still, she caught Misty's eye and gave her a warm smile. It was Thanksgiving, after all.

"Hi, Misty. It's so nice to see you again."

"You, too. I like your house. It's nice."

"Thank you. Hey, you can give your coat to Kyle if you want. Are you thirsty? I've got drinks — fresh iced tea, Diet Coke, orange soda, beer, juice . . ."

"Diet Coke would be good, thanks."

Claudia nodded. "Would anyone like something to drink?" she asked everyone in a louder voice.

After her guests had given her their preferences, she turned to go back into the kitchen, but Peggy intercepted her and laid a hand gently on her arm. "Now, Claudia," she said in a low voice, "Kyle tells me you've done an amazing job cooking. I thought for sure you'd be needing some help, seeing as how this is your first time fixing Thanksgiving dinner. I brought my lucky apron, you know." Claudia looked down and had to giggle when she saw that Kyle's mother really was holding a rolled-up kitchen apron.

"There are a few things left to do," she replied. "Besides, it's always nice to have company when you're cooking."

"Oh, trust me, you wouldn't want me in there with you," Misty said loudly, even though the invitation to help cook hadn't been extended to her. "Me and the kitchen don't exactly get along."

"Um, well, that's okay," Claudia said with an awkward grin. She was relieved when Kevin called to Misty to come sit with him in the living room. "I'll just get you that Diet Coke."

Once Claudia and Peggy were alone in the kitchen, Peggy sighed and rolled her eyes. "I don't know what Kevin sees in that girl. I think she has a lot of growing up to do." Her mouth pressed into a thin line, as if she were forcing herself to stop talking. "But I don't say anything to him, and I won't say anything more to you, either. I always promised my boys that I'd accept whoever they brought home, so long as they loved her — or him, if things turned out that way. The last thing they need in their relationships is a meddling mama."

Claudia smiled. "I totally hit the mother-in-law jackpot."

"Oh, that's very sweet of you to say, dear, but Kyle's the one who's hit the jackpot, and the rest of our family. You make him so happy, and I couldn't ask for a nicer daughter-in-law. Now," Peggy said as she unrolled her apron and tied it around her waist, "it's time for you to put me to work!"

With Peggy's help, the rest of Claudia's to-do list seemed to get done almost instantly. Kyle's mother took a genuine interest in Claudia's quinoa stuffing. "I'm partial to the regular dressing, but this *is* delicious," she said when Claudia gave her a sample. Once they had all the food arranged in serving dishes, Claudia went out into the living room and called everyone to the table.

Everyone ooohed and aaahed when Kyle brought out the turkey. His father offered a prayer and then a toast before the meal. "To my son and my wonderful new daughter," Dave said in his quiet, humble voice. "We're all so thrilled about your upcoming marriage. May this first home of yours be filled with happiness and the site of many family gatherings to come."

Claudia held her breath as the dishes she'd prepared were passed around and universally praised. She was especially happy that, for several minutes after everyone's plates were filled, everyone seemed to be eating too enthusiastically to talk. Everyone, that is, except Misty. From the corner of her eye, Claudia watched her pick at her food, pushing various bits to different positions and occasionally putting small bites in her mouth. Kevin noticed, too.

"You okay, sweetie?" he asked Misty. "You don't seem to be eating much."

"I am too eating. Just not as much or as fast as you."

All of a sudden, no one at the table made so much as a sound.

"Well, it *is* Thanksgiving," Kevin said awkwardly in his own defense.

"I know," Misty said. "I just don't eat much, that's all. It's real good, though, Claudia. Everything tastes good."

"You can say that again," Kevin said. "Everything is delicious. I really love this cranberry sauce. It doesn't taste like Ocean Spray."

Claudia giggled. "Thanks. And it's not. I made it from scratch with fresh cranberries."

"She's a keeper, bro," Kevin said to Kyle before he shoved another big bite in his mouth. Claudia couldn't help noticing

Kyle's smug grin and the unhappy expression that flickered across Kevin's face before the conversation veered off into football.

"Excuse me for a second," Misty said as she stood up. "I just need to use the little girls' room."

Claudia nodded and put a hand over her mouth, which was full at the moment. "It's just down the hall," she said after she swallowed quickly, pointing back over her shoulder. "Right before you get to my bedroom."

Misty nodded and disappeared.

While she was gone, Claudia leaned closer to Kevin. "I take it Misty doesn't do much cooking?"

"Nah," he said. "She mostly heats up canned things. And she can make toast."

Claudia waited a moment, expecting Kevin to laugh as if he had made a joke, but his expression remained serious and sincere. "That's it?" she finally asked. "Canned food and toast?"

"Yeah. I do most of the cooking, but that's okay. I don't mind."

Claudia smiled. Somehow, judging by Misty's long, flawlessly polished nails, she didn't think Misty was the kind of girl who would do dishes, either.

Later that evening, Claudia couldn't help but remember her conversation with Kevin as she and Kyle stood in the kitchen packing up leftover food and scraping plates after Rowen had conked out on the sofa and everyone else had left. What Kyle lacked in the cooking department, he more than made up for in cleaning up, and Claudia was especially grateful for his help tonight.

"Typical Thanksgiving," she said as he passed rinsed dishes for her to load into the dishwasher. "Hours of cooking, an hour of solid eating, and then more hours of cleanup. You know, I really appreciate all your help today."

"Are you kidding? You did pretty much everything. The turkey was perfect, and everyone liked the side dishes. My mom was really impressed, you know. And my dad doesn't usually say much, but I caught him lurking around the leftover pie, snitching spoonfuls, after we were all finished eating."

"Really? He had two pieces after dinner."

"Yeah, I know. He isn't usually big on sweets, so that should tell you something."

"It was a lot of work, but I'm glad everyone came here for Thanksgiving.

Seemed like everyone had a good time, even Misty, except for that one nasty crack she made about Kevin's eating. I felt bad for your brother."

"I did, too," Kyle said, "but there isn't anything we can do about it. Kevin would be offended if I criticized her. I think he'll come to his senses about Misty eventually, but it's something he has to do all by himself."

"Probably," Claudia agreed.

"Well, we're about done with the kitchen, I guess, so I'm going to wake Rowen. We'll probably all sleep in tomorrow morning and then go out somewhere for lunch. I can swing by and get you if you want to come along."

"Sure. I mean, I can't think about eating right now, especially more turkey. Maybe we can go someplace in Rutland and save leftovers for Saturday."

"Okay." Kyle yawned. "If I stay here much longer, Ro and I will both end up zonking over here." He got his daughter up and walking, and pecked Claudia on the mouth as they headed out the door. "Love you."

"Love you, too. See you tomorrow."

Finally alone in her house, Claudia was straightening up the pillows on the living room furniture when she spotted Kyle's phone on the end table. *If he realizes he left this here, he might come back for it tonight,* she thought. She picked up the phone, fully intending to move it to the little table in the entryway where she kept her car keys. Instead, she stared at the dark screen for a moment before swiping her finger across to illuminate the icons.

This is wrong. This is so wrong, she thought, but she touched the screen again to bring up Kyle's text messages.

A new message from Misty was on the top of the list:

Loved talking with you tonite. Was serious about my offer 4 fun b4 your wedding. Let me know. xoxo Misty

Claudia didn't know everything that Misty and Kyle had said to each other during the evening, but this text, which Kyle hadn't seen yet, made abundantly clear what Kevin's girlfriend was after. Her first instinct was to write a text back telling Misty exactly where she could go. Another option would be to delete the message, which she very nearly did. And, the fact that Kyle had said nothing to her about Misty propositioning him was really starting to upset her. But, it was Pauline's voice in her mind, plainly repeating the most recent advice, that prevented her from doing either of those things.

What you don't want to do is let somebody or something come between you two and drag you down. Trust each other, enjoy the present, and focus on your future together.

As enraged as she was, Claudia knew the seamstress's advice was sound. It had been wrong of her to go snooping in Kyle's phone. He was soon to be her husband, and she owed him more respect for his privacy. Also, as much as she hated to admit it, she could also understand why Kyle might not want to tell her about Misty's antics. He'd been the one to ask her to host his family for Thanksgiving, after all. And, she was as confident in his love for her as she was in his disgust for Kevin's girlfriend. So, as much as she wanted to yank out Misty's hair and every one of her long fingernails, she would return the phone to Kyle and trust him to get rid of the bitch.

As Claudia's guests were finishing up their meal, Thanksgiving dinner was just getting started in the Wykowski house. Karen and Ben had joined Ron and Jean and their boys. Father O'Brien was seated at the table, too — a last-minute addition about

464

which everyone seemed happy. For Karen, having the elderly priest as a guest was an extra measure of comfort that made the difficult holiday a bit easier to bear.

It was her first Thanksgiving without her father. Seeing George and his family at the funeral had been little comfort. She struggled daily with the feeling that she should be going to the facility to visit. Concern for her father's health and well-being had been a constant presence at the back of her mind for so long, she was having trouble adjusting to this new reality without him.

Weeks had passed since she'd received any news about Nick. She called his company every few days, but the representatives always had the same answer. "I'm so sorry, Mrs. Cooper" was how it always began. "We don't have any new information about your husband, but we will call you immediately if that changes." The company had strongly discouraged her suggestion that they take Nick's situation to the media for fear that, if her husband were alive, the coverage might anger whoever was holding him captive.

Not knowing what other options for help remained, she'd emailed her congressional representative and her two U.S. senators. Their staff members had responded quickly with promises that they would look into the matter, but she had yet to hear anything more from them. It was as if all of her pleas for assistance disappeared into a black hole. Only when she spoke with Father O'Brien, when his clear blue eyes looked into hers before he bowed his head to pray for Nick's safety, did she feel any measure of relief. It wasn't peace, exactly, but the feeling that someone was finally listening to her — someone who could make a difference and bring a happy ending to the nightmarish limbo in which she and Ben were stuck.

She managed to choke down some of the food on her plate, but it was difficult to do when Father O'Brien's blessing before the meal had included a request for Nick's safe return. What she truly wanted was to disappear. Her soul was tired, and her ability to be strong and maintain some semblance of hope was fading. As horrible as it was to admit, a growing part of her was convinced that she would never see Nick alive again, and she knew that learning definitively about his death wasn't something she was strong enough to survive. She was already a broken, unfixable person. Ben deserved someone better to raise him, and it hurt too much to try to go on in her current situation.

The darkness had fully overcome her again, and she could think of only one way to escape it.

"Ron, Jean, this was such a lovely dinner. Thank you so much for inviting me," Father O'Brien said as he paused at the Wykowskis' front door on his way out. "You, too, Karen. It was a joint effort, from what Jean told me."

"You're welcome any time, Father," Jean said. She handed him a large plastic food container. "It wouldn't be Thanksgiving without leftovers. There's a little bit of everything in here, enough to hold you for a few days."

"More than a few days," he said as he accepted the container and felt its weight. "I appreciate it very much." Secretly, he had a satisfying sense of accomplishment in that every one of the spoons he'd touched or used during the dinner was still safely in Jean's possession.

He stepped outside and headed toward his truck. Karen and her son came with him, on the way to their house next door. When he looked down and caught her eye, Karen managed a smile, one of only a few he'd seen from her the entire evening.

"You look like you could use some rest,"

he told her.

"Cooking that much is hard work," she replied wearily.

"Maybe it's the tryptophan in the turkey," Ben chimed in. "They say it's supposed to knock you out if you eat a lot of it."

"Probably a little of both," Karen said. "Ben, could you take these things in and stick them in the fridge? I'll be there in a few minutes."

"Sure, Mom." Ben extended a lanky arm. She handed him the two food containers that she was holding and watched him lope off toward their front door.

"He's such a good kid," Karen muttered.

"I was just thinking that very thing," Father O'Brien said. "He still does well in school?"

"Very well. He's never not made the honor roll. Even with Nick missing, he's kept his grades up. Said he knows that's what his father would expect of him, and he's right."

"He's strong, like his mother."

"He is, but I'm not, Father. I'm just existing, that's all. Existing and trying to keep hoping for the best." Karen's eyes teared up as she spoke, as if her feelings and extreme fatigue had finally caught up with her.

"That's all we can do," Father O'Brien said. "Will I see you at Mass this Sunday?"

Karen hesitated before answering, and something about the way her eyes looked when she spoke bothered him. "I plan on coming. Unless something unexpected happens, I'll be there."

"All right. You'll call me if you need anything, yes?" She nodded, and he got into his truck for the short drive back to the parish house.

At home, he put his leftovers in the fridge and lowered himself into his favorite recliner. His mind was focused on Karen and her son and how bravely they'd handled the emotional hardship of the holiday. He was increasingly worried about Karen, who had endured a lifetime of stress and sadness in the past few months. And even though Ben seemed the picture of youthful resilience, Father O'Brien knew that Karen's son was as worried and as frightened as his mother over what had happened to his father.

Michael could empathize with Ben. He'd been in much the same position, with his own father far away and his family facing numerous hardships, on the last Thanksgiving he'd spent at his grandmother's farm. It had been his last Thanksgiving at home before everything changed.

Chapter 28

Fall 1934

By mid-September, Michael's routine had changed yet again. He now rose early to help with farm chores before heading to school. After school let out at three o'clock, he gathered his books and went straight to the loan office, where he worked until closing time. Then he walked home, did more chores, ate supper, did his homework, and collapsed into bed until the whole cycle started over in the morning. It was a grueling schedule, but he was determined to do his part, especially when he saw his mother standing before the stove holding the small of her back, her feet unusually swollen.

It seemed they were all waiting — for word from his father about his brother's trial, for the happy day when he would be able to send them money again, for the new baby to be born, for the family to be reunited. On the evening of the day

Seamus's trial was supposed to start, Michael arrived home to find his mother sitting at the kitchen table, weeping.

"What's wrong?" he asked, dropping his book bag by the door. "Did you hear from Father?" He noticed a telegram on the table and experienced a sinking feeling. He had never heard of a telegram delivering good news.

"Yes," his mother said. "Just before they all went into the courtroom this morning, the prosecutor offered your brother a new plea deal. He said he'd drop the charge of attempted murder if Seamus would plead guilty to second-degree assault. It's still a felony, but a lesser one, and the prosecutor said he'd ask for only one year in prison, since your brother had no other convictions."

Michael was quiet, processing all the information. "So Seamus took the deal? He's going to prison?"

"He took it. The lawyer said he'd better, since the government's case for assault was a lot stronger, and he was liable to get more time if he went to trial on the amended charges and was found guilty. It's a terrible thing, but it could be worse. A year isn't so long. It'll free up your father from paying legal expenses so he can start helping us again. He said in the telegram that he should be able to send us something as soon as he makes the final payment to the lawyer. And it means he'll be home for the baby's birth, and for Christmas."

"He's coming home? It's for certain?" Michael asked. His father's four-day visit in June was a blur, and the firm assurance that he'd be home in December had been gradually growing softer in Michael's mind.

"Yes," his mother said. She began crying harder, shaking her head as she tried to speak. "I've never felt so sad and so happy at the same time. All my feelings are scattered and swirling because of the baby, but I'm thankful he only got a year and that the whole thing is almost over. And to know that Niall will be here with us again. Oh!"

"Shhh, take a deep breath, now, that's it." Michael wrapped her up in a hug. "Everything's going to work out. We'll keep doing what we're doing, and we'll be fine here until the baby comes."

"I know you're right, Michael. I've been crying over nothing these days," his mother said as she backed away and pulled up her apron to wipe her eyes. "And I shouldn't be sitting here when there's supper to be served. You must be starving. Let me get you a plate."

His father's telegram renewed Michael's determination. He rose extra-early the next morning and had a spring in his step throughout the day. Mr. Borisov looked at him strangely a couple of times that afternoon. Even the long walk home in the evening didn't seem as long as usual.

The months leading up to the Thanksgiving holiday passed quickly. The money from Michael's part-time hours was just enough to cover their necessities until his father could send twenty dollars in late October. Ten dollars followed a few weeks later in a letter dated November 8. The week of Thanksgiving, despite her awkward size and increased fatigue, his mother gleefully planned out an ambitious menu.

"Are you sure you're up to all that, Mother?" Michael asked, although his belly rumbled at the thought of roast goose and pumpkin pie.

"I'll manage. We haven't had much to celebrate in a long time, and now that things are looking up, we're going to do it properly, even if it's just the two of us and Frank."

The Wednesday before the holiday, Michael expected the loan office to close a bit earlier than usual, but Mr. Borisov insisted on staying open an extra half hour after closing time.

"Busy today, Michael O'Brien. Very busy," Mr. Borisov said, and before he had finished speaking, three more people entered the shop.

The only downside to the part-time schedule, working the last two hours the loan office was open, was the fact that it was when most of the desperate customers appeared to speak with Mr. Borisov. Perhaps it was because they thought it would be the slowest time of the day, when folks were on their way home and the atmosphere in the loan office might be most conducive to privacy. Unless Mr. Borisov had something specific for him to do at the front of the store, Michael stayed toward the back, away from the counter and the heartbreaking stories of hardship told there.

At ten minutes after five, the loan office had cleared out, and Michael wondered whether Mr. Borisov would change his mind and call it a day. He busied himself by tidying up the back shelves and checking the tickets for the items in the storage cubicles to make sure all was in order. When he heard the front door open, he didn't think much of it, other than to realize that the store would remain open late as planned.

The voice of the woman who had entered, though, immediately drew his complete and undivided attention. "Mr. Borisov," the woman was saying, "I brought something in the hope that you might see fit to loan us a small amount. Just enough to buy some groceries for dinner tomorrow. I've got my grandmother's Sunday brooch. It's got real jewels, a few diamonds and some rubies, I think." The woman paused as she reached into her pocketbook and withdrew something small wrapped in cloth, which she handed to him. "It's the only valuable thing we have, but I'd rather part with it than see my children go hungry on Thanksgiving."

Michael didn't see the piece of jewelry that Mr. Borisov unwrapped, nor could he have, from where he was standing. But he wasn't looking at the brooch. He stared instead at the woman who stood at the counter wringing her hands.

It was Clara Whibley, his next-door neighbor.

Mr. Borisov took his time looking at the brooch. He peered at it through a loupe, carefully inspecting the gemstones. Mrs. Whibley looked around the shop as she waited. She glanced at Michael and made brief eye contact before he could lower his face and turn his back to her.

"I think I can help you," Mr. Borisov said.

"You're looking for a loan, yes? Not sale?"

"Y-yes," Mrs. Whibley said, turning her focus back to the shop owner. Michael's hands began to tremble as he continued to work, so much so that he took refuge in the water closet. When he emerged, Mrs. Whibley was gone, and Mr. Borisov was putting on his overcoat.

"You haf happy Thanksgiving, Michael O'Brien," he said as Michael came to the front of the store. "And here, for you." He held out two one-dollar silver certificates. "Pay for week and little extra for holiday."

"Thank you, sir," Michael said. "I appreciate it very much. A happy Thanksgiving to you as well."

Michael put on his coat, and they stepped outside together. "See you Monday," Mr. Borisov said as he drew the bars across the front door and locked up the office.

She probably didn't recognize me, Michael thought as he started his long walk back to the farm. *It's pretty dim inside the loan office, and I was all the way at the back. Besides, I can't remember the last time I was in the same room with her.* By the time he reached home, he had talked himself into believing that the secret of his employment was safe.

The next morning, he heard his mother working in the kitchen before he got out of

476

bed. He entered the room in time to see his mother try to put a roasting pan containing a large goose into the oven.

"Wait, Mother, let me," Michael said. He grabbed the roaster from her and maneuvered it into the oven. "It's too heavy for you. You should have called me to help."

"I didn't want to wake you. You need the extra rest. But that was quite a goose you got. I think it's the biggest one I've ever cooked. It'll be nice and tender, and I'll make lots of gravy."

"You make the best gravy. Grandma always loved it, and your mashed potatoes, too."

"I remember," his mother said from her place by the stove. "I know we'll both be missing her today."

Michael nodded. "And Father and Seamus."

She brought him a plate of eggs and toast and then sat next to him to peel potatoes. He ate at a leisurely pace, thoroughly enjoying the fact that he didn't have to rush off to catch the school bus. His uncle Frank showed up before he was halfway done.

"Happy Thanksgiving!" his uncle said. "I brought a little something. It's not much, but since today's special . . ." Frank held a flat yellow box out to Anna, and Michael recognized it as a Whitman's Sampler.

"Frank, you shouldn't have," his mother said, but she looked delighted all the same. "I can't remember the last time we had something so decadent."

Michael's mouth watered at the thought of the bite-sized chocolate candies inside the box, but he didn't dare ask for one.

"Why don't we each pick one now and save the rest for after dinner?" his uncle said. He winked when Michael looked at him.

"My goodness, I've never heard of eating chocolate so early. We've all barely finished breakfast. There's some coffee left, Frank, if you're interested."

"Sounds good," he said. "I think it would go better with something sweet." He held up the box of candy and looked at her with raised eyebrows.

"All right, all right, you win," his mother said. "It figures you'd feel that way, seeing as how you were the one who taught me to snitch sugar when we were kids."

After Frank lifted the lid of the box, his mother chose a small round candy. When the box was presented to him, Michael selected a small, lumpy mass of chocolate. He was guessing there were peanuts inside.

Frank's surprise helped them enjoy the

day despite the three empty chairs at the table. They lingered in the kitchen, talking and laughing, as he and his uncle tried their best to help his mother or stay out of her way, whichever she needed. In midafternoon, they sat down to one of the most delicious meals Michael had ever had. He steadily ate his way through pieces of succulent goose, a pile of mashed potatoes with gravy, giblet dressing, and several other dishes. When his stomach was filled to capacity, he and Frank cleared the table while his mother went to sit on the sofa with her swollen feet elevated.

The only blemishes on the holiday were the absence of his grandmother, father, and brother, and the memories of countless people, especially Mrs. Whibley, begging Mr. Borisov to help them scrape by. Michael realized again just how much he had and how thankful he was to have it.

There was no school on the Friday after Thanksgiving, and the loan office was also closed, so Michael took the opportunity to finish his homework for the week. It was clear and bright outside and unseasonably warm, so he also spent some time outside cutting wood and playing with Tabby in the puddles of sunshine that moved slowly across the floor of the barn. He fed and watered Onion and the chickens before he walked back to the house. There were lots of Thanksgiving leftovers in the icebox, he knew. He didn't think he could ever get tired of them.

When he came inside, his mother was sitting on the sofa, but she wasn't alone. He had neither seen nor heard Clara Whibley arrive at the house, but there she was, wearing an expression as unhappy as his mother's.

"Michael, sit down, please," his mother said. She spoke in a strange, soft monotone, and the stare she leveled at him as he obeyed could have melted iron. "Mrs. Whibley came by to return some empty milk bottles, and she mentioned that she saw you in the city the day before yesterday . . . in the loan office."

Michael glanced at each of the women in turn but remained silent.

"I told her there must be some mistake, that you work at Radcliff's and have since the beginning of the summer. But she insisted it was you there, working alongside Mr. Borisov. Would you care to explain why she might be so sure of that?"

He swallowed, thinking frantically of what he could say and how he should say it. His mother's expression made it clear that he had very little time to think.

"That day I went into Burlington to look for a job, I did inquire at Radcliff's. Forelli's, too, and the grocery, and every other place all up and down Church Street and the whole downtown area. Nobody had any jobs open. The loan office was the last place I stopped, more out of curiosity than anything else. And I talked to Mr. Borisov, and he told me he'd give me a try as a clerk."

His mother made a little choking sound and covered her mouth with her hand.

"Please, Mother, I know you don't approve of the loan office, and I almost didn't take the job because I knew how you'd feel, but I had to find work somewhere, something that would pay enough to settle up our bills and keep us going until Father could help again. I even told Father about it, when he was here back in June, and he agreed I should keep the job and not tell you where I was working. Please, please, don't be angry, Mother. I know I shouldn't have lied about it, but I didn't know what else to do. I felt I didn't have any other choice. I promised Father. I promised him."

"Your father knew? He allowed —"

His mother's response was interrupted by her sharp intake of breath, followed by a loud cry. She clutched at her belly and grimaced as Mrs. Whibley leaned over and touched her arm. "Anna, are you all right? What is it?"

"The baby," his mother gasped. "It hurts, but not like it should. It hurts so much."

CHAPTER 29

On the Sunday after Thanksgiving, Emily was working in the marble mansion by herself. Gus was lounging on his dog bed, as usual, but Matt was up in Maine visiting his family for the long holiday weekend.

It was a relief to have Thanksgiving over with. They'd gathered at her mother's house, and it had been special in a way because it was the first holiday when she and Rose had been together on speaking terms in over a decade. Now, she was having trouble imagining a holiday dinner without everyone — including Rose and her husband and son — being there.

There was a downside to having a close-knit family, though, and that was the lack of privacy. Between her mother and Rose pumping her for information about Matt, it had been all Emily could do to prevent herself from covering her ears and running for the door. Her relationship with Matt was so new. She wasn't ready to share it with anyone. Finally, within the solid, quiet walls of the old McAllister house, she was feeling relaxed.

Her work was nearly done. She had subcontracted out the replacement of the corroded pipe. That had been finished on the Friday after Thanksgiving, although she'd had to pay a holiday rate to the plumber. She had spent the rest of the holiday weekend replacing the waterlogged wall and ruined hardwood flooring in the bedroom she'd flooded. Miraculously, the water hadn't soaked all the way through to the dining room ceiling beneath it. She was especially thankful for that, because having to replace a ceiling might have jeopardized her ability to finish the house on time.

The remainder of the new furnishings was scheduled to arrive over the course of the following week, and she hoped to take Ruth and Fitz on a walk-through. That would be quickly followed by the necessary state inspections. The Fitzgeralds would then have a green light to open for business, with just enough time to prepare for Kyle and Claudia's wedding.

The two projects Emily had yet to complete were minor ones. She had created a stained glass window as a gift to Ruth and

Fitz, and she'd obtained their permission to install it above the front entry in place of a drafty window that needed to be replaced. The other issue, which she was nearly ready to address, was the drain in the old antique tub in the owners' suite. It was so slow that it took hours to empty a full tub of water, and plunging it had done nothing to improve the situation. She had no idea how heavily the tub had been used over the years or what might be clogging the drain. Most likely, it was the typical mix of soap, hair, and grime, the kind of clog she'd dislodged countless times in the past.

Emily double-checked to make sure she had turned off the water supply to the house. Then she carried her toolbox up to the bathroom and set it beside the bucket of water, coiled plumber's snake, and air compressor that were already there. Flashlight in hand, she climbed into the tub. A visual inspection of the drain didn't reveal the problem. Fortunately, the drain and overflow pipes of old claw-foot tubs were easily accessible. Instead of being beneath the tub in the floor or behind it inside a wall, the drainpipe protruded upright from the floor, right next to the end of the curved cast-iron tub. Emily grabbed her pipe wrench. Although the drain assembly and overflow pipe were somewhat corroded, she was able to disconnect them from the drainpipe. After she had everything in working order, she would install new pipes and fixtures for the tub.

The thin, coiled plumber's snake passed from the entrance to the drain and all the way through the disconnected drain assembly beneath the tub with no resistance, which meant that whatever was impeding the flow of water from the tub was in the drainpipe itself. With a sigh, she reconnected all the pipes. She wouldn't be able to tell if the clog had been cleared unless she could observe water exiting the tub down the pipe.

Once everything was put back together, Emily climbed into the tub and pushed the end of the snake into the drain. She then began to turn the crank on the reel, which fed the snake farther into the pipe. Three feet went in, then a couple more, before the end of the snake encountered a barrier. She continued to turn the handle, but the snake moved forward only another half foot or so. When she cranked the reel in reverse to withdraw it, the corkscrew-shaped hook at the tip was covered in thick sludge but had not pulled out any sort of clog.

Typical, Emily thought as she wound the

snake back onto its reel. Old houses often had small, corroded pipes that were difficult to clear. Those leading from sink and tub drains were usually only an inch and a half or two inches in diameter. In her experience, a snake often failed to remove a clog in houses like this. But she was sure that her trusty air compressor would succeed where the snake hadn't.

She pulled the compressor closer to the tub, plugged it in, and turned it on. The motor hummed quietly for a few moments until the regulator indicated that the pressure level had risen to twenty pounds per square inch. Carefully, Emily pulled the hose over the edge of the tub, inserted the nozzle into the drain, wrapped a rag around the hose where it met the drain to prevent air from escaping backward, and squeezed the trigger. There was a muffled *whump* as air was forced into the drain.

Emily plugged the drain, got out of the tub, and poured in the bucket of water. When she removed the plug, though, the water didn't budge.

She repeated the process with the air compressor, this time waiting until the regulator read forty pounds per square inch before repositioning the nozzle and again releasing the air. Another *whump* sounded.

Again, the water in the tub didn't drain.

With sweat beading on her forehead, she cranked up the pressure on the air compressor to one hundred pounds per square inch. *Surely this'll do it,* she thought as a third *whump* sounded in the bathroom.

A second later, there was an enormous *BOOM!*

The walls shook as the sound reverberated throughout the house. Instinctively, Emily sank lower into the tub and covered her head with her arms. Her first thought was that she had blown out one of the old pipes leading from the bathroom. It was then that she realized some sort of wetness had sprayed her. A strong septic odor filled the bathroom just as she looked down to see hundreds of slimy gray and black droplets clinging to her arms and clothing.

Emily stood up and turned around. The sink had obviously been the source of the geyser-like explosion, because the counter, mirror, walls, floor, and ceiling were coated with copious amounts of the same disgusting sludge. Beyond that putrid blast radius, the sludge had been dispersed in smaller droplets like those that covered her.

The sink drain.

It had apparently been connected to a pipe on the same branch as the bathtub.

Even though she knew better, she had completely forgotten to close the sink drain and weigh it down to prevent whatever the air compressor dislodged from being ejected through it.

As if to point out the silver lining in her situation, a loud gurgle caused her to glance down just in time to see the last of the water in the tub disappear down the drain.

"Emily? Emily, are you up there? I heard an explosion. Is everything okay?"

Matt's voice echoed through the marble mansion, and she heard footsteps coming up the stairs. *What in the hell is he doing here? He's supposed to be in Maine,* she thought.

"I'm fine," she yelled. "I'm in the owners' suite bathroom, but you might not want to come in here right now."

"What? Why not? Are you all right? Oh, God."

It was too late. Matt appeared in the doorway to the bathroom, made a gagging sound, and immediately pulled up the front of his shirt to cover his nose and mouth. His eyes grew wide as he looked first at her, then at the colossal mess around the sink.

"I unclogged the tub drain," she explained matter-of-factly. "I forgot to stop up the sink before I shot compressed air into the pipe."

What else could she say? She was disgusted with herself for the amateurish oversight and embarrassed to have Matt see the result of it. Just when it had seemed like there was great potential for their budding relationship, she'd made a complete and utter fool of herself. She didn't know whether to cry or laugh or throw up from the smell.

"Okay. Okay." Matt's voice was muffled under his shirt. He was looking all around, from the mess surrounding the sink to her and back. "Tell me what you want me to do. Should I go get some stuff to start cleaning?"

Emily fought back tears and tried to think through her next steps. "I need disinfectant cleaner, something with bleach. A clean bucket and mop, sponges, and rubber gloves. Paper towels and plastic garbage bags. I'm going to have to scrub down everything, even the walls. I'll need soap and shampoo and some clothes I can put on after I wash all this off. After everything that's happened, you'd think I would have brought a change of clothes over here."

"Don't worry, I've got plenty of stuff you can throw on." Matt fixed his gaze on her and chuckled a little.

"What?" She felt her temper rising, and

her chin trembled. "Do you think this is funny?"

"No, of course not."

"Then why are you laughing?"

"I was just thinking about that old saying. You know, that there's shit in every job."

Emily snorted. She still felt like crying.

"The other thing I was thinking is that even covered in it, you're still the most beautiful, amazing woman I've ever seen."

As Father O'Brien straightened up in the sanctuary after Mass, he grew increasingly worried about Karen. She'd been there in her usual pew, but she'd seemed distant and distracted. She hadn't made eye contact with him once. It was easy to tell which of his parishioners were actively listening and connecting with his message. This morning, unusually, Karen hadn't been one of them.

Father O'Brien walked slowly down the aisle back to his church office. Once there, he tried to call Karen several times, but each time, his call went directly to her voicemail. He couldn't quite put his finger on it, but something about the way Karen had stared vapidly during the homily continued to bother him. It was a nagging feeling of déjà vu, and the association with whatever similar prior experience he'd had lingered stubbornly out of his grasp.

The feeling preoccupied his thoughts throughout the evening and as he shifted restlessly in bed. It was when his mind had started to enter the realm of sleep that the answer came to him, and it shocked him back to full wakefulness. In only one instance had he seen eyes like Karen's, with the light of vitality having faded so completely.

On the last night he'd visited her, Mary McAllister had looked at him like that. After he had left for the evening, she'd taken her own life.

In her house a few blocks from St. John's, Emily was also retiring for the night. After scrubbing and bleaching and rinsing, she'd finally rid the owner's suite bathroom of every trace of the sludge that had exploded from the sink. When Matt had returned with the supplies she'd requested, he had offered to stay and help, but she had insisted on doing the job herself.

Once the bathroom was clean, she'd stripped off her soiled clothing, climbed into the now-functional bathtub, and scoured every inch of herself with shampoo and soap. She'd opened all the upstairs windows in the mansion, hoping the smell would dissipate overnight, and she'd showered all over again at home in her own bathroom before changing into her pajamas. Never in her life had she felt as filthy, and never had she been so thankful to be as completely, mercifully clean.

Emily had every intention of going to sleep early, but when she reached toward her night table to turn off the light, her hand brushed a bundle of letters from the briefcase. How long had it been since she'd read any of them? She thought for a moment. It had been a few weeks, at least. In fact, she hadn't touched them since Matt had started helping her in the marble mansion. Part of the reason was that she'd been completely exhausted and basically falling into bed each night. Also, the allure the letters once held, of being able to peer into the private conversations between two people of the past, had faded dramatically once her own life had taken an unexpected, romantic turn.

Still, there were many she hadn't read, and she wasn't so tired that she couldn't stay awake a few more minutes. The mere possibility of finding something juicy prompted her to grab one of the bundles.

Emily looked at the postmark of the top letter. It was dated May 1971, the latest date of any postmark she'd seen on the correspondence. The envelope was different, too. It was light pink and larger than the common white envelopes containing the other letters. She opened it to discover that it contained *two* letters: one from Anna to Mary, and one from Mary to *Father O'Brien* and dated a few years after the first. She removed each one and began to read. When she finished them, Emily let her hand drop onto the covers and fell back against her pillow. At that moment, she realized two things.

The first was the extent to which her decision to read the letters in the briefcase was a gross and shameful invasion of privacy — both Ruth's and Father O'Brien's. She wouldn't read another word, but she would atone for her actions at the earliest opportunity.

And second, the letters she had read weren't just gossip from a bygone era. They revealed a long-held secret, one with the potential to change Father O'Brien's world.

On Monday morning, Karen was already dressed and in the kitchen when Ben came downstairs.

"I made you your usual breakfast sandwich," she said, sliding a plate and a glass of juice toward him.

"Wow, you're up again! Are you going out?" he asked as he began to eat.

"Yes. I didn't sleep well last night, and I need to go shopping. I can drop you at school on my way, if you'd like."

"Cool! That means no waiting for the bus this morning!"

They left the house a few minutes later, and she had him in the middle school's front drop-off zone right on time.

"Thanks for the ride, Mom," Ben said. He had already unfastened his seatbelt and had one foot out of the car when she gently took hold of his wrist.

"Wait just a sec," she said, and Ben turned to her with a quizzical, slightly annoyed expression. "I just want you to know that I'm really proud of you, and that I love you so much. You remember that, okay?"

"Um, okay. I love you, too, Mom." He paused, studying her face. "Are you all right?"

"I'm fine. Can't a mother tell her son she loves him?"

Ben shrugged. "Yeah, sure. I'll see you later." He got out of the car and shut the door.

Her eyes brimming with tears, Karen watched his lanky form enter the school building and disappear down one of the main hallways before she pulled away.

She drove back into town and parked in a space outside Turner's Hardware. It wasn't yet nine o'clock, so she got out and walked down to the bakery.

"Good morning," Ruth Fitzgerald said from behind the counter when she entered. "I haven't seen you in a few days. How are you?"

"Okay," Karen replied. "I was thinking this morning how coffee and cherry pie sounded really good for breakfast."

"You're in luck. I just made a fresh pot of coffee, and there's one piece of cherry pie left. I'll be baking a few more later on. Why don't you sit down? I'll bring it all out to you."

Karen took her time, watching from a corner table as other customers came and went. She had no appetite, but she tried to take a few bites of the pie. A familiar voice caught her attention, and she looked up to see Emily at the counter, placing an order.

"Hey, Karen," Emily said. "Could I sit with you for a few minutes until my stuff is ready?"

"Sure," Karen said, although she wasn't particularly in the mood for company. "So, are you headed to the hardware store?"

Emily came over to her table and pulled out the chair across from her. "Not today. That's just a part-time thing. My main job right now is renovating that big marble house on the hill so Ruth and her husband can open a bed-and-breakfast. We're rushing to get it done in time for a wedding."

"Claudia Simon's wedding, right? She told me about it. I'm the aide in her classroom."

"Really? I didn't know you work with Claudia. I guess I shouldn't be surprised, though. Everybody knows everybody around here, and news travels fast."

"That's true."

Emily's expression changed to one of sympathy, and Karen kept talking to answer the question she knew had popped into Emily's mind.

"I haven't heard anything about Nick in months, not since they found his Jeep shot up and abandoned. His traveling companion's body was still in the front seat. Nick wasn't there, but the driver's seat was bloodstained. His company insists they're still searching for him, but in all honesty, Emily, I know he's not coming back."

"Karen, you can't give up hope until —"

"Nick is dead." Karen felt an overwhelming sadness and a surge of adrenaline, speaking those words for the first time, and it was as if doing so removed a barrier and allowed her to acknowledge aloud that she didn't have the strength to resist the darkness anymore. "They haven't found him yet, but I can feel it. I'm just trying to hang on and convince myself that it's worth going on without him."

Emily looked at her with wide eyes. "Worth going on? Karen, you don't mean you're going to . . . You're scaring me, talking like that. You *can't* give up. What about Ben? He needs you more than ever. And so many people care about you."

Karen shook her head. Part of her knew that what Emily was saying was true, but the darkness suffocated any emotional impact the words should have had.

"Karen," Emily tried again, "I know what it feels like to lose someone you love more than anything. I *know*. When I was in college, the guy I planned to marry was killed in a car accident, and for years, I thought I'd never get past it. There are still days when I feel sad, remembering him, wondering what we might have had together. But I'm still here. I know he would've wanted me to go on with my life, to try to find happiness. And it's been hard, but I'm doing that now."

Just how many years has it taken you to get over your fiancé's death? Karen thought. *You weren't even married. You hadn't built a life together. Losing a husband is worse, so much worse. I just want the hurt to go away.*

She didn't speak her thoughts, though, and Emily kept talking. "You can't jump to conclusions about Nick until you have proof. You can't give up hope, at least not yet. I want you to promise me that you won't go and do something rash. You call me if you're even considering it, okay?" Emily fished around in her purse for a pen and began writing on a paper napkin. "Here's my cell number. You call me anytime, day or night. Do you have anyone who can stay with you? Or anyone else you might be able to talk to?"

Karen shrugged. "Father O'Brien knows what's going on, and I've talked with him quite a bit."

"Maybe you should go see him now," Emily suggested. "I can drive you over to the church on my way to the mansion, if you'd like."

"Maybe I will go see Father O'Brien," Karen said slowly. "I don't need a ride — my car's outside — but thanks." She rose from her seat, and Emily quickly grabbed up the napkin and pressed it into her hand.

499

"Don't forget this," she said. "I'm serious about you calling me if you need to. Are you sure you're okay right now?"

"I'm fine, don't worry." Emily didn't look at all as if she believed her, so Karen forced a smile as she stuffed the napkin into her jacket pocket. "Thanks for listening."

"Anytime."

Karen left enough money on the table to cover her bill and then some. Ruth was waiting on several people who had come in around the same time, and Karen was able to slip out of the bakery without another conversation. Instead of going to her car, though, she walked next door to the hardware store, where Henry Turner greeted her and asked if she needed help finding something.

"I need a new dryer vent hose."

"Oh, sure. They're right over here." Henry came around the counter and led her down one of the aisles. "Here you go. These are actually dryer duct kits. We've got 'em in eight-foot and twenty-foot lengths. Do you know how long of one you might need?"

"The longer, the better, I think. How wide is the hose?"

"They're both a standard four inches. They come with two clamps, one for each end. The clamps should make the connections airtight, but you could always use a little duct tape around each end if you wanted to."

"I have plenty of that at home. It's what I got the last time I was here, actually."

Henry nodded and took a twenty-foot duct kit from the shelf. "I'll carry it up front for you."

When she arrived back at home, Karen pulled into her garage and lowered the door. She left her purchase resting on the trunk of the car while she went inside and got her roll of duct tape. She also retrieved the two sealed envelopes — one addressed to Ben, and the other to her brother, George — that were sitting on her dresser. She then opened the duct kit and knelt on the floor of the garage beside her car's exhaust pipe.

A half hour later, she climbed into the driver's seat, laid the letters on the dashboard, and started the engine. The duct functioned perfectly. The end attached to the car's tailpipe was clamped and taped, and she had made sure the area surrounding the end of the hose secured in one of the back passenger windows was also airtight.

Exhaust from the engine poured into the car. Karen inhaled deeply, her eyes closed and her head fully supported by the headrest. Her faith told her that what she was doing might prevent her from ever seeing Nick again, but her heart hoped to see him and hold him again, or at least for relief from the crushing burden of her life.

CHAPTER 30

November 1934

Michael sat with his uncle in the hospital
waiting room. He'd been there over an
hour, having arrived with his mother in Mr.
Whibley's truck. By the time they'd made it
to the hospital, she'd started to bleed heavily. Michael had never felt so disappointed
and helpless — disappointed that everything
he had done to make sure she and the baby
would be all right might not have been
enough, and helpless to do anything to
improve the situation.

Another hour passed, and then a nurse
with a clipboard appeared and called,
"Anna O'Brien?"

The two of them practically jumped off
the bench. "I'm Frank Lynch, Mrs.
O'Brien's brother," his uncle said. "This is
her son Michael. Her husband is working
out of state, I'm afraid."

The nurse nodded and made a note on

her clipboard. "Please follow me. The doctor would like to speak with you." She turned and pushed open one of the double doors leading from the waiting room and held it for them to follow. She led them to a small consultation room in the maternity wing, where a doctor in surgical garments soon joined them.

"Anna is resting comfortably," the doctor said. "She had a serious placental abruption, which means that the tissue connecting the baby to her body suddenly separated. We were able to stop the bleeding after we delivered the baby, although she needed a transfusion."

The doctor paused, and the momentary silence in the small room was ominous.

"The baby —" his uncle began, and the surgeon nodded.

"The baby survived, but she's very small, not even four pounds. She wasn't due for a few more weeks, from what I read in Mrs. O'Brien's medical records. The early delivery, and the sickness that Mrs. O'Brien suffered for a good part of her pregnancy, probably kept the baby from reaching a normal size."

"Will she survive? The baby?" Frank asked.

"She could. It's hard to say. She's in the

nursery, and I can assure you she's receiving the best of care."

"When can we see them?" Michael asked.

"Your mother is unconscious from the anesthesia. I expect it will be tomorrow morning, at least, before she's able to receive visitors. There's no reason why you can't see the baby, if you wish. I can ask a nurse to escort you there."

"Yes, please, Doctor. And thank you for all you've done for Anna," Frank said, extending his hand. "Our prayers have been answered tonight."

The hospital nursery was conveniently adjacent to the maternity wing. Through a glass window, Michael could see rows of wheeled bassinettes, many of which were occupied. The nurse who had walked with them went inside and spoke with one of the pediatric nurses, who nodded. Instead of going to a bassinette, she approached a large, boxy structure against one of the walls. The front of the structure was open and divided into three small beds.

"What is that?" Michael whispered.

"An incubator," his uncle said quietly.

The pediatric nurse bent slightly and lifted a tiny bundle from one of the incubated beds. Carefully, she positioned the baby in one arm and walked over to the window.

The nurse who had escorted them to the nursery came back out the door and stood with them to see the infant.

Michael could scarcely breathe. His baby sister was a delicate vision. Although her eyes were closed, he marveled at the tiny perfection of her facial features. Her minuscule eyelashes matched the slight wisp of blond hair on her head, and her clenched fists were no bigger than the end of his thumb. The rest of her was hidden, well swaddled in a receiving blanket.

"Well, Michael, you're a big brother now," his uncle said quietly.

She has to survive. She will survive, Michael thought. Somehow he had done it. He had seen his mother through, and he would continue to do anything he could to make sure his sister grew and thrived. Michael wiped a tear from the corner of his eye and grinned up at his uncle, who was smiling, too.

"Uncle Frank, we have to call Father. I promised we'd contact him if anything happened with Mother or the baby."

"I'll do that as soon as I drive you back to the farm. You'll need to tend to the livestock, yes? Will you be all right alone for the night?"

Michael nodded.

506

"Tomorrow morning I'll come get you for another visit. Hopefully, we'll be able to see your mother then, too."

The next morning, Michael was ready to leave the house at ten o'clock, when his uncle had promised to be there. When Frank hadn't arrived by ten-thirty, he started to pace around the kitchen. The Colchester parish sedan finally turned into the driveway at five minutes before eleven, but the expression on his uncle's face as he exited the vehicle kept Michael from saying anything about his tardiness.

"Michael, something terrible's happened. Please come back inside with me for a minute."

Michael focused on his uncle's eyes, which were uncharacteristically watery. They sat down at the table.

"I tried to call your father last night, but I couldn't reach him. I figured it was late, that there was no one in the company office at that hour. This morning I tried again. I got through to one of the foremen, and he passed the phone to one of the managers. I don't know how to say this . . . The manager told me that he was killed in an accident three days ago."

Michael stared blankly, unable to find his voice.

"It was an accident," his uncle said. "A fall. He was working up on one of the steel supports. Apparently, no one saw what caused him to lose his balance. They only realized he was in trouble once he'd slipped and was hanging on by one arm, and he fell into the river before they could get to him."

"No. No," Michael said. "Father's so strong. He'd hang on, even if he did fall. And if it happened three days ago, we'd have heard before now. Someone would have called you or sent us a wire."

"I know it seems like that's what they would do. I said the very same thing. I guess it took some time to retrieve his body from the water and identify him, and the company decided not to try to notify us on Thanksgiving Day. They tried to call my office yesterday, probably while we were at the hospital with Anna. The manager sent a telegram for her to my office after we spoke by phone, said we should consider it official company notice." Frank produced an envelope from his pocket and gave it to Michael to open. "I was late coming out because I waited for it to arrive. I knew you'd want to see it for yourself."

Michael took the envelope and opened it.

WESTERN UNION
1934 DECEMBER 1 AM 10:13

DEAR MRS. O'BRIEN,
I DEEPLY REGRET TO INFORM
YOU THAT YOUR HUSBAND,
NIALL MICHAEL O'BRIEN, DIED
AFTER FALLING FROM A STEEL
SUPPORT TRUSS AT THE TRIBOR-
OUGH BRIDGE CONSTRUCTION
SITE. A LETTER OF INFORMA-
TION FOLLOWS.
OTIS P. MACARTHUR, MANAGER
TRIBOROUGH BRIDGE AUTHOR-
ITY

Michael looked up with tears welling up and spilling out of his eyes. "Why?" he asked his uncle. "Why would this happen to us right now, after everything? Why would God *let* this happen?"

Before Frank could answer, he'd dropped the telegram and was out the door, running, running through the fresh snow. He cleared the back pasture and kept going, not knowing where he was headed or when he would stop.

In every difficult situation he'd experienced since his father had left, he had figured out a way forward. Now, though, he couldn't think. He didn't know where to turn or what to do. He was lost.

CHAPTER 31

Once Karen had left the bakery, and before she herself went up to the marble mansion to begin the day's work, Emily stopped at the counter again to speak with Ruth. The morning rush had cleared out, and Ruth was putting on a fresh pot of coffee.

"I have some good news," Emily told her with a grin. "I think the house is about ready for you and Fitz to see. I'm going to be installing the stained glass window today, and I'll probably swap out the fixtures on the antique tub we kept for your guys' bathroom, but after that, we'll be all set."

"Oh, this is so exciting! I'm sorry I haven't been up there recently, but it'll be better to see everything you've done all at once. When do you think we should come?"

"How about Wednesday afternoon, around three o'clock?"

"That'll work for me. Rose will be here to cover the counter. Let me just call Fitz at the station and see if that time's good for him."

Emily waited while Ruth phoned her husband, who sounded equally thrilled to see the mansion.

"I'm really pleased with how it turned out," Emily said, "but don't forget that we can make adjustments in the future if we need to."

"Kyle and Claudia's wedding should give us a good opportunity to see how the space works for guests. Maybe it'll give us some more ideas."

"Sure." Emily paused and took a deep breath. "There's one other thing I wanted to talk with you about. While I was refinishing the floors in the former master suite, I found a briefcase hidden in the closet. I probably shouldn't have opened it before telling you about it, but it was locked, and I wanted to see if I could open it without damaging the locks, as a favor to you. The whole briefcase was filled with letters between Mary McAllister and a lady named Anna O'Brien."

"Anna O'Brien? Any relation to Father O'Brien?"

Emily nodded. "His mother. I read some of the letters. I shouldn't have done that, either, but I'm thinking that even though

the briefcase was in the mansion and technically yours, it should go to Father O'Brien.
If you agree, that is."

"Absolutely," Ruth said. "If the letters
were between Mary and his mother, my
goodness. He'd probably be so grateful to
have them."

"Good. I'll take the whole thing over to
him today. I really am sorry for opening the
briefcase, Ruth. It wasn't any of my business." *And when I see him, I can make sure
he knows about Karen and how fragile she
seems,* Emily thought.

"Don't worry about it, Emily. Chances
are, if you had brought it to me locked, I'd
have asked you to open it. And both of the
people who wrote the letters have passed. If
we get them safely into Father O'Brien's
hands, I don't see that there's any harm
done."

In the parish house, Father O'Brien hung
up the phone and pulled on his coat. He
glanced at the briefcase that Emily had
brought over. Although he hadn't quite
wrapped his mind around what it was and
what it contained, he couldn't focus on it.
Far more important was Karen's well-being.
She hadn't stopped by to see him, as she'd
told Emily she would, and she still wasn't

answering his calls. He was so worried that he thought it best to go see if she was home.

Halfway from the door and his truck, he felt an odd sensation. It wasn't dizziness, but more like the ground under his feet was uneven. *No wonder,* he thought. *I hardly slept last night.* The sensation passed quickly, though, and he felt fine as he got behind the wheel.

Karen's home seemed empty as he pulled into her driveway. It was a school day, so Ben wouldn't be there. He got out of the truck, intending to go ring the doorbell, but a humming noise coming from the garage caught his attention. He checked to see if his hearing aids were in the proper positions and then snapped his fingers on each side of his head to test them. The noise was definitely coming from Karen's house.

Quickly, he went to the garage door and flattened his palm against it. It didn't feel out of the ordinary, but when he pressed his ear against it, the sound of an engine idling inside was unmistakable.

Father O'Brien stooped down and took hold of the handle protruding from the lower half of the door, but he wasn't strong enough to raise it manually.

He looked over at the Wykowskis' house and noticed that there were two vehicles in the driveway. Ignoring the painful protests from his arthritic knees, he hurried across the lawn to Karen's neighbors' house and pounded on the door. "Ron? Jean? Are you home?"

Ron Wykowski, eyes baggy and half-open, came to the door in sweats and a T-shirt. His hair was mussed and standing straight up on one side. "Father? What's wrong?"

"There's a car running in Karen's garage next door. I think she might be trying to kill herself."

Ron's tired expression vanished. "Jeanie! Jeanie, call 911, and come next door, quick!"

"What?" Jean's voice sounded from another room in the house. "Did you say to call 911?" She appeared, dressed in her work scrubs, just as Ron put on his shoes. Rather than stay behind, she grabbed the handset of a cordless phone and followed her husband outside, dialing as she went.

Back at Karen's, Ron also tried and failed to lift the garage door.

"She keeps a spare key taped to the back of her porch light," Jean said with the phone to her ear. "Hello? Yes, I'm calling to report a possible suicide attempt." While she gave the emergency dispatcher the address, Ron ran to the front porch, found the key, and let himself into Karen's house.

Father O'Brien and Jean followed him into the house. Ron quickly went to the interior garage door and threw it open. A huge, warm cloud of automobile exhaust engulfed him as he found the keypad and hit the button to open the exterior door.

None of them spoke as sunlight illuminated the inside of the garage and the exhaust dissipated. Father O'Brien made the sign of the cross. Karen's sedan was still idling. It was obvious from the hose apparatus extending from the tailpipe into the rear window that she had indeed used the car as a means to attempt suicide. Strangely, though, the driver's door was open, and Karen was nowhere inside.

"Why would she do this and then get out?" Jean asked. "Maybe she had second thoughts? Oh, please, let that be it."

"We need to search the rest of the house," Ron said. He came back inside, and the three of them spread out, checking all of the rooms.

"In here!" Jean yelled. Father O'Brien followed Ron back to the master bedroom, where Karen lay on the bed. There was an empty prescription bottle on the nightstand. "Xanax," Ron said when he looked at it.

"I can't get a pulse," Jean said. As she and

Ron began to administer CPR, Father O'Brien crossed himself again and began to pray. So much of this scene was reminiscent of how Mary's life had ended, except he alone had gone to her home and found her. A siren in the distance was growing louder, and he hoped that somehow, with emergency help, Karen's outcome would be different than Mary's. Karen had suffered through a tremendous amount of pain, but she was young and healthy. She had a beautiful son who needed her. There was still hope that her husband would be found alive. It wasn't right that she should die today.

On the dresser next to where he was standing, a ringtone sounded from a phone tucked in Karen's purse. He didn't know much about how to work cellphones, but the melody played over and over, and it was so loud that he was afraid it would distract Ron and Jean from their frantic efforts. Father O'Brien tried to reach out and pick up the phone, but his arm remained motionless. The strange sensation he had experienced before getting into his truck returned. It was much more pronounced, and the room was swirling. He felt his leg give way, as if the floor had disappeared out from under it.

"Help," he managed to say before he fell. "I think I need —"

CHAPTER 32

Sunday, December 2, 1934

On Sunday afternoon, having spent a second night alone at the farm, Michael stood outside the door to the maternity wing, waiting as his uncle broke the news to his mother about the death of his father. "You've been through more than a boy of fifteen should," his uncle had said before going in. "She'll be incredibly upset. You needn't have that memory to further burden you." Even so, Michael heard his mother's screams plainly through the heavy double doors.

He stood, head bowed, with his hands in his trouser pockets. To distract himself from his grief, he forced himself to think about various trivial problems and their solutions. The Whibleys were caring for Onion and the chickens. He wouldn't be attending school on Monday, and his uncle had already written a note to the principal, explaining what would be a lengthy absence. His uncle didn't know about the loan office, but Michael hoped his boss would understand when he didn't show up for work on Monday.

A few minutes after his mother's cries had quieted, Michael began to wonder whether he should go in to see her when a nurse approached him. She carried a tiny bundle in her arms, and he recognized her as the nurse who had held his infant sister in the window of the nursery for the family to see.

"You're Mrs. O'Brien's son, aren't you?" she asked. "I've heard the news about your father. I'm so very sorry." The bundle in her arms stirred, and the nurse began to gently pat it. "It's not quite feeding time, but I thought that holding the baby might bring your mother some comfort."

"Maybe so," Michael said. He craned his neck closer, trying to get a better look at his sister. "Would it be all right . . . do you think . . . *I* could hold her?"

"I don't see why not, but only for a moment. The doctor doesn't want her outside the incubator for long. Make sure you keep her swaddled, and support her little head at all times. There, that's it." The nurse carefully transferred the baby into his arms and helped position her properly.

Michael gazed down at his sister's face, marveling again at how perfect and small it was. He could scarcely believe that a human being could be the size of his tiny sibling. Even Tabby the barn cat was easily twice her weight. Carefully, gently, he brushed his lips against the baby's forehead. Her skin was softer than velvet.

"How long will she have to stay in the hospital?"

"If everything is stable with her growth, until she gains enough weight that the doctor feels she's strong enough to go home. I expect both she and your mother will be here for some time. Now let's bring her inside," the nurse said.

"I can carry her?"

"Yes. Walk slowly and carefully. Keep both hands on her and your arm beneath her head, and she'll be just fine."

They entered the maternity ward. It was smaller and slightly more private than the women's ward, and there were only two women besides his mother. The nurse led the way to the last bed on one side of the room, where a privacy curtain had been pulled. Inside the curtain, his uncle Frank sat on a chair beside the bed.

"Mrs. O'Brien? I brought two people who'd like to see you," the nurse said. She stepped sideways, making room for Michael to approach with the baby.

"Oh," his mother said as she looked at the two of them. Her eyes were swollen and bloodshot, and tears continued to leak out of them as she spoke. "Is it the first time you've held her?"

"Yes," Michael said. He came closer, bent down, and placed his sister in his mother's arms. Before he straightened, he wrapped his arms around them both as best he could. "I'm so sorry, Mother. I feel like I should do something, and I can't."

"Just your being here is a comfort, Michael. There's nothing any of us can do."

Frank quietly slipped out of the curtained area and returned with another chair for Michael.

"Mother, what's her name?" Michael asked.

His mother smiled down at the tiny infant before she answered him. "Your father and I . . . we always said that if we ever had a baby girl, we'd name her Grace. We talked about it when he was home those few days last June. Maybe we can use Elizabeth as a middle name, after your grandmother. After everything that happened, and how she took care of me all that time . . ."

"I think Lizzie would've loved that," Frank said.

"And Father, too," Michael added. "Grace Elizabeth."

His uncle cleared his throat. "Anna, circumstances being what they are, I wanted to suggest to you that we give Grace the sacrament of baptism right away, if you're willing." He reached into his jacket and removed a small glass bottle of clear liquid. "I brought a bit of holy water with me."

His mother looked at Frank with vacant eyes, but she nodded and carefully turned Grace in her arms so that the baby's downy head was accessible. Frank bowed his head to pray before he removed the stopper from the bottle and softly began the rite of baptism. As he sprinkled a few droplets on her head, Grace blinked. Rather than cry out, though, she flung her tiny arms free of her blankets and open wide, as if to accept the love flowing from all of them into her soul.

"It's not right for you to stay at the farm by yourself indefinitely, Michael," his uncle said as they ate dinner at the Holy Cross Mission rectory. "You can stay here until your mother is well enough to go home. I'll have to talk with her once she's strong enough and figure out what we need to do."

Michael nodded. He realized he had no other option.

"We need to go out to the farm tonight, though," his uncle continued. "You'll need to get some clothes and whatever personal things you'd like. Your mother asked me to get some things for her as well. We'll drop them off at the hospital on our way back into the city."

"What are we going to do, Uncle Frank? Without Father, I don't know if I can earn enough. What if Mother has to sell the farm? And the hospital bill for Mother and Grace . . ."

"Don't worry about that now, Michael. I know you feel responsible, but your mother is the one who has to decide how to handle things when she's up to it."

Everything's changing too quickly, Michael thought as they arrived at the farmhouse. It didn't feel right being there alone, and yet it seemed just as wrong to be packing up his things, preparing to sleep elsewhere for an uncertain length of time. It was almost a relief when his knapsack would hold nothing else. He carried it down the hall and set it by the door.

His uncle was in his mother's room, putting her things in a suitcase. Michael's gaze traveled to the back door. Quickly, he slipped outside and opened the trapdoor to the root cellar. He ran to the pile of burlap sacks in the corner, pawing through them with fervor until he found the case containing his mother's secret silver. It was a small miracle that, in the many months that had passed since she'd revealed it to him, she hadn't moved her prized possession to another hiding place.

Michael assumed his uncle didn't know about the flatware, since his mother had kept it a secret even from her own husband. The burlap sacks strewn all around were large enough to hold the flatware case, so he slid it inside one of the newer-looking ones and slung it over his shoulder. Back upstairs, he transferred several of his larger books to the sack and twisted the top closed.

Frank emerged with a large suitcase and a smaller satchel. "All set?" he asked, and Michael nodded. As they were putting the bags in the backseat of the parish sedan, one of the books slid out from the burlap sack and onto the ground.

Wuthering Heights," Frank said as he retrieved the book and handed it to him. "Never cared for it much."

"Me, neither," Michael said. He dropped the book back into the sack and twisted the top closed more tightly than before.

Back at the hospital, they hurried to reach the maternity ward before visiting hours ended for the evening. Carrying the smaller of the bags, Michael followed his uncle toward his mother's bed. She was awake, sitting with her hands in her lap and staring blankly straight ahead.

"Anna, I brought you the things you wanted. Do you want me to set them on a chair so they're easier for you to reach?"

His mother turned her head toward Frank. "All right," she said, and then she looked curiously at Michael. "Is he a friend of yours?"

Frank looked at her with a furrowed brow before glancing in Michael's direction. "Anna?"

"Hmm? I just wondered if he's a friend, since he's here with you. Or is he someone Niall knows?" She craned her neck to peer at him over his uncle's shoulder. "Are you helping Frank with the wedding?"

A chill ran down Michael's spine. His mother was looking directly at him, but her eyes were strangely empty.

She didn't know who he was.

"Anna," Frank said in a calm, careful voice, "this is Michael. Your son. Don't you remember him?"

His mother gave a strange, high-pitched giggle. "Oh, don't be silly, Frank. I don't have a son! Why, Niall and I won't even be married until next week!"

Michael opened his mouth to say something, but a sharp look from his uncle warned him against speaking.

"I'll check in with you tomorrow, Anna. You get some rest tonight," Frank said. He bent to kiss Anna on the forehead and then quickly ushered Michael away from her bedside. "We need to find a doctor right away. And we need to make sure they don't bring the baby to her while she's in this state."

"What's happening? Uncle Frank? Why didn't she recognize me?"

His uncle didn't answer him until they were completely outside the maternity ward. "I think your father's death has affected her mind. The grief and maybe the stress of everything that's happened. Somehow, her mind has taken her back in time and blacked out all the painful things that have happened."

"She's . . . she's gone insane?"

"I couldn't say. I saw the same sort of thing happen one other time, to one of my parishioners who lost her son in the Great War. She lost touch with reality, although she eventually recovered."

"Mother's a strong person."

"She is," his uncle said. "I know that probably better than anyone. She'll make it through this, and I'll see to it that she gets the care she needs."

On Monday morning, when he opened his eyes, Michael was confused about where he was. The spare room in which he was sleeping was furnished with only a bed and a chair. The windows lacked curtains, allowing the sunlight to shine into the room unimpeded.

He sat up and rubbed his eyes. There was a note from his uncle on the seat of the chair:

Michael, help yourself to anything in the kitchen. I have church business to attend to today and tonight. We'll visit the hospital tomorrow.

Frank

Michael looked at the burlap sack in the corner of the room and got out of bed.

By midmorning, he was walking along the main road from Colchester to Burlington, the burlap sack slung against his back. Every so often, when he heard a car approaching,

he extended his arm with his thumb sticking upward, hoping for a ride. It was about
six miles from the mission to the loan office, and the case of flatware in the burlap
sack was getting heavier with each step.

An old pickup truck finally rattled to a
stop several yards ahead of him, and Michael jogged up to meet it.

"Where're you headed?" the driver asked
through a window.

"Burlington."

"What's in the sack?"

"Just some personal things. Clothes,
books, and such. I'm going to stay with my
aunt. She lives a few blocks from Church
Street."

The driver was grizzled and wrinkled, a
good fit for the rusty truck he was driving.
"I'll be passing through there," he said after
a long pause. "Don't trust hitchhikers in
the cab, but you can climb up in the back,
if you want."

"Thank you, sir. I really appreciate it."

Michael scrambled into the bed of the
pickup. The late autumn air was frigid
against his face, but it was far more comfortable than carrying the flatware into Burlington.

The driver pulled over at the corner of
Church and Main, and Michael jumped

down from the truck. He wished so much that he had more to offer the driver than his thanks.

Mr. Borisov already had customers milling around the counter when Michael walked into the loan office. Obviously, he had arrived far earlier than his regular starting time, but he ignored the look of surprise on his boss's face. Instead, he took the burlap sack directly to the back of the store, where the containers holding the scrap gold and silver were kept. He breathed a sigh of relief when he saw that they were full. It meant that the gold buyer hadn't yet arrived for his monthly visit.

While Mr. Borisov dealt with his customers, Michael took the flatware case from the sack and opened it. The pieces were neatly in their compartments, and they shone enough that he could see his reflection in the spoons. His mother had managed to keep them polished.

He had wrestled with the idea of what he was about to do, but he'd decided that he had no choice. His mother was recovering from surgery and now was apparently sick in her mind. His new sister was weak and fragile. A great deal of money would be needed to pay for their medical care and afterward, and his father and grandmother were gone. His uncle had sworn himself to a life of poverty. And he himself was only fifteen, unable to command the wages of an adult, even if he could find a job paying them, and even being as willing and able as he was to shoulder the responsibility of a man who was fully grown.

His mother's secret insurance policy was all they had.

On Tuesday, Michael went with his uncle to the hospital, where they found that Anna had sunk deeper into her delirium. When she wasn't sleeping, she alternately babbled nonsense or stared blankly at nothing in particular. His uncle was receiving regular updates from her doctors, who seemed to feel that her mental recovery would be lengthy. His mother seemed to recognize Frank, but Michael was a stranger to her.

Grace was hanging on, although her health, too, was precarious. She weighed little more than she had at birth. Michael hadn't been allowed to hold her again, though he saw her through the nursery window in the arms of the nurses.

The rest of the week, he stayed at the rectory. His uncle was uncharacteristically grim and busy. They rarely saw each other except at dinner and during their visits to the hospital that took place every few days. Michael thought about trying to go back to school, but he could barely focus on reading, and he couldn't imagine sitting in a classroom with his mind so dulled by sadness.

On Friday morning, he was awakened by his uncle gently shaking his arm.

"Uncle Frank?"

"Michael, wake up. We need to talk."

He sat up in bed, and his uncle took a seat at the end of the mattress. "The hospital called an hour ago. Grace passed away last night."

Michael said nothing. He thought he might not have heard his uncle correctly.

"They did all they could for her. She grew weaker and weaker, despite having the best care, and in the end, the doctors couldn't save her. She was too small and born too soon." His uncle cleared his throat. "Your mother's doctors think it best that we not tell her. She doesn't remember Grace right now, anyway. They want to send her to a hospital called the Brattleboro Retreat. It specializes in compassionate care for the mentally ill. It requires the consent of her closest living relative who is of age. Since Seamus is in prison out of state, they're looking to me to make the decision, but I wanted to speak to you first."

Michael felt his body trembling, still trying to adjust to the shock of hearing his sister had died. "Will this place — the retreat — will it help her get well?"

"It might. I think she has the best chance of getting well there."

"Does it cost anything for her to go there?"

"The Brattleboro Retreat is a private facility. I'm working on getting her a charitable admission, with the assumption that the farm will be sold to help cover the expense. It's also possible that your mother will receive some sort of death benefit from your father's employer in New York."

"I can help, too," Michael said. He got out of bed and went to his knapsack, where he withdrew a roll of bills and a thin object wrapped in cloth. "Mother had a set of old sterling flatware that she kept hidden. She got it from her mother after she married Father. It was a secret. Nobody knew about it but me. She told me her mother gave it to her so she'd have something valuable in case of an emergency.

"She was upset with me, that day she had Grace, because she found out I've been working in the loan office in Burlington since early summer. I know the gold buyer who comes around each month. Monday, I got a ride into the city and sold the flatware." He held out the money to his uncle. "There's almost a hundred dollars here. It might not be enough to cover everything we need or already owe, but it's a start."

His uncle took the bills and looked down at them, then nodded.

"I kept this," Michael said as he unwrapped the thin object. "It's the sugar spoon from the set. Mother told me her mother had it engraved especially for her. I didn't think it'd be right to part with it. Do you think I could bring it to her in the hospital?"

The little sugar spoon shimmered in the light of the morning sun. His uncle picked it up, looking closely at its engraving.

"I worry that seeing you right now would upset your mother further," Frank said. "She's still confused and wouldn't recognize you. But I can keep the spoon and give it to her once she starts to recover."

Michael looked from the spoon to his uncle. "It's important that she have it."

"I understand," his uncle said before he sighed heavily. "There's one more thing I wanted to talk to you about. You're not an adult, Michael, which means someone has to take responsibility for your care. I wish you could stay here with me, in the rectory, but the diocese won't allow me to assume custody of a child, even one as mature as you are. Your brother is in prison, and your mother isn't able to care for you right now."

"What will happen to me? Am I going to St. Joseph's? The orphanage?"

"Not if I can help it. I don't believe that's a safe place for children, although I can't voice that opinion openly. I'm working on having your father's body transferred here from New York, and I'm planning to have a joint funeral Mass for him and Grace this month with a burial in the spring. In early January, I've arranged for you to enroll in the minor seminary at my alma mater, the Cathedral College of the Immaculate Conception. I'm good friends with the rector there, and he's arranging financial aid to cover your expenses. You'll board there, which will keep you out of the orphanage. We'll also seek legal emancipation for you — that means we'll ask a judge to declare you an adult legally. Either way, once you come of age, you'll be free to decide whether to stay on or take your life in a different direction."

Michael bowed his head, willing himself to keep control of his emotions when everything else about his life had escaped his grasp. At last he managed to look his uncle in the eyes. "Where is the Cathedral College?"

His uncle's voice was almost apologetic. "New York City."

The Vermont landscape was snow-covered in early January. Michael sat in a window seat on the train, watching mountains and forests and farms he had never seen fly past. He couldn't help but think of his father, how he and Seamus must have traveled through some of these same places on their way to New York nearly ten months ago. His own journey was bittersweet, not like the wide-eyed adventure for which he had wished back in March.

He had said goodbye to his mother two days ago. The Brattleboro Retreat had indeed been good for her. Physically, she looked well. She recognized him now, though she was fragile and prone to bouts of memory lapse and despondency. She had been happy to hear that Michael would continue his education. In time, with the help of the doctors and nurses caring for her, he was hopeful that she would find herself again.

The train had stopped in the southern city

of Rutland and was now picking up steam as it left the station. A few miles farther south, after the train passed through rougher terrain and over a lengthy trestle, he caught sight of a tiny village in the distance. It was nestled in the hills and, like so many in Vermont, barely more than a cluster of houses with snowy roofs and smoking chimneys. There was a tall steeple, too, sprouting up from a stone church in the heart of the town.

For some reason, the village fascinated him. He had never laid eyes on it before, but the sight of it was comforting, as if it beckoned to him with the promise of home. It seemed to be something out of a storybook, the kind of magical place made of love and hope that he would never forget.

Michael clung to that feeling as the train continued on and the village disappeared from view. The events of the past few months had left him numb and nearly bereft of emotion. He didn't know what lay ahead of him or what path his life would take, but the tendril of warmth he felt at seeing the little town seemed to push through the numbness and stoke what few embers of feeling he had left. He knew then that he would somehow find the strength to build a new life for himself. And someday, as soon as he was able, he would return to Vermont and find that lovely little village again.

CHAPTER 33

At the marble mansion, Emily stood with Ruth and Fitz as she unlocked the back door. "Are you ready?" she asked with a huge grin.

"Are you kidding?" Ruth asked. They all laughed as Fitz took Ruth's hand and followed her into the house.

The kitchen hadn't changed much since Ruth had seen it last, but it was new to Fitz. He glanced around at the gleaming new cabinetry and appliances and nodded with approval. "Sure looks like you could do some damage in here, Ruthie."

"I fully intend to," she said with a smile. "And look! This door goes right into the dining room, so it'll be easy to serve meals!"

Emily led them into the great room, where the couple gaped together.

"Oh, Emily, this is . . . this is wonderful!" Ruth said. "Everything is so new and bright, and the lighting fixtures, and the — Oh,

Fitz! Look at that gorgeous chandelier! I've never seen it lit up like that!"

They went through each future guest room, some of which were partially furnished. Emily nearly held her breath as they looked into the bedroom where she'd drilled into the pipe. No damage was visible, as she'd replaced the drywall and ripped up and relaid a good portion of the wood floor.

Fitz's face lit up when they entered the owner's suite. There was a large living room and kitchenette, a separate bedroom, and the bathroom. "It's only one bedroom, but the rest of the space is more than we have in our apartment!" He rubbed his hands together, as if he were planning some mischief. "I'm thinking that corner right there would be the perfect place for a new TV. A big flat-screen with high def."

Ruth and Emily laughed. "I can see it, too," Ruth said. "Plus, having one bedroom here in the suite is no big deal. If the girls and their families want to come visit us, we'll have plenty of other rooms where they can sleep!"

Emily smiled as Ruth's words reminded her of her own childhood in Mill River, of growing up with Rose and her mother and Aunt Ivy in their snug little houses. She could see, too, how Ruth missed her own children and how her face lit up at the prospect of them coming to visit. It was the same way her own mother looked, even after months of Emily pushing her away every time they saw each other. It had been her mother who'd insisted that Andy would have wanted her to find happiness in her life. She'd continued to repeat that to herself since then, and strangely, with Matt, she felt it beginning to happen.

She had a sudden urge to find her mother and give her a huge hug.

"Oooh!" Ruth said. "I want to have a look at my tub."

They went through the bedroom to the owner's bathroom. Every surface was clean and sparkling. For added reassurance, Emily had placed a vanilla-scented plug-in air freshener in one of the outlets. The antique tub sat regally against a wall with a shiny new faucet and hardware at one end.

"How beautiful! This is going to be fantastic in the winter," Ruth said. "When the weather's frigid, I'll be soaking in warm bubbles."

"For the last thing I want to show you, we'll have to go outside," Emily said. They went back downstairs to the front door and out onto the stoop. "This is my gift to you," she said, pointing to the new stained glass window above the door. It was an image of several horses in a pasture, with a backdrop of vibrant autumn trees. "I wanted to create an image that paid tribute to Mary. The horses are colored like the ones she used to have on the property."

"Emily, it's stunning," Fitz said, his voice rough with emotion. "I think Mary would have loved it and everything else you've done with her home."

"Father O'Brien talked with me about the horses while I was in the process of shaping the glass. He remembered them well."

For several seconds, no one spoke. Everyone in town knew what had happened to him.

"I pray he'll be well enough to see it," Ruth said in a quiet voice. "Claudia told me that the diocese will provide another priest to marry her and Kyle if Father O'Brien isn't able to do it, but she was pretty cut up just thinking about it."

Emily nodded. The elderly priest was so loved by everyone in Mill River. The little town wouldn't be the same without him.

Father O'Brien was dreaming of spoons. They were everywhere — lying in clusters on his countertops at the parish house kitchen, in the drawers of his bedroom bureau, in the bathroom in the cup where he kept his toothbrush. None of them matched, but he didn't care. Every one of them was beautiful.

He adored the spoon that he kept separately, in his desk drawer. It was Mary's spoon, given freely to him, unlike the hundreds of others he had once stolen, those hundreds that he had shipped away to a soup kitchen months ago, that were cluttering his dream.

He longed for one spoon in particular, the petite sugar spoon he had saved for his mother from her precious secret flatware. It was a relic of his past, lost long ago in the maternity ward of the hospital in Burlington, or maybe after she had been transferred to Brattleboro. Every spoon he'd seen since then, every one he'd ever held in his hand or slipped up his sleeve, reminded him of that one he hadn't seen in decades. Maybe the lost spoon and his emotional connection to it were what had triggered his horrible obsession in the first place. Had a part of him been searching for that spoon all these years?

In his dreams, he could feel it in his hand, a perfectly balanced specimen of elegance. He could see the delicate handle etched with clover leaves, the bowl with a spray of leaves and scalloped edges, the engravings from a grandmother he never knew. Every spoon was beautiful, but that one was unique and irreplaceable, a lost treasure from his youth.

At that moment, he became aware of strange, rhythmic beeping noises nearby and opened his eyes. He wasn't in his bedroom or his favorite recliner in the parish house. His current bed was elevated with rails along either side. Father O'Brien turned his head and blinked.

Fred Richardson, Mill River's longtime doctor and a close friend, was at his bedside. "Michael? Can you hear me?"

"Yes. Why am I in the hospital?" His voice was craggy, and he had to put more effort than usual into forming his words.

"What do you remember?"

"I was . . . I was at Karen Cooper's. She tried to kill herself. Her phone went off, and I reached for it . . ." He looked down at his arm, the one he had tried to use to grab Karen's phone. It hadn't responded then, but he was able to move it now.

"You had a stroke, Michael, the kind caused by a blood clot moving to your brain."

"How long have I been unconscious?

What day is it?"

"Today is Wednesday, December fourth."

"Two days." Father O'Brien looked again at his arm and flexed his hand open and closed several times. "This arm wasn't working so well two days ago."

"You can thank Ron and Jean Wykowski and tissue plasminogen activator — tPA for short — for that," Dr. Richardson said. "They realized right away what was happening to you and marked the time. When they got you here to Rutland, the doctors confirmed the ongoing stroke and administered tPA to dissolve the clot. It's a drug that can be given only in the first three hours after stroke symptoms begin, but if you can administer it in that window, especially within the first hour, it often prevents permanent disability in patients."

Father O'Brien remained silent for a moment. "It seems I was very lucky."

"You were, but you're not home free. I expect you'll be here the rest of the week, at least. You'll need to be monitored for brain hemorrhage, and we'll start you on some sort of blood thinner to help reduce the risk of this happening again. You might also need a bit of physical therapy, although the fact that you're moving that arm when you say you couldn't earlier is encouraging. Your speech is quite good, too."

"What happened with Karen Cooper?" He was afraid to hear the answer.

Dr. Richardson looked evenly at him. "She survived, but she's still in a coma, in critical condition. The good thing about Xanax — that's the drug she took — is that people often survive overdoses of it, even really large amounts. And Ron and Jean got her here quick, just like they did you." Dr. Richardson shook his head. "The police report indicated that she'd tried suicide by carbon monoxide poisoning first."

"Yes. Her car was running in the closed garage. She'd rigged a hose from the tailpipe to the interior."

"The woman must have nine lives. It's tough to use car exhaust to commit suicide nowadays. Modern cars have catalytic converters to strip out almost all the carbon monoxide from the exhaust. Karen probably realized it wasn't working and went back inside to try with her pills."

"I should have gone to her sooner. I waited too long."

"No, you didn't. Look, Michael, I'm not her attending physician, but I spoke with him yesterday, and he's optimistic that she'll recover completely. What Karen will really need is some good psychiatric care and support from her family and friends once she's discharged. And thanks to you, she probably will be. You weren't too late — you were just in time."

"Mom? Are you waking up? It's Ben. And Uncle George. We're both here with you."

Karen opened her eyes slowly. At first the images she saw were nothing more than a blurry mass of light and color. Slowly, her vision came into focus. There were two faces nearby, both with expressions of combined worry and elation. She was having trouble forming thoughts, but the faces held her attention.

"Karen, it's Georgie. Can you squeeze my hand if you can hear me?"

She became aware that her left hand was being held. Her gaze traveled down to their linked hands, and slowly, slowly, her fingers curled around to tighten her grip.

"Good! That's really good, Karen! Ben, stay here with her. I'm going to go get a nurse."

Her hand was disengaged as the larger of the two faces left, and the one that remained moved closer.

"Mom? Do you know who I am?"

Karen blinked slowly and raised her now-lonely hand to touch the cheek of the one remaining face. "Ben."

"That's right, Mom! You remember!" A grin nearly split the face in two, but at the same time, tears appeared in her son's eyes. His lip began to quiver, and he quickly pressed his face down against her, draping an arm over her body to hug her as best he could.

Karen raised her hand to touch Ben's head. A movement near the door caught her attention, and she shifted her gaze. "Georgie," she said as her brother reentered the room, followed by a man wearing scrubs.

"I'm back, Karen. This is Ed," he said, pointing to the nurse. "And your doctor will be here soon. We just called him."

"Keep talking with her. Nothing too heavy or complicated, but encourage her to speak," Ed said. He checked the IV line inserted into her right hand and the readings on several of the monitors surrounding the head of the bed and nodded approvingly. "Her vitals are good. Stable. The doctor will be pleased."

Gradually, her perception and awareness improved. The grogginess was diminishing. It was then that she remembered what had happened, what she had tried and failed to do, and why.

Her face crumpled as she stared at her brother and son, saw the love with which they looked back at her, and realized how badly she must have hurt them. How could she have decided to go through with her plan when it would have inflicted unimaginable pain on these two people she loved with everything in her? What horrible mother and sister would do such a thing?

And yet there was still the darkness, festering inside her, made more painful by Nick's absence. The tug-of-war between the need to fight for her life for others' sakes and the desire to swallow twice as many pills next time was overwhelming.

"Karen, listen to me," her brother said. "We're not going to talk about why you're here right now. The important thing is that you're still with us and that you start helping us help you get better."

"Nick —"

Ben nearly yelled as he interrupted her. "He's coming home, Mom! Dad's coming home! They found him, and he's on his way right now!"

Karen looked at her son's overjoyed face, then at the smile on her brother's. Had she heard them correctly? Was it possible that they were lying to give her false hope, to keep her from wanting to finish what she had failed to do? She was having trouble articulating everything that she felt and wanted to ask, but George read her face and answered her questions.

"Karen, today's Thursday. Nick was located in Yemen last Sunday. He'd been kidnapped by militants, and the U.S. sent a commando unit in to rescue him. We didn't get any sort of notification until Monday evening. Nick's company couldn't reach you, so they tried my number. He has some minor injuries — a broken arm, broken ribs, and some cuts on his face. The company rep didn't have a lot of information, so we don't know very much, but apparently, he was abducted in Saudi Arabia by a group of militants, part of an Al-Qaeda offshoot, looking to rebuild an American military drone they'd managed to shoot down. They targeted Nick because of his background in aerospace engineering and smuggled him into Yemen. There's an investigation under way into how they managed to access that kind of personnel information, but that's not important now. What *is* important is that he's *alive* and on a jet heading home as we speak. He should be here tonight."

"Oh," Karen said. She raised her hands to her face, covering her nose and mouth as she was overcome by a rush of happiness such as she hadn't felt in years. The joy was followed by deep shame. "What will he think of me?"

"Shh, sis, the only thing he'll be is happy to see you, and Ben, too." George took her tear-moistened hands in his. "You have nothing to be sorry for. You've struggled with depression for a long time. Nick knows that, and he'll understand. The stress of what you've been through would be tough for anyone to handle. If anyone should be sorry, it's me. I should have realized what you were dealing with and spent more time with you out here, especially after Dad got sick. You've been carrying our whole family for so long. I should have done better by you. But I promise you this: Ben and I, and Nick, when he gets here, are going to make sure you get all the help you need to get well. You've got a lot of life left and a lot of happiness ahead of you, and we're all going to be there with you when it comes."

In her dim hospital room, Karen opened her eyes. She heard the usual beeping of monitors and the muffled sounds of activity outside her door, but it had been something else, a slight movement, a soft intake of breath, that had interrupted her sleep.

He was sitting in a chair at her bedside.

At first she was convinced she was dreaming. Certain details, though, were not the sort she would expect to see in a dream about her husband. His left arm in a bright white cast. The white Steri-Strips adhered to his forehead. His hair, longer, ragged, framing a face that was thinner than she had ever seen it, even when he'd been a wily young thing fresh out of basic training. The tears that moistened the thin face.

"I never get tired of watching you sleep. You're so beautiful."

"Nick."

The dream was real, and they were in each other's arms as quickly as his broken bones and her sluggish post-comatose body would allow.

They didn't speak for a long while. Karen couldn't have said anything had she tried, as the sobs and the heaving breaths would have prevented it. Eventually, they quieted together and just held each other.

"I'm sorry," Karen finally managed to whisper. "I gave up."

"Shhh, honey, don't talk, just listen," Nick said. His uninjured arm kept her pulled tight as he kissed her temple and spoke softly next to her ear. "I'm the one who should be sorry, for leaving you, for not understanding that what we needed was to be together regardless of our finances or anything else. I never should have risked leaving again for any reason."

"I don't deserve to live," she choked.

"That's the depression talking, and it's not true," Nick replied. "You deserve it more than anyone I know. You're stronger than anyone I know. All this time, you've kept going. You took care of your dad and Ben all by yourself, even when you were hurting inside. What happened to me by itself would be enough to make anyone crack under the pressure, and you were dealing with so much more."

There was another long silence.

"You must be exhausted," Karen whispered. She reached over and pulled back the covers, motioning for him to crawl in with her. It took some maneuvering, but they were able to find a position comfortable for both of them and Nick's cast in the hospital bed. She still couldn't believe that he was here with her, alive and relatively unharmed. She had been so sure she would never see him again.

"Tell me what happened to you?" she asked with her forehead nestled against his jaw. "George said you were kidnapped by militants wanting you to fix a drone."

"Yes. They surrounded my Jeep once I was

off-base, and my colleague and I couldn't hold them off. They shot Elliott, the guy I was driving with, and took me across the border to Yemen. They had the drone in an old warehouse. The thing was damaged beyond repair — at least there was nothing I could do to get it to fly again — but I couldn't tell them that. I let on like I was fixing it, that it would take a long time, but really, the only thing I could do was rewire it and program it to send out an encrypted SOS, in the hope that our guys could track my location and send help."

"How did this happen?" she asked, lightly touching the cast on his arm.

"When they first got me," he said. "The ribs, too. I didn't make it easy for them."

Karen had many more questions, but they would wait. Nick's voice had taken on an edge, and she changed the subject so that he wouldn't have to relive his ordeal further. "Did you hear about Father O'Brien?"

"No, what about him?"

"He had a stroke. He's here in the hospital, too. Came to see me earlier this afternoon."

"He's all right, then?"

"He told me his doctor says he will be. He'll have to take medication and be a little more careful, but he seemed like his regular self. He thinks he's going to go home in time to say Mass this Sunday."

"Amazing, especially at his age," Nick said. "There are miracles all around us."

"There are," Karen agreed, and she felt her eyes well up again. "I'm so thankful we're both here to see them."

"I am, too," Nick said. "And when we go home, I promise you that every day for the rest of our lives is going to be a celebration of living, and each other."

CHAPTER 34

By Friday, Father O'Brien was getting frustrated. He felt fine physically. Miraculously, despite a moderately severe stroke on the right side of his brain, he had no paralysis on his left side or other lingering effects except a bit of numbness in his left big toe. He'd had two physical therapy sessions, both of which had gone well. Out of an abundance of caution, Fred had restricted visitors until Thursday afternoon, and since then, it seemed that practically everyone in Mill River had come to see him.

Not that he wasn't grateful for such an outpouring of love and support. Or having been allowed to visit Karen Cooper in her hospital room down the hall, where they'd joked about which one of them had won the race to the hospital. Or the fresh cherry pie that Ruth had brought over.

But what he wanted more than anything was to be able to go home to the comfortable parish house he loved, to sit in his chair in his office at St. John's and work on a homily for Sunday's Mass.

At least he was able to do the third thing. After he'd showered and changed into fresh clothes, one of his nurses had brought him a lap desk and some lined paper. He was scribbling away, absorbed in thought, when yet another knock sounded at his door. He sighed and set down his pen.

"Father O'Brien?" A woman with shoulder-length black hair peeked into the room. She looked familiar.

"Yes? Come in," he encouraged her. She smiled and entered, along with an older woman with curly white hair whom he didn't recognize. He focused again on the younger lady. "You're the one who interviewed me a few months ago, aren't you? Julia Tomlinson?"

"I am. It's nice to see you again, Father, although I'm sorry about the location."

"Believe me, I'm more than ready to get out of here. But I'm curious why you tracked me down. What brings you back up this way? Did you run out of stories to cover in New York City? And who did you bring along with you?"

Julia laughed. "I'm glad to see you're doing well. They told me what happened to you when I arrived at the church. Some lovely woman there — I think she said her name was Elsa — told us where we could find you and encouraged us to visit you here, since you'd been having other visitors from the congregation. Father O'Brien, this is Mrs. Elizabeth Montgomery," Julia said, gently ushering her companion forward. "She contacted me a few weeks ago, after she read my interview with you. May we sit down?"

"Please," Father O'Brien said. Julia pushed the two chairs in the room closer to his bedside, and she and Elizabeth each took one.

"As I was saying, Elizabeth contacted me after she read the interview because she was interested in meeting you. At first I thought she might be — what is the best way of describing it — a fan of yours? In which case, there was no reason why she couldn't call you or write to you or come up to Mill River herself. But when she explained why she wanted to get in touch with you, I could see that it would be better for her to reach out with me along so you wouldn't think that what she has to say is some crazy concoction of her imagination. That, and also because I could see the potential of an amazing article in the reason why she wanted to meet you."

"The truth is, Father," Elizabeth said, "you still might think I'm crazy after I tell you why I'm here, but could you hear me out before you make that decision?"

He was utterly perplexed and very curious. Neither of the women seemed anything but kind and normal. "All right," he said to Elizabeth.

"I grew up in New Hampshire, in a little town called Suncook, just south of Concord. I was an only child, but my parents were wonderful and loving, everything you could ask for in a mother and father. We were very close.

"They've been gone a long time now — my father almost fifty years and my mother nearly thirty. After my father was gone, my mother and I became even closer. There wasn't a day that went by when we didn't see each other or talk on the phone. I thought I knew everything about her. When she passed away, though, I learned that wasn't true.

"She left me a letter telling me that she and Dad had adopted me when I was a newborn. They couldn't have children of their own, and their priest came to them one afternoon and asked whether they'd be willing to care for a child whose mother was so ill that she no longer could. Of course they said yes. I was sickly as a baby, underweight and colicky, but my mother was determined. With her constant care, I found good health and thrived.

"I don't know why she never told me that I was adopted while she was living. Maybe she was afraid my love for her would change somehow, which is ridiculous. But back then, adoption wasn't so common, and some folks looked down on couples who couldn't have their own children. I suppose I'll never know some things.

"My mother didn't have a lot of information about where I came from, other than the fact that the whole thing was arranged illicitly by her priest and a priest who knew my birth family. She also told me that my original surname was O'Brien, and my birth mother's name was Anna."

Father O'Brien opened his mouth, but he quickly closed it as he remembered his promise to let her speak uninterrupted.

"You told me in our interview that your mother's name was Anna," Julia said quietly.

"I did, and it was. But —"

Elizabeth held up her hand. "You promised to let me finish," she said gently, and he sighed and waited for her to continue.

"After I read my mother's letter, I didn't do anything with the information for a long time. It took some getting used to, learning that I'd been adopted. But eventually, I started to wonder about where I came from. About that time, something called the Internet had started to pick up steam, and suddenly, there were ways of finding out about your ancestry that people hadn't dreamed of before then.

"My daughter and grandson helped me a lot, I'll admit. I still don't know how to work a computer very well, but my grandson sure is a whiz, I tell you. The other thing that was difficult is that our country sure has a lot of Anna O'Briens."

Father O'Brien had to chuckle. "I imagine that's true. Have you gone through all of them?"

"Almost," Elizabeth said. "We've been working at our own pace, trying to narrow down the possibilities, including those Annas who have already passed. When I read Julia's article in *America,* I thought it was a good lead. The names matched up, at least. I wondered if you might be willing to share a little about your family with me, to see if your mother might be the Anna I'm looking for."

"I'm sorry to have to tell you this, but I

don't think that's the case. Yes, my mother's name was Anna, and I had a younger sister, but she died in infancy. I attended her funeral. My uncle Frank officiated."

A strange look passed between Julia and Elizabeth.

"Maybe you should show him," Julia said. Elizabeth nodded, reached into her purse, and took out a yellowed, folded piece of paper and a small flat box.

"Besides the letter, my mother left me this. There was a note tucked inside. It's barely legible now," she said, unfolding the paper and holding it out to him, "but it was an instruction that the box and its contents should go with the baby. And it was signed by someone named Frank."

Father O'Brien reached out to take the note. When he saw the faded handwriting and signature, his hand began to tremble so violently that he could no longer make out the letters.

Elizabeth stood up and came closer to him. She carefully lifted the lid on the box, but he already knew what he was about to see. He closed his eyes. When he had reopened them, the shimmering spoon resting inside the box was exactly as it had been in his dreams.

"May I?" he whispered. Elizabeth nodded, and he took the spoon from the box. The name Anna was engraved on the front of the handle; on the back, as he knew it would be, the inscription read, "My sweet girl."

"This . . . this was my mother's," he said. "I thought . . . I thought it had been lost." He looked into Elizabeth's eyes — blue eyes that were exactly the same shade as his own — and acknowledged the truth of who she was. "I held you once," he said, trying unsuccessfully to stifle a sob. "I held you when you were three days old. Your given name was Grace Elizabeth."

"It still is," she said, bending her tear-streaked face toward his to kiss his cheek. "I go by my middle name."

EPILOGUE

No one is to be despaired of as long as he breathes. (While there is life there is hope.)
— DESIDERIUS ERASMUS

Late in the afternoon on Saturday, December 20, just before it was time for her to walk down the aisle, Claudia Simon stood before the mirror in the dressing room at St. John's. Everything was perfect — hair, makeup, veil, and gown. Pauline had made the veil to match the gown, and it was just as stunning. Claudia touched the combs and pins holding it in her hair and straightened the sheer fabric that flowed past her shoulders.

"You about ready, Claudia?" her father asked as he came into the dressing room. "The music is about to start. And wow, you are beautiful." As if on cue, she heard the organ begin "Wedding March." She took a deep breath and smiled as she slipped her hand through her father's arm.

Even though she had sworn to herself that she would not blubber all the way down the aisle, the sight of Kyle standing at the altar beside Father O'Brien unlocked the floodgates. As she passed the pews filled with people she loved, she couldn't help thinking that a wedding was a real-life version of Facebook. People from all stages of her life were gathered here with her, all in one place, ready to celebrate this huge happiness with her and Kyle. All of these people standing as she passed were her current and future friends list. The thought was ridiculous, of course — who in her right mind would be thinking about social media on her trip down the aisle? — but it helped her to smile more and cry less.

The wedding Mass passed in a blur, and before she knew it, Kyle was sliding a ring onto her finger, Father O'Brien was announcing them as Mr. and Mrs. Kyle Hansen, and Kyle was lifting her veil for their first kiss as husband and wife. He kept it classy, which made her happy, although he couldn't help grabbing her up and spinning her around in a hug as they began their walk back down the aisle to form a receiving line.

Kevin was standing with the other groomsmen and their dates, but Misty wasn't with him. Strangely, Claudia didn't remember seeing Misty in the church as she'd walked down the aisle. Kyle had never mentioned the text messages Misty had sent him, and Claudia couldn't help but wonder whether her absence was his doing. Had he privately disinvited her from the wedding?

"Congrats, bro," Kevin said as he hugged Kyle. "And Claudia, I always wanted a sister. Well, that's not really true, but it's awesome that my new sister is you. Welcome to the family."

"Aw, thanks, Kevin," Claudia said with a laugh as he kissed her on the cheek. "I already have a brother, but I'm glad to have another one! So, are you ready to give the big toast at the reception?"

"Yeah, I think so. I've practiced a bunch of times."

"You'll be great," Kyle said. "Best best man ever."

"I haven't seen Misty," Claudia said. "Did she step away for a minute?"

"Uh, no," Kevin said, and the jovial look on his face vanished. "She's not here. I mean, she was going to come, but that was before we — Well, we're done. I'll tell you about it later. I don't want to hold up the line."

"Oh, man, I'm sorry," Claudia heard Kyle say. "Come find me later, all right?" Kevin nodded, and she struggled to keep from smiling before Kyle gently took her elbow and nudged her toward the next person in line.

After they had gone through the receiving line and had their photos taken, they freshened up in the dressing room. The guests were awaiting their arrival at the marble mansion, but Claudia had a little trouble convincing Kyle to leave the church.

"You are stunning," he said, pulling her close and kissing her neck. "Everyone's almost gone. And since we're officially married now . . ."

She scoffed at him. "Kyle Hansen, I am not about to consummate our marriage in the church basement!"

"I'm kidding, kidding," he said. "It's just that you are so irresistible —"

"We have a mansion full of guests waiting for us," she said, "and what about this surprise wedding-night venue you have planned? You really don't want to spoil that, now, do you?"

"No," he admitted. "But I'm thinking that maybe we should leave the reception early."

They left the church to go to Kyle's truck and were surprised to see snow falling heavily. Already, the ground was covered, and the tree branches were quickly becoming lined with white.

"Could it *be* more perfect?" Claudia said.

"Nope. Not for a winter wedding, anyway."

Kyle helped her get into the truck and tucked the long train on her dress in over her legs. It took only a few minutes to drive from St. John's to the big house on the hill. They parked in a space reserved with a sign and a display of red roses.

"I can't wait to see inside," Claudia said as they hurried to the front door, holding hands and shielding their faces from the snow. A new sign was affixed to the front of the house: MARY'S MARBLE INN BED-AND-BREAKFAST, EST. 2013. Beneath that, a temporary sign read, "Hansen Wedding Reception."

The door opened suddenly, and Ruth was standing there, beckoning them inside. "Come in, come in, before you freeze!" Once they were safely in the foyer, she smiled and clasped her hands. "All right. Everyone is waiting, so just follow me."

Ruth led them around a corner and to the double doors that led into the enormous great room. Claudia gasped. Everyone from the wedding was there, but the room itself was transformed. There were beautiful sofas and chairs around the perimeter of the room, where people could comfortably sit and visit. Large bouquets of red roses were strategically interspersed along the walls and next to a table overflowing with gifts, and the disc jockey they had hired had set up his equipment in one of the far corners.

The guests began to applaud as they made their entrance, accompanied by the announcement of their arrival over the sound system. As they mingled, Claudia began to realize that what she'd heard was true. One of the hardest things about weddings was having so many people you love around you and so little time to spend with each one. Her family was there, of course, and several of her fellow teachers from Mill River and her hometown of Dryden, New York. Her best friend from high school had flown in, as had her college roommate. There were other familiar faces. Dear Father O'Brien was slowly working the room. When Claudia spotted Karen Cooper standing with her husband and son, she immediately went over to them.

"Claudia," Karen said with a smile, holding out her arms to hug her as Kyle and

Nick shook hands. "You look so beautiful. Congratulations."

"I'm so glad you're here today. And you, too, Nick! I'll always look back and remember what a blessing it was that you were both able to share this day with us."

"It is a blessing," Karen replied. She gazed at Nick's face, and he squeezed her against him with the arm that wasn't in a cast and sling.

Claudia was looking around, trying to see where Rowen was, when a short little woman with gray curly hair approached her.

"Oh, Miss Claudia, this is the most perfect wedding I've ever been to," Daisy Delaine said in her distinctive singsong voice. "Well, you know that it's the only wedding I've ever been to. I'm so happy you invited me. I hope you and Officer Hansen have a long and joyful life together."

"I hope that, too, Daisy, thank you," she said, and bent down a little to embrace her.

"Oh, and you know, Miss Claudia, I made you a real special potion as a gift. It's an early batch of my famous love potion. There's no fresh wintergreen ready yet, but I had just enough left over in the freezer from last year. Anyhow, it's on the table over there, but I thought I'd tell you that the one that has 'Fragile' on it is from me."

"I'll keep an eye out for it, Daisy," Claudia said. "And thank you so much for thinking of us. I'm sure it'll be great."

As Daisy tottered off into the crowd, Claudia noticed Emily, who had helped Ruth set up for the reception, standing with Matt Campbell in a nearby corner. Claudia had been meaning to compliment Emily on the stunning renovation of the mansion, but she and Matt were holding hands and talking, seemingly oblivious to everything around them.

"I'm so thrilled with how everything turned out," Emily was saying to Matt. "If you hadn't helped me so much . . . I still can't believe you offered when I was so cool toward you in the beginning."

"Eh, I like challenges. I didn't have anything better to do, and I figured it was worth a try to get what I really wanted."

"Which was?"

Matt gave Emily a naughty grin. "A woman of substance," he said. "Smart, good sense of humor, and one who . . ." He leaned over to whisper in her ear. Claudia didn't catch everything he said, but she couldn't help smiling to herself when she heard him say "tool belt" and "smoking hot."

The evening seemed to speed by, faster

and faster, in a blur of champagne and hors d'oeuvres, cake, dancing, more champagne, and more cake. All the while, the snow continued to fall outside. A few hours after they arrived at the mansion, Ruth took them aside.

"Fitz just told me they've issued a winter storm warning for the whole area. They've upped the snow totals, too. You might think about getting on the road if you want to get to . . . uh, wherever you're planning on spending the night."

"She's probably right," Kyle said after Ruth went to check on the appetizers set up in the dining room. "Why don't you have a quick word with anyone you haven't talked to yet. I'm going to go find Rowen to make sure she and my parents are good to go, and then I'll meet you back in the kitchen."

"Okay," Claudia said. She couldn't help giggling as Kyle grabbed her up and kissed her passionately before letting her loose. When she returned to the kitchen, she was surprised to find Kevin lounging against the counter. He'd removed his bow tie and held a half-empty bottle of beer.

"Hey there, sis," he said as she came in. "Great party out there. I guess you and Kyle will be taking off soon?"

"I think so. We heard that the weather's

going downhill fast." Kevin was a pitiful sight, with bloodshot eyes and hair that was mussed on one side. "I'm really sorry to hear about you and Misty," she said carefully. "I wanted to tell you that earlier, but it's been kind of crazy tonight. I haven't had much time to talk with anyone for more than a few minutes."

"Thanks. I was hoping no one would notice Misty didn't come, especially you guys. It was your special day, you know? I didn't want the whole mess with her to take away from that."

"It didn't, and it wouldn't have," Claudia said. "Are you sure you're okay?"

Kevin took a swig of his beer and nodded. "Yeah. I was kind of pissed about it at first, but it's been a week or so since she ended things, and now I'm not as upset. I'm even starting to feel glad. I mean, she was really beautiful, you know? The prettiest girlfriend I ever had, hands down. But I found out that she was sleeping around on me."

Not with Kyle, Claudia thought with smug satisfaction, though she wasn't at all surprised about Kevin's revelation. Remembering Misty's proposition to Kyle, she felt the urge to wallop the woman all over again. What *was* strange was the fact that her new brother-in-law was sharing so much with her. *Maybe it's the alcohol,* she thought. *Or maybe the poor guy just needs someone to talk to about it.*

"Oh, Kevin, I'm so sorry. That's awful."

Kevin snorted. "Yeah. Some guy she met at the gym. They took a naked selfie together, which she texted to me, along with a few choice words about how much better-looking he was than me, to break things off."

"Oh, God."

"Yeah."

"That's *really* horrible." Secretly, she was relieved that Kyle hadn't been the one to reveal the truth about Misty to Kevin.

"I know. Ol' Kevin struck out again. But I figure I'm better off without her, if that's the kind of person she is. I just wish I could find a really nice girl."

"You will," Claudia said. "It's hard to be patient when you're ready for a relation-ship, I know, but it takes time to meet the right person, time to get to know her."

"I'm trying. Have been for a while, but I never seem to find the right one. Mostly, it's tough to get anyone interested in going out with me." Kevin twisted the beer bottle as it sat on the countertop. The bit of liquid left inside sloshed rhythmically against the brown glass.

Claudia chewed on her bottom lip, trying

to think of what she could say to bring him some comfort. Finally, she took a deep breath. "There was a time not long ago when I didn't think I'd ever meet anyone, especially someone who loved me for *me* — the person I am on the inside. I was pretty overweight and had been all my life. No one wanted to get close enough to me to see what kind of person I was. Or maybe I was so insecure that I convinced myself of that.

"Once I committed to getting healthy and got myself in shape on the outside, I figured things would be really different. But, you know what? On the inside, I didn't change that much. I realized after a while that I'd never have a real relationship unless I met someone who truly loved me for who I was inside . . . and unless I loved myself. That was scary. No amount of running on the treadmill would take away my insecurities, so meeting people hadn't gotten any easier for me, despite the change in how I looked. I realized that outward appearances aren't the important thing.

"With Kyle, things just fell into place. It happened fast — faster than I ever imagined it would — and there are still days when I pinch myself and marvel at how happy I am with him. Like today. But my point is, you're a lot like him, Kevin. You're a nice guy. You *are* good-looking, regardless of what Misty said. You obviously value what a person is like inside, and you deserve someone who shares that quality. I know the right girl *is* out there, waiting for you. It may take a little while, and a strikeout or two, but eventually, you'll find someone you love for who she is, inside and out, and she'll feel the same way about you."

"I hope so," Kevin said. "And I think Kyle is really lucky. You don't have any sisters, do you?"

Claudia laughed. "Nope, just my brother, but I've got a lot of friends. A lot of *single* friends. Maybe I can set you up on a blind date once we're back from our honeymoon."

"Really?" Kevin finally cracked a smile. "Are you serious?"

"Sure, if you're up for it."

"Huh. Well, what the hell? I guess it's worth a shot."

Claudia beamed. "It definitely is."

A moment later, Kyle entered the kitchen. "All right," he said. "I think we should get going. You ready?"

"Yes," Claudia said. She stood up and took Kyle's hand.

"Have a great time," Kevin said with a wink at Claudia. "And I'll be looking forward to my date."

"Date?" Kyle asked with a puzzled expression as they left the kitchen.

"Oh, I'm going to try my hand at playing Cupid," she said. "I'll explain later."

They quickly changed out of their formal attire and said goodbye to their families and guests. Their overnight bags were already packed and in the cab of Kyle's truck. Ruth handed them a small portable cooler just before they got inside. "I didn't see either of you eating much, so I packed some food for you to take. There's some of the cake in there, too."

"That's so nice of you, Ruth. Thank you so much for everything," Kyle said.

Claudia hugged her tightly. "We couldn't have asked for a more beautiful reception. And congratulations on your new bed-and-breakfast. It really is amazing."

Rowen ran up to Kyle and grabbed him around the waist. "You be good," he told her as he squeezed her around the shoulders. "Don't you run your grandma and grandpa ragged. We'll be back tomorrow night."

"Don't worry, we're going to have a great time," Peggy said. "Now get going, you two, before the snow gets too deep and you end up stuck on the side of the road on your wedding night."

"Are you finally going to tell me where we're going?" Claudia asked once they were on the road.

"Ummm, no. I'd rather you see it," Kyle said. "You only have to wait another hour, though."

"Thank goodness," she said, sliding her hand along his thigh.

"So, what was Kevin saying?" Kyle asked. "About the date?"

"I was trying to cheer him up. Misty cheated on him with another guy — treated him like crap. I feel so bad for Kevin. He really deserves to meet a nice girl, so I'm going to try to set him up on a blind date with one of my friends."

"Really? That would be awesome!" Kyle grinned at her. "You know, I didn't say anything to you, because I didn't want you to think it was a big deal or that I wouldn't handle it, but Misty made a couple passes at me. She even texted me after Thanksgiving, wanting to hook up for fun. Can you believe it?"

"What?" Claudia looked at him with her mouth slightly open. "Are you serious?"

"Oh, yeah. I texted her back and told her that I was madly in love with you and that she should fuck off and stay the hell away from Kevin. Not that I usually use words like that, but I was so disgusted. I wanted to use language she'd understand. I blocked her number, too."

"There aren't words bad enough to describe her. It's a good thing you didn't tell me all this before now. I trust you completely, but I really might've killed her."

Kyle chuckled. "I know. So, you're not mad? I didn't want it to ruin our wedding or the time before it. I made it clear to her that she was no longer invited, but I haven't told Kevin what she did. I've been trying to figure out how to do that."

"I don't think you have to," Claudia said, and she filled him in on the details of Kevin's breakup. "He's done with her and looking toward the future, so he's in a good place. And so are we." She rubbed his thigh gently, and Kyle put his free arm around her so she could rest her head against his shoulder.

After several minutes, they managed to get out in front of the storm, and they made great time the rest of the way.

"Lake Placid?" Claudia asked as she saw a sign.

Kyle just smiled.

A few minutes later, her eyes grew wide. " 'Mirror Lake Inn Resort and Spa,' " she read as they pulled into the parking lot. "Oh my God, I've heard of this place. It's supposed to be incredible!"

Kyle smiled again. "It is."

They had the Adirondack Suite, one of the lake-view signature suites with a stone fireplace and a whirlpool tub. Claudia could only stare at the columns of birch bark, twig, and cedar and the rustic wooden frame on the enormous king-size bed. Through the window, they could plainly see the rush of snowflakes flying past as the storm caught up with them.

"It really is just like our first time," Claudia breathed. "I think this might have been worth the wait."

"What do you say we try out the tub first?" Kyle asked. He came up behind her and slipped his arm around her waist.

Claudia stroked his hand with her own and reached out to lower the window shade. Then she turned toward him and began unbuttoning his shirt. "First the tub," she agreed, planting a light kiss on his bare chest. Feeling the warmth of his skin against her lips sent a rush of electricity down her body. "And then?" She looked past him, toward the bed.

Kyle took her face in his hands and lowered his mouth to hers. "And then I intend to take my wife into that huge bed and make love to her for the rest of the night."

In his office in the parish house on Saturday night, Father O'Brien read over his homily for the next morning's Mass. Every so often, he glanced around and felt a renewed gratitude that he was still there, able to enjoy and be a part of this place. And then there was Elizabeth, the wonder of her finding him and of feeling a love reawakened after eighty years.

He looked down at two envelopes sitting on the corner of his desk. The first was a business letter from a medical laboratory confirming that he and Elizabeth were siblings. After seeing the spoon, he'd had no doubt, but the modern marvel of DNA testing had made it official.

The second envelope held two old, handwritten letters. One of them was from his mother to Mary, written when they'd been corresponding. He'd had no idea that they would develop the friendship they had. When he'd suggested they start writing, it had been merely to give two similar individuals — one isolated in a great white house in Mill River and the other a long-term patient at the Brattleboro Retreat — a constructive activity.

And yet, his mother had confided to Mary so much. He'd read all of the letters since Emily had dropped them off in Patrick McAllister's old briefcase, and it gave him joy to know that his mother had regained her memories over the years. Mary, with her penchant for helping, must have seen in his mother another person who needed her, albeit from a distance.

Father O'Brien unfolded the first letter and read it again:

October 24, 1971

Dear Mary,
I write this letter with a heavy heart, for I have learned that my older brother, Frank, has died. I visited him in the hospital two days ago, and we said our goodbyes then, because the doctor told us his infection wasn't responding to treatment and his organs had begun to shut down.

Frank told me something very upsetting during my visit, something he had kept from me for nearly forty years. My baby girl, Grace — the one I told you about, who died only a few days after she was born, didn't actually die at all. I don't remember much from back then, as I was very ill, but I do remember her. She was born prematurely at less than four pounds. I named her with Michael and Frank sitting beside me, right before her baptism.

Frank told me that he knew I would've done anything for that baby, but in my condition, I wasn't capable of taking care of an infant. I was so grief-stricken over Niall's death that I didn't even recognize her or Michael, and the doctors couldn't tell Frank when I might be myself again or if I ever would be. Frank also detested orphanages. He told me he'd heard about too many orphans being mistreated . . . or worse. So, he arranged for Grace to be adopted by a childless couple — good people, he assured me — although back then he told me she'd died. She was so small and weak at birth that the doctors didn't expect her to survive, and Frank felt that if I ever got well enough to realize my daughter was gone, it would be easier to come to terms with her death than her having been adopted. Plus, I imagine Michael would have objected strenuously if he knew Frank was attempting to find a new home for Grace.

Mary, I find myself pining more for

my lost child than my late brother. That may be terrible to say, but it's true. There aren't words to describe how upset I was with him when he finally told me the truth. The difficulty I had carrying that baby, and all the trouble Michael went through to provide for me when his father couldn't . . . I fought harder for Grace than I'd fought for anything my whole life. In the end, she was taken from me, and I was too sick to realize it.

Frank didn't have any information about the child — the names of the adoptive parents or where they lived. He worked with another priest in New Hampshire to arrange it, but it was done quickly and in secret. I've made inquiries to various state agencies and offices of the church, but no one has been able to find any record of her other than a funeral Mass conducted in the spring of 1935, which I now know was not reflective of the truth.

I'm nearly eighty, Mary, and I don't expect that I'll live long enough to find my Grace. But you're younger than I, and you have more resources at your disposal. Could you find it in your heart to take up the search? I have no idea whether she is still living or where she might be. She might not be alive, and if you discover as much, or if you fail to locate her, I pray you'll not say anything to Michael, for it would break his heart all over again. But if she can be located, it would mean the world to Michael to know what happened and to meet her. After all he did for his baby sister, he deserves it.

My fondest wishes,
Anna

The second, shorter letter was written by Mary and addressed to him:

March 14, 1973

My dearest Michael,
I hesitate to even write this letter, knowing how it would upset you to read it, and not having even decided whether to give it to you, but I feel I must put what I know to paper.

I'm enclosing this note with a letter I received from your mother concerning a baby sister you once had. I won't repeat everything in Anna's letter here, but I wanted you to know that I used every means at my disposal to try to determine whether your sister had in fact survived and been adopted. My written inquiries and telephone calls uncovered very little information about her. I arrived at the same conclusion your mother had, that no paper records exist beyond the church record of her funeral.

I did, however, have Jack Gasaway look into the matter. I didn't know whom else to ask, but since the Gasaways had handled my legal affairs for years, I knew I could trust them and that confidentiality wouldn't be an issue. Jack and his son were able to travel to the Burlington area on my behalf and meet with officials of the Colchester parish. The officials put them in touch with a woman who had worked as Frank's secretary years ago. She was quite old, but she remembered clearly one night when Frank arrived at the church with an infant and asked her to hold it. Together, she and Frank drove with the baby to New Hampshire to meet another priest waiting to take the child to an adoptive family. This woman trusted Frank implicitly, and she never questioned what he was doing or why. Unfortunately, the Gasaways weren't able to find any further information about the baby.

I know that your mother wished you not to know anything about your sister if I couldn't confirm that she was alive and locate her. I wanted so much to be able to do this for you, Michael. You're my closest — my only — friend. You've given me so much over the years, and here was something precious — the gift of your sister — that I might be able to give to you in return. It pains me terribly that I couldn't find her. But I believe she lived when you had been told otherwise, and that she might still be out there somewhere.

You know that I am not a devoutly religious person, but I do pray that somehow, someday, you and she will find each other again.

With all my love,
Mary

Sitting in his chair, Father O'Brien closed his eyes. It was clear that Mary had decided not to share the letter with him while she was living, or to reveal what she knew about his family and sister, but he wasn't angry with her. He was sure she'd made the decision in order to spare him certain agony. Just as Grace had said, there had been no

Internet back then, and if he'd known she was alive and couldn't find her, it would have cast a painful shadow over decades of his life.

Mary's face materialized in his mind. She was smiling, and he got the feeling that wherever she was, she was overjoyed. He, too, was happier than he had felt in years. For so long, he'd thought of Mary McAllister as the sister he'd never had. It seemed almost too good to be true to think that his real sister had survived, and that he had the chance to get to know her and the rest of her family — *his* family — in addition to the lifetime of memories he had of his time with Mary.

Father O'Brien opened his desk drawer and removed the two spoons that he now kept there: Mary's silver teaspoon, and his mother's clover-patterned sugar spoon. He could almost feel the warmth in his heart radiating down his arm to warm the metal in his hand. It was a sign, he was sure, that Mary and his mother were together, happy, and smiling.

He'd already accepted an invitation to spend Christmas with Grace — or Elizabeth — they hadn't quite worked out what he should call her. But it didn't matter. Regardless of the challenges ahead, regardless of any changes that might come with the New Year, he'd been given a bit more time on Earth. He intended to continue spending as much of it as he could with *all* of his family — his sister, his congregation, and his beloved community of Mill River.

ACKNOWLEDGMENTS

Writing a novel is a valuable and enjoyable experience for many reasons, not least of which is that the research required allows me to expand my understanding of subjects about which I know little or nothing. I am grateful to many people who kindly took time from their busy lives to answer my questions or direct me to information that I needed. In particular, I would like to extend my thanks to Mary Jo Kriz, executive assistant to the rector at St. John's Seminary in Boston, Massachusetts, for information about the history of St. John's during the 1930s and '40s; to Irene Dey, Esq., for clarification of criminal legal procedures and lesser included offenses; to Shandra Andry, RN, CNM, for help researching the treatment of hyperemesis gravidarum in the 1920s and '30s; to Sherri Miller, for sharing with me her deeply personal experience caring for a parent with Alzheimer's disease; to

Timothy Chan, M.D., Ph.D., for answering myriad general medical questions; to Brian Woods, for teaching me about home repair and remodeling (and home repair disasters!); and to Dennis Tomasallo, for similar information about home repair and remodeling, as well as for giving me a crash course in various tactics for and methods of hunting wild game.

I must also thank my wonderful test readers — my friends Lena Ottusch, Elizabeth SanMiguel, and Brian and Deidre Woods, as well as members of my family, namely Linda Tomasallo, Carrie Tomasallo, Molly Tomasallo, and Dennis and Susan Tomasallo. I appreciate so much the insightful and honest feedback you offered to help improve this book.

To my friend and fellow author, Elizabeth Letts, thank you for your continued advice and camaraderie. I am also grateful for the encouragement and moral support given by my close friends Angie Swedhin, Deidre Woods, Sherri Miller, Elizabeth SanMiguel, Michele Knorr, and Lena Ottusch. And, to Nina Arazoza and Jenny Stephens, assistants to my editor and agent, respectively, I know you both do a great deal behind the scenes, and I appreciate it very much.

I would like to thank my publisher, Libby

McGuire, as well as Kim Hovey, Matthew Schwartz, and Jennifer Hershey. I can't tell you how much I appreciate all of your support, feedback, and enthusiasm. Many thanks also to my publicist, Lindsey Kennedy, and to Susan Corcoran and Alex Coumbis in the publicity department; to my marketing manager, Maggie Oberrender, and to Kristin Fassler, who heads up the marketing department; to my production editor, Jennifer Rodriguez; to Marietta Anastassatos, the artist who designed the gorgeous cover for this book; and to the rest of the lovely and talented people at Penguin Random House and Ballantine Books, whose great care and effort have gone into the publishing and launch of this novel.

To my brilliant editor, Kara Cesare, thank you so much for another fabulous editorial experience and for loving my Mill River books as much as you do. I am thankful that our working styles and goals are so in tune, and your advice and expertise are invaluable. I couldn't ask for a better in-house advocate or friend on the road to publication.

To my superb, longtime literary agent, Laurie Liss, thank you for your wisdom, humor, honesty, and friendship, and your tireless efforts on my behalf. I am so grateful for everything you've done and continue to do for me.

Finally, I would like to acknowledge the members of my immediate family whose support and encouragement are constant and unfailing. To my mom, Linda, my dad and my stepmom, Dennis and Susan, my sisters, Carrie and Molly, my husband, Tim, and my little dude, Gavin — all of you mean so much to me! Love you always!

■ ■ ■ ■

THE PROMISE
OF HOME
A MILL RIVER
NOVEL

DARCIE CHAN

■ ■ ■ ■

A READER'S GUIDE

A CONVERSATION WITH DARCIE CHAN

Random House Reader's Circle: The fictional town of Mill River, Vermont, serves as the setting for all of your novels, and many characters overlap across all three books. What was the biggest challenge in creating and maintaining such an interconnected community?

Darcie Chan: Strangely, when I was writing the first Mill River book, I had no inkling that it would become the first of at least three novels with a common setting and many common characters. It was simply my first novel, one that I hoped would be published someday.

When it became clear that I would have the opportunity to write more books set in Mill River, I had to think carefully about how to proceed. Consistency is key. Characters who appear in more than one book must be consistent across, not just within, the books. At the same time, I think it's vital that I continue to explore and develop those characters.

I also view the town of Mill River itself as a central character in my books, if not the heart of each story. It's important to keep the details of the town consistent — not only the physical details, such as the location of certain buildings and streets, and their positions in relation to others — but also the town's safe, cozy, and welcoming feel.

The residents of Mill River play a large part in achieving that latter goal. As I plan each story, I'm constantly focused on which of the townspeople should be involved, which would have some connection to or know about the events taking place, and what kinds of people I might like to meet were I to actually visit the town. Should I involve a character who is already known to my readers, or should I introduce someone new? What kinds of things might happen in a small town that would involve and intrigue the people there? And why would the people of Mill River want to live there in the first place?

In a way, building the Mill River series and maintaining its interconnectedness are much like trying to re-create the structure of a hurricane. The town itself, calm and peaceful, is at the center, with the actions and stories of the town residents swirling around. Everything is held together as part of a single, consistent system. And as with the path of a hurricane, what happens in a small town like Mill River can often be unexpected or unpredictable, as my readers well know.

RHRC: What is your writing process like? What helps you when you get stuck?

DC: Before I start writing a new book, I need to have the main characters and a central plot in mind. I must also know how the story will begin, how it will end, and a few "main events" that will take place in the middle. Unless I have that bare minimum of information, I don't feel ready to put anything on paper (or my computer screen, as is more often the case).

Once I've planned out the basics, I try to do a brief chapter-by-chapter outline to serve as a roadmap. Some chapters start in that outline completely blank — as was the case with my most recent novel — and I end up filling them in as the plot unfolds and ideas come to me while I'm writing.

I've been fortunate in that I haven't yet

had a serious case of writer's block. I do two things to try to keep that from happening. First, I end each writing session knowing what it is that I'm going to write next. That's hard to do sometimes — stopping when I'm on a roll — but knowing exactly how I'm going to start the next writing session makes doing it much easier. And second, before I start writing for the day, I read over and edit the pages I wrote the previous day. Doing so helps refine the draft and helps me to coast into writing whatever comes next in the story.

RHRC: Who was the first Mill River character you ever came up with? What was the inspiration behind him/her?

DC: Mary McAllister was the first character I developed, and she did indeed have a real-life inspiration.

In the 1940s, a Jewish gentleman named Sol Strauss fled Nazi Germany and settled with his mother in my hometown of Paoli, Indiana. There, he opened a dry goods store on the town square. Even though his business was successful, Mr. Strauss quietly lived alone above his shop and never seemed to be fully embraced by the town's predominantly Christian population. Still, he considered Paoli his adopted community and its people *his* people. When Mr. Strauss died, the town was shocked to learn that he had bequeathed to it millions of dollars, which were to be used for charitable purposes to benefit the residents.

The Sol Strauss Supporting Organization Fund is still in operation today. Among other things, it provides clothing and additional necessities for needy children and an annual supply of new books for the high school English department. Residents of Paoli may also apply to the fund for assistance in carrying out a project that would benefit the town. The fund is the legacy of Mr. Strauss, who continues to be remembered for his extreme and unexpected generosity.

I had Mr. Strauss in mind when I was brainstorming ideas for a first novel. I thought it would be interesting and challenging to build a story around a character who is misunderstood or different in some way, and to show that even someone who is seemingly far removed from his or her community may be more special and loving than anyone could imagine. I liked the idea of an older woman peering down at a small town from her window and knowing that she was helping the people who lived there — her people — even though most of them knew little or nothing about her. This woman, of course, became the character Mary McAllister, and her life story became *The Mill River Recluse.*

RHRC: Do you have a favorite character? Why?

DC: I really love the character of Father O'Brien. Writing scenes involving his "spoon problem" are such fun! I also like the fact that he is an incredibly kind and gentle person, and that even at his advanced age, he's an active and beloved member of the Mill River community.

I'm also fond of the character Emily Di-Santi, first introduced in *The Mill River Redemption.* I suppose it's because Emily shares some personal qualities with my youngest sister, Molly. Both love dogs — Emily's dog, Gus, is based on a dog my sister used to have. Molly has a degree in landscape architecture, so she's very artsy and outdoorsy, with a skill set to match. I think it's really cool that she can drive a dump truck and refinish furniture, and she has her own hip waders for trout fishing. Molly can also grow *anything.* She somehow managed to raise perfect artichokes during the short, cool summers in Green Bay, Wisconsin! I really admire my sister's self-reliant, can-do attitude, and I wanted the character of Emily DiSanti to have that same state of mind.

(I should add that my other sister, Carrie, is also a fabulous person with her own set of unique talents . . . which might be borrowed for a future character!)

RHRC: Readers have met Father O'Brien before, but in *The Promise of Home,* they find out so much more about his backstory. When did you first start to think about the details of his personal history?

DC: Over the years, many readers have written to me wanting to know why it is that Father O'Brien is so obsessed with spoons. Once I was able to turn my attention to developing the plot for my third book, I realized that I wanted to give my readers an answer to that question. Gradually, a story took shape in my mind — Father O'Brien's story — and it seemed it would make a good addition to the two Mill River books I'd already written. I wanted to let my readers see a bit of his childhood and learn what experiences shaped him into the priest they know. And, I wanted to contrast that historical portion of the book with events in the present to reveal how his past still had the ability to change his life.

I was fascinated by my research into living during the Great Depression. It was a time of struggle, when little was taken for granted. Children grew up much more quickly and were expected to do more at a much younger age. Father O'Brien, or Michael, as he was called back then, certainly would have experienced this, and I think that reality is borne out in this third book.

RHRC: How did you decide which Mill River residents you wanted to focus on in *The Promise of Home*?

DC: Once I came up with a story and plot for *The Promise of Home,* I knew that Father O'Brien, both as an elderly priest and as a teenager, would feature heavily. Since this book was to be crafted as the third in a series, I thought it was important to continue with certain previously established plotlines and characters. Kyle and Claudia appeared in the first two Mill River novels, and their relationship continues to evolve in this one. Both DiSanti sisters from *The Mill River Redemption* are put through an emotional wringer in that story, and I wanted to follow their journey — especially Emily's — in this new book.

Of course, I am always striving to further develop the town of Mill River itself. New characters help expand and enrich the fictional community and play important roles in this new story. And I always like to let established characters make cameos in new books, even if they're not heavily involved in the plot. My readers like to find out how and what they're doing, and so do I!

RHRC: Do you think of your novels as having any overarching messages or themes?

DC: Although I can see certain themes — particularly emphases on the importance of kindness, family, and community — in the finished books, I don't sit down to write a new story with any particular message or theme in mind. Rather, they seem to take shape along with the story.

I've often wondered why these themes have emerged in my writing. Each of them is important to me personally. But I think the real reason is my feeling that our society has changed over the years, and is continuing to change, in a way that isn't good. I think an argument can be made that in many places, kindness, family, and community are under siege. Crime and racial tensions are often in the news. Families of all kinds are struggling economically and socially. At school or neighborhood events, people who manage to leave work early to attend, and who might once have struck up conversations and gotten to know each other, now sit silently glued to their smartphones. For all the digital and electronic interconnectedness in our current society, I sometimes feel as if we're actually *disconnected* from one another and from a focus on human qualities and in-person relationships. Even in Mill River, life is neither easy nor perfect, but an effort to be kind, to help families thrive, and to develop relationships that foster a strong sense of community could make life more meaningful and enjoyable for many people.

RHRC: What is your favorite thing about Mill River?

DC: My favorite thing about Mill River — other than its wonderful residents — is the way it offers a sense of safety, comfort, and community. If I close my eyes, I can easily picture its quaint houses and shops and its neat, quiet streets. I can imagine peering out the window of one of those houses, listening to crickets and tree frogs singing on a summer night or the howling wind of a blizzard during the winter. I would feel cozy and safe, surrounded by neighbors I knew in a community steeped in kindness and caring. Mill River really is the little town of my dreams, a place I wish existed in real life. I would move there in a heartbeat!

QUESTIONS AND TOPICS
FOR DISCUSSION

1. *The Promise of Home* rotates among the perspectives of several different characters: Karen, Claudia, Emily, and Father O'Brien. Were you drawn to any one of their storylines more than the others? Why do you think that is?

2. A significant portion of the narrative includes flashbacks to Father O'Brien's youth. Why do you think the author chose to include those flashbacks when the rest of the novel takes place in the present day? What would the novel be like without them? How might the other sections change?

3. "The very hands that rested on his knees, the hands that were suddenly unable to do what he wanted them to, had held a rifle and ended a man's life. Up until now, he hadn't allowed that realization to sink in. . . . The weight of it, regardless of the

man's actions toward his mother, was immense" (page 113). This quote is from the moment Michael O'Brien begins to process what he's done. Do you think he is too hard on himself, considering the circumstances? How do you think you would react in a similar position?

4. After deciding that it's best to conceal what happened with the intruder, Frank says to a young Father O'Brien, "This is one of those tough situations, Michael, where there are no good solutions. It isn't possible to do something right without somebody else getting hurt or paying a price. These situations will come up every once in a while during your lifetime, and you need to recognize them and choose which solution does the least harm and who should suffer that harm" (page 308). Do you agree with this statement? Why or why not?

5. After reading one of the letters from the briefcase, Emily learns that Father O'Brien killed a man and ultimately finds his actions, under the circumstances, to be "perfectly justified and understandable" (page 232). How do you think some of the other characters would react to the news? Why?

6. When Claudia goes in for a wedding dress fitting, Pauline offers her this piece of advice: "Falsehoods and little white lies never lead to anything good. And be careful when you decide what's false and what isn't. Sometimes things and even people aren't what they seem" (page 131). How is this advice relevant at different points throughout the novel? Are there any moments in *The Promise of Home* when you would disagree with it?

7. Mill River is clearly a unique place to live. Why do you think so many people are drawn to it from other places, and why do you think so many people return after years away?

8. When Emily first meets Matt, she is offended by his advances and pushes him away. Do you think she is too quick to judge him based on her past experiences, or is she justified in her reaction?

9. When Father O'Brien suspects the worst has happened to Karen, he rushes to find her, putting his own health at risk. Can you think of other times when he acted selflessly? In what way(s) is he a pillar of the community? Give examples.

10. Throughout the novel, Karen struggles

with suicidal thoughts and even acts upon them, but she is ultimately given a second chance. In what way do you think some of the other characters were afforded second (if less obvious) chances?

11. Claudia tolerates Misty, the rude girlfriend of her future brother-in-law, with a smile on her face, and she even bites her tongue when she realizes Misty is making inappropriate passes at Kyle. Where do you think she finds the strength and faith to stay out of the situation? What do you think her silence on the matter says about her character and her relationship with Kyle? Could she have made her concerns known to Kyle in a constructive way?

12. Frank makes some difficult decisions to help spare Michael and Anna more pain and difficulty. Do you agree with his decision to tell them that Grace died as an infant? Given his opinion of orphanages, were there any other reasonable options for him at the time?

13. What do you think of the title, *The Promise of Home*? In your opinion, does it fit the novel? Why or why not?

ABOUT THE AUTHOR

Darcie Chan is the *New York Times* bestselling author of the eBook sensation *The Mill River Recluse* and the novels *The Mill River Redemption* and *The Promise of Home.* She has been featured in *The New York Times, USA Today,* and *The Wall Street Journal.* For fourteen years, Chan worked as an attorney drafting environmental and natural resource legislation for the U.S. Senate. She now writes fiction full-time and lives north of New York City with her husband and son.

darciechan.com

Find Darcie Chan on Facebook

@DarcieChan